The Luthier's Diary Series:

Written to inspire, entertain and give hope to those that have the courage to dream.

These original books come from deep within the world of the Master Luthier (violinmaker) and contain the lives, loves and fantasies of those who play upon true master instruments.

Book Two: Choice of Loves

Mary Anderson has *saved herself* and waited most of her life, looking for the perfect man; a *knight in shining armor*, *Prince Charming* and *Superman*, all wrapped into one handsome package. She is still desperately clinging to her dream when she looks into the eyes of "...a drunk, sleazy guy in black leather...". Now she must decide between her principles and her passionate *love at first sight*.

Steve Miller is a lone, desperate man, living what most people would consider a worthless life. Neglected and abused as a child, he grew up to be one of the toughest Marines in Vietnam. Now, haunted by his past, with little chance of ever succeeding, he decides to order a master violin from the Luthier while searching for the greatest father in the world.

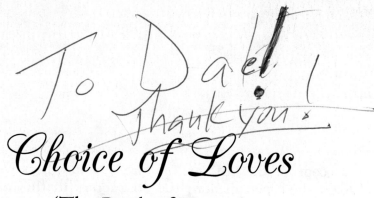

To Dale!
Thank you!

Choice of Loves

(The Book of Honor)

March 17, 2002

Kevin Lee Luthier

Luthier's Press

(A division of Lee Instruments)

000316

Printed and bound in the United States of America.

* * * *

Publisher's note:

This Luthier's Press edition of Choice of Loves (The Book of Honor) was printed and bound in the Luthier's library mentioned in this book.

This book is dedicated to my father and all the other brave veterans of the United States who can hold their head high because they fought with honor when their country called.

Warning: **Those who find the terms "Honor," "Morals," and "Patriotism" offensive, should not continue reading this book.**

...on the other hand, maybe you should.

"True love at first sight" is looking deep into someone's eyes and seeing what your own soul lacks; and in that same person, everything it needs to make it whole.

True love is only a fairytale to those who have not yet experienced it.

For those that question, I have.

...Kevin Lee Luthier

Chapter 1: Steve

The crunching sound of gravel and the accompanying thump, thump, thump of the *Harley Davidson's* engine caught the Luthier's attention. He opened his eyes and looked down at the old, oak schoolteacher's desk before wiping a few beads of perspiration from off his brow. It was the end of a very long day and the summer sun was hanging low on the horizon.

Usually the violin shop was kept very comfortable, but the air-conditioner and large fan used to blow dry air between the pieces of wood hanging from the ceiling were turned off, allowing the temperature to rise until it was as hot as the scorched, desert sand outside.

Dragon's Blood must be filtered while still very hot and without any dust or drafts. It's a simple fact of life for a Master Luthier, and he thought nothing of the discomfort. Instead, the Luthier used the time to relax and let the cares of the world melt away.

He had watched the varnish dripping through the cotton filter for almost an hour before closing his eyes. This batch was darker and had been cooked longer than any other in order to satisfy the wealthy patron's request; that her viola be "as mournful as possible."

The violin shop, itself, had taken on a feeling of deep sorrow while the viola was taking shape, and heavy gloom lingered thick in the motionless air. The cinnamon-colored instrument was supported on a wooden stand at the back of the desk, awaiting this final coat; the one that would give it the color and character the woman truly needed.

The water cooler by the front door had tempted the Luthier earlier, but he had wanted the varnish to be completely finished and put away before giving in to its enticings.

The sound of the motorcycle had interrupted the peace and tranquility of the shop, but the Luthier didn't mind. He had opened his eyes just in time to watch the last drop of varnish fall into the jar.

He lifted the bottle with a smile of approval and carefully tightened the lid so its contents would remain free of dust. The varnish was now perfect and he quickly wrapped the jar with thick, black tape to protect it from any light that might change its character before being applied to the instrument.

The Luthier opened one of the large, glass-paned doors in an old varnish cupboard his grandfather had made almost a century before and placed the jar inside. He gently closed it, tilted his head back and stretched his limbs before turning on the fan and air conditioner.

After lifting his drinking cup off an old square nail driven into the wall, he walked across the entry. He could tell that the motorcycle was passing through the orchard while he filled his cup with cool, refreshing spring water.

Acid-rock music mixed with the percussion of the engine's exhaust began beating against the walls, then it began shaking the front window. The Luthier closed his eyes and tried to savor his drink while the sounds got even louder and more obnoxious. Everything went quiet a split-second before the heavy front tire of the *Harley Davidson* bumped against the freshly-painted white wall outside.

The Luthier lowered his cup and walked back to the cupboard while a kickstand squeaked and rotated, then ground its way into the dirt under the shifting weight of the massive motorcycle. He turned toward the door while large boots made their way across the gravel. The uneven steps sounded as if the rider had been sitting for a long time and was now trying to loosen himself up.

There was a sign on the door that read, "Come in. You

are welcome," so the Luthier waited to see if the unexpected visitor would enter on his own, or if he would knock.

After only a slight hesitation, the brass doorknob turned and the hinges creaked. There was something about it that made the Luthier watch with more than his usual amount of interest. He turned and replaced the cup on its nail without making a sound.

The door moved slowly at first, one inch at a time, until the Luthier could see three military dogtags hanging from a sweaty wrist. A large, soiled hand firmly grasped the handle and it paused just long enough for the dogtags to stop swinging. The door was then pushed and let go a moment later, giving the Luthier a brief glance at a brightly-colored scorpion tattooed on a large, muscular forearm.

The scorpion quickly disappeared behind the wall with the accompanying clinking sound of the three dogtags. The door opened the rest of the way on its own, allowing the afternoon sun to shine directly into the shop.

There was an uncomfortable stillness in the air and a silence outside that seemed to heighten the Luthier's anticipation that something unusual was about to happen. He quietly walked across the entry and stood by the counter containing the cash drawer.

Suddenly, a dark silhouette appeared in the doorway and stood there motionless. It cast a long, menacing shadow across the floor. The Luthier squinted his eyes and looked down. The sun was behind the stranger and the Luthier quickly scanned the image the best he could while his eyes adjusted to the light.

Old, military jungle boots stood on the threshold. They were cracked and rotten, still covered with traces of dirt from years gone by. They looked like they were ready to fall apart.

The left boot had a bullet hole just above the ankle and a jagged opening on the other side with dried blood beneath it. Black leather pants were tucked into the boots and a heavy, stainless steel chain was draped out of the right pocket and riveted to the belt.

A large, bone-handled knife protruding out of a thick, leather sheath finished off the lower half of the inspection.

As the Luthier's eyes became more accustomed to the light, his gaze quickly worked its way up the rest of the figure. The man wore a military, camouflage shirt with the left sleeve rolled up as far as it would go. The right sleeve was torn completely off, revealing a large, deep scar running most of the way up his arm. A dark, gnarly tattoo of a rattlesnake ran over the scar; it started at his wrist and the rattles of its tail ended on his shoulder.

The name REBER was sewn above the left pocket and there were single, silver bars on either side of the collar, designating that he was a 1st Lieutenant, or at least the shirt had once belonged to one. It was unbuttoned and revealed a sweaty, *wife-beater* undershirt that had once been white. The thin cotton fabric was stretched tight and helped accentuate his thick, muscular torso and large, tattooed arms.

His coarse, unshaven face was that of a weathered, middle-aged man with dirt settled deep into every line and pore. The tangled ends of his ragged, brown hair hung past the bone handle of the knife on his left hip but was only half-an-inch long on the right side, where there were three crosses shaven into it above his ear. Large, silver, skull-shaped earrings with flaming, gold eyes swung back and forth as his gaze shifted from side to side.

He seemed to be carefully surveying the violin shop and all its contents. His demeanor was that of nervous paranoia, mixed with those of an animal of prey, ready to strike.

After eyeing the Luthier, the man asked in a harsh, throaty tone, "Are you the violinmaker?"

The Luthier directly faced the stranger and deliberately answered, "I am."

Without any notice, the man lunged at the Luthier with his large arms stretched out.

The Luthier ducked and rotated in response. As he

instinctively slid behind the counter, his right foot carefully lingered behind, tripping the man's feet while he advanced. The stranger fell, but just before he landed, he tucked and rolled over with the sure gracefulness of a panther.

He sprang back up and faced the Luthier again, now holding the long, menacing bowie knife in his right hand, ready for a more serious assault. His eyes looked up just in time to see the Luthier's black, matte-finish Glock, model 27, 40-caliber pistol aimed directly between his eyes.

The intruder stopped advancing and froze instantly when he heard the distinct click of the Glock chambering a round. He slowly moved his head to the right until his left eye was directly in line with the very short, three-inch barrel of the gun. Six, shiny, copper serrations at the top of a forty-caliber hollow-point demanded his undivided attention. His eyes widened and his jaw slowly moved back and forth, while the rest of his body remained completely motionless.

"Never underestimate your enemies," declared the Luthier. His finger was on the trigger, waiting to see what the stranger would do next. Every visible muscle of his adversary was well defined and taut as spring steel.

After hesitating a few seconds, the man slowly lowered the knife. To the Luthier's surprise, a smile spread across his face while he continued looking directly into the barrel of the gun.

"I am not your enemy," he replied. "I have travelled over two thousand miles, without sleeping, so I could be here today and talk with you."

The stranger's expression then became solemn while his hand came around and slid the long, razor-sharp blade back into its sheath. His fingers instinctively snapped the leather strap as though it were second nature to him.

He stood straight up. As he did, he quickly brought both heels of the old, rotten boots together in military fashion and held his arms rigidly at his side. His eyes looked straight forward across the room.

After standing at attention for one second, he quickly raised his right arm and saluted. "My name is Steve Miller, Sir. I need a violin, and I need a father. I will be your friend from this moment on, whether you are mine or not."

After a short pause, he dropped his salute, directly faced the Luthier and added with a smile, "Damn, you're good!"

Chapter 2: Bill

The Luthier looked at the two silver bars and the name REBER on the shirt while thinking about Steve Miller's announcement about needing a violin and a father. He looked back into Steve's face and slowly squinted his eyes. The old, torn shirt was obviously someone else's and Steve had to be nearly fifty years old.

The Luthier assessed the situation and considered his options. His only reply to Steve's request so far was the unwavering barrel of his Glock and a firmly set jaw.

After the tension had subsided a little, Steve took a cautious step forward. The Luthier responded by backing away the same distance. Steve understood the reaction and immediately stopped. He then decided to wait for the Luthier to make the next move, no matter how long it took.

After a few minutes, the Luthier closed the front door without losing eye contact. He carefully slid the pistol between his belt and the small of his back while walking back over by the counter.

"Continue," the Luthier told him. Then he pointed to a cello chair on the opposite side of the entry resting between the water cooler and a padded bench.

Steve sat down while the Luthier slid a chair over to the opposite side of the room.

After the Luthier was seated, Steve admitted, "I don't know where to begin. I've been trying to think of the right words for the past thirty-four hours while I rode out here."

Instead of responding, the Luthier looked directly at Steve's left arm. It was brushing up against the fine, blue, silk covering of the bench beside him.

Steve pulled his arm away and apologized, "I guess I'll start with, 'I'm sorry.' And that's the first time I've said those words in over forty years."

Steve became frustrated when the Luthier showed no reaction to his sincere apology. He knew the Luthier was in complete control of the situation and that he could call the police at any time. He continued to explain, "I had the worst father in the world and the only thing he ever taught me was how to fight. I've fought most of my life for one reason or another.

"I figured that if you were half the man I was told about, you would be able to defend yourself. It was the only way I had of seeing if you were the right man for the job and if I could respect you."

The Luthier's face was solemn. "I had the best father in the world and he taught me how not to fight."

"That's exactly what I heard!" Steve exclaimed, his hopes raising after hearing the comment.

The Luthier's eyes narrowed, "And exactly where did you hear this?"

"On a shooting range, outside Detroit, just three days ago," Steve answered. "From Hardcore. A sniper I met in Vietnam."

The Luthier's eyes opened wide, "Lieutenant Bill Hardy?"

Steve nodded and grinned. "He was shooting his Barrett 82-A1 (fifty-caliber rifle) at the 1000 meter range. We are the only ones left out of our original platoons and we talk every once in a while."

Steve then added a little sheepishly, "Usually when I'm in trouble."

The Luthier relaxed in his chair while Steve began telling his story...

"What's bugging you today, Chip?" asked Bill Hardy, better known as *Hardcore* in Vietnam and by the members of his SWAT team where he had earned his living as a sniper over the years.

Even though the mood was serious, Steve had to smile

when he looked directly at Bill. He still talked with his lips stretched far enough back to clearly show his chipped, uneven teeth. He never changed much, he just added a few more grey hairs along his temples each time they met.

"A woman," replied Steve. Steve had been nicknamed *Chip* when he was seven; just after his mother died. He was a good-humored, high-spirited boy full of optimism before that. But after his mother was gone, everyone said that he acted like a "chip off the old block" when compared to his father. He arrived at boot camp with a large chip on his shoulder and everyone thought the name still fit him perfectly, so Chip was the name Steve went by the entire time he was in Vietnam.

It didn't surprise Steve when Bill lifted his rifle and turned toward the shooting range in response. Steve knew that *Hardcore* always thought better when he was shooting, so he picked up the spare electronic muffs and put them over his ears. The special earmuffs would allow them to talk, but also deaden the sound of the large-bore rifle when it went off.

"You've had plenty of women before, Chip. Do what you always do. Have fun. Then when you get tired of her, or if she actually wants you to do something, dump her like all the rest and find another." That was Bill's half-joking, half-serious answer as he lowered the barrel of the large, military-green rifle and pulled the trigger.

"BOOM!"

The shock wave from the rifle's large, muzzle-brake ports (gas vents on the barrel to reduce the kick) pushed Steve back a few inches while the blast echoed across the valley. About one second later, a small puff of dust kicked up behind a target at the base of a hill on the other side.

Steve instinctively looked down at a lap-top computer sitting on a folding table between them and commented, "Four inches, seven o'clock."

Just as the words left Steve's mouth, the large rifle replied, "BOOM!"

One second later, another small white dot appeared on the green screen.

"Two-and-a-half inches, three o'clock"

"BOOM!" was the immediate reply of the rifle again.

"Three-quarters-of-an-inch at twelve o'clock," Steve commented.

Bill clicked on the safety and lowered the butt of the rifle onto his steel-toed boot. He then turned toward Steve to hear what more he had to say.

"This is a real woman," Steve emphatically explained. He glanced up from the computer screen to see the surprised look on Bill's face.

Bill dropped out the clip, unchambered the next round and blew out the smoke remaining in the barrel. "And what were all the others? *Barbie dolls?*"

Steve just stood there, not knowing what to say.

The silence said a thousand words to Bill.

"Chip's in love?"

When there was still no response from Steve, Bill added, "You're going to tell me that after all these years, *Chip's in love?*" Bill shook his head in disbelief, "No way!"

Steve looked back with a hurt, puppy-dog expression. He knew he deserved Bill's comments and didn't know how to respond.

"Oh, man! There is justice!" Bill declared while watching a sad, pouting look, spread across Steve's always tough, emotionless face. "Man, give me a camera. I've got to remember this *Kodak moment!*"

When Steve's expression still didn't change, the mood turned serious. Gradually, their faces became somber, and without saying another word, they both turned and gazed across the valley toward the target in the distance.

Bill was always a cool thinker and Steve knew it. When he had come back from Vietnam, he was one of the few that had blended back into society without much trouble. Bill ignored all the rude comments and personal insults. Even when he stood up for his country, it was in a way that didn't attract too much attention to himself.

It didn't take Bill long to find a good job, then a good woman to marry. He had always respected women and now he had three wonderful daughters; two were happily married, while the youngest was attending her senior year in high school.

Steve, on the other hand, did not blend in well when he got back.

When he enlisted to go to Vietnam, he felt it was his duty to protect his country and what it stood for, especially the women and children. Then, when he stepped off the plane after fighting and watching his friends die around him, he was greeted by dozens of women throwing rotten fruit and manure at him while they screamed, "Baby killer!"

The women had even brought their children and had them hold up signs that read, "Hell no, we won't go!" Then they stood on American flags cut up and thrown on the ground for the special occasion of welcoming him home. Steve loved his country and had never looked at women or children the same after that day.

There were a lot of protests going on during the war and if anyone ever said anything bad about him or his country, he would fight. When a group of students started burning an American flag in front of the city library, he plowed into them and took them on, one by one. He knocked them down, then walked over the top of them with his army boots. Most of them were cowards and backed away, but there were ten people lying on the ground and Steve held the burning flag in his hands by the time the police came and hauled him away in handcuffs.

All added up, Steve had spent over three months in jail since the war, mostly one day at a time. Some of them were for what he considered noble causes, but after a few years had gone by, most of them were not. Bill and Steve both knew that he had a long, tough road ahead of him if he were to ever become a gentleman and be able to keep a wife happy.

Bill turned and looked at Steve again. After seeing that he was really serious, Bill smiled and asked, "Do you want to give it a try?" Then he popped the clip back in, chambered a round and held up the Barrett.

"I've never shot a Barrett before, Hardcore. And you

know I haven't pulled a trigger since 'Nam."

"You're going to have to do a lot of things you've never done before if you're going to go falling in love, Chip. Hitting that bull's-eye at 1000 meters is going to be easy compared to changing your life!"

Steve had never hesitated or backed down to a challenge before, so he reached out and grabbed the rifle with his left hand. When Bill let go, Steve had to quickly bring his right hand around to help support it. It was heavier than he thought and he strained to hold it out in front of him like Bill had.

Bill smiled while he watched Steve struggle to lift the Barrett to his shoulder. He wasn't surprised when Steve had to set it back down on his boot with a grunt of frustration.

Without another word, Steve took a deep breath and tried again. This time he held the barrel up vertically first and managed to get the butt of the rifle against his shoulder so he could lower the sights toward the target.

As soon as the heavy, deeply-fluted barrel levelled into firing position, Steve's left arm started shaking. Within a second or two, before he had time to aim or take the safety off, he had to lower it again with another grunt and a loud exhale.

"I'm no weakling, but this is ridiculous," Steve exclaimed. Then he handed the rifle back to Bill with both hands.

Bill was no larger than Steve, but he grabbed the heavy gun with his left hand and held it out before bringing it up against his shoulder.

BOOM!
BOOM!
BOOM!
BOOM!
BOOM!
BOOM!
BOOM!
Seven shots in less than two seconds.

Steve turned and watched the dust spots kick up on the hill, one after the other. Then he watched seven white dots appear on the computer screen while Bill lowered the rifle onto his left boot. They were all within the three-foot circle.

"That's impossible!" Steve exclaimed while staring at the screen in disbelief.

"So are women," replied Bill with his large, toothy grin.

Bill pushed the small lever next to the trigger guard and popped out the large, empty clip. He reloaded it with ten fresh rounds and added, "So we better start at the beginning."

Bill handed the rifle to Steve, then walked over to his car and opened the trunk. He pulled out a camouflage, canvas tarp and spread it out on the ground. He unfolded the Barrett's bipod and extended the legs a couple of notches before telling Steve, "Lay down and give it a try. It doesn't kick any more than a normal, high-powered rifle, this one just pushes a whole lot more, so don't flinch because you're worried about it hurting your shoulder. I've put a thousand rounds through it in a day and I didn't even feel it."

Steve smiled in reply. He knew that Bill had not received the nickname *Hardcore* for nothing.

Steve laid down with the rifle, pulled its heavy, steel bolt back and let it go, chambering the first fifty-caliber round he would shoot. As he rotated the safety lever to the *fire* position, he realized that the bullet in the chamber, and each round that would follow, cost between four and five dollars each. Steve also thought of the thousands or possibly millions of rounds that Bill must have shot over the years, all at the government's expense. He then thought about how it was all worth it, and much, much more.

"I will never be able to thank you enough, Hardcore."

Bill just grinned. They both knew what Steve was talking about, and nothing more had to be said.

Bill coached Steve until the white dots started appearing on the green screen and his shoulder began aching. Then Bill showed him how to *really shoot*.

It was "poetry in motion" for Steve, watching his friend laying on the tarp and using the bipod to steady the rifle for more accuracy.   There was absolutely no quiver at the end of the barrel as Bill smoothly pulled the trigger, time after time, with the accompanying white dots consistently appearing on top of each other in the center of the computer screen.

After Bill was through shooting for the afternoon, they sat down under a small canopy and talked while Bill began cleaning the Barrett.

"How many people own a rifle like this, Hardcore?"

"Other than the government, there are only a few scattered across the country."

Bill pulled out a cloth and wiped if off.

"Can anyone else shoulder it like you?"

"Only one, that I know of," Bill replied. Then he laughed.

"Who's that?" Steve was interested in Bill's reaction to his own statement.

"A luthier I know."

"A what?"

"A violinmaker," Bill clarified. He turned toward Steve so he could see the look on his face.

Steve was surprised, but he still accepted the answer without any further questions. He knew that Hardcore never made anything up or ever exaggerated a story.

Steve looked back across the valley at the target well over a half-mile away and asked, "Can he shoot as good as you?" Steve would be surprised if anyone in the world could shoot half as well as Bill.

"No. But I can't make violins as well as he can, either," Bill joked. Then he continued in a more serious tone, "We shoot together when he travels here on his business trips, and whenever I go out West, we shoot on his 1000 meter range. He has one right by his violin shop."

"He doesn't sound like a normal violinmaker to me."

"He isn't," Bill replied.

While Steve thought about a violinmaker who shot fifty-caliber rifles, he asked, "You remember Tiny Tim, don't you? The one who wore glasses and played the violin?"

Bill nodded very slowly.

Steve could tell by the look on Bill's face that he didn't want to talk about Tiny, so he quickly changed the topic, "How did you and this violinmaker meet?" Steve was still curious about someone who shot Navy Seal sniper rifles and made violins.

"The day I came home from 'Nam. I was stupid enough to step off of the bus wearing my *dress-blues*."

Steve nodded after thinking about his own homecoming from Vietnam again.

Bill continued, "There were flower children, hippies, and what looked like normal old-folks standing behind them. They were all gathered around when I stepped out of the door and onto the sidewalk. At first I thought they were actually there to welcome me home. After all, 'I served well,' I thought.

"When I smiled at them, they started screaming and throwing things. Some of the mothers standing in front even covered their children's eyes so they wouldn't have to look at the 'terrible monster!'"

Steve was listening intently while Bill continued, "When they really got riled up and tempers started to flare, a small, ten-year-old boy pushed his way right through the middle of them. He was yelling and screaming as loud as he could, 'Stop it! Stop it everyone! He's a hero!'

"They all turned toward the boy and one lady screamed, "No he's not. He's a killer! Go home and ask your mother.'

"The little boy looked her right in the eyes and yelled, 'My mother is an American!'

"He spit on the woman's shoes, then ran toward me. I didn't even know who he was and he gave me a hug. Then the crowd started throwing all their insults and garbage at both of us.

"No one else stood with me that day or said anything in my defense but that ten-year-old boy. Even though they threw everything they had, from what I heard later, it would have been a lot worse if it hadn't been for that little boy standing there with me.

"After the crowd finally started wandering off, I told him,

'I'm no hero, Boy. You better go find your parents and go home now.'

"'Yes, you are! No matter what these stupid people say!' and he pointed his finger at the people still standing there, one by one. Then he ran right through the middle of them and back down the sidewalk.

"That little boy is now a master violinmaker."

Chapter 3: The Bet

Steve stopped to take a breath and to see what the Luthier's reaction to the story Hardcore had told about him would be.

The Luthier simply nodded. Then he offered, "Would you like a drink of water?"

Steve filled a cup from the dispenser and drank it all before continuing...

"So, tell me about this girl," Bill asked while sitting in the shade of the canopy. "What's her name and how old is she?"

"Mary," Steve answered. "Mary Anderson, and she's thirty-seven."

Bill was shocked when Steve answered both questions. Steve was usually lucky to even remember the *names* of the women he had been with.

"Where did you meet her?"

"In a restaurant," Steve answered. "A nice restaurant."

"And what were *you* doing in a *nice* restaurant?" Bill asked as he deliberately surveyed Steve from head to toe with a look of disbelief.

"I made a bet with Jared. He bet me thirty bucks that I couldn't walk in and order a meal without being thrown out."

"If it really was a nice restaurant, I would have taken that bet myself," Bill chided.

"Well it *was* a really nice restaurant, and I walked right in the front door..."

"May I help you?" asked Raúl, the maitre d', in a snobby voice that let Steve know he was not welcome. Then he looked Steve over in disgust.

Steve stood out like a sore thumb with his long, ratty hair, colorful tattoos, black leather vest and dirty motorcycle boots.

"Yea, I want to eat dinner," Steve replied.

"Here?" asked the maitre d' with a look of surprise.

Steve kept his cool because he wanted to win the thirty-dollar bet that would pay for his meal. There weren't many things in Steve's life that were free and he was really hungry.

He straightened himself up and replied, "Yes, and it's even okay if you put me in a back corner, my Good Man."

Steve had had enough experience with the police and being thrown out of places to know that, if he kept acting civilly, the police wouldn't come, no matter how much they begged. He didn't see anyone around that would dare to physically throw him out themselves, so he folded his arms, smiled at the maitre d' and waited.

Raúl walked over to the manager who had come up from the back of the restaurant when he saw Steve walk in. They both looked back over at Steve, then began arguing.

After Raúl shook his head and stormed off, the manager came over with a forced smile, "My name is Frederick. Please follow me, Sir." He led Steve back to a table in the far corner by the kitchen.

Steve sat down and waited. It was late on a Tuesday and the restaurant was almost empty.

After a few minutes, Steve realized that the waitress was either ignoring him or didn't know he was there. He still didn't want to create a disturbance, which always seemed to happen whenever he confronted anyone, so he sat back, took off his black leather gloves with no fingers in them, let out a slow, deep breath, and relaxed. Next, he cleaned his fingernails with his knife and looked around the restaurant in boredom.

While trying to balance a salt shaker on three grains of salt, he heard two waitresses talking behind a partial wall by the kitchen and looked in their direction.

"I give up Mary!" the first waitress exclaimed. "I am so tired of men and their hollow promises. Dave just gave me the brush off, and it's over!"

Steve could hear the other waitress gasp. "He took your ring back?"

"Yes," was the reply.

Steve quickly glanced at the people on the other side of the room, making sure that he was the only one who could hear the conversation. Then he sat back and listened out of idle curiosity.

"I've decided to give up trying for a meaningful relationship, Mary. I'm going to have a little fun before I get too old."

"You're kidding, right Cindy?" Mary asked.

There was a long silence.

Cindy finally answered, "I don't know, Mary. The older a woman gets, the tougher it is to land a good one. I'm tired of holding out for the trophy winner. At least for now."

Steve glanced toward the front door. Raúl was standing in the entry and didn't seem concerned that Steve had not been given a menu yet. In fact, when he looked toward Steve and noticed the empty table in front of him, he smiled.

Mary responded, "I know I'm dreaming, Cindy, but I will never give up. Someday, I don't know when, but someday, I will look my *Prince Charming* in the eyes and we will fall deeply and madly in love. Then we will live *happily-ever-after*, and I'll be glad I waited."

"Oh, stop fooling yourself, Mary. You and your *Prince Charming, love at first sight, knight in shining armor* and *Superman*; all rolled into one, big, pipe dream. Get real! I'm only twenty-six, I'm trying as hard as I can to get a decent man, and look how things are going! You're thirty-seven years old and still a virgin!"

"Shh! Someone will hear you!" Mary pleaded.

"Hey, everyone! There's a thirty-seven-year-old virgin back by the kitchen!" Cindy yelled out, though it was just barely over a whisper.

Steve then heard another frantic "Shh" come from behind the wall.

"Oh, relax, Mary. No one is going to hear us, except maybe Charlie. And he's so old and tired that he's probably asleep on a pile of pots and pans in the back. There's only one family in my section and no one in yours," Cindy assured her.

"I heard the door bell about ten minutes ago," Mary responded. "Where did Raúl seat them?"

When there was no answer, Mary's voice raised a pitch, "He didn't give me any signal. I wonder if Frederick took care of them for some reason?!"

A moment later, a woman with short, black hair, wearing crimson lipstick cautiously poked her head out from behind the wall. She gave a startled jerk and her eyes widened when she saw Steve sitting in the booth right in front of her. She quickly disappeared from sight and Steve heard her let out a stifled scream.

Steve listened while agitated, angry and defensive whispers exchanged back and forth between the two waitresses. Next he heard some rustling and commotion, alternated with stamping and kicking, then finally an "Ow!" He couldn't tell which one had said it.

Mary walked around the corner a minute later. Her step was firm, almost with military airs, and she walked with her chin up. Her short, black hair swished back and forth and her face was as red as her lipstick.

"My name is Mary, and I will be your waitress for the evening," she announced, trying to hide her embarrassment. Her hand was noticeably trembling when she handed Steve a menu.

"I will also be servicing your table, since it is a Tuesday." Then she glanced down and exclaimed, "Oh, pardon me," before dashing behind the wall again.

Mary came back with a glass of water and placed it in front of Steve while trying not to stare at the tattoos on his arms.

She took a step back. "I will return when you are ready

to place your order, Sir. Is there anything else I can get for you now?"

Steve's gaze went from Mary's polished black shoes, up her slender legs to the hem of her short dress. His eyes moved around her hips, hesitated for a moment at her slim waist, then ran on up her torso. His smile grew larger with each stop along the way.

Mary's eyes widened while she watched him look her over. His gaze lingered where it shouldn't have and he ogled her figure for an unbearable amount of time before finally looking up at her face. It sent a cold chill through Mary and she noticeably flinched and shuddered.

It made her nervous at first, then extremely angry, but before she could turn, his eyes met hers.

The smile on Steve's face instantly disappeared and his jaw dropped. He looked at Mary like he was in shock.

Mary had started to walk away, but her eyes remained fixed upon his. She even stopped and turned back around until she was squarely facing him again.

The chill and anger she had felt only two seconds before, melted into a warm, rushing feeling that flowed through her entire body. Then it consumed her. It became the feeling of wild abandon and ecstacy that she had fantasized about her entire life.

She couldn't look away and stood gazing into Steve's eyes while her innocent soul melted into one of hot, passionate desire. Her tightly clenched jaw relaxed and her small, red lips parted. She involuntarily let out a soft, "Oh," before she even realized it.

Mary froze and was unable to register anything around her. She knew, that instant, that she was looking deep into the eyes of the love she had dreamed of and waited for her whole life.

Steve sat straight up and leaned forward, looking into Mary's eyes in disbelief. He felt like he had just been kicked in the stomach by a mean drill-sergeant's well-aimed boot, only he liked it. Then, for the first time in his life, he cleared his mind of the physical attraction and desires he felt and really looked at Mary. That's when he knew he was in love. Serious love.

Somehow even he knew that what he was feeling was special and not limited to the normal kind of love shared between men and women who live together their entire lives. Though his life had been totally void of any caring or positive feelings for years, he knew this was not pretend or second rate; this was, in fact, *the real McCoy.*

They stared at each other in disbelief, neither one able to move. Their mouths hung wide open and they looked like they were in a trance. For that moment, it was as if they were looking deep into each other's souls.

Steve's face softened, then he acted as though he was trying to speak, but couldn't. Mary's eyes began wandering and she quickly took a good look at the rest of him again.

She shook her head and whispered, "No."

Terror quickly replaced the feeling of passion while Mary looked at him over and over again. She wrenched her head from side to side and screamed, "No!"

The family sitting on the other side of the restaurant turned toward Mary. Raúl, who was still standing at the front desk, looked at Frederick and pointed in her direction.

"No!" Mary screamed again. She started trembling and backed away from the table. Tears flowed down her cheeks and she shook uncontrollably.

"No! No! NO!" she screamed in horror. She dropped her notepad to the floor and covered her face with her hands. Her knees almost collapsed as she stumbled back behind the wall by the kitchen.

Raúl and Frederick marched over to Steve's booth and glared at him. His body was frozen and he sat spellbound, still staring at the wall that Mary had disappeared behind.

Mary screamed, "It can't be HIM!" Then she sobbed something between her tears that Steve couldn't understand.

Cindy poked her head out from behind the wall and looked at Steve. He was struggling to get up.

Steve felt dizzy and Cindy watched him stand with a

dazed expression. She pulled her head back behind the wall and anxiously asked, "The drunk, sleazy guy in black leather?"

"Yes!" Mary bawled.

Cindy reappeared as Raúl and Frederick firmly grabbed Steve's arms. Steve stood helplessly looking at Cindy with eyes like that of a deer staring into the headlights of an oncoming car.

"Please leave, or we will call the police," Frederick demanded in a firm voice of authority while he and Raúl pulled even harder.

Steve resisted at first. Then for the first time in his life, he gave in without a fight and allowed himself to be escorted through the tables and out the front door.

After the doors swung closed, Steve turned around and looked back into the restaurant, stunned. He couldn't move. He just stood and stared while trying to figure out what had just happened to him. The feeling was so new to him, so powerful, so unbelievable that he couldn't decide what to do next.

"Give it up, Chip," came a man's voice from down the sidewalk behind him.

After a minute, Steve straightened himself up, forced a smile and turned around. Then he firmly tramped over to where two *Harley Davidson's* were parked along the curb. There was a dirty, mean-looking man standing between them. He was leaning against a parking meter with his arms folded, wearing black leathers and a studded collar. A dirty grin spread across the man's face as he held out his hand when Steve approached.

Steve pulled on the stainless steel chain and lifted his wallet out of his pocket. He reached in and pulled out thirty dollars in worn, folded bills and crumpled them between his hands. He worked them together and wadded them into a tight ball before slapping it firmly into Jared's outstretched palm.

"See, I told you, you couldn't do it!" Jared gloated.

Jared looked down at the money and smiled. After stuffing it into his pocket, they both swung around and started their motorcycles at the same time. Then they rode away from the restaurant and into the night.

Chapter 4: Tom

"That was three days ago, Hardcore," Steve added while lifting one of Bill's noncarbonated, natural drinks out of the cooler.

Steve didn't complain about the sparse selection of beverages and quickly downed the unsweetened fruit juice. He knew Bill was highly-disciplined and took his health and mental awareness very seriously. Bill rarely drank alcohol or caffeine and didn't allow any at the range.

Steve couldn't remember the last time he had drunk anything that could be considered "good for him." He thought about it for a minute, then crumpled the can and tossed it into the trash.

Steve continued, "I went back to the restaurant, first thing the next morning, just so I could see Mary's face again. But she wasn't there." Steve's face saddened and he looked away to hide his emotions.

"Man, you've got it bad," Bill sympathized.

Steve nodded. "I called the restaurant and asked to talk with her. When they told me that she had called in sick and asked who was calling, I hung up.

"I must have driven past the restaurant a dozen times the next day. Every time I looked in the window and thought about how beautiful she was, I saw my own reflection and felt worse.

"By the time she showed up, I decided that I better not let her see me. So I waited around until the restaurant closed and followed her home. She lives on the second floor of an apartment by the university.

"After she went to bed, I went back to my place and

changed my clothes. Then I slept in an alley across the street so I could find out more about her..."

An angry driver woke Steve up early the next morning. The man was honking his horn and yelling at a woman in a stalled car in the middle of the street.

Steve opened his eyes and looked over at Fred. The old wino groggily smiled back and propped himself up. They had shared a full bottle the night before and it was still lying on the ground between their feet. It had been Steve's *treat* in order to keep the old man happy, and so he wouldn't raise a fuss.

A few minutes later, Mary walked out of her apartment wearing a backpack and carrying a violin case. As soon as she started down the steps, everyone on the sidewalk greeted her with a cheerful, "Good morning, Mary!"

They acted surprised when she halfheartedly mumbled, "Good morning," in return.

Steve could tell that Mary didn't normally act this way. It was obvious by their reaction when she had to force a smile.

He quickly slipped on a baseball cap and a pair of sunglasses. He stood up as soon as she started down the sidewalk. His hair was tucked into the collar of the only long-sleeve shirt he owned and he kept at a safe distance.

Mary stopped a couple blocks later and pulled out some money to put in a blind man's cup. His hair was pepper grey, his skin was dark and his clothes were old and simple. Before she ever said a word, the old man asked her in a concerned voice, "What's wrong, Mary?"

Steve stopped close enough behind to hear her softly reply, "Nothing, Tom."

The man shook his head. "Yous can'ts fool me, Mary. You may can fool others, but I can see a whole lots better than mos'. And where's yous been?" His ebony face lifted up, even though two glass eyes sat behind the jet black lenses of his glasses.

Mary let out a sob while Tom scooted over on his small,

folding bench. There was just enough room for two, and by the way he scooted over and Mary sat down, Steve could tell that Tom was more than just a chance acquaintance.

"I'm sorry, Tom," Mary apologized, "but now I know what love at first sight feels like."

Tom was startled.

Mary continued, "I became so sick that I couldn't get out of bed. I still couldn't keep anything down yesterday, but I got up and went to work anyway."

Steve glanced over and finally noticed how pale Mary's face was.

Tom's expression went from surprise to concern and he shook his head back and forth, "Yous finally meets the man o' yous dreams an' that makes yous throws up? An' now it makes yous feel like crying and dragging yo' feet?" asked Tom.

"Yes," cried Mary. She pathetically put her head in her hands and sobbed, "He's a nightmare!"

Mary leaned over and put her head on Tom's shoulder. Tom quickly set his cup down and put his arms around her. After a few minutes of comforting her, he sat back and felt her face with his hands.

Steve backed off a few more feet and leaned against the building. He looked the other way and tried to act unconcerned while other people passed by.

"Tells ol' Tom what's really goin' on, Mary," asked Tom as he reached for his handkerchief.

"Do you believe in true love at first sight, Tom?"

Tom scrunched up his face. "I knowed a might about love once, but I don' knows much about seeing it at firs' sights, Mary."

Tom held up the handkerchief and added, "I does either likes or don't likes people right away though, an' I don't knows that I ever changed my min' 'bout 'em after that."

"Well I've always believed in love at first sight, Tom. I knew that someday I would look *Prince Charming* in the eyes and boom! That would be it. Fairy tale come true. Just like in the story books.

"Well, I looked into those eyes two days ago, but they were attached to a dirty, greasy man wearing black leather with tattoos all over his body. His hair hung down past his waist and it was all tangled up. His nasty earrings were the size of half dollars! Then, to top it all off, I learned last night that he rides in a motorcycle gang!"

Mary had a frightened look in her eyes and she glanced up toward Steve. He quickly faced the other direction again, trying not to look obvious.

"I don't knows, Mary, you may want to trade eyeballs with old Tom." Tom smiled, trying to cheer her up. "Do you want me to pop thems out so yous can takes a better look at him?"

Tom began pulling off his glasses and Mary laughed through her tears. Then they both went quiet as each tried to think of something more to say.

Finally Mary blurted out, "Oh, I know, Tom! I just can't help it! I can't stop dreaming about the look in his eyes.

"You've been so kind to me, but I've still felt so alone for the past twenty years, waiting for that look. I've tried to be good and save myself so I would be ready and able to give myself to my true love when he finally showed up. But I just can't stomach the rest of the picture, or the thought of what someone is really like who looks like that!" Mary shook her head and leaned against Tom again.

Steve flinched at Mary's remark, especially when he added it to the other comments she had made earlier. He hated it when people judged him just because of how he looked. It lit his fuse because they were also the people who say, "don't judge a book by its cover." The more he thought about it, the more his anger boiled.

He finally pushed away from the wall and began walking away.

Steve stopped a few feet down the sidewalk and considered taking off his hat and glasses so he could confront Mary. But when he turned and saw her crying against Tom's shoulder, he thought about the feeling he had in the restaurant again. He thought of his reflection in the window and finally realized how he must have

looked to a girl like Mary, especially sitting in the
restaurant dressed the way he was.

His emotions got all twisted up and they ended turning
into shame. Steve knew he was not the ideal man, or
any woman's dream come true for that matter. Then he
realized that he was probably what Mary expected to find
at the very bottom of the barrel of her worst nightmare.
The funny thing was, it was the first time in his life that
he had ever cared or thought about any of these things.

Tom started talking while Steve stood on the sidewalk
trying to decide what to do next, "Yous better stops and
thinks this one through for a long time, Mary. An' yous
better hurries up or yous be late for class."

Tom placed his large, clean handkerchief into Mary's
hand. Mary wiped her eyes and blew her nose, then she
tried to build up a little courage, "Thank you, Tom. I
will."

Mary stood up, then turned back toward Tom before
continuing on her way. She shook the handkerchief and
asked, "Can I borrow this, Tom?"

"Everything's mine, is yours, Mary," Tom replied with a
smile. Tom's everything was his cup, his folding, wooden
bench, and a large paper bag sitting next to him.

"Thank you again, Tom," Mary said, as she turned and
headed down the sidewalk toward the university.

Steve watched Mary walk away. He was still trying to
decide what to do.

Tom was soon holding out his cup again and Steve
watched the people walk by, one after the other. Every
time someone dropped in some change, Tom would smile
and thank them. Sometimes he even called them by name
without them ever saying a word.

Steve wondered if he could ever make someone like Mary
happy. He also wondered if he could ever be happy settled
down with a woman.

A thought then struck him while thinking about Mary's
conversation with Cindy in the restaurant. He became
obsessed with the idea until it replaced all reason in his
mind. Finally he walked over and stood in front of Tom.

He reached into his pocket and pulled out about two dollars in change and dropped it into his cup.

"Thank you, and good mornin' to yous," Tom perked up.

Steve didn't answer, instead he pulled on the stainless-steel chain attached to his wallet.

"I hain't done nothing wrong, Sir! I promise! Old Tom's jus' bin minding his own business here! Please put those cuffs away! I'll tell yous whats yous wants, ifs that's it."

Steve still said nothing while Tom continued, "Though I cans think of nuthin' I know."

Steve pulled out a few bills and dropped them into Tom's cup.

"Thems feels pretty heavy," Tom commented.

"I need to know a lot," Steve answered.

"Yous ain't no police officer," replied Tom with his voice becoming serious.

"I am Mary's nightmare," admitted Steve.

Tom acted surprised at first, then he said, "I see," while nodding his head.

Steve sat down on the sidewalk beside Tom's bench. "And I love her."

"Whoa! Now we's got's the fish jumpin'," exclaimed Tom. "Are yous goin' to tell me yous believes in loves at firs' sights too?"

"Not until two days ago," Steve answered while reaching down and scraping some dirt off one of his boots with his fingernail.

"Never thought I'd see the day!" Tom remarked while leaning back and scratching above his ear as though in deep thought. "Whos is you, anyway?"

Steve sat up a little straighter, "Steve Miller, at your service, Sir."

"Military?"

"Vietnam."

"What does you do now?"

"Nothing. I'm nobody," Steve answered, shaking his head and slumping back down.

Tom reached over and put both of his hands on Steve's

head just as Steve started shaking it. He pulled off the baseball cap and felt the hair tucked into his shirt. Next his hands came around and worked over the surface of Steve's face.

"Yous a mess, but there's coulds be a little somethin' there," Tom commented.

After a minute, Tom's fingers pulled at both of Steve's cheeks, "Or somethin' little." Then Tom let go and added, "Yous mights could have been somebody, deep down, if yous had tried. Maybe, maybe nots."

Tom shook his head. Then he leaned back with a large, proud smile on his face, "But Mary's somebody. Mary is everything."

"Somehow I knew you were going to say that," responded Steve with disappointment.

"Well, what yous 'spects, man? How old are yous?"

"Forty-some," answered Steve.

"Forty-plenty," remarked Tom, and what has yous done wit' yo'self? Other than serve yer time?"

"Nuthin," answered Steve.

Before Tom could say any more, Steve interjected, "But for the first time in my life, I'm willing to change that."

"Yous thinks yous can change that, as old as yous be?" questioned Tom, a little surprised at Steve's comment.

"I can try."

"You'll haf' t' do better than that!" Tom declared.

Tom pulled the money out of his cup and put it in his pocket. Then he held it out toward the people as they walked by.

"I will, Sir," replied Steve with conviction in his voice. Then he stood up.

"We'll see," replied Tom. Then he turned the other way.

Bill sucked in his breath when Steve finished telling him about Mary and Tom.

"Do you know what you're saying, Chip? Do you have any idea what you're doing?"

"Yea," answered Steve. Then after a pause, he added, "I think I do."

Bill whistled and shook his head. He could tell that
Steve was serious. "What else do you know about her?"

"I went back and dropped some more money into Tom's
cup the next day. I talked to him as nice as I could and
it wasn't long before he told me everything about Mary.
He talked so proud that you'd think he was her father.
Mary loves music and has played the violin since she
was a little girl. From what Tom says, she's really good.
That's what helps keep her going. Other than her visits
with Tom and her friends in front of her apartment
building, she's all alone.

"Her whole family died in a car accident years ago. Tom
said she really had a hard time paying off all the bills
and emotionally getting over it, but now she's going back
to school and finishing her degrees, or whatever. All I
know is, she is really smart and talented."

"And she fell in love with you?" Bill just couldn't help
himself. But when he noticed that Steve was actually
hurt by his remark, he apologized, "I'm sorry, Chip. You
really are changing, aren't you?"

Steve nodded, "I know. I can't believe it either. Mary
works at the restaurant to pay for her schooling. Tom
says that she's been going to the university for years and
she knows and does almost everything. She acts, plays
concerts, runs track and does science experiments. Tom
went on about her forever. He talked like she was the
most talented, most beautiful person alive.

"And I believe him," Steve added. He looked out across
the valley at the target in the distance, "I guess my
chances of ever getting together with Mary are probably
the same as hitting that bull's-eye over there with a BB
gun."

Bill's voice became serious with Steve's last remark, "No
matter how hard you try, Chip, it will still take the right
tools and a lot of time and sacrifices."

"I wish I could start my whole life over again, Hardcore,"
Steve groaned.

Instead of responding to Steve's last comment, Bill
started disassembling the Barrett.

Steve walked over to the tarp and picked it up while Bill started cleaning each of the pieces of the rifle. He went down wind with the tarp so he wouldn't get any dust on the Barrett and started beating the dirt out of it. While folding it up, he looked back over to where Bill was swabbing out the barrel. Bill worked the cleaning rod in and out until a fresh cloth came out perfectly clean.

"I wish I could clean up my life like you clean up your rifle-barrel, Hardcore. Or, I wish I could have chosen a different father. Maybe then I would have turned out to be the man Mary wants. I feel like I had the worst father in the world and never got a chance to be someone decent."

Bill had to nod his head in agreement. He had met Steve's father once. It was the first time he visited Steve after Vietnam. Right after Steve's father had his right arm amputated from sleeping on it wrong during one of his drunken stupors and just before he died of liver failure.

When everything was packed up, they climbed into Bill's car and drove out to the target. It was riddled with holes, just like the computer-screen had shown. Bill picked up the sensors and transmitters that lay behind thick, angled, armor plates and carefully packed them into their padded boxes.

"Those can't be cheap," Steve commented while Bill placed the electronic equipment into the trunk of his car.

Bill shook his head and responded, "Neither are women." Then he smiled at Steve with his toothy grin again.

Steve smiled back. "When I asked Tom what makes Mary happy, he said, 'mostly simple things. But she also likes beautiful things; everything from flowers to fine art.' He told me that if Mary ever gets rich, the first thing on her list is a truly-fine violin." Steve added, "If I can work things out, I think I'll buy her one."

"Do you have any idea how much fine violins can cost, Chip?"

"I think so," Steve answered.

"Tens of thousands of dollars, and that doesn't include

the old ones that sell for over a million!"

"That's what Tom said," Steve answered, seemingly un-phased by Bill's last comment.

After getting back in the car, Bill pulled it around while Steve explained, "I never told anyone this before, but when my father died he had a life insurance policy."

"What did you do with it?" Bill asked, surprised.

"Just like everything else, nothing," Steve answered a little sheepishly. "When the lawyers handed me the money, I secretly wished that I could buy a *real* father with it. When I realized I couldn't, I put it away and forgot about it, just like I tried to forget about him."

Steve thought about his childhood and his dream of having a real father while they drove back toward his motorcycle.

"It's hard to imagine actually having a father you like, Hardcore."

After pulling the car to a stop, Bill turned and asked, "How about the best father in the world?"

"What are you talking about? Your father wasn't that much better than mine!"

"But I know someone whose father was," replied Bill.

"Who?"

"The violinmaker's."

Chapter 5: A Chance

Mary decided to eat her lunch on the same bench that she and her mother used to sit on when she was a little girl. It was far enough away from the campus buildings that it had a feeling of privacy. Her mother had always wanted to go back to school and she made this one of their regular stops.

Mary pulled her lunch out of her backpack, unwrapped the peanut butter sandwich and opened her thermos full of fruit juice. After taking her first bite, she closed her eyes and smiled.

She dreamed that she was sitting at a large banquet table in a beautiful silver castle on a forested hill. She was at the head of the table, wearing an elegant, silky-blue dress with flowers pinned on the sleeves and a small gold-and-diamond crown in her hair. After all, she was the princess.

It was the same dream Mary had every time she ate her lunch there.

Her mother and father (the king and queen) were also sitting at the table, but the chair right next to Mary was empty. The prince had sent a message that he would be a little late and to begin dinner without him. He was rescuing a maiden (a child, a helpless widow, or even a small village) from a dragon (an ogre, or a band of thieves). It all depended upon the day and the mood Mary was in what the prince looked like, who he was rescuing and what the villain was.

She knew her prince would prevail over anything evil and that everything would be perfect when he arrived, so she had no worries. In the meantime, she was surrounded by the most wonderful guests who had come to congratulate them on their recent marriage.

"I'm sorry I kept you waiting my love," came a deep, mellow voice from behind her. Mary immediately stood up and turned around so she could greet her prince with the passionate kiss that he deserved. She closed her eyes and pressed her lips lovingly at first, then passionately against his.

It took a second for Mary to realize that she was kissing the motorcycle guy in her daydream. Mary gagged on her sandwich and started choking. It had never ended that way before!

Mary opened her eyes and looked around the campus. Luckily she was still alone with no one nearby to have to explain anything to.

She wiped the crumbs off and picked up her juice. Now the reality of her life all came back and slapped her in the face when she realized that her true love had long greasy hair, an unshaven face and tattoos.

"Gugh! Gag!" she said out loud. Then she took a drink and tried to calm herself back down.

The juice tasted funny in her mouth while she wondered what it must be like kissing someone like that. She thought of his large earrings and ratty clothes, then how his breath must smell if he drank and smoked. It got to the point where she couldn't bear to imagine it any longer and tried clearing her mind.

Her mother had taught her to only date "nice, clean-cut, young men" and to stay away from all the others. "Never date anyone you wouldn't want to marry," were her mother's exact words.

Clarice Anderson was a religious woman, but she was also a realist. She didn't believe it would be a sin if Mary chose someone with a lot of money. "Men can be nice and have money too," she would often remind Mary.

Her mother had a lot of character and everything she said had always made good sense to Mary. She liked that best about her mother and always tried to follow her advice.

Her father, on the other hand, was the one who insisted that Mary was a princess. "There are no limits in life, Mary. You deserve a *Prince Charming* that passionately loves you. Dream all the way, no matter what anyone else ever tells you."

Mary's father and mother constantly gave her advice while she was growing up. Her mother had her lofty ideals, but her father was the dreamer and the one that had influenced how Mary really looked at life.

One month before the accident, her father had told her, "When it comes time to choose who you're going to spend the rest of your life with, remember this: There are a lot of dreamers and talkers in the world, Mary. Men that will claim that they would do anything for you. Choose someone that actually will."

Mary tried to imagine her family's reaction and the look on their faces if she brought home someone like the motorcycle guy. Mary laughed at the thought. Then, when she thought about her family again, she missed them more than ever.

Mary finally wiped away the tears and put her lunch away so she wouldn't be late for her next class.

The Luthier stood up and turned on the light. The sun had dropped behind Pine Valley Mountain and the sky outside had taken on a dark, purplish hue. Steve's lack of sleep was catching up to him and he leaned over and rested his arm against the bench beside him.

The Luthier sat back down, looked at Steve's elbow on the clean, soft silk and winced. Steve looked down at his dirty arm and immediately pulled it away. "I'm sorry," he apologized again. "I'm tired, and I really have a long way to go."

After brushing the spot on the silk with his fingers, Steve continued, "Then, Bill told me all about you."

The Luthier's expression looked like he doubted Steve's last comment.

"Well, from what I hear, maybe not *everything*, but plenty

anyway. He told me how you claimed that you had the greatest father in the world, and from what he saw, he believed it. By the time Hardcore was done, I realized that I needed what you have and it gave me hope."

"What he apparently didn't tell you was that I buried my father years ago," responded the Luthier.

Car headlights panned across the violin shop's window and both the Luthier and Steve turned at the same time.

While the car approached and parked beside the motorcycle outside, Steve told the Luthier, "Hardcore told me that your father had died. But he still believed you could help somehow. He said you can do things that no one else can."

The Luthier raised his eyebrows.

Steve continued, "I went back to Hardcore's house and talked with him and his wife about women late into the night. The next morning, I decided to go back and visit Tom one more time. I told him, 'Tell Mary that what she saw in my eyes is really who I am. Tell her that I will be back when I have repainted the rest of the picture, and that I will try with all my soul to make it worth the wait. And tell her to pray for me.'

"I packed my things and headed out that afternoon." Then Steve patted his chest and declared, "So here I am!"

The Luthier stood up without saying a word, and walked toward the door. "Good evening, Dianne," the Luthier greeted a somewhat-elderly woman of obvious status.

Steve remained seated while Dianne stepped into the doorway. He found himself staring at the gnurled handle of the Glock still protruding out of the Luthier's belt. He had almost forgotten about it while they were talking. He also noticed that the Luthier was watching him very closely out of the corner of his eye.

"What on earth is that?" Dianne asked before she was completely inside. She was looking at Steve's motorcycle.

Before the Luthier could reply, Dianne turned and stared at Steve. "Oh," she added. Dianne's expression immediately turned to distaste.

Steve eventually had to look away while he struggled

not to lose his temper.

"Dianne, this is Steve Miller. Steve this is Dianne Adams, a customer of mine."

Steve looked in her direction and nodded. Instead of acknowledging Steve, Dianne turned back to the Luthier and commented, "I think charity is a good thing and my foundation gives food to the needy all the time, but do you think it's wise to associate with *them*?"

She said it in a condescending tone and as if Steve wasn't even there.

Steve's jaw tightened and he looked at Dianne with obvious hate. The Luthier could tell that there would have been trouble if he were not standing directly between them.

"What can I do for you Dianne?"

Dianne's expression quickly changed and her voice became eager, "Is it finished? Can I see it yet? I debated whether I should stop in unannounced, but I was passing by on the freeway and I just couldn't wait any longer."

Though Dianne was in her late fifties or early sixties, she was on the verge of jumping up and down. "I haven't felt like this since I was a little school girl!" she added.

"It still needs one more coat of varnish," replied the Luthier.

"But you let me see the other one before it was finished," she pleaded.

Steve figured from the way Dianne acted, that she had been spoiled her whole life. He wondered why someone like the Luthier would patronize her.

"This one is different, Dianne. I will call you when it's ready," responded the Luthier in a calming tone.

Dianne quickly snapped back, "I'm paying you more money than you have ever received and you're telling me that I can't see it?"

"Not until it's done," reaffirmed the Luthier. He seemed unaffected by her sudden flare-up.

Dianne became outraged. Not knowing how to respond to the Luthier, she glared over at Steve and lashed out, "What are you staring at, Gutter-Trash?"

Steve instantly flew out of his chair. Before he had taken two steps, the Glock was aimed directly between his eyes again.

Dianne screamed. Then, when she saw Steve was held at bay, she yelled obscenities and swore profusely at him. Finally she took a step further behind the Luthier and added, "How dare he threaten me. It makes me wonder why I even bother trying to help people like that."

"I think it would be best if you left us alone, Dianne." The Luthier didn't move or take his eyes off Steve while he spoke.

"Do you want me to call the police?" she asked while reaching into her purse for a cell-phone.

"I will make the call in a minute," replied the Luthier. "I know you're anxious for the viola and I will call you the minute it's ready. Rest assured, it will be worth the wait."

Dianne dropped her phone back into her purse and backed away. She looked at the Luthier like she believed he would shoot Steve as soon as she was gone. She even glanced down at the carpet as though contemplating the mess it would make.

After glancing back at Steve one last time and shrugging her shoulders, as if to say, "Oh well. No big loss," she walked out.

Steve and the Luthier were looking into each other's eyes. The gun was directly between their faces and neither of them moved until the car could no longer be heard in the distance.

The Luthier slowly backed away a few steps. Sweat was beading up on Steve's forehead. He couldn't think of anything to say. He knew he had just blown his chance and he felt like a cornered animal.

The Luthier stepped around the counter until the telephone was within his reach. He picked up the receiver and began dialing while Steve looked for some way out. Steve twitched each time the Luthier pushed a button like it was stabbing him in the flesh.

"This is par for the course," he thought, after the Luthier finished dialing.

He heard a woman's voice come from the receiver. It was sweet and gentle.

The Luthier replied, "Sheryl, we will be having a special guest for dinner this evening, and we will be walking down the path."

The Luthier hung up the phone and stood silent for a moment. Then he commented, "For the taxes."

"What?" Steve replied, not sure what was going on. The gun was still pointed directly between his eyes.

"That's the reason Dianne donates money to good causes. For the tax write-off," the Luthier clarified while lowering the gun and putting it away.

The Luthier then held out his hand. After a second, Steve shook it in disbelief.

The Luthier stood back and his voice became firm, "I want everything to be crystal clear between us, Steve, so let's make sure I fully understand. I don't want there to be any misunderstandings later on."

Steve nodded and the Luthier continued, "You were raised by a man you consider a worthless, drunken slob. He was a terrible father, and yet your friends call you Chip because you are so much like him and you always carry a chip on your shoulder.

"You have lived a pretty-much worthless life for almost fifty years and it has led you nowhere. The only thing you have ever done that could be considered good was serving your country in what most people consider a worthless war.

"You respect almost no one, especially not women. In fact, until eight days ago you have despised women, but you still use them as you like, when you feel like it, then thoughtlessly 'dump' them."

The Luthier paused for Steve's reaction.

"A little blunt, but yes," Steve replied with a cringe.

"Now you have looked into the eyes of a beautiful woman for thirty seconds. A woman that wants a '*Prince Charming*, *knight-in-shining-armor* and *Superman*' all wrapped up into one handsome package that can make her truly happy forever. And by some miracle you want me to help transform you into all of those things in the time it takes to make her a violin?"

The Luthier didn't wait for Steve's response.

"Then, you expect to enjoy living the life of a perfect gentleman from that moment on? In other words, you think you can totally change *who you are*?" asked the Luthier.

Steve wondered if the Luthier was serious or mocking him. Then he realized, "People never change! You can't teach an old dog new tricks!" His countenance dropped while he thought about his worthless life again.

He turned away from the Luthier and thought of the many nights he got plastered until he couldn't see straight, just to forget who he was and what his life could have been like. He remembered his dreams as a boy. He had wished he could have had a real family who would be proud of him when he did good things, or just give him a smile if he succeeded at something worthwhile. He knew that could never happen now. There was nothing he, nor anyone else, could do to change the past.

Steve then looked back into the Luthier's eyes and remembered what Bill had said about him. He wondered if Bill was right and if the Luthier really could help. Maybe the Luthier knew of some way to make up for the past. Somehow.

He thought of Mary, living all those years alone, keeping herself pure, working hard, and waiting for someone special. If only she could look into his eyes and embrace him. If only he could become someone that she would be proud of. If only!

Steve would have done the kinds of things that Mary had done if it wasn't for his father. But his father made sure that all of Steve's dreams were torn up and thrown away until none of them were left. Steve could have changed after his father died, but his father had also taught him how to blame everyone else for his failures, whether it was their fault or not.

"If only they had lived in a good neighborhood. If only he had a good mother who had stayed with him. If only he had a teacher who he could relate to. If only the war hadn't come along. If only people would stop judging him by the way he looked. If only..."

Steve had learned every excuse there was from his father; even how to blame his father and to create new excuses whenever a situation required it. Now he was tired of all the excuses!

The Luthier's gaze began to remind him of his mean, old drill sergeant's face when telling the new recruits, "It's time to find out what you're really made of, deep...down...inside."

Steve looked into the Luthier's eyes and realized that they were both crazy if the Luthier said he could do it. But he felt like this was his only chance. For the first time in his life, there was someone standing in front of him that might be able to help him succeed. And now he had the best reason in the world to try.

Courage began building up inside Steve.

"YES, SIR!" Steve found himself answering the Luthier. "To everything you have said, YES, SIR!!!"

The Luthier looked surprised at Steve's answer at first, and the confidence that he delivered it with. Then he quickly changed and mirrored Steve's determination. "Okay then, let's do it!"

Steve, in his turn, was shocked when the Luthier accepted his answer. After thinking about the logistics of the situation, he forced a smile. "Do you really think I have a chance?"

The Luthier's eyes narrowed and he answered in a slow, deliberate voice, "A chance. If it really is 'true love', then you have 'a chance'."

Chapter 6: The Path

"*T*rue love can do the strangest things to a man and melt the hardest of hearts, but you have no idea what you're getting yourself into," the Luthier cautioned Steve.

"I don't care. I'm ready to go in, Sir," Steve replied in true military-fashion.

The Luthier looked Steve over one more time before taking on the posture of a hardened, veteran, drill sergeant. His words then became intense and brutal, "The road you have chosen is longer, harder and covered with more blood than any battlefield anyone has ever died upon. The dead and mangled bodies of millions of brave men lie strewn upon it. Few, *if any*, have ever made it to the other side alive.

"If you choose to take this path of your own free will and choice, you will suffer more than you have ever suffered before. More than you ever thought humanly possible.

"If I am the one to accompany you, you will do *anything I ask*." Even louder and with more severity, the Luthier continued, "WHEN I ASK IT!

"And you will do it, whether you believe it to be right or wrong, good or bad or whether you think it has anything to do with your final objective or not, WITHOUT RESERVATION AND WITHOUT HESITATION!"

The Luthier's countenance now changed to that of an insane, commanding officer going forward into battle, knowing that what lies ahead is a suicide mission. "If you fall, you will get back up and charge, no matter how many times you are struck down. Even if your bowels fall out on the ground and get trampled upon, YOU WILL STAND!

"I will not take the first step on this path with you until you *really do* vow *with all your soul* and with *your word of honor* that you understand and that you accept all of these conditions. I will show no mercy and I will give you no quarter." From the tone in the Luthier's voice Steve could tell that he was dead serious.

"I will not kill anyone," replied Steve.

The Luthier put his face right up to Steve's, "I *WILL* ask you to KILL ONE PERSON!" demanded the Luthier.

"Who?" asked Steve. He was startled at the look in the Luthier's wild eyes.

"The man that walked in my door two hours ago," answered the Luthier. He relaxed and backed away, "Only leave the man inside alive."

After taking a deep breath, the Luthier finished in a somber tone, "If you will try with all your soul, I will fight beside you and I will share my father with you."

Steve took one more minute and thought about it; he had always taken his oath of honor very seriously. More serious than his life.

"Yes, I understand," Steve firmly replied.

The Luthier raised his eyebrows again, as though that wasn't quite good enough.

Then, with deep resolve, Steve added in military style, "Yes, Sir! I understand, Sir! I will do it, Sir!" Steve stood straight up while bringing the old, rotten, jungle boots together and saluted the Luthier with firm determination.

To which the Luthier replied, "So be it," while returning the salute.

"If we are going into battle, call me Chip, Sir."

"We are going in together, Chip," replied the Luthier. "You can call me Luthier, or Sir. Whichever seems appropriate at the time, but do not salute me again."

"Yes, Luthier," Steve answered. Then they both dropped their hands to their sides and walked out the door.

Even though Hardcore had told Steve about the Luthier,

it seemed strange how quickly he could go from being a violinmaker to his new drill sergeant. He also began to wonder just what kind of man the Luthier really was.

"There are many rules that you must learn and follow before becoming a *real man*," the Luthier told him while locking the door behind him. "There are so many that I will not be able to tell them all to you, and some of the most important ones, I will only have time to mention once. I still demand that you follow each and every one, absolutely and flawlessly. DO NOT MAKE ME REPEAT MYSELF! Is that understood?"

"Yes, Sir!" Steve replied.

The Luthier had accepted Steve's proposal so quickly that many things Steve hadn't thought about before started running through his mind. It was only then that the seriousness of what he had just committed himself to dawned on him. Yet he had given his word of honor.

It was dark. Thick clouds had gathered outside while Steve had told the Luthier his story.

"Will your things be all right if it rains later?" asked the Luthier. He was referring to Steve's motorcycle and the belongings strapped to it.

"Everything's bundled. It should be all right," Steve answered. Then he walked over and gave it a quick check.

"Oh, #*!" Steve exclaimed after pulling out his small flashlight and turning it on. He reached down and felt his motorcycle's flat front tire. "There must have been a nail in that #*! board I ran over!"

Steve quickly scanned the rest of the *Harley*. His bags were still securely tied to it with small chains.

The Luthier came up behind Steve, and in a stern voice, he demanded, "The first rule you will obey without exception is: *no swearing.*"

That was one of those things Steve hadn't thought about.

He had sworn since he was five years old. His father had sworn profusely, his mother even swore. Everyone in the military swore except Tim, and all his other friends he ever knew, swore.

Steve turned around with his flashlight and looked at

the Luthier. He reacted to the expression on the Luthier's face by turning it off and putting it back in his pocket.

"Oh, #*!" Steve thought. "What have I gotten myself into? Stop swearing? Cold turkey? *!#*&!#,#@!"

Steve now realized that the Luthier had psyched him up and made him commit so quickly in order to get him to vow and commit to *anything* he asked. "%&*#&#*@%*!......."

It didn't matter now, though. Steve had given his word of honor and he would lay down his life before he would break it voluntarily.

"Yes, Sir," was Steve's only verbal response.

"And, as a bit of advice, it's a whole lot easier if you don't even think swear words," the Luthier offered.

"Yes, Sir." "You miserable #*@!" But Steve only thought the last part to himself.

"All right, Chip. We will start this journey, *now*." When the Luthier said the word "now," he quickly turned and started walking into the darkness.

The Luthier's footsteps became firm and steady. The uniform rhythm of their feet marching through the sand and sagebrush reminded Steve of the military. Steve couldn't see a thing, so he followed close behind the Luthier, listening to the sound of his footsteps. Suddenly, they changed and dropped down, then they were gone altogether.

Steve stopped instantly. He could sense something very different ahead of him; something very wrong. It was the feeling that there was nothing there!

He reached into his pocket and pulled out his flashlight. He turned it on as a gush of wind came almost straight up in front of him. The small light verified his feeling. He was standing at the edge of a solid, rock cliff!

Steve panned the flashlight across its surface until he saw the Luthier. He was over twenty feet below, standing on a small ledge.

Steve knelt down and looked for steps or handholds to climb down on. The only thing he saw was a large rock shelf hanging out in space about ten feet below him on his left. Its edge was out past where the Luthier was standing and too far away to swing back to where he was.

There was black, empty space below the ledge, so Steve continued looking for another way down. The last thing Steve ever did was to ask for help.

The Luthier looked up and silently waited.

After a good ten minutes, Steve finally gave up and pointed his flashlight back at the Luthier. He asked, "How?"

"Jump down on the ledge," was the answer.

Steve walked over to the edge of the cliff. It was a long drop, but he had taken on worse before. So he crouched down and jumped. As he dropped, he realized that it was further than he thought and he rotated a little too far in the air.

When he landed, both of his hands went down and hit hard. The flashlight was knocked out of his grasp and went spinning out into space. It flew into the night with its small, white beam rotating as it dropped. By the time Steve recovered and looked down, the flashlight was nowhere to be seen.

"Now what?" asked Steve in complete darkness.

The Luthier answered, "You must hang from the edge, swing yourself back under and drop onto a shelf that lies beneath you.

"You will drop about five feet before you land. Do it."

Steve felt the edge of the rock shelf he was on. It tapered under for as far as he could reach. He wished he had his flashlight. The wind was picking up and it blew his long hair across his face. It didn't affect his sight though; he couldn't see anything.

He pulled out his cigarette lighter and tried lighting it. Only sparks flashed, without any flame. Even when he cupped his hand around it, the flame wouldn't stay lit. He still didn't give up. He cupped his hands downward and sparked the lighter until he thought he could see something below.

He put the lighter back in his pocket and turned around so he could lower himself over the edge. He hung by his arms for a few seconds completely surrounded by the darkness of the overcast night with the wind swirling around him.

Steve kicked his legs and swung back and forth until his forearms touched the edge of the rock, then he blindly let go and dropped.

It seemed like eternity, then when his feet finally hit the shelf below, he stumbled forward and bumped up against the face of the cliff. Just as he caught his balance and stood up, he heard a loud buzzing or rattling sound.

Steve froze, then slowly backed away until the heels of his boots rested on the outer edge of the rock shelf he was on. He could tell that the large rattlesnake was only a couple feet away and level with his stomach.

The snake's hiss grew louder and the rattling more intense while he balanced in the darkness with sweat pouring down his face. A hopeless panic seized him when he realized that there was nowhere to go.

A light flashed on and he saw the large rattlesnake poised in front of him, ready to strike. A gunshot followed and Steve watched the head of the large, venomous snake fly apart and fall at his feet while he lost his balance and fell backward.

Steve screamed the exact same swear words he had thought about only minutes earlier while he plunged through the blackness with his arms flailing, trying to hopelessly grab onto thin air.

Mary walked down the front steps of the music department and across the campus with her violin in her hand late that afternoon. There were times that playing music was the only way she could get her mind off her troubles and she was still an emotional mess from the other night.

As Mary approached the sidewalk, she had a strange feeling come over her. She turned around to see if someone was following her, but no one was there.

She was alone for as far as she could see and it sent a chill running down her spine, even though the afternoon was still warm. The lonely feeling made her think about her family again, then of the husband that she had never found. She desperately wanted children of her own, yet she knew her biological clock was ticking and would someday run down.

Mary began to feel like it was a good thing that she had looked into the eyes of the disgusting stranger. She had been dreaming of the perfect man for so long that maybe it was time she woke up. If she remained too picky and grew old, she would never have children, and that's the kind of man she would probably end up with.

Mary thought about Cindy's words while she continued on her way home. Was it really just a "pipe dream" that would never come true, or was it still possible for her *Prince Charming* to come riding up on his white horse and make everything right? Was there still time for her to live *happily ever after*?

Mary just didn't know, and it began weighing heavily on her mind. By the time she stepped onto the corner of the sidewalk where Tom had spent the last half of his life, she was depressed.

She looked at Tom and smiled though. Just the fact that he was there cheered her up. Mary knew that if it wasn't for Tom she would have been all alone, without anyone she could call family. It was difficult to see the family resemblance between Tom and Mary, but that had never bothered Mary.

She stopped and took a moment to look at the buildings and cars lining the street, noticing how much everything had changed since the first day she met Tom. Then she froze.

Her mouth dropped open and she gasped outloud, "It's been over twenty-seven years!"

Mary was pushing a baby carriage made of brown plastic, gilded with dozens of bright-yellow daisies. It was old and worn, but very clean. John and Clarice Anderson had purchased it from some friends just before Mary was born.

Clarice said it made "good, common sense" because it was inexpensive and they could use it whether they had a boy or a girl. It had been Mary's when she was a baby, and now her younger brother Joey was riding in it.

Clarice worked very hard as a housewife and loved things that made good, common sense. Mary loved her mother and tried to help her in any way that she could. That's why she was pushing the baby carriage while Clarice carried the groceries.

"Mary, watch where you're going," cautioned her mother, when they came to the corner of the sidewalk.

Mary had been skipping and humming the whole time. They had moved into their new home a few days previous and it was the first time they had been to the grocery store together.

"I will," replied Mary as her gaze went from her mother's face to the other side of the street.

Mary looked both ways and stayed close by her mother's side until they reached the other curb. Mary loved her little brother and she carefully worked the baby carriage wheels through the gutter and up onto the sidewalk without jarring him. It was a big job, but Mary was a big girl. She was ten years old.

As soon as they were safely off the street, Mary started skipping and humming her happy tune again.

Just a few feet later, Mary pointed up the sidewalk and asked, "Mother, what's in that chocolate man's cup?"

Clarice immediately stopped and gently tugged at the back of Mary's dress until she turned around and looked at her. She bent down and whispered very quietly, "That's not a chocolate man, Mary. That's an ordinary man, just like your father, except he's blind."

Everyone Mary had known in the small, country town where they had lived before was white.

"So, even though he's dark-brown all over on the outside, he's just like Daddy inside?" Mary asked in a quiet whisper. She always tried to follow her mother's example.

"Yes, Mary," Clarice whispered back.

"Okay. But what's in his cup?" Mary asked again.

Clarice stood for a moment and watched the people walk by. Most of them acted as though the blind man wasn't even there, while others looked at him in disgust.

"Probably nothing," Clarice answered. "He looks sad."

Clarice reached into her purse and pulled out two dollars, "But let's change that."

Mary knew that the two dollars in her mother's hand was all the money they had left after buying groceries. Her mother was always helping others and the statement didn't surprise Mary at all.

Clarice handed the two dollars to Mary and told her, "Put this in his cup when we walk by. I think he needs it more than we do."

Mary took the money from her mother and started happily pushing the stroller again. The man didn't move as they approached and Mary agreed with her mother; he looked very sad. Mary stopped the baby carriage directly in front of the blind man and dropped the two dollars into his cup without saying a word.

"Thank yous little princess," he quietly told her.

"You're welcome, Tom," replied Mary in a happy tone as a big smile spread across her face.

Then Mary took two steps forward and wrapped both of her arms tightly around the blind man and gave him a big hug. Next she gave him a gentle kiss on the cheek and said, "I love you, Tom," before stepping back.

The man lifted his head and large tears began rolling down his cheeks from behind the dark glasses he wore.

Mary looked up at her mother. Clarice was speechless, both at what Mary had done and now at the blind man's reaction.

Mary looked back at him and asked, "Why are you crying, Tom?"

"How does you knows my name is Tom, and why does yous loves me?" he asked through his tears.

"That's easy," replied Mary with a smile. "Your lunch bag has your name written on it, and my mother told me that you're just like my father inside."

Tom smiled with the tears still streaming down his

cheeks.

Mary then asked Tom, "How did you know that I'm a princess?"

Tom smiled and wiped away his tears, "That's easy. Yous walks like one."

It had been twenty-seven years, and Tom had always been there for her.

Mary stood a little taller and walked more like a princess should as she thought about that day and continued on her way up the sidewalk toward Tom.

The fall was less than twenty feet and the piles of leaves were deep and soft, but the impact still violently knocked the wind out of Steve and he almost passed out for lack of oxygen. While he lay struggling to inhale, something violently jerked his long hair and started dragging him mercilessly across the ground.

He couldn't breathe while he was being drug indiscriminately over sharp rocks, cactus plants and thorn bushes. His head was pulled hard to the side every time his body hit each new obstacle and it twisted his neck painfully, over and over again.

After a couple of minutes, when Steve thought he couldn't hold out any longer without breathing or from being beaten to death, he finally caught a painful breath of air. His body instantly started to recover, and after choking in a couple more lungfulls of oxygen, he flipped himself over and tore his hair free from whatever was holding it. He drew out his large bowie knife and stood in the darkness facing whatever was there, ready to kill or be killed.

"Am I going to have to carry you the whole way?" barked the Luthier. "And do I have to repeat myself? No swearing!"

Steve stood speechless wondering, "Who is this guy?

"That's what my father would say," declared the Luthier. "You want the greatest father in the world? Then follow me, *Boy*."

Steve had never let anyone call him "boy" like that before and he wasn't about to now. He gripped the handle tighter and ran into the darkness where the Luthier stood, waving the blade out in front of him. He heard the Luthier's footsteps head off to the left and followed at full speed, ignoring the branches and rocks scraping and cutting at him as he advanced.

After a minute of missing any target he hoped to find, he stopped and listened. All he could hear was the wind through the trees and a few raindrops starting to fall on the dry leaves.

Suddenly the knife was torn from his hand and he heard the large razor-sharp blade swish up past the left side of his head. Something fell down onto his shoulder as he turned by reflex. While he wondered how badly he was wounded, he felt his hair and left earring fall down across his arm to the ground.

"My father would tell me over and over to cut my hair," the Luthier barked out again, then he quickly retreated into the night.

Steve was even more furious now. No one had ever dared taunt him before. He ran through the trees in a blind rage toward the Luthier's footsteps. He was flying through the darkness when a large, jagged rock sunk into his shin, sending him down in agony.

He held his leg and screamed out at the top of his voice, "You snivelling coward! Come face me like a man!"

Blood poured from the gash and ran down Steve's leg. His thick leather pants had not stopped the rock's sharp edge from cutting him deeply. He was still hunched over in pain when lightning flashed and he saw the Luthier's face right in front of him for that instant.

The Luthier's voice came from the darkness ahead, "You and my father must have had the same drill sergeant, Chip. My father used the words 'snivelling coward' many times when referring to men like you, but he never let anyone ever call him one."

Steve stood up and faced the Luthier. He couldn't help it: he clenched his teeth, doubled up his fist and took a swing.

The Luthier grabbed Steve's wrist and turned him around. Then he reached up and pulled out the other large, skull-shaped earring, tearing Steve's right earlobe into two pieces.

"My father told me that if I ever walked through the front door of his house wearing an earring, he would rip it out, along with half of my ear before I could cross the threshold."

Before Steve could respond, the Luthier pushed him away and headed back through the trees. The lightning flashed a moment later and the rain came pouring down in torrents.

The Luthier led Steve even deeper into the valley, then waited for him. When Steve passed by, the Luthier hit him in the back of the head with a branch. The next time the Luthier ambushed him, it was with a rock. In the wildest, thickest part of the valley the Luthier hid many times, giving Steve's body one more gash or bruise after another.

Steve pursued the Luthier through the darkness in all directions. He was wearing down fast and engulfed in so much pain that he could barely stand. He only stopped momentarily each time he ran his face into a branch or when one of his shins dug into another sharp boulder, dropping him to his knees in unbearable-misery again.

Steve figured they must have travelled over two clicks (kilometers) from where he fell off the cliff as he lay trying to nurse his twisted ankle and the latest gash in his leg.

"Coward!" The Luthier's voice came out of the darkness. It was raspy and mean.

Steve painfully stood up while the rain poured down on him. "What do you mean, coward?" he replied in the darkness.

"You will fight to the death in agony for nothing and yet you don't have the courage to be a *real man*," the Luthier barked at him in what sounded like the voice of his old drill sergeant.

Steve hated his old drill sergeant and he crept forward

while the Luthier spoke. With his arms up and his hands trying to reach for the throat he knew was behind the voice, he leapt forward. The Luthier stepped aside and tripped Steve, then pushed him down hard into an old, jagged tree stump.

"'Loser'," barked out the Luthier. "That's what my father would say! Then he would leave your poor, pathetic ass sitting in the mud so you could go back to your same, old, worthless life tomorrow."

The Luthier turned and walked away.

Steve sat against the tree stump, holding his head and shoulder while rocking back and forth in pain.

The Luthier stopped and slowly turned around, "I say, if you really think you have it in you to be a man, you will quit feeling sorry for yourself, get up off your lazy haunches, and follow me. That's what *I* say.

"My father taught me that there was always someone meaner, tougher, faster, and better trained with his fists and weapons than I was."

Without any warning, the Luthier threw the large bowie knife through the darkness and into the tree stump Steve was leaning against.

It easily cut through the thick bark and sunk deep into the hardwood beneath. Steve could barely see the knife in the darkness but the sharp blade hung about a quarter of an inch away from his nose and his heavy breath blew against it when he exhaled.

Steve remained hunched over in pain while the Luthier continued, "My father claimed that he could tell what kind of soul was inside each man that he met, regardless of what was showing on the outside. I'm sorry Chip, I don't have that gift. But I truly believe that if you will stand up one more time and leave that knife forever in that stump, you can succeed at this noble quest of yours. *I* believe that you have it within you to make the greatest woman in the world proud of you, and in doing so, you will become the happiest man alive.

"I also believe that you have it within you to waste away the rest of your life as a pathetic, miserable cuss!"

The Luthier now yelled louder than he had ever before, "STAND UP NOW! And you choose, once and for all, whether it is with or without that knife, and let's get on with it!"

The Luthier walked over to a tree while he spoke, turned on the flashlight that Steve had dropped earlier and placed it between two branches so it lit up the small clearing. The rain slowed to a drizzle and Steve turned his head back toward the Luthier. The Luthier was standing in the middle of the clearing, challenging him.

Steve slowly drug his feet up under him while leaning against the stump. He rose to his feet and grabbed the handle of the knife. He squinted his eyes and clenched his jaw. Then he stopped.

His tight grip loosened and he slowly turned back toward the Luthier. His fingers began caressing the bumps of the carved bone handle.

"It belonged to a friend of mine that died in 'Nam. He was a good man."

"He'll understand then," replied the Luthier.

Steve staggered over to where the flashlight hung between the two branches and lifted it up. He followed the Luthier through the trees without a word, leaving the knife and his anger deeply embedded in the stump.

They trudged through the thick growth and crossed a stream three times. Steve was breathing hard and struggling to keep up because of the beating his body had taken and the three days he had gone without sleep.

The Luthier was standing by a large tree when Steve finally caught up. The flashlight was very dim and almost ready to go out. The rain had come and gone since they left the stump, but for the last few minutes it had stopped altogether.

"You can think of this evening as your life up to this point," declared the Luthier, "Walking through the darkness, falling off cliffs, being drug through a wilderness, beating yourself senseless against senseless obstacles, danger on every side, struggling, fighting, and not knowing where on earth you are going.

"Now, since you have chosen another path, it is my job to open your eyes." After the Luthier finished speaking, he reached behind the tree and flipped on a switch.

The entire valley lit up with hundreds of bright lights. They were standing at the edge of a lush, green lawn and looking at a large, colonial-blue, Victorian-style farm house. It was surrounded by flowers and gardens that were beautiful beyond Steve's wildest imagination.

Steve leaned against the tree and stared all around at the beautiful sight for what seemed like an eternity. It was truly amazing. Then he turned and looked at the dark, wild, jungle he had just been through and shook his head. When he looked forward again, he told the Luthier, "It looks like heaven."

"It is heaven," the Luthier responded. "And there's an angel in that house waiting to serve us dinner."

As Steve staggered away from the tree, the Luthier looked at him and added, "Let's get you cleaned up."

They headed across the grass, side by side, looking like two comrades after the battle.

Chapter 7: Steven

*A*s they walked toward the house, Steve turned to the Luthier and asked, "I thought your father taught you how 'not to fight'?"

The Luthier stopped in front of the metal stairs leading up to the porch and replied, "I said *he* was the greatest father in the world. I never said *I* was very bright."

The Luthier gave Steve a smile and started scraping the mud off his shoes on the open wire steps, then motioned for him to follow suit.

Steve had never seen house steps like the Luthier's, but it seemed to make sense and he followed the Luthier's example. They then rinsed their shoes and boots off with a garden hose before stepping up onto the porch.

While they were removing their shoes, Sheryl, the Luthier's wife, opened the front door and announced with a smile, "It sure took you two a long time to come down the path. Dinner will be reheated in about fifteen minutes." She disappeared behind the large, round-top door without saying another word.

Sheryl had given Steve a glance and a smile, but she didn't seem to notice that the walkway was covered in blood mixed with water. She also hadn't reacted or commented about how he looked.

Steve couldn't believe it, and he took a quick assessment of himself and how he must have appeared to her:

His left arm and shoulder felt separated, so he started feeling the top of his head with his right hand. His scraped and bleeding fingers carefully ran over dozens of bumps, bruises and lacerations, then tugged at the short, jagged clump of hair remaining on the left side. When he lowered his hand, it was covered with blood, small twigs and bark mixed with mud.

He heard and felt a rough, crunching sound as he took his broken nose between his fingers and straightened it out the best he could. "Not the first time," he thought to himself.

He wiped his hand off on his T-shirt and felt his right earlobe tenderly with his fingertips. He flinched when he touched it. As he continued down his scraped, bruised and bleeding arms, chest, and legs, he realized that he must look worse than many of the mangled corpses he had found in the jungle during the Vietnam War.

When he pulled off his left boot, it tore in half, right across the two bullet holes in the ankle. He turned it over and almost half a cup of blood poured out. Both of his legs had bled profusely from the sharp rocks that had dug into them.

When the Luthier offered to take the two pieces and throw them away, Steve declined.

The other boot stayed together, but it wasn't much better and the laces were separated into half a dozen pieces. The olive-green socks were just a pile of mush lying in the bottom of the boots and there were threads and pieces of them all over Steve's feet.

The Luthier turned the hose back on and helped Steve rinse his feet off, then he washed the mess off the porch.

"Those aren't your boots and socks, are they?" asked the Luthier after noticing that there were no scars on Steve's left ankle.

"No, Sir. They belonged to *Tiny* Tim. Died in 'Nam, Sir."

The Luthier looked at the name above the pocket of the shirt and asked, "Since your name is Miller, who is Reber?"

"Lieutenant Joe *Ruckus* Reber. Died in 'Nam, Sir."

"And the knife?"

"Steve *Slaughter* Slader. Dead. 'Nam, Sir."

"And the rest is yours?"

"What's left of me, Sir." replied Steve with a grin. Dirt and blood were mixed together and it was dripping down between his lips and in his teeth when he smiled.

The Luthier smiled back and shook his head.

After taking a quick shower and doing some preliminary first-aid, Steve changed into some of the Luthier's clothes. He joined the Luthier and Sheryl downstairs where formal introductions were then made. He was amazed again when Sheryl simply smiled and replied, "Hello, Steve, it's a pleasure to meet you." She looked at him and shook his hand as though he really was someone special.

They sat down together at an elegantly set table with the finest of foods. It was late, and the Luthier's three children had gone to bed, so there was a quiet, peaceful feeling in the house while they ate.

After finishing dinner and laying his napkin down, Steve asked, "Is the violin shop and this whole valley yours?"

"Pretty much," replied the Luthier.

"How do you pay for all this?" he asked in amazement.

"He is a Master Luthier," replied Sheryl. She then turned and smiled at the Luthier.

Steve glanced over at Sheryl before looking back at the Luthier, "You make that much money making violins?"

The Luthier shook his head. "No. As much as I love them, and as much as I sell my instruments for, they never seem to make any more money than they cost. Most of the things you see around you were bought with the money earned from writing books."

"Violinmaking books?"

"Not exactly," replied the Luthier. "I write about the world I live in and the people who buy my violins. A lot of readers find their stories quite interesting."

"Maybe you'll put me in one of your books someday?" Steve asked jokingly.

"Perhaps," replied the Luthier with a mischievous grin.

After dessert, the Luthier accompanied Steve to the bunkhouse. It was a small building about twenty feet wide and thirty-five feet long with rows of beds running up the walls in military style. There was a bathroom and a shower at the far end and it looked like it was fully outfitted for a large platoon.

"There is a complete first aid kit built into the back wall by the sink. Supplies and clothes are on the shelves with food stored in the cupboard and refrigerator. You are welcome to everything here for as long as you stay," the Luthier offered while flipping on the light switch and showing Steve around.

"I suggest you sleep in. You look like you need it. When you rise tomorrow, eat here, then follow the paved road up to the violin shop."

The Luthier turned and squarely faced Steve, "I remember what you asked Tom to tell Mary. If you do believe in God, I suggest that you get down on your knees tonight and ask him for some help."

The Luthier then walked out and closed the door.

Mary couldn't sleep that night. Her mind felt like it was going a hundred miles per hour.

She rolled over and looked at her violin case in the dim moonlight. It was late, but she knew that her heavy practice mute would allow her to play almost any song without disturbing the other tenants in the building.

She had used quiet music at night to soothe her many times over the years. She debated it for a minute, then rolled back over and looked at her nightstand.

Mary smiled and turned on the light. She reached down and picked up an old photo album. It was her grandmother's...

"They're absolutely perfect, Grandfather!" twelve-year-old Mary Anderson exclaimed while seventy-five-year-old Fred Anderson held up the two sparkling wedding rings that he had finished the day before. "But weren't you going to give them to Grandmother last night for your anniversary?"

Fred Anderson loved making fine jewelry. He had been doing it in his spare time for many years and these were the finest pieces he had ever made.

It had taken him over four months to design the rings, carve the wax, cast them, then find the two matching diamonds and finish them off. They were exquisite by anyone's standards and Mary thought that they would be perfect for any king and queen, or prince and princess, she could imagine. Everything about the rings represented royalty, fairytales and dreams.

Mary had suggested making them because her grandmother's and grandfather's rings were so old that they were almost completely worn through. She had also helped her grandfather design them and did some of the polishing herself.

"I did give them to her," he replied with a smile. "Then she told me to give them to you!"

Mary gasped and held both her hands up to her mouth. She spun around when she heard her grandmother's footsteps behind her. The camera flash went off while Mary's mouth was still wide open.

Her grandmother loved to catch people like that and she had a very large collection of interesting photographs. She absolutely loved them.

"Grandma!" Mary exclaimed. She ran over and gave her a big hug.

Mary's parents appeared next, and they were both smiling.

Mary then informed her grandmother, "But Grandfather made them for you!"

"I know, Mary. But we realized last night that there was no way of getting our old rings off without cutting them."

She held up her hand and showed Mary her old, worn ring, then tugged on it to show her that it wouldn't come off. Mary's grandmother had gained a little weight over the years and had not taken it off in so long that it was now deeply inset into her finger. Mary's grandfather pulled at his ring, showing Mary that he had the same problem.

"That's just something we could never do, Mary," her grandmother added. "Besides, I have a funny feeling that the rings we were married with will last just long enough."

Mary was only twelve years old, but she was smart and could tell that something was up. She carefully pulled the ring out of the small jewelry box, took her grandmother by the hand and tried it on her finger. It was way too small.

Everyone was silent while Mary tried the other ring on her grandfather's finger with the same result. Mary carefully looked at the size of each of the rings, then dropped both of them onto her own, slender, twelve-year-old wedding finger.

She gave her grandfather a wink, "Who do these rings *really* fit, Grandfather?"

"Your mother and your father!" he blurted out. Then he quickly looked up at Mary's grandmother with a big grin. All three turned toward John and Clarice just as the flash on Grandmother's camera went off again, adding yet another picture to her collection.

Mary's mother and father had not worn wedding rings since Mary was a baby. Mary was too young to remember, but she had heard the story of how John and Clarice were held at gunpoint, then robbed of almost everything they owned, including their wedding rings. The two "motorcycle hoodlums," as Mary's parents called them, even threatened to cut off their fingers when they hesitated and struggled to remove them. They were always short on money after that and had never been able to afford new ones.

After discussing it, they all agreed that John and Clarice would use the special wedding rings as their own until they could comfortably afford to replace them. That way they could stop worrying about the money and finally get back on their feet financially. Then someday, they would give the rings to Mary and her husband when she got married.

After everyone had kissed each other a dozen times, Mary's grandmother put the camera on timer and lined them all up for one final picture. Just before the flash went off, she stepped on a *whoopee-cushion* so she could add that photograph to her collection also.

Mary looked at the three pictures and smiled at each one before closing the photo album. She turned off the light, then dreamed of her grandmother and grandfather.

The shades were down in the bunkhouse and it was early afternoon before Steve woke up the next day.

There was only a sliver of light coming in around the edges of the windows and Steve looked around very slowly. His eyes felt like red-hot pokers had been shoved through them.

He had a throbbing headache, every inch of his body was screaming in pain, and he was so stiff that he could barely move. Those were all pleasant things compared to his dream the night before.

Steve had no trouble drawing the covers off with his bruised arms and torn up hands. There was no hesitation as he swung his gruesomely-mutilated legs out of bed and planted both feet firmly on the floor.

Even though most men in his condition would have buckled under in agony if they tried walking, Steve stood on his swollen ankle, ignored the excruciating pain and dizziness, and took a shower.

Every inch of his body screamed and tormented him while forcing it to move against its will. But no matter how much he hurt, he acted as though nothing was wrong.

After eating breakfast, Steve selected a set of military fatigues from off the hangers on the wall and put them on, then he picked up a pair of military boots out of the lineup on the floor. Most men would have passed out in reaction to the pain of pulling a stiff army boot over the deep-purple, swollen ankle, yet it was nothing for Steve this morning. He had dreamed about his father all the night before and he clenched his teeth, stood up and walked to the other side of the bunkhouse in spite of him.

His eyes quickly and painfully adjusted to the light after

opening the door. He then staggered past the Luthier's house on the only paved road in the valley. Even though they had not crossed it the night before, the Luthier had told Steve that it would lead him back up to the violin shop.

He had been in a lot of fights over the years, but this was the worse shape he had ever been in. He had also been mangled pretty good back in Vietnam, but that was many years ago and it felt much worse now that he was a middle-aged man. Even though he was feeling his age, his gait evened out to a mild limp by the time he reached the cliff where he had fallen the night before.

It didn't seem as high and menacing in the daylight and he looked around, trying to figure out where the Luthier had led him in the darkness. As he surveyed the valley, he realized that the Luthier had carefully taken him back and forth and around and around without running into any signs of civilization. The valley wasn't nearly as large as he had thought it was.

As Steve headed up the hill toward the violin shop, the temperature rose very quickly. It changed more than he thought it should have and he found himself looking back down at the lush, green valley in wonder.

When he arrived at the violin shop, he noticed that his motorcycle tire had been repaired. He kicked it just to make sure he wasn't dreaming. No one had ever done him a favor like that before.

He knocked this time and waited for the Luthier to open the door, even though the sign said, "Come in. You are welcome."

The Luthier appeared in the doorway. "Hello, Chip."

"Hello, Luthier. Thank you for fixing the tire."

"I heard a crack when you hit the tree last night. I figured you would need to take it easy on that shoulder for a while."

Steve nodded and now wondered at how nice the Luthier was treating him.

The Luthier suddenly stood up straight and harshly barked out, "But I won't be taking it easy on you," while waving his finger in Steve's face.

Steve drew back under the sudden harshness of the Luthier's voice, then his body straightened up, even though it hurt him to do so. Only then, did the Luthier relax and smile at him again.

Steve forced a smile and replied, "You mean yesterday wasn't just a bad dream?"

The Luthier shook his head.

In a joking tone, Steve put his hands over his face and wailed, "Oh, no..!"

"Yep, you're in this one for keeps, Chip. I have your word of honor and I'm here to make sure that you keep it. The real question is, do you still want 'IT'?"

Steve wasn't quite sure what "it" was, and asked, "What?"

"The world," replied the Luthier.

Steve nodded.

"Then let's get started, Chip. You will need to pay for your violin up front. Cash on the barrelhead." The Luthier held out his hand with the palm up.

Steve turned and walked back out of the violin shop. In less than two minutes, he returned with a large stack of one hundred dollar bills. He crumpled them between his hands and wadded them up into a large, ragged ball. He then slapped it into the Luthier's outstretched hand with a smile.

"Hardcore said this is how much you charge," Steve declared.

The Luthier hefted the wad of bills and eyed it. It looked like he was weighing the ball by gently lifting it up and down. He nodded, walked over to the cash drawer and tossed it in.

"As for our other agreement," the Luthier informed him, "You can never begin to pay me what it is worth, and I can never accept a penny for it." The Luthier offered his hand and Steve shook it, thinking that he understood.

The Luthier led Steve into the workshop area and stopped by a bench that had pieces of wood sitting on it. They were very old and grey.

The pieces were larger, thicker and cut differently than all of the others hanging from the ceiling, yet they looked like they had just been pulled down. The Luthier blew the dust off one of the pieces and handed it to Steve, "Tell me what you see."

Steve looked at it and replied, "An old piece of wood."

"Is that really all you see?" asked the Luthier.

Steve looked at it a little closer and replied, "An old, dusty piece of wood that is weathered and dry with a piece of wire running through it, so you can hang it from the ceiling, I guess."

The Luthier nodded. "Feel it."

Steve knocked it with his knuckles, twisted it the best he could with his bad shoulder, then hefted it up and down. He tried to think of something more intelligent and added, "It's hard and strong, but it feels light."

"Very good," said the Luthier with a smile. "Now taste it."

Steve gave the Luthier a puzzled look, like he thought the Luthier was crazy.

The Luthier's face suddenly flared and he snapped out more viciously than Steve had ever heard his father or any drill sergeant, "DO YOU FORGET AND FAIL YOUR VOW OF HONOR SO QUICKLY AND SO EASILY?"

The Luthier's face was red and the veins were sticking out of his neck as he drew back his fist in the air.

Steve could not believe how quickly the Luthier could change emotions and expressions, and he wondered if the Luthier really was insane. Yet the reality was, Steve had hesitated on a direct order, again!

The Luthier continued yelling with his fist threatening Steve the whole time. It was all Steve could do not to raise his arms in defense of the blow that he felt was sure to follow. The Luthier's face contorted and his temper flared to an even higher level, "Just because orders are not yelled and forced down your throat does not mean they are not orders!"

The Luthier finished by putting his clenched fist into his other palm and grinding it with massive force to reinforce his point.

"Yes, Sir," was Steve's humble reply.

The Luthier lowered his voice two notches but still maintained a serious, harsh tone. Steve felt like the Luthier's eyes were drilling right through him while he spoke, "If you ignore Mary until she has to scream at you, your married life will become a living hell."

The Luthier's voice instantly changed and became very soft and mellow. A peaceful expression even spread across his face as though nothing had happened.

"From this moment on, I will never yell an order in anger or reprimand you with a loud voice or hard words again. If you will not listen unless you are yelled at by the time we are through," the Luthier's eyes moistened and his voice saddened, "in the words of my father, 'You are not worth the sweat off my brow'."

Steve could tell by the way the Luthier acted that the Luthier's father had indeed yelled at him and said those exact same words.

"From now on I will ask politely and talk as a gentleman should talk. Even though I do, you will still take everything that I say as a direct order and obey it immediately. Do you understand?" the Luthier asked in a soft, mellow voice.

"Yes, Sir," was Steve's reply.

After letting that sink in, the Luthier continued, "Do you plan on having any children with Mary?"

"I haven't thought about it," replied Steve.

"She will want them." The Luthier spoke as though there was no doubt in his mind. "Even if she can't have them herself, she will want to adopt. When that time comes, will you be the same father to your children as your father was to you?"

"Never," was Steve's defensive answer.

"Will you viciously punish *your child* every time he doesn't listen or if he isn't what you want him to be? And will *you* hold your child down and mercilessly beat him until Mary shoots herself in the head with *your* pistol?"

Steve's face grew pale, then rage tore across his face. "How do you know about my mother?"

The Luthier stepped back a foot and the most serious expression spread across his face. He answered in a profound, absolute tone that Steve had never heard anyone speak in before, "I...just...do."

The Luthier continued, "If you want to be a good father to your children, you must never yell at them in anger.

"A father yells at his child, trying to get him to listen. He screams louder and louder until the child no longer hears him at all. He eventually screams so loudly that he couldn't hear the answers anyway. Then that *bad* father starts beating the child and wonders why the child never listens.

"Before I go on, I am going to make something absolutely plain, Chip."

"Yes, Sir?"

"Everything I will do will be based upon the assumption that you are special, and that what you have really is *true love at first sight*. Not just true love that happens upon occasion, but true love *at first sight* which I have only heard of happening five times in the entire history of the world.

"I am also assuming that you have fallen in love with the most wonderful woman in the world and that she has also experienced this same *true love at first sight*. A woman of such character that she will forgive you of your past and only judge you by what you are when we are done. Even though you come from two completely different worlds, I am also assuming that it really is possible for you to live *happily-ever-after* together."

Steve thought it over for a minute, but that really was how he felt and what he hoped for, so he replied again, "Yes, Sir."

After hearing Steve's response, the Luthier continued, "I ask all of this because, no matter how strong you are, that's what it will take."

The Luthier turned away from the bench and walked through the shop, looking up at all the other pieces of wood hanging from the ceiling. "Some of the things I will tell you along the way will not make any sense, or will seem totally outlandish and unreasonable. No matter what you or other people might think, you must totally open your mind and free yourself of everything you thought you knew before today. Do you understand?"

"Yes, Sir."

"In order for you to succeed at this quest, you must become as close to the perfect man as is humanly possible." The Luthier smiled and his expression became strange, almost diabolical. "I know of only one individual that has ever laid claim to that title." The Luthier's words and his gaze made Steve feel uncomfortable.

The Luthier looked into Steve's eyes to make sure he really understood. "Do you realize that you're asking me to make you a saint?"

Steve looked dumbfounded. He wasn't sure if the Luthier was still serious or joking now.

"What is your *real* given name?" asked the Luthier as though he knew something Steve wasn't telling him.

Steve hesitated at first, then admitted, "My mother named me Stephen, after the apostle in the New Testament. She even pronounced it Stefen."

"Saint Stephen," the Luthier repeated as though he were pondering it.

Steve had the strangest feeling come over him. It felt really weird now that he knew the Luthier was serious.

The Luthier looked into Steve's eyes while repeating the words, "Saint Stephen," over and over.

The Luthier's gaze wandered down to the black rings surrounding Steve's eyes, then to his swollen, purple nose and the ragged clump of hair on the side of his head and he burst out laughing.

"Pardon me, but even I can't quite picture it yet. But I will call you Steven, and that is the name you will go by starting right now. Your name is no longer Chip or Steve, it is Steven."

Steven's face went through a whole series of contortions. But after a minute, he brightened up and actually thought he liked the sound of it.

He found himself looking up at the roof of the shop while he thought about his mother again.

"Steven," he said outloud.

"Steven," he repeated while still looking up.

Chapter 8: Bone Guys

Steven lifted the old grey piece of wood to his mouth and placed his tongue against it. It only took a second before he tasted the distinct flavor of salt. He drew it away with a sour look on his face.

"Salt!" he declared, and he looked back at the Luthier for an answer.

"Sea salt," replied the Luthier.

Steven looked at the piece of wood and nodded. He had heard of curing things with salt before. While in the Marine Corps, he had also seen old wood at the docks that had similar characteristics.

"From a pirate ship that sank in 1712," the Luthier added. "It was found off the coast of Jamaica over a hundred years ago."

The Luthier took the piece of wood and replaced it on the bench by the others. Next, he reached into his pocket and pulled out Steven's silver earring. He held it up to the light so Steven could clearly see its golden eyes sparkling at him, then he tossed it on the bench. It flipped over and came to rest against the board he had just set down.

"That skull's pattern was taken from that pirate ship's flag. It was the only piece of wood recovered from the ship good enough to go into a master instrument. It will now become the scroll of your violin."

The Luthier ignored Steven's reaction and handed him the next piece of wood.

As soon as Steven looked back up, the Luthier softly ordered, "Taste it."

Steven did not hesitate this time. He lifted the old,

greyish-brown board and placed his tongue against it. He was not surprised when he tasted bitter sea salt again.

"From the floundering ship *Bon Homme Richard*, from which John Paul Jones declared, 'I have not yet begun to fight!' It will become the back and ribs of your violin."

Steven's jaw dropped and the Luthier calmly took the wood back out of his hand without saying another word.

The Luthier reached down and slowly grasped the last piece of wood. It was totally different than the rest. It was almost black with age and its uneven surface was worn smooth and glossy.

It felt strange in Steven's hand. By the way the Luthier handed it to him, he knew it must be the most valuable of all.

He felt the wood and rolled it over in his hands while he waited for the Luthier to tell him where it came from. The Luthier looked into Steven's eyes without saying anything. It made him wonder, more than ever, what he was holding.

The Luthier finally spoke, "From Jerusalem, nearly two thousand years ago. You can believe what you like."

Steven stared at the piece of wood in disbelief. He didn't know what to think. His mother was a Christian, but the only time she took him to church was when his father was passed out beyond comprehension on Sunday morning. Then they would sit in the back of the church wearing their everyday clothes just in case his father woke up before they got back home.

His mother told Steven never to admit to his father that they went to church. She would pretend that they had gone for a walk or to the park if he was awake when they got back. The last time Steven had been in a church was the morning of the day his mother shot herself. Steven never told his father that they had ever attended and he never went back.

After his mother was gone, Steven gave in and followed his father's example. He pushed every thought of being a good Christian so far out of his mind that, by the time he went to Vietnam, he considered himself an anti-Christ, and did everything he could to act the part. Even though his father had raised him with the slogans "victory or death" and "duty to country," his cigarette lighter had the words "Jesus is dead!" scratched into it.

Steven didn't really "hate Jesus" like the back of his helmet said while marching through the jungle in Vietnam. He simply needed to say something mean to make himself feel better and that's what got the biggest reaction from everyone.

When Steven was talking to Tom on the sidewalk the second day, Tom told him that Mary was a Christian, and it was then that Steven started thinking about God again and wondering who or what Jesus really was, if anything.

Steven handed the piece of wood back to the Luthier not knowing what to think, and it showed.

"I just wanted to know what you would believe," commented the Luthier. Then, holding it up to the light, he announced, "It was removed from the basement of Solomon's temple while it was being destroyed. It is said to be from the original cedars of Lebanon mentioned in the Jewish Tora and the Christian Old Testament. The original trees had much finer grain and were stronger than those found there in the last two thousand years. It will make the top or "belly" of your violin."

The Luthier gently placed the piece of wood back on the bench with the others. "Think of these pieces of wood as *what you are* standing here today. We shall see *what you become* by the time you give this violin to Mary."

The Luthier took a deep breath and smiled. He seemed to change character as he changed the subject, "We've been pretty serious since you came in that door yesterday. To be a good father you must also know how to have fun.

"What do you do for fun, Steven?"

The question caught Steven totally off guard. He could only think of what he had been doing for the past twenty-some years: getting drunk, women (not nice ones), and lately, hard drugs and running from the police on his motorcycle. He thought about the word "fun" and wondered what the Luthier meant.

"Fun?" he asked.

"Good, wholesome things that allow you to let off some steam and enjoy yourself. Something you could do with your children," replied the Luthier.

The words "your children" stuck in Steven's mind. What he told the Luthier was true, he had never really thought about children. Now, if he succeeded, it could actually happen.

"Whoa!" he thought to himself, he needed to think more about that one later.

Steven put his mind back to the question and found that he couldn't think of anything he had fun doing that he could do with children. He then tried to think about what *normal* people might do with their children and finally answered the Luthier with the only thing he could think of, "Bowling?"

The Luthier smiled. He could tell that Steven was having a difficult time. "Yes, that's pretty good. But I'll tell you what; we'll do fun backwards to help you get in the spirit of things. Have you ever played with *play-doh*?"

Steven could remember playing with the small cans of colored clay and replied, "Yes. But that's starting backward?"

"It's a game my father taught me and I think it is one you might enjoy also. Follow me."

The Luthier headed out the door and led Steven away from the violin shop. They didn't follow the road Steven had driven on the day before. Instead, they walked through the orchard where the Luthier pointed out many of the different trees. Then they crossed the road on the other side and walked across a large, open field.

They stopped in front of a steel door surrounded by concrete and embedded in the side of a small hill. The Luthier pulled out a set of high-security keys and unlocked two deadbolts, then he twisted a large combination lock next to the handle. When the Luthier finally opened the heavy steel door, there was a space of about six feet, then another door!

The Luthier noticed the look on Steven's face and commented, "I like to keep this building *well insulated*. You can never be too careful with *play-doh*."

The Luthier pushed a rubber pad on the wall and an eerie greenish-yellow light glowed above them. While he closed the outer door and fastened the locks, he noticed that Steven was looking back and forth between the special switch on the wall and the strange sealed light on the ceiling.

"No electrical spark and no heat," the Luthier responded to Steven's expression as he turned to unlock the next door.

When the second, solid-steel door swung open, Steven understood. Then his jaw dropped and he stared in amazement. He was looking at every kind of explosive and demolition ordnance he had ever seen. Now the barricades and special light switch made sense.

There were stacks of crates, and rows of cans and pails. They were all marked with various, colorful *danger* and *high explosive* stickers.

While Steven continued looking around, big smiles spread across both of their faces.

Steven's attention finally rested on something he had never seen before. A row of large, flat boxes, each painted red and black with a very large, white skull and cross-bones in the middle. The cross-bones formed an "X marks the spot" in the center of each box and there was a warning that read, "UNBELIEVABLY HIGH EXPLOSIVES! MUCH MORE THAN DANGEROUS!" in bright orange letters. They looked like a row of large pizza boxes except they were four feet square.

The Luthier noticed Steven's gaze stop at the boxes. "We will need two of those. You can carry them both in your right hand if it feels like too much weight for your left shoulder."

The Luthier's expression suddenly lightened and he chuckled. "When my youngest son Colter was four years old, he called skeletons, 'Bone Guys.' He doesn't call them that anymore, but the name stuck on those boxes and it still seems fitting.

"Please, pick up the *Bone Guys* by the handles. And please be very careful," he added.

The word "please" sounded very strange to Steven. Not only because it was the first time the Luthier had used it, but because he couldn't remember the last time anyone had spoken it to him nicely. He knew the simple request was really a direct order, but it still felt different when the Luthier used the word and Steven couldn't help smiling.

Steven headed toward the *Bone Guys* while the Luthier walked over to a row of white, two-and-a-half-gallon plastic pails and picked up one in each hand. Then he announced, "That's all we will need from this room."

Steven noticed that the first *Bone Guy* in the row looked like it had been buried in the dirt before. It seemed strange because all the others were clean and spotless.

The boxes weren't very heavy, but he still carried two of them in his right hand while following the Luthier to the opposite side of the room. They went through two more steel doors, just like before, but they exited on the opposite side of the mound.

Steven found himself looking out across a large shooting range. It was a lot like the one he and Bill Hardy had been on just a few days before. There was a large, flat valley and a mountain on the other side with targets set up at different distances.

Out in the middle, slightly off to the right, was something that wasn't at the other range. Twenty large, granite boulders about four feet in diameter were sitting between what looked like two solid-steel launching pads. About a hundred feet beyond them were two large, fluorescent-orange circles painted on the ground.

The Luthier laughed at the expression on Steven's face. "My father loved this game, Steven. He helped write the original *Handbook of Explosives* and loved bowling and golfing. He thought of this as a *real man's* version of the two sports put together.

"He played the game back and forth between circles or

with fifty-gallon barrels. I added the *Bone Guys* after he died. It adds a little extra thrill to the game."

While the Luthier and Steven walked over to the launching pads, he continued, "The game works like this:

"Each of these buckets contain sticky, medium-velocity, explosive *play-doh*. It's easy to mold and will stick to the bottom of a boulder quite well. By molding the explosive into a shape-charge and placing it on the bottom of the boulder *just right*, it is possible to launch a boulder, sail it through the air, and land it in the center of your circle where one of the *Bone Guys* will be placed. We blow the charges simultaneously and the first person to land their boulder on their *Bone Guy* wins.

"It doesn't count unless you land your boulder on your own *Bone Guy*. It's not as hard as it looks and I'll demonstrate once. Then, if you would like, I'll help you the first time or two."

As they walked from the launch pads to the circles, Steven looked back to where the boulders were, up through the air and then to the circles again. He smiled, then looked down at the boxes he held in his hands and exclaimed, "Wow!"

"Exactly," replied the Luthier.

Chapter 9: The Game

*A*fter the Luthier and Steven placed the *Bone Guys* in the center of each of their circles, they headed back to get rubber gloves, blasting caps, wire and an old-fashioned dynamite plunger. Those items were kept in a separate room, located in the same mound that they had come through earlier. Steven had been trained in the military that igniters and blasting caps had to be kept separate from the main powder for safety reasons. He had also been taught most of the basics of explosives, so he didn't need much explanation from the Luthier.

Steven noticed that the Luthier had nice electronic equipment in the bunker and questioned the old-fashioned plunger that the Luthier chose instead.

"It adds a rustic thrill to it all," the Luthier repled while carrying out the old wooden box with the T-handle sticking out of the top. Did you ever watch the *Addams Family* when you were a kid?"

Steven nodded, then smiled when he remembered Gomez, the father, blowing up his toy trains with dynamite, using an old-fashioned plunger just like the one the Luthier was carrying.

The Luthier put on a set of rubber gloves and opened his pail while explaining the basics of shape charges. He then showed Steven how to mold the explosive *play-doh* into cup shapes with just the right angles and thicknesses, and the philosophy behind it.

Steven normally didn't like listening and learning about technical things. In fact, the Luthier reminded him of his old chemistry teacher in high school that he had ignored and gotten an 'F' from. But this was different, and he took it all in. He found himself listening to every word.

The Luthier grabbed a large crowbar and rolled one of the round boulders onto his launch pad. There were hardened steel nubs protruding out of a hollow in the center of it and he rolled the large boulder onto them using a special fixture to pry with. It left a gap between the rock and the launch pad where he placed the shape charge.

"I will place your boulders because of your bad shoulder," he told Steven.

Steven started to open his mouth to object, then he realized it was a statement, not an offer, so he didn't. He was a *dyed in the wool* military man, and even though he was a little rusty and the Luthier wasn't really military, he was slowly taking these quiet, polite orders just as serious, if not more, than the loud ones his superiors had barked at him in boot camp and Vietnam.

The Luthier carefully positioned the blasting cap in the *play-doh* while he explained how important its placement and angle were to Steven. Steven was *eating up* the information and his excitement was building as the Luthier rolled the detonation wire over to a bunker that faced the boulders and rings.

The bunker wasn't any further away from the launch pads than the rings were and Steven gave the Luthier a puzzled look as they walked in.

"Yes," the Luthier replied without Steven uttering a word. "Though the boulders cannot get close to the storage facilities, they can reach us here." When the Luthier finished speaking, a large grin spread across his face.

Steven looked at the roof of the bunker. It was made of heavy steel beams and thick steel plates, but he still wondered...

The Luthier wrapped the wires around the two copper posts sticking out of the box and tightened the copper wingnuts. "Are you ready?" he asked.

Steve hesitated a little. He still wondered if the Luthier

wasn't just a little bit crazy, but he went ahead and answered, "Yes, Sir!" anyway.

The Luthier got an excited childish-grin on his face when he lifted the old wooden handle and the plunger box clicked.

"Fire in the hole!" he announced, before quickly pushing the handle down. They both looked out the small, but thick, bullet proof glass window of the bunker together.

"BOOM!" Smoke burst out from beneath the rock, and it sailed into the sky like a golf ball hit with a sand wedge. It floated through the air for about five seconds before landing twenty feet shy of the Luthier's circle with a loud "thud" that they could feel in the bunker.

"Cool!" exclaimed Steven as he rushed out the door, carrying his pail toward the launch pad.

When the Luthier caught up to Steven at the pad, he asked, "Would you like to give it a try?"

"Yes, Sir!" Steven's adrenaline was rushing.

The Luthier rolled a boulder onto Steven's launch pad and explained how to judge each rock; how to place it, and how to determine where the charge should be placed, depending upon the exact size and shape of the boulder. It was then that Steven realized that the boulders were not perfectly round or exactly the same size.

After Steven placed his charge, the Luthier adjusted it a little and explained why. Steven found it strange that he could take the advice from the Luthier; normally he fought being corrected by anyone.

Steven even asked, "I don't mind taking advice from you. Why?"

"Two reasons," answered the Luthier. "I really do care about you, and you believe that I can beat you to a bloody pulp." Then after that same little pause that Steven was getting used to hearing, the Luthier smiled and added, "That's what my father would say."

"Your father really was something else," Steven remarked after thinking about the two statements.

"Yes, he was," reinforced the Luthier.

Steven followed the Luthier over to the other launch

pad and watched him set his charge. The Luthier continued, "My father was a hard man. He wasn't a large man, but some of the things he did would make most men whine and cower like yellow dogs. He enlisted in the Navy during World War II, but came home early after contracting rheumatic fever. He was in a military hospital for months and ended up with a badly scarred and perforated heart.

"That hospital was where my father said he learned to hate doctors. Even though he knew there were good doctors around, he never took us to one when we were growing up unless it was for something life threatening, or if a limb was completely severed off.

"He told us how he watched many men limp into that hospital, be operated on, then never walk another day in their life. Or how they ended up six feet under, instead. Those same doctors released him and told him that he had anywhere between two weeks and four months to live. Then they sent him home with a military disability pension that ended up at seventeen dollars a month.

"He slowly recovered, but he must have figured that he didn't have long to live. Especially if *those* doctors gave him *that much time,* and he took his life around some strange twists and turns. My father's caliber would never allow him to purposely hurt or kill himself, but one does have to wonder what was running through his mind when you look at his life.

"To earn money, my father took a job in a carnival as a shallow diver. He would climb a ladder eighteen feet high, then dive from the platform into a tub of water eighteen inches deep. He even succeeded a few times before breaking his neck." The Luthier paused just a moment, then added, "The first time."

Steven found himself wondering, "This is the greatest father in the world?"

"He recovered," the Luthier continued.

"Next he took up figure-eight racing, which is now outlawed of course."

Steven nodded and followed the Luthier back to the

bunker. He had heard of figure-eight racing but he had never seen it for himself.

"Of course the whole reason people went to watch was to see the drivers misjudge their timing when the cars crossed in the center of the track, or when the drivers simply played chicken.

"Every time there was a bad crash, the crowd would go wild. It wasn't uncommon for most of the cars to end up in the center of the track, all piled up. And it wasn't that rare that someone got killed.

"He only stopped racing when he blew his last engine and couldn't afford another one. That was a few years after the doctors told him that he would be dead, so he decided to settle down and get a real job."

The Luthier tightened the large copper wingnuts again and continued, "That's when he went to school and entered the field of explosives. Would you like the honors this time?"

"Yes. Please." Steven's response was followed by the ratcheting sound of the old handle. Then he followed the Luthier's example and yelled, "Fire in the hole!" before pushing it quickly down.

"BOOM!"

Both rocks sailed into the air at the same time. The smoke and shockwave was definitely bigger with the two charges and Steven grinned with pleasure. The rocks sailed through the air, almost side by side at first, then they separated and headed toward their respective targets.

"Thump. Thump." The boulders both landed right next to each of their circles before rolling past their respective *Bone-Guys*. When the smoke had cleared, they headed out of the bunker with the two pails full of play-dough.

"This time you can try it by yourself," the Luthier offered as they approached the launching pads.

Steven nodded and went to work. He put on a pair of rubber gloves and started shaping the charge and placing his blasting cap while the Luthier worked on his own and continued talking.

"He must have figured out that he was going to live after

all and married my mother. She was runner up for Miss Idaho in the Miss America contest and had a promising career as a concert pianist. They were happy enough, yet my father continued living dangerously.

"Next he took up ski jumping, which was a fairly new sport at the time. He became very good very quickly, but a gust of wind caught him in midair and he over-jumped the hill and landed upside down in the parking lot at the bottom. That's how he broke his neck the second time.

"He made an elaborate contraption of his own design after that accident to relieve the pressure from off his spine. I know it sounds cruel and unfeeling, but I still remember us laughing at him every time he hung himself in the corner of the living room with it. His friends at the ski jump had taken him to the hospital with his broken neck but he just wouldn't go back to the doctors unless his very life was directly threatened, no matter how much pain he was in.

"My brother Ben, who loved everything in the wild outdoors and seemed to open himself up on a regular basis, always carried a needle and sutures with him so he could sew himself back up when he got hurt. He knew my father wouldn't take him to the hospital, so he figured he might as well learn how to take care of everything as it happened. I think he actually liked the idea of fixing himself.

"My father taught us to be able to control ourselves like we were machines. 'Show a little backbone and some self control,' he would say if we ever flinched from pain."

After looking at Steven's shape charge and connecting the wires to the blasting cap, the Luthier stood back and smiled. As they entered the bunker, the Luthier's smile got bigger until Steven asked, "What?"

The Luthier silently fixed the wires to the posts, lifted the handle and hollered, "Fire in the hole!" with a little extra, added zeal.

With the handle still held high, he hesitated just a moment and commented, "This should be interesting." Then he quickly pushed it down.

"BOOM!" and both rocks flew into the air.

The Luthier's boulder split in two as it headed toward his circle and Steven's disappeared altogether!

There was just enough time for Steven to holler out, "Where did it go?" and for the Luthier to calmly reply, "Incoming."

Steven and the Luthier crouched down against the wall and looked into each other's eyes just before it hit. Steven's eyes showed fear, but when he looked over at the Luthier, he saw what looked like the face of a five-year-old boy smiling back at him.

"CRASH!" The ceiling of the bunker was instantly three feet lower in the center than it had been the moment before and the sound was deafening! Dirt flew from all directions as the walls buckled. The steel supports were pounded a good six inches deeper into the earth.

Steven couldn't see the Luthier because of the dust in the air. After a minute, Steven could barely make out the bent steel beams still holding the twisted roof of the bunker up and he knew the boulder was sitting right on top.

"I always wondered if it would hold," commented the Luthier in a slow contemplative tone.

As soon as the dust cleared, Steven could see that the Luthier sat smiling with dirt and dust covering him from head to toe. The only thing Steven could see that had any color were his eyes and smiling teeth.

"My father would also say, 'If at first you don't succeed...'"

"...try, try again," finished Steven as he excitedly grabbed his white pail full of play-dough and started to get up.

"No. If at first you don't succeed, don't try parachuting," laughed the Luthier as he quickly wiped off the window with his sleeve, grabbed his own pail, and followed Steven out the door of the bunker.

The bunker looked pretty much demolished with the boulder sitting right in the middle of the roof, but as they headed back to the launching pads, the Luthier insisted that it should still hold.

The two pieces of the Luthier's boulder had landed on either side of his circle and about twenty feet short again. "It happens," the Luthier commented. "If the boulder had held together it would have been a perfect shot."

After the Luthier pushed two more boulders onto each of the pads, Steven watched the Luthier set his charge before heading back over to his own.

"Would you like some help this time?" asked the Luthier with a smile.

"No, I think I know what I did wrong," replied Steven.

The Luthier looked surprised, but stood back and waited until Steven was finished. He didn't even check Steven's shape charge before hooking up the wires.

"So, what's in those *Bone Guys* anyway?" asked Steven as the Luthier fastened the other end of the wires to the plunger back in the bunker.

"'Patience,'" replied the Luthier. "That's what my father would say." Then, he added with a big mischievous grin, "Lots of patience."

After a second, the Luthier looked out the window and yelled, "Fire in the hole." He lifted and pushed the plunger down, all in one motion.

"BOOM!"

Steven's head instantly turned to watch the boulders launch.

Both boulders arced elegantly across the sky. Steven watched them peacefully float down, but he never saw either of them hit their respective *Bone Guys* in the center of the circles.

"KA-BOOM! ! !" The ground shook violently as the two boulders instantly vaporized and the explosion sent a shock wave that jarred Steven's teeth.

After the ground stopped shaking, Steven started toward the door.

"STOP!" ordered the Luthier above the rumbling that could still be heard echoing across the valley.

It startled Steven to hear the Luthier yell and he instantly stopped and turned.

The Luthier just stood there. Steven walked back over

to the window where the Luthier was and looked out as it started to rain. It sounded like rain, and it looked like rain at first, but then Steven noticed that it was thousands of small rocks falling from the sky. The Luthier held up a stopwatch he had pulled out of his pocket and after forty-five seconds, he announced, "All clear."

They both rushed out to survey the damage. It was beautiful.

Steven smiled and laughed as he admired the large craters that now replaced the two circles and *Bone Guys*.

"Yes!" he hollered out across the valley. Then he did a little victory dance that looked like he was a wide receiver in the end-zone at the *Superbowl*.

"What do you think of that, Mr. Luthier?" asked Steven as he danced through the bottom of his crater.

"Beginner's luck," replied the Luthier, still a little amazed.

Without another word, Steven came up next to the Luthier. He was beaming with pride.

They both stood back and looked at the two large craters again.

"And the very first tie game ever," thoughtfully added the Luthier. Then a big childish grin spread across his face.

Chapter 10: Raising Children

The sun was low on the horizon and the warm autumn air started to cool. The detonation box and white pails were put away and Steven whistled while he washed off the large, steel launching pads with a hose. He swept the small rocks off of the walkway by the bunker while the Luthier drove a large, green, earth-moving loader and filled in the craters. The Luthier took away the broken boulder, then hauled the good ones back and put them in the pile with the others.

After finishing up, the Luthier parked the loader and came back over to Steven. He asked with a twinkle in his eye, "Did you have fun?"

Steven smiled and responded, "Yes, Sir!"

"Good," nodded the Luthier. "I'm sorry, but it's too late for another game today"

"That's okay. But what about that?" Steven asked while pointing at the boulder sitting in the middle of the bunker's roof.

"I think I'll leave it there for a while," the Luthier responded with a smile. "It seems to add a rustic charm to the place. Are you ready for dinner?"

"Yes, Sir! Very much, Sir!" Steven was still hyped from the game and now realized that he had worked up quite an appetite.

As they turned and walked toward the violin shop, Steven thought about the night before and asked in a somber tone, "Will we walk down on the road tonight, or will we take the path again?"

"I would prefer the road," answered the Luthier.

"So would I," Steven agreed with a sigh of relief.

Mary put her violin away and was thankful that she had her music memorized. Also that it had only been a dress rehearsal. She had always been an emotional musician and had made it a point to memorize pieces like this. They were performing Mozart's Requiem Mass (the one Amadeus was working on when he was sick and dying) and Mary thought about her family the whole time.
She couldn't read the music after the first few bars because of her tears...

"Mary has grown into such a beautiful young woman," Grandmother Anderson commented to John and Clarice while watching Mary and her younger brother, Joey, walking along the edge of the pond in their bare feet.
They were gathering rushes so Mary could weave them into decorations and baskets. The whole family had been visiting with Grandmother Anderson for two days and they were almost ready to go back to the city. Mary was staying behind so she could visit and help her grandmother for two weeks before college started.
"She has always been beautiful," Clarice replied. "Inside and out."
"A true princess," added John. "Just like I raised her."
Clarice jabbed John in the ribs.
"We," he added. "Just like *we* raised her. And now she's ready for college. It's unbelievable how the time flies."
"Look how much Joey has grown," Grandmother commented as Joey put another handful of rushes into Mary's basket.
"Joey's a good kid too," replied John. "I've never seen either of them argue or say a cross word to each other."
"That's because you're always at the hardware store, John," Clarice informed him with another soft fingertip in his ribs. "But they are as wonderful as a mother could hope for."
A look of contentment spread across Clarice's face and

she leaned back against John.

"I wish we could spend more time, Clarice. But I need to finish off the inventory before I go to bed tonight. It has to be done first thing in the morning. It's time we got going."

"Ten more minutes?" Clarice pleaded.

John looked at his watch and commented, "Okay, ten more minutes." They all sat back in silence to enjoy just a few more minutes together.

John looked at his watch after the ten minutes were up, but waited until Mary called out, "That's enough," to Joey before standing up.

Then they walked back to Grandmother Anderson's house together and started packing.

After the hugs, kisses and good-byes were done, Mary's mother, father and brother got into the car.

As they pulled away, Mary excitedly called out, "I'll see you in two weeks!"

Yet Mary never did.

When the Luthier and Steven stepped out of the other side of the bunker, they were greeted by the most beautiful sunset imaginable. They watched in silent awe as the colors changed and the little white wisps of clouds drifted by.

For a few minutes, the sun was at just at the right angle so it lit up the clouds like dazzling, silver jewelry floating in the sky. It gradually dropped lower, softening the clouds with glowing mixtures of indescribable colors that blended and flowed together.

Steven had never seen anything like it and he wondered if this moment was a once in a lifetime experience or if he simply hadn't taken the time to look. It was so calm and peaceful that he found himself closing his eyes and drifting off to sleep.

The sound of the Luthier's footsteps on the gravel woke Steven out of his trance and he quickly caught up.

"Beauty is everywhere, if we will stop and notice it," the Luthier commented. Then he picked up the pace and continued with their earlier conversation, "The secret to making children happy, or anyone happy for that matter, is putting yourself into their world and freeing your mind so you can enjoy it with them. So far, I have only mentioned things that my father has said. On the other hand, my father never said and would never allow his children to say these words:

"'I'm not interested in that.'

"'I can't do that', or 'it's too hard.'

"'I give up.'

"'That's only for girls,' or 'that's only for boys.'

"'That's childish.'

"And worst of all was, 'That's impossible.'

"As I grew up, I realized that most people forget what it feels like to be young. To experience the world for the very first time is exciting. The real secret is being able to enjoy it like a child does, no matter how old you get.

"Most people fall into their narrow, little ruts and become so closed-minded by the time they have children that they can't possibly relate to them and become their friends."

"If you want to experience joy and have your child love you, get down on your hands and knees and see life through their eyes. Play with their toys. Get into it; let yourself go. Watch the ants and bugs with them.

"Get excited about what's important to them. You'll find that even if you simply pretend to have fun, you will start to get excited. Then it becomes fun for everyone.

"Take my father's advice seriously: ride bikes with them, play with their dolls, read their books, listen to their music, and don't ever limit their imagination.

"It is more important to be able to relate to them than to be able to control them. They will be their own person sooner or later, like it or not."

"Your father sounds too good to be true," Steven finally commented. "But if you let your children do anything they want, won't they get spoiled?"

"There was a catch with my father," replied the Luthier.

They walked past the violin shop and headed down the paved road into the valley.

"My father would never make anything easy for us. In fact, he seemed to make many things as hard as he possibly could."

"What?" Steven asked. He didn't understand.

"My father would never go out and buy something new. Instead, he would go out of his way to find something old and broken, or best of all, broken with pieces missing. Then he would tell us how it worked, how to fix it, and then how to make it better than it ever was. We didn't have a choice, even if he had to sit on us until we did it.

"When I wanted a bicycle, I had to pull the pieces out of the town dump and put them together before I had something to ride. My first few cars started out as wrecks in people's back yards, put together with parts that also came from the old town dump.

"It was tough and frustrating at times, but anything we got excited about, he was excited right along with us. My father's attitude didn't even change after I left home and got married. When I started making violins, he made his own tools and templates and began carving a violin of his own."

The Luthier stopped and turned toward Steven, "He would learn and do anything, Steven. That's what made him so great. Nothing was too outlandish and nothing was impossible. My father was a man who loved racing cars and testing nuclear bombs in the morning, then relaxing with his knitting and sewing that same evening."

The Luthier let that statement sink in while they walked the rest of the way into the valley.

When they reached the bottom of the hill, the Luthier added, "People often accuse me of making things seem easier than they really are. They ask me why I am so *lucky* to be able to do all the things that I do. Then they tell me how jealous they are because they could never see themselves doing these things."

The Luthier's tone became very solemn as he looked out across the valley with all the wonderful things in it, "If I am someone special, it is because of my father, and if I am not, I have failed my father."

Steven now agreed with Hardcore. The Luthier really did have the greatest father in the world.

When they walked through the front door, Colter ran up and jumped on the Luthier, wrestled him to the ground and asked, "Was that two *Bone Guys*?"

"Yes," replied the Luthier. Then he rolled Colter over and pinned both of his shoulders to the ground.

"Him?" asked Colter, with his eyes wide open, looking up at Steven in the doorway.

"Yep," replied the Luthier. Then he stood up and held out his hand to help Colter up. "Him."

"I've only done it once," Colter explained to Steven, "And I've tried lots of times."

Steven stared back in amazement. Colter was only eleven years old.

"Never too young and never too old, Steven," the Luthier told him with a smile. "Free your mind. Children can accomplish anything they believe they can. They can grow up and do anything if you will just believe in their dreams with them."

"My dad always talks like that," Colter added.

Dinner was a little more haphazard and rambunctious than Steven had imagined it would be and the conversation covered a dozen different topics. Some of them would be considered acceptable at most dinner tables and some, Steven was sure, would not.

Tessa, the Luthier's sixteen-year-old daughter, finally commented, "Looks like you were in a fight."

Steven nodded in reply. He had forgotten what he must still look like with all the distractions of the day.

Colter smiled at Steven and announced, "It isn't right to start a fight, but if you're in it, win it!" and he held up both of his fists in front of him.

Steven looked over to see the Luthier's reaction. The Luthier smiled and nodded his head. "My father said that, also."

"Did you win or lose?" Tessa asked.

There was a noticeable moment of silence while Steven

turned from Tessa and looked at the Luthier.

"Both," he replied.

"I can trim that hair if you want," Tessa offered.

Steven reached up and felt the clump of hair on his head. He had trimmed it using the scissors in the first aid kit, but he knew he hadn't done a very good job. Sheryl gave Tessa a look of reprimand, but before anyone else spoke, Steven accepted her offer, "Yes, please, I would like that."

Everyone smiled. The Luthier even looked a little amazed at Steven's polite response and reaction to his children.

Skyler, the oldest son, who had just gotten back from basic training for the Army National Guard, had been very quiet during dinner. He finally asked his question, "Were you in Vietnam?"

Even though Steven was in a set of the Luthier's military fatigues, he was surprised by the question. The way Skyler asked, he didn't know if it was good or bad that he was.

Finally Steven turned and answered, "Yes, United States Marine Corps. Two tours of duty."

There was another moment of silence at the table.

"I'm honored then, Sir," and Skyler stood up and held out his hand with a smile.

"I really don't deserve the 'Sir'," replied Steven while he shook Skyler's hand. "Most people think Vietnam was a worthless war."

"No matter what value people place on the war itself, the men who were willing to stand and fight for their country are great," replied Skyler.

There was silence around the table as all of them nodded in agreement. Steven could tell that the Luthier really was that ten-year-old boy at the bus stop when Hardcore stepped out in his dress blues.

As he finished dinner, Steven thought it was strange that none of them ever asked why he was there or what his plans were. They just acted as though he were someone special and they all seemed happy he was there with them.

After dinner, the Luthier announced that they would watch a movie while Tessa trimmed up Steven's hair.

"We have no time to waste, Steven, and consider this movie two of your most important lessons: How to look at the world, and how to treat a lady." The movie was *Man of La Mancha,* starring *Peter O' Toole* and *Sophia Loren* and it was one of the Luthier's favorites.

Tessa was sixteen but she handled the clippers and scissors with skill. Steven's hair was all evened up and the edges were neatly trimmed by the time Don Quixote (the hero and knight-errant) met Aldonza (the kitchen maid) and called her Dolcinea (the name of a princess).

Steven was amazed when the whole family sang along with some of the songs. He could tell that they had all seen the movie many times. He never cared much for musicals, but he found himself drawn in as the show progressed and he even related to some of the characters in the prison.

When the movie was over, Steven was invited to follow them upstairs, where the Luthier told his children in a loving voice as each went to bed, "Never stop dreaming. Never give up. And that's how a lady should be treated." He finished with Tessa, "And that's how a lady should expect a gentleman to treat her." Then he gave her a good-night kiss.

After they came back down the stairs, he talked with Steven some more, "My worst fault in life is that I don't spend enough time with my children. Most parents, especially fathers, never do. It is very difficult, and never underestimate the challenge. Earning a living and doing all that has to be done in life will never leave you with enough time to spend with your children. If you ever doubt where to spend your time; tighten your belt, eat sack lunches and give them more."

Steven nodded in agreement. He thought of all the times he wished his father would have helped him, had fun with him or just taken him somewhere he needed to go. He had never wanted very much. All he really wanted was someone to be there and act like they cared.

The Luthier could see Steven was deep in thought and he waited before continuing, "If you think you can put up with me, for better and for worse, we will start on a regular schedule tomorrow."

"Yes, Sir!" was Steven's reply.

As the Luthier opened the front door, he added, "If you think I was tough on you yesterday, and if you think you had a good time today, *you haven't seen anything yet.*"

Steven turned back toward the Luthier. He was amazed at what the Luthier had said, yet somehow, deep down inside, he knew that it was the truth. He shuddered at the thought of it.

"Sleep well, Steven. We will dive in deep tomorrow. Meet me up at the violin shop at 0-seven hundred, ready to go."

"Yes, Sir," replied Steven. "And thank you."

Chapter 11: Dragons and Dinosaurs

Steven woke up early, made himself breakfast and walked up to the violin shop before dawn. He paused to watch the sun crest above the east horizon before going in. As he turned the handle, he smiled. It amazed him that there really was someone like the Luthier willing to help him, and that he was out here in the middle of nowhere.

"Stop where you are!" came the Luthier's voice from back in the violin shop. He was around the corner of the entry where Steven couldn't see him.

Steven instantly froze.

The Luthier's voice was intense, "Slowly close the door and lock it, then carefully come over where I am with as little movement as possible. Do not touch anything and walk as lightly as you can. Whatever you do, do not drag your feet, and don't come too close."

"What on earth?" Steven wondered as all his senses became keen and heightened. He closed the door and surveyed left and right, ceiling to floor, then listened carefully before slowly caressing his feet silently across the entry.

There was an eerie, *dead* feeling in the shop and Steven couldn't shake it off. He hadn't felt this way since he was in Vietnam. It was the same kind of feeling that he had when approaching the fallen dead.

His sensitive ears had been trained for reconnaissance, and they could now hear a soft, licking sound coming from around the corner.

Steven didn't know what to expect and he couldn't imagine what the warning in the Luthier's voice meant. All he could think of as he listened, was that a tiger was either softly licking the carcass of a recent kill or a piece of raw flesh in the Luthier's hand. He didn't think these thoughts were too outlandish, after coming down the path his first night and then yesterday's *game*.

He rounded the corner with stealth and prowess. The Luthier was applying a blood-red liquid to the surface of Dianne Adams' viola. The Luthier only glanced at Steven once between brush strokes, then continued varnishing without saying another word.

Steven relaxed when he saw what the Luthier was doing, but he still crept slowly and stayed at a safe distance, just as the Luthier had ordered.

When the Luthier had finished with the largest brush, he explained, "Usually I apply this last varnish coat in the clean-room where everything is absolutely dust-free. Other times I feel I must do it here.

"When I do, I turn off the fan that blows the air between the wood, then wait. After every particle in the air settles and is dusted away from around me, it is then time to start. Once I open the container I am committed to the task, and once I begin applying the varnish, the slightest movement outside this area can place small pieces of dust on the instrument. It is amazing how the varnish gathers and builds up on each particle that falls upon it. I would ruin this viola if I allowed any dust to reach it now."

Steven stayed where he was and breathed very slowly. He was surprised that the Luthier would even let him in during such a critical step. He knew there was a lot at stake since a viola would have to cost a lot more than the violin he had just ordered.

The Luthier motioned toward a plain-looking wood box about five feet tall standing by the varnish cabinet and told him, "Once the varnish is applied, the instrument is placed in that large box with the two doors. It remains there, in *black light*, until its surface is dry to the touch and can go out into the direct rays of the sun.

"I never allow normal people in the room while I varnish, but it was a calm morning outside and I could tell that you have been trained in the martial arts."

Steven thought of his special instructor at Force Recon School after boot camp. He could walk across rice paper placed on the barracks floor without leaving a trace and had shown the men how to do it. Steven had never reached the end without leaving a trace, but he did the best of all of the enlisted men by the time the training was over.

"How long does the varnish take to dry?" Steven was staring at the sparkling liquid on the surface of the viola.

"About a week for this coat," replied the Luthier as he pulled out a smaller brush to apply the thick, red varnish to the scroll.

The varnish looked like dark blood, only more transparent. Steven watched the Luthier apply it and he wondered if it really was blood. He was about to ask when something else suddenly struck him. The room was dead calm, yet some of the pieces of wood were swinging above his head! His eyes quickly glanced up, then his head slowly followed.

Some of the pieces were hanging perfectly still while others right beside them were gently swinging back and forth from the ceiling. After watching them for a minute, Steven looked back down at the Luthier.

When the Luthier had finished varnishing the scroll, Steven asked, "Why are some of the pieces of wood swinging? And doesn't dust fall from them?"

The Luthier set his brush down and answered in the same profound tone that he had used before, "They...just...do."

The Luthier began touching up around the edges of the viola with an even smaller brush and added with resolve, "The dust *never* falls from them."

The tune from the *Twilight Zone* began running through Steven's mind as he silently watched the Luthier finish off the last touches of varnish. The Luthier then opened the doors of the large wooden box and placed the viola inside. An eerie, purplish glow came out of the darkness and shone on the Luthier's face. It added even more to the strangeness of the mood.

Steven silently watched while the Luthier closed the doors. He was almost afraid to ask any more questions, even if they didn't have anything to do with the wood hanging above his head. He felt as though Rod Serling would step out at any minute and announce that Steven Miller had just entered the "Twilight Zone."

Steven looked at the varnish bottle sitting on the Luthier's bench. It still had some of the blood-red mixture left in it and all kinds of wild ideas started filling his head. Finally, he couldn't help it, "What's in that varnish?"

The Luthier turned around and acted more casually now that the doors were closed. He smiled and answered, "Dragon's blood." Then the Luthier walked over to the varnish cupboard and pulled out a bottle.

He opened the lid and dumped out a large, red rock into Steven's hand. "Dried dragon's blood."

Steven didn't say a word.

The Luthier continued, "That wouldn't surprise you if you were a witch or sorcerer in medieval times."

"Real dragon's blood?" asked Steven while he held it in his hand.

"As real as it gets," replied the Luthier.

"From *real* dragons?" asked Steven in amazement.

"From a real dragon tree," replied the Luthier. "There are dragon trees found here and there around the world, but this particular kind of dragon tree was thought to be extinct for over two thousand years."

Then a big smile spread across the Luthier's face. "That was, until June 2, 1754 when Montai Franqui found one near the town of Orotava on the island of Teneriffe. He immediately recognized what it was, then built an elaborate garden and shrine around it.

"You see, the *real* dragon tree grows very slowly and its shape evolves as it grows like that of a dragon standing up. When it reaches maturity, which takes a minimum of a thousand years, it looks like a ferocious dragon standing against the sky with its arms outstretched and its claws poised, ready to strike."

"A thousand years to grow?" Steven had a hard time believing that, as well as the images of the tree that were now in his mind.

Instead of responding to Steven's question of doubt, the Luthier's eyes went wild as he continued, "After they reach maturity, you must sink a long, sharp knife deep into their chest, and it must be done at the right time of year; between the sixth and sixteenth of August when the blood flowing through its veins is the purest. The dragon tree will then bleed a clear, ruby red liquid called dragon's blood."

Steven didn't know what to believe. He waited for the Luthier to stop and say, "Just joking," but instead, he continued even deeper into the unbelievable.

"Some say that the tree moans and cries as it is cut. But if the operation is done properly, the tree will not only recover, it will grow stronger and with that strength it grows more arms."

"You expect me to believe that?" asked Steven.

"It is not necessary for you to 'believe that'," replied the Luthier. "Each person can choose for themselves what they will believe. But if you would like to read about some *real* explorers finding the tree and reporting about it in a *reliable* magazine, just open your copy of *The People's Magazine*, Saturday, April 6, 1833. The magazine, if you recall, always lists at least two independent and reliable sources before printing any such articles. I can't say as much for the newspapers and magazines that are printed today."

Steven just smiled and responded, "I have a few magazines in my saddlebags, but I didn't bring that particular one with me. Can I borrow yours?"

The Luthier turned and opened a drawer in the varnish cabinet. Even though Steven was joking, he found he wasn't that surprised when the Luthier presented him with a very old magazine. It was entitled "The People's Magazine," dated Saturday, April 6, 1833, "published every other Saturday."

Steven wasn't that surprised, but his jaw still dropped and his mouth hung open as he turned the pages of the old, yellowish-grey magazine and saw a woodcut picture of a massive dragon tree. There was an explorer leaning against it with a gun in his hand but Steven could barely make him out because of the size of the dragon tree!

"Read the article while I go take care of a few things and fill up my jug with hide glue crystals. It will take me a little while, so just wait here until I get back."

The Luthier picked up a small jug and headed to the back of the shop. As soon as Steven heard the door close, he began reading.

Steven was glad that the Luthier had left him alone with the article. He had never been a good reader. He wasn't "slow" or "dumb" like some of the teachers and kids in school had called him. In fact, he learned very quickly. But when it came to reading out loud, something just didn't click and he sounded like some "freak" talking. At least that's the word one boy had used when Steven was a junior in high school.

Steven broke both of the boy's arms and beat him unconscious before three teachers could pull him off. That was halfway through his junior year and it was also Steven's last day in school.

The magazine article was fairly short and half of it was the picture of the large tree, so Steven read it all the way through.

Steven thought it was funny how he couldn't decide whether the dragon tree was real or not when the Luthier told him about it. Now, as he held the magazine article in his left hand and the large chunk of dragon's blood in his right, he believed it.

The article never said why it was called the dragon tree

and it didn't mention violin varnish. But everything else was there, including its huge size, its two thousand year age and rarity, along with the people who verified the special tree's existence. The Luthier's words had simply filled in the details and missing parts of the story.

The tree had many branches, or arms, like the Luthier had described, and as Steven took them away, one by one, in his mind, he could clearly see the dragon with his two massive arms and claws raised in the air. It gave him an eerie, almost disturbing feeling as he held the dried piece of dragon's blood in his hand and thought of the fresh blood dripping out of the dragon's huge chest. Steven started to imagine the Luthier sinking a large knife deep into the chest of the dragon and the sound that it made as it was being cut...

Steven jumped and swung around when he heard a deep breath exhale immediately behind him.

"I didn't mean to startle you, but I walked quietly to allow you to finish reading without being disturbed," apologized the Luthier.

Few people had ever snuck up on Steven before, and no one had ever done it when it was quiet.

The Luthier didn't seem to react to the startled look on Steven's face and he continued, "The other main ingredient is Baltic amber. It is tree sap that is over 65 million years old. It is dug out of the sands of the Peninsula of Samland (north of Kaliningrad), or if a deeper red color is required, it is mined from deep in the heart of Italy."

The Luthier then traded a large, clear, yellow rock for the dark, opaque-red one Steven was holding. Steven held the amber up to the light where it glowed between his fingers.

"That piece you hold in your hand drained from the trunk of a tree millions of years ago, probably when a Tyrannosaurus Rex had a tooth ache or just needed to flex his jaw muscles on a tree."

"Dinosaurs?" asked Steven.

"Didn't you ever watch *Jurassic Park*?" asked the

Luthier.

Though Steven normally never went to movies, a couple of guys at a bar had told him that it was *pretty cool* and he went to a late showing with them. "Yes," he admitted.

"Though no one has made a dinosaur out of the mosquitoes in amber yet, it does make the finest violin varnish in the world."

"I thought the movie was fiction," commented Steven.

"Most good stories are based upon as many facts as possible," replied the Luthier. "The storyteller just tells the facts in a way that will keep our interest, and adds just enough *make believe* to spark our imaginations. That way many of the wildest, outlandish stories eventually do come true.

"Remember that thought as you teach your children. Tell them about Leonardo DaVinci, Jules Verne, Ray Bradbury and Gene Roddenberry. Don't ever stifle their dreams of visiting the stars or building robots and holding cold fusion in their hands.

"Don't let them waste their life dreaming, but never discourage them from pursuing their dreams, no matter how impossible or crazy they may seem to you or others. That's what my father would say."

"How did you ever find amber and the dragon tree?" asked Steven.

"My father taught us how to hunt for treasure. He taught us that needles are easy to find in haystacks with the right tools. This world of ours is not as large and impossible to explore as most people think. We panned for gold and silver, we metal detected and prospected, then we worked our way up to lost caves, sunken ships and cities.

"He also taught us that some of the greatest treasures are sitting in dusty books that no one reads any more or in the back of people's minds down the street.

"I have learned the art of violinmaking out of many books that *do not exist* and from people who *don't know anything*. Some of my ingredients *aren't real* and come from places that are *just make believe* to the rest of the world. I also *treasure* a piece of steel that can be used to carve a violin much more than other people treasure pure gold."

Steven thought the Luthier's words about comparing steel and gold sounded a lot like Don Quixote from the movie he had watched the night before. Steven also realized that, deep down inside, he was really a dreamer, just like the Luthier.

"There are no limits or bounds to what I believe is possible, Steven. Or to what will go into each of my instruments." The Luthier held out his hand.

Steven handed the amber back to the Luthier. He felt that it was real now; in fact, somehow he *knew* that it was real, just as real as his dream of changing his life.

The Luthier smiled when Steven nodded his head in reply, and he added this encouragement, "There are no limits, Steven. Dragons and dinosaurs are just the beginning."

Chapter 12: The List

$\mathcal{M}$ary closed her apartment door, turned the two deadbolts and fastened the chain. It was late. Symphony practice had lasted over three hours. She turned around, leaned back against the door and closed her eyes.

The apartment was quiet and she felt tired and lonely. She stood in the darkness and began thinking about her life.

Before allowing herself to get too melancholy and depressed, she smiled and thought, "It could be worse. I could have married George Humphries!"

Mary rolled her eyes. She was grateful that she hadn't...

"I guess it's about time to say good night. I..."

Mary realized that this was her chance, maybe the only one she would ever get.

"Good night, George." Mary quickly stepped inside and closed the door as fast as she could.

Mary had never interrupted anyone like that before in her life, but tonight she knew she had to. Otherwise she may have died of old age before George Humphries quit talking!

Mary stood against the door and debated whether being rude was really necessary. Then she heard George babbling to himself outside. It was over ten minutes before George finally walked away. Even then, he was still rambling on about something.

"Oh brother!" she exclaimed. "I'm never going to find

the man of my dreams at this rate." Mary leaned against her door for another few minutes. She wanted to make sure that George wasn't coming back.

Mary had believed in love at first sight since she was a little girl, but over the years, she had decided that "first sight" might have to include at least a date or two.

When George's car finally pulled away from the curb, Mary reached over and turned on the light switch. It was her first date with George Humphries and Mary had already decided that it would definitely be the last.

She fastened the latch and turned the deadbolt with a sigh of relief. It was Mary's thirty-second birthday and she had been playing the *Dating Game* since she was nineteen.

George was just the most recent of many disappointments, so Mary casually walked into her small bedroom, flipped off her shoes and changed into her nightgown. She brushed her teeth and got ready for bed while thinking about them all.

George Humphries was actually one of hundreds and Mary stood at the foot of her bed trying to add them all up in her mind.

"Hundreds!" she exclaimed. Then she flopped backwards in frustration and looked up at the ceiling.

Mary had mentally scratched off George, just like every other available bachelor she had ever met, yet she still didn't feel over-judgmental.

From the moment George had picked her up, until the time he walked away, he never quit talking. Even while he ate his spaghetti dinner at the fine Italian restaurant, he was constantly rambling on about absolutely nothing.

It was not a pretty sight watching him eat and talk at the same time, but Mary had seen worse, much worse, and "eats with his mouth open" was still on her list of "not desired, but I can live with" attributes for her knight in shining armor.

After all, she didn't want to disqualify suitors for small, nitpicky things like that, otherwise there would be absolutely no hope in finding *Mr. Right*. There were always plenty of big things that disqualified every man she had ever gone out with. With George it was the inability for her to say a single sentence without being interrupted, and not being able to start that sentence without struggling to jump in somewhere.

Mary closed her eyes and thought about men. Ever since she was a little girl she had always been serious about choosing wisely.

"Maybe that's my problem," she told herself. "Maybe I'm too serious." Yet, as she opened her eyes and looked over at the picture of her parents on the wall, she knew she wasn't. She wanted to spend the rest of her life with someone special.

She was only thirty-two, but most of the women Mary associated with had been divorced at least once, and she knew she couldn't live with that. About half of the others were unhappy with their husbands and only stayed married out of loyalty, not love, and that was also not an option for Mary. She would be loyal to whoever she married, but what she wanted, most of all, was love. She still dreamed of finding her true love and passionately loving him for the rest of her life.

The happily married women Mary knew just seemed to have lucked into it, and Mary hadn't been very lucky during the past thirteen years. She honestly didn't feel like she had passed up her *Prince Charming* yet, and it wasn't because she hadn't tried.

When the years had started clicking by and her choices seemed limited, Mary decided that she needed to broaden her horizons and widen the playing field. Even though she was supporting herself and finances were tough, she gave up her job at the lab and started working at the college cafeteria so she could meet a wider variety of men.

It had worked too; she did get exposed to a wider variety:

First, there was Rob Williams. He was the best prospect behind the counter and he had asked her out the first day she worked there. But by the time Friday came around, Mary knew that she was already well on her way to scratching him off her list. He was a slob.

Rob was a food handler, but that didn't stop him from doing his job with dirty hands or picking up food and utensils off the floor and putting them back in the trays. Still, he seemed so nice otherwise that she tried to keep up a little hope and went out on the date with him anyway.

He picked her up in an old car with torn seat covers and trash strewn across the floor six inches deep. He was sweaty, and now that he wasn't wearing his hair net she realized that it was unwashed and uncombed. When he offered her his hand, it was dirty, sticky and slimy, all at the same time.

He also insisted that they eat at his favorite restaurant; a greasy diner with ketchup and mustard spills dried on the table. When Mary grabbed the edge of the table top and slide over, her fingers squished into a large wad of chewing gum. She pulled her hand away and large pink strings spanned the gap.

When Mary decided that she just had to look underneath, there were dozens of large wads of different colored chewing gum stuck to the bottom of it. Mary always liked to make the most out of a bad situation and she tried to lighten the mood by pointing it out to Rob. He looked at her hand and shrugged his shoulders as if to say, "So what?"

By the expression on his face when he looked under the table, Mary thought Rob was going to grab a piece and put it in his mouth.

Mary finished the date, only to find that his initial nice manners were only on the surface. His dirty demeanor went right to the bone and also applied to women.

The other men that Mary met at the cafeteria were numerous and varied, but the next one that stood out during the "cafeteria episode," as she called it, was Harold Parker. He was almost the opposite of Rob; neat and clean to a fault. It was only later that she found out he was wealthy and the only reason he ate at the cafeteria that day was to ask her out.

*   *   *

Mary heard a car horn honking outside her window.

"It can't be," she thought to herself as she walked over and looked down. But sure enough, there was Harold, sitting in a white Mercedes 500SL convertible with his hand pressing down hard on the steering wheel. Mary took a moment and tried to decide what to do next.

She gathered her courage and told herself, "It's not his fault if his parents didn't teach him how important good manners are. I'll at least give him a chance and the benefit of the doubt." Mary had always tried to give each man she met more than a fair chance, regardless of her expectations, so she grabbed her purse and headed out.

When Harold saw her walking down the steps, he stopped honking and looked at her with a smile, "You look beautiful, Mary." Then he looked at the apartment building, as if to say, "I can't believe you live here."

It wasn't until later that she realized he honked because he couldn't bring himself to be seen in a building like the one she lived in. It was bad enough having to park on her street.

"Thank you," she replied with a forced smile.

Mary hesitated just long enough to see if Harold would get out and open the door for her. When he didn't, she smiled again and got in. "Always give him the benefit of the doubt," she reassured herself.

Just before they pulled away from the curb, Harold smiled and asked, "Would you mind keeping your feet flat on the floor? Sharp edges are hard on the carpet."

Mary quickly looked down. She realized that the automobile cost more than any house she had ever lived in and the toe of her right foot was tilted up, leaving only the edge of her heel on the floor. The stories and tests of true princesses that her father had read to her when she was a child began running through her mind, especially *The Princess and the Pea*.

"I'm sorry," she apologized, and she lowered her foot. That's when Mary took a good look at the car and Harold.

There wasn't a speck of dust or dirt anywhere. Not a smudge on the interior or a single insect stain on the windshield, nothing.   Harold was wearing the finest clothes and, even though he was riding in a convertible, there wasn't a single hair out of place. As the car sped up and Mary's hair started to move around, she wondered if he had glued his in place because it remained so perfect.

"This is probably as close to a fine carriage as a prince can get these days," Mary told herself. "And he definitely looks the part." Her hopes started building again.

Mary smiled and waved at one of her girlfriends as they passed by. Harold gave her a look of disapproval, like it just wasn't proper to acknowledge others on the street. It gave Mary a strange feeling and she tried to decide if she was really that uncouth or if Harold was, as she was starting to expect, overly eccentric.

When they pulled in front of the nicest restaurant in town, the valet greeted them with a smile.   Harold responded by reaching over and pulling two white handkerchiefs out of the glove compartment. He handed them to the valet, along with twenty dollars and told him, "Please use these, and take extra care with my car."

Mary could tell that Harold was different than anyone she had ever gone out with, so instead of overreacting she decided she would give it a try and play along. Why not?

The doorman opened Mary's door and as she swung her left foot out, it hit the door jam leaving a small, black mark on it. Harold's eyes instantly went wide and Mary found herself quickly kneeling down and wiping the spot off the best she could with her fingernail and a hanky. That seemed to appease Harold and they walked into the restaurant, arm in arm, without saying a word.

They were waiting to be seated when another couple walked in.

Harold greeted the man, "Good evening, Mark."

"Good evening, Harold," was his friend's reply as they quickly looked at each other's dates.

Harold was the first to start introductions, "Let me introduce you to Mary Anderson, principal violinist at the university. Mary this is Mark Cooledge."

Mary politely shook Mark's hand. As she did, she had the distinct feeling that her looks, added to her credentials as lead violinist, were being sized up and rated.

Mark then replied, "Mary, Harold, this is Julia Gingold, daughter of *the* Preston Gingold."

Mary shook hands with Julia while Harold took his turn and gave Julia the once over. She was blonde, about twenty years old and would barely tip the scales at a hundred pounds. While Mary and Julia visited, Harold's gaze went back and forth between them, seeming to compare Julia's anemic looks and her father's vast wealth with Mary's figure and her talents as a musician. As the maitre d' walked up, Harold looked back at Mary with a smile. It made Mary feel like she had just passed muster.

When Harold escorted Mary to their table, he held his head high and made sure everyone noticed them as they walked by. It was a whole mixture of feelings for Mary. On the one hand, she felt complimented that he was proud to be seen with her and that her looks and talents could compare with the rich and famous. Yet, at the same time, she felt like it was the only reason that Harold had asked her out that night, so he would look good.

While they sat and talked, Harold didn't seem interested in what kind of person Mary was, just how good he and she looked together. He also tried to nonchalantly look at every other woman in the restaurant and size them up also. He only relaxed and turned back toward Mary when he was satisfied that she was the best looking woman in the room.

"Julia seems like a very nice girl," Mary finally commented.

"She's a little too thin," he flatly replied.

Mary couldn't believe how shallow Harold actually was. Julia did seem like a nice girl, it wasn't just a hollow compliment; Mary never gave hollow compliments. She also didn't care for hollow people.

"What does how much she weighs have to do with how nice she is?" Mary found herself asking.

Harold looked from Julia and Mark's table back at Mary

as her comment registered.

His whole demeanor changed. He eyes now wandered down and looked at Mary's figure with just a hint of disapproval.

Harold ignored Mary's question. Instead he asked her, "Would you like dinner tonight, or just a small salad without any dressing?" There was a hint of snideness in his voice.

Mary found herself looking down at her stomach. She was not fat, and she knew it.

"What are you having?" Mary asked with her voice tightening.

"Dinner, of course," he replied, matter-of-factly.

Mary's patience was wearing thin and she decided that she was through playing along.

"I'll have the same as you," replied Mary.

Harold replied by puffing his cheeks.

Mary's jaw dropped open in shock, then she glared at him defiantly.

That's when their evening really began. It was personal now, and it was a wonder that they weren't both thrown out of the restaurant by the time they finished eating their meal together.

Mary rolled over on her bed and started laughing...

Harold ordered the largest dinner on the menu for each of them with all the side trimmings, plus dessert. Then every time Mary took a bite, he would make a different animal sound.

Mary, on the other hand, *accidently* spilled or flipped a little of everything in front of her all over Harold's new, spotless designer clothes and eventually his face. She even stepped on his feet three times before they reached the front door.

Harold proved to have a reasonable sense of humor and threatened to frisk Mary for food before he would let her back in the car, but she could tell that it was only because he didn't want the stigma of a woman walking out on him. That would have been as bad for his image as dating an ugly girl.

He was good natured enough about it all, but he also made it very plain when he dropped her off that Mary would not fit into his world.

That was fine with Mary because she didn't have any desire to fit into his hollow, spotless world. The sad part was, Harold was as close to a prince on a white stallion as Mary ever found.

After working at the cafeteria one year, Mary tried other jobs, one after the other, with basically the same results. No matter how lenient she tried to be with their personalities, the men she dated turned out to be sucker-fish and she had to throw them all back.

Mary thought about her date with George that night, then about Harold, Rob and all the other men she had been out with over the years as she looked over at a large piece of paper pinned to her wall. She had originally made it up when she was taking a marriage and relationships class in college, then she had added to it over the years.

At the top it read, "THE MAN OF MY DREAMS." Under it were three columns labelled MUST, MUST NOT and NEGOTIABLE. The last one was subtitled further down in smaller letters, "Not desirable, but I can live with."

There were dozens of things listed under each heading, many of them very serious. But even though the NEGOTIABLE column had started out serious, the things she had added after particularly memorable dates were the ones that always made her laugh.

Mary was tired of hunting for the man of her dreams and she needed a good laugh, so she started reading her favorite column for the millionth time...

NEGOTIABLE:

Age, looks, income, race, in-laws, handicaps, musical background, education, etc., etc., etc..

Then came the "Not desirable, but I can live with," part:

"Baldness, nervous twitches, excessive ear, nose and

back hair, chews with mouth open, constantly quotes movie lines, cross-eyed and bucktoothed, stutters, picks nose openly, chews fingernails and spits, bad dandruff and sheds, large warts, scratches himself... the list went on and on and got worse.

Mary laughed when she started reading the list, then she began crying by the time she reached the bottom and tried to picture the man of her dreams based upon all the NEGOTIABLE items added together. It was a horrible image and when she couldn't get it out of her mind, she reached up and tore the list off the wall, wadded it up and threw it in the garbage.

Mary was exactly thirty-two years old that night and she was tired of hunting. She decided after dating George Humphries that she was going to stop spending all of her time aggressively looking for her prince. The man of her dreams was simply going to have to find her.

Chapter 13: Tiny

"This is hide glue," the Luthier explained as he poured a small amount of clear, tan colored crystals into his glue pot.

"It is the finest of all glues for making violins and it will hold wood together for thousands of years. There have been many examples of wooden furniture and toys recovered from the oldest Egyptian tombs with the hide glue joints just as strong and stable today as they were five thousand years ago.

"To make hide glue, skin is taken from young calves and the hair is removed. The skins are soaked under water in a large tub until they swell and soften. Then they are cooked and stirred until the skins turn into a fluid, jellylike substance that resembles light maple syrup."

To most people this operation might have seemed morbid and gruesome, but to Steven it was new and exciting to learn how something was made, and each detail that the Luthier explained sparked his interest and made him want to learn more.

"The liquid is then allowed to settle and the center portion is drained off through a spout. To finish, the glue is dried and ground into the crystals you see here.

"It can be stored for almost any length of time in crystal form, but once water is added, it is only at its best for one day. A fresh batch is made by mixing cool water with some of the dry crystals, allowing it to soak for a half-hour or more, then heating it in a glue pot until it turns into a fluid, jellylike substance again.

"If done properly, a hide glue joint can be stronger than the wood itself, without leaving any thickness between the two pieces. I know of a fine Stradivari violin that was run over by a truck in New York. By gluing each of the hundreds of pieces of wood together with hide glue and proper varnish touch-up, it is barely possible to tell that it was ever scratched."

Steven took it all in. He had always fixed things himself and he did all the repairs on the many motorcycles he had owned over the years. He also liked working with wood but the only woodworking he had done was framing houses. The only glue he used there was the construction adhesive in the big tubes, so this was all new to him.

Once the glue was soaking in the pot, the Luthier turned to Steven and announced, "It is now time to see what you are made of."

Steven didn't know if that meant another walk down the path, or if the Luthier was going to draw some blood. Either way, he decided to patiently wait for the answer.

"Tell me what those mean?" asked the Luthier as he eyed the three crosses shaved on the side of Steven's head.

Steven relaxed a little and answered, "After I talked with Tom, I went back to my place and gathered up my things. I wasn't sure why I told Tom to ask Mary to pray for me. I haven't been in a church since I was seven years old. Maybe it was because of how religious Tom said Mary was and I was trying to impress her. Maybe because there really is a God or a Jesus. I don't know.

"I just knew that I needed some help and the only people that had ever helped me or acted like they cared were my friends in Vietnam.

"They were willing to die for me, and I was willing to die for them. You already know Hardcore."

The Luthier nodded in response.

Steven continued, "The others were *Tiny* Tim Williams, Steve *Slaughter* Slader, and Joe *Ruckus* Reber." Steven pointed to each of the three crosses when he said their names.

"I figured if I was ever going to become somebody that

would impress Mary, I would have to take the best of those guys and put it all together. Crazy, huh?"

The Luthier nodded. "Go on."

"The boots were Tiny's. He wasn't tiny, he was as big as the rest of us, he just spoke very quiet and usually kept to himself. When it came to taking fire or dishing it out to the *Gooks* (Viet Cong), he was as good as any man. He was *true-blue* when it mattered, but when it came to standing up for himself, he let people walk all over him. My mother would have considered him a humble and religious man, and I figured Mary would like that..."

"Hey, Tiny!" whispered Steve Slaughter Slader.

Private Timothy Williams answered without moving or even turning his head from the group of trees he was surveying fifty meters away, "What?"

"Do you have a hot *McDonald's* hamburger in your knapsack that I can have?"

The half of the platoon that could hear Slaughter's question laughed and snickered.

"Wish I did," was Tiny's response, "I would give it to you."

"Then I'll have to dream of one!" Slaughter announced. There was absolute silence in the platoon now.

Slaughter closed his eyes, and with a dreamy voice, he primed the men around him, "Hot and juicy with an ice-cold *Coke* running down my chin."

The men in the platoon that could hear him moaned, but they moved closer so they could hear more. They knew Slaughter wasn't going to stop there.

"I'm holding the soft, fresh, sesame seed bun in my clean, freshly washed hands right now. I'm slowly rotating it all the way around, just to make sure it's *just* right; and it is... It's so... soft and perfect. And it's so... fresh that my fingers gently sink into it as I lift it up. I'm opening my mouth wide in anticipation and lifting it even closer."

Slaughter paused just a moment to let the description sink into the other men's minds. Most of the platoon had moved within earshot, sitting around him in the hot, miserable jungle, enjoying the fantasy as much as he was.

"My mouth is closing and my lips are resting on the sesame-seed bun, right now. Oh...! My teeth bite through the tangy pickle and it squishes the warm, smooth ketchup out onto my tongue. Now my teeth are entering the prime, hot, juicy, one-hundred-percent American beef; hot off the grill. The hot juice oozes out the side of my mouth and trickles down my face onto my chin. Oh... Oh..."

More moans and laughs came from behind the trees and bushes separating each of the ten men who were listening.

"I've chewed all the warm flavors together and I'm reaching for my ice-cold *Coke* to wash it down. The red and white cup is covered with cold beads of water on the outside because I've ordered *extra ice*. The ice is floating down deep and swirling around in the sweet, brown heaven."

"Shut up!" hissed *Raunch* Jones.

All the other men listening, instantly turned and aimed their M-16 rifles at Raunch's head. His eyes grew wide and he started shaking. He was a new Marine (what the Marines usually referred to as "new meat"). He had been trying to act tougher and meaner than all the others since he arrived. Most of the men usually ignored him, knowing that the jungle would soon change his attitude, but they were not willing to give up one of Slaughter's descriptions of ecstacy.

"Go on!" "Don't stop now!" the others begged. All of them still had their rifles aimed at Raunch's quivering face. Only after Slaughter spoke again and Raunch kept quiet were their rifles lowered.

"I'm resting the edge of the cup against my lips and opening my mouth, letting it all pour in at once." Then he made slurping and gurgling noises that sounded like "*the real thing*."

Half of the men simultaneously took off their helmets, wiped their foreheads and faces with their sleeves and took a drink from their canteen.

The water was warm and had a smell to it. It was hard for the men to decide whether it was more enjoyable listening to Slaughter with the water in their mouths helping their imaginations or not. This afternoon was extra hot and humid, even for Vietnam, and they hadn't been back to *the hill* for over three weeks.

It was days like this that could really get Slaughter going good.

Slaughter, and most of the rest of the platoon, had their eyes closed and their heads were tilted back as they went through the motions of drinking a Coke.

"The ice is so... cold, it almost hurts as I hold it in my mouth for a few seconds before crunching it up between my teeth and swallowing.

"Now for the hot, juicy burger again... Oh... Now the Coke... Oh......... Oh..............!"

There was a profound silence as the rest of the men listened to Slaughter go into spasms.

After Slaughter was done and a few minutes of silence had gone by, Sergeant Reber spoke, "I'm dreaming of Julie Munford."

Only a second later, Chip asked, "What part of her Sarge?"

They all laughed together. A little too loudly.

"Everyone back to their posts!" hoarsely whispered Lieutenant Murphy, the commanding officer. The men quieted down and scooted back to each of their own trees again.

After a couple of minutes, Chip asked, "What about you, Tiny? What do you dream about on a day like today?"

Tiny's soft voice came from behind Chip and to his left, "I dream of discovering a cure for cancer so I can help people and take away their suffering. I dream of coming up with the right words that could end this war and sending them to Chou En-lai and Mao Tse-tung . Then I dream of marrying Amy Hopkins and having a family..."

"You make me sick," interrupted Raunch. "You're gonna tell me that's all you ever dream about?"

Tiny wasn't sure if he should answer Raunch or not.

Unless he said something crude or vulgar he knew Raunch would just make fun of him.

He also knew that if he didn't answer, Raunch would just razz him more. So Timothy thought he would compromise just this once and give it a try. After all, they were out in the jungle on the other side of the world where no one would ever know. "I dreamt once that I played a love song on my violin and seduced Amy Hopkins."

Raunch laughed and replied, "Your idea of seducing Amy Hopkins would be to shake her hand." Then Raunch continued in a rough tone, "If Amy Hopkins were here right now I'd..."

"Shut up!" screamed Tiny in a whisper.

Raunch continued talking about Amy Hopkins until Tiny was ready to snap.

"Shut up, Raunch!" Chip demanded.

"Are you gonna make me?" challenged Raunch.

"Yes."

There was silence, and every head in the platoon turned and tried to see the look on Raunch's face. No one that had ever stood toe to toe with Chip was left standing or even conscious when it was over.

There was more silence, and eventually all their heads turned back.

After a minute, Chip spoke again, not to anyone in particular, "If Tiny wants to dream about shaking Amy Hopkin's hand, I say let him. If Raunch wants to grab Lucy Goose and she wants to grab him, I say go for it. I like to think that's what we're out here dying in the jungle for. The American dream."

Most of the helmets scattered through the trees were nodding as various voices came floating back through the foliage to Chip, "Yeah, man." "That's where it's at." "I'm in."

"Hot apple pie," came another voice.

"My pickup truck," Slaughter added.

"*Playboy* magazines," Raunch even joined in, and there was a snicker and a hoot.

"Wine, women and song," came another.

"My mother, and Aunt Bee," laughed another. Then they all laughed together.

"Tiny Tim was just different than the rest of us," Steven told the Luthier. "He never lied, drank, smoked, or looked at a dirty magazine. Most of the men made fun of him at one time or another, and it seemed like it was up to me to keep anyone from crossing the line. He was as big as the rest of us, but we all knew that any one of us could eat him alive hand-to-hand because he wasn't willing to hurt us. I've hurt many men, but only if they deserved it."

The Luthier looked like he doubted Steven's last statement.

"I thought they deserved it at the time!" defended Steven.

The Luthier still sat with the same expression on his face. He acted as though he was waiting for Steven to think about his statement a little more.

Steven looked away while thinking about the past twenty five years. "They deserved it," he thought. Then he remembered the times when he had "just gone along" with some of the things his motorcycle friends did at the expense of others.

"All right, I haven't been a saint," admitted Steven, "but Tiny Tim seemed to be and I did stand up for him." Steven looked at the Luthier like that should count for something.

The Luthier nodded as though it did, so Steven continued, "Two days later, we were back on *the hill*. The hill was the only place we could really rest or take a break without worrying about killing or being killed. Our company would spend a few days there *cutting loose*, then we would head back out into the jungle for another two to five weeks of *recon* or 'hunting'.

"All of us got a little crazy on the hill, and the longer the war went on, the crazier and crazier we got. We had to, just to keep going. Everyone but Tim. He was different.

"By the way Tiny acted while he was on the hill, I wondered if he had even gone through boot camp or if he could really pull a trigger. But each time I saw him in action again, I would stop wondering. He had six confirmed and at least three unconfirmed, and he took a hit once without even flinching.

"It was just too weird to see how he acted when he got back on the hill after shooting Gooks in the jungle. While everyone else was partying and carrying on, just glad to be alive, he was writing poetry and playing a violin that his parents had sent him from back home. It was probably the only violin in 'Nam, and it wouldn't have survived if I hadn't rescued it more than once. I never considered playing one myself, but I kind of liked listening to him.

"One night when we were side by side on the hill doing *hole watch* duty (sitting in a hole, watching for the enemy), I asked him, 'What's hummin' in your brain tonight, Tiny?'

"'Home and my future,' he answered.

"'You really think any of us have a future?' I asked him.

"'Here or the hereafter,' answered Tiny. 'I've decided that if I make it back home I'm going to become a priest so I can help some of the people this war has messed up.'

"That was Tiny," Steven told the Luthier. "He never said anything mean or dirty. He always helped anyone he could. And his favorite saying was, 'Don't judge a man until you've walked in his shoes.'

"Or boots," Steven added.

Chapter 14: Slaughter

After the hide glue had soaked in water for almost an hour, the Luthier placed it in an electric glue pot.

"From the looks of everything else, I expected you to start a fire or something," Steven commented.

"I only use fire when absolutely necessary," replied the Luthier, "and then only outside. While most of my processes are hundreds of years old, being old does not necessarily make things better."

Steven then watched while the Luthier scanned dozens of large, flat drawers in a large military-green cabinet. It looked about fifty years old and was against the center wall of the shop toward the back. The Luthier then pulled out a drawer containing a set of templates and a mold for making a violin.

Steven was still looking at the green paint after the Luthier had turned to go back toward the front of the shop. "Were those Military?"

"Yes," replied the Luthier. "When I heard they were closing down the base where these were located, I went and purchased them."

"You can afford this violin shop and all this land, and you buy your cabinets army surplus?" Steven questioned.

"Take a good look at these drawers, Steven. They are the finest of their kind and I purchased them for under a tenth of their original cost. Even though I insist upon the very best, I do not waste my money, and I suggest that you don't either. Especially when you have a wife and children to feed. Never be too proud to shop at surplus or thrift stores."

Steven was surprised to hear the Luthier talk of being *thrifty*.

"A real man knows when to buy his wife something new and special. He also knows when to tighten his belt and make do. If you can do each of these things with love and in the right attitude, they will both make her love you that much more.

"Mary is very special. For a woman of beauty and culture to be able to embrace a poor, blind man on the street and ask his advice is rare. Truly rare, and she will appreciate you more than you can imagine, if you succeed.

"Even though you feel that she has judged your appearance too harshly, it is probably from experiences that she has had, and I would not hold it against her. You have probably forgotten what it's like to be fragile and feel defenseless, and I would give her the benefit of the doubt."

Steven knew the Luthier was right about Mary. Even though he had never admitted it to anyone, he still remembered what it was like to feel helpless.

"You must also learn everything you can from whomever or whatever you can, Steven. Not only during the next month or two, but for the rest of your life. Some of the things I will tell you come from the greatest men and women in history, while others come from small children or drunks lying face down in the gutter. No matter where wisdom comes from, it is always priceless.

"A wise Pope studies the words of Confucius. A wise Rabbi will listen to the words and advice of Jesus. Even an atheist should be wise enough to learn wisdom from the different religions of the world.

"There are many secrets of life, and I will tell you as many of them as I can. Just like violin making, none of them is really secret; they are just not sought after, or not thought important enough to sacrifice for.

"You have probably heard of lottery winners losing all their money and being more miserable than when they started?" asked the Luthier.

Steven replied, "Yes, of course."

"The money was just as valuable as if they had earned it, but most people simply cannot appreciate something unless they have paid the price for it. Part of the secret of life is to be able to appreciate things for what they are worth instead of how much they cost.

"If Mary had thrown her arms around you as you were, you would not be happy, and you would not have been able to make her happy because you had not earned her. If you do *indeed* pay the price you claim you are willing to, you just might appreciate her enough to be able to make her happy."

With the Luthier's statement, Steven began to understand happiness and how to appreciate things for the very first time.

Steven thought of himself in his leathers, with his long hair, earrings, drinking, womanizing, and the friends he rode with, then about Mary. The vision of himself and who he was, standing in front of Mary, then kissing her, now slapped him in the face.

Without saying a word, Steven turned away from the Luthier, walked over to the large, full length mirror hanging by the bathroom door and took a good look. He still saw the man who had looked at his reflection in the window of the restaurant a few days before. Though, as he looked closer at his bruised, beat up face, he saw someone that was at least trying to become the man Mary could love. Also someone that could appreciate her.

Steven had only thought of becoming a gentleman until that moment. He had never tried picturing it.

"How are we going to do this?" asked Steven. "What will I be like when we are done?"

The Luthier walked over and stood beside Steven. "There will be changes in your appearance, but the most drastic change will be in your heart. If you look at yourself again you will notice that you have already taken a very large step."

Steven knew what the Luthier was talking about. He looked at his own face again and *knew* he saw someone who was trying to be better.

The Luthier walked back over to his bench, "As I make your violin, you need to watch and learn all that you can. At the same time, we will work on making you a better person."

The Luthier picked up the mold that Mary's instrument would be built around and started explaining the process to Steven, "This mold will determine the violin's size and shape, which in turn, helps determine its character. A Master Luthier must choose the right mold, or all is lost."

The Luthier then started working on small pieces of wood that would become the cornerblocks and endblocks of the violin. He continued, "To answer your question, 'How are we going to do this?' I must first know what I have to work with and what you want to become. Tell me about the next one."

The Luthier was referring to the second cross on the side of Steven's head.

"Slaughter," replied Steven. "A southern gentleman, with a twist..."

"Time to go *snoopin* and *poopin*," Lieutenant Murphy announced one afternoon after spending only three days on the hill. "Tomorrow, 0-five-hundred, full gear. It'll be a *long hump*," he added.

The party ended earlier than normal that night. As wild as the men got on the hill, when it came to going back into the field, they all took it seriously. They were, after all, Marines, through and through; a hangover could cost a man his own life as well as the lives of others.

The next morning, Chip looked over and watched while Slaughter packed his extra *ditty bag* full of grooming supplies and *who-knew-what* else.

Slaughter always looked good. He even smelled good. In the jungle that meant he didn't smell at all.

He always acted good, too. "Good" meant just the right amount of crazy in the jungle, cutting loose the right amount on the hill, and then firm, but polite, when he went to a *vill'* (village) or town.

While all of the other Marines were suffering from jungle

rot on their feet, Slaughter's looked like *Sunday morning*. No one knew how he did it. Whenever they would ask him, he would answer, "That's just the way a gentleman's feet *should* look. In the jungle or in the statehouse, grooming is a sign of being a gentleman."

Even at the end of a month in the jungle, Slaughter would walk back to the hill with white teeth, combed hair and a clean, shaven face. His clothes were even cleaner than anyone else's. No one knew how he did it. They all went where he went, they all did what he did, but even when a *long hump* was done, he finished it out clean.

Every time anyone asked him about it, his answer would always include the word "gentleman," sometimes more than once in one sentence. He used the word "gentleman" a lot.

Everyone knew he came from the South, though Chip thought Slaughter must have come from the South one hundred and fifty years before and been a mental patient. His demeanor was that of a wealthy plantation owner, yet he would quote Booker T. Washington as though he were his own father. Chip knew he even carried a copy of *Up From Slavery* in his ditty bag and he could tell by Slaughter's tone of voice when he was quoting words or ideals from it...

"A man must rise above his circumstances," Slaughter answered.

The rest of the platoon members sat in disbelief around the two tables. They were in front of a restaurant visiting one of the friendly *vill's*.

Slaughter had just turned down a *free introductory offer* from the most expensive prostitute from the city. There were no "free introductory offers" to anyone else, ever. Especially not from her.

Slaughter had bowed and smiled while answering, "No thank you, Ma'am."

She violently screamed what English insults and swear words she knew at Slaughter in response. Then slapped him and kicked him with her sharp, pointed shoes.

Finally, she cut loose with a long list of swear words in her own language before turning and strutting away.

Slaughter didn't even flinch. He just got a sad look on his face and waited for her to walk completely out of sight before putting his hat back on, sitting down, and facing the other men.

"His large bowie knife and his dogtags were the only way I could identify his body," finished Steven.

The Luthier looked down at the three dogtags still hanging from Steven's wrist. He nodded, then turned back to the task at hand.

Chapter 15: Ruckus

"*The* last cross is for Lieutenant Joe *Ruckus* Reber. Though, no one could ever pin a name on him that stuck until four months before he died..."

"Lieutenant Murphy, Sir?" questioned Chip. He had come forward, out of file, and approached the commanding officer. "Shouldn't we swing north, Sir?"

"Fall back, Private Miller. When I want your advice, I'll kick a hole through your teeth and stomp on your chest till the words come out," was the angry Lieutenant's reply. He then put his field glasses back in their case and led the men down toward the large, open field.

It was a vast clearing, hundreds of meters across, with only short grasses and a few dozen, random dirt mounds where the Viet Cong buried their dead. The mounds and a few dry stream beds were the only things interrupting its otherwise large, flat surface.

The mounds were low enough that the platoon could see all around them from the hill they were descending, but most of the men still didn't like it. Probably the only reason they followed, despite the Lieutenant's order, was the fact that the rest of the company was only two clicks beyond, then they were on their way back to the hill for a some serious R and R (rest and relaxation).

As they went lower in altitude, the trees got thicker until Chip and the other men had to cut their way through, even though many of the others had passed that way ahead of them. At times Chip could only follow the platoon by the swishing sound of their machetes and KBARs (large knives).

As they reached the edge of the trees, the Lieutenant stopped and took one last look. "Fall in," he gruffly ordered. Then they started across the field.

Joe was *tail end Charlie* that day. It was his job to bring up the rear and make sure there were no Viet Cong following or surrounding them from behind. Joe had been *taking care of business* when the rest of the platoon had started to move, so he was lagging behind more than he normally would.

Just as the platoon reached the center, Joe was approaching the edge of the trees. Shots rang out and the Lieutenant was the first to fall. Viet Cong appeared from nowhere and opened fire on the platoon from behind the mounds. Within seconds, the bullets from the enemy's AK-47 automatic rifles sounded like a vicious swarm of bees in the air.

Chip and the others crouched down and started spraying the mounds with their M-16s, while trying to find cover. One man after the other fell, until the few remaining rolled into a shallow stream bed that offered a minimum amount of protection.

After looking back at the bullet-riddled radios, they knew the possibility of calling for support had been eliminated. Chip's gaze went further back across the field to where they had just come from while the dirt flew in his eyes from the enemy's bullets hitting the ground in front of his face. He had told Joe to hurry up before heading out across the field and knew that he was still back in the trees somewhere.

"I wonder what Joe will do?" Chip asked himself.

As he looked around at the mounds, he realized, "What can he do? Other than cause a small distraction that might prolong the inevitable a minute or two and get himself killed."

A moment after Chip turned back around to face the enemy, there was a lull in the machine gun fire.

Floating out across the valley from the edge of the trees came a distinct cry from a running figure in green yelling,

"I will rise!"

Chip and the others first looked at Joe coming their way, then over at Slaughter. He was laying in the streambed brandishing a large, pure-white smile. The words were *his* words. Words and ideals that he had taken from Booker T. Washington. Slaughter had said them many times, almost as a recited prayer or creed, each time he went into battle. "No matter where I am placed, no matter whose fault it may be, no matter what odds are against me, I will rise!"

Most of the enemy fire was directed toward Joe as he charged across the open field and ran behind the first mound. Without even hesitating, he came out from behind the mound still yelling.

One after another, Joe disappeared behind the mounds and came screaming back out the other side, victorious. Dirt was flying up in all directions and his equipment was torn to shreds and ripped off his sides, piece by piece, but he kept going.

When Joe cleared the fifth mound, a bullet took the heel off his left boot and the force sent him down on his side. Without hesitation, he rolled over and jumped back up screaming, "I will rise!"

After Joe had cleared the first mound, the other men in the platoon realized that the enemy had been distracted. Slaughter looked at the other men lying in the streambed and started his chant, "No matter where I am placed..."

They looked back at Slaughter, then reloaded their rifles with fresh clips of ammunition.

"...No matter whose fault it may be," Slaughter continued as they turned and faced the direction of fire.

"No matter what odds are against me..." His voice raised to a yell.

Then all the men stood up out of the shallow streambed and screamed together, "I will rise!" as they charged forward, into the face of the enemy.

"There were thirty-five enemy confirmed dead that day and four of us left standing," Steven told the Luthier.

"Joe, Slaughter, Tiny, and myself."

The Luthier had stopped working and set his tools aside while he listened. His eyes were misty.

"Joe held the highest rank in the platoon. Later he was field commissioned Lieutenant back at the hill. But while we were still in the jungle that night, we started celebrating and getting louder than we should have. Joe came over and told us in an agitated voice, 'Hold that *ruckus* down!'

"His voice was gone from yelling, and he was half-jokingly trying to impress us with his new authority. He was forcing his voice so hard to give the order that it cracked or hiccuped right in the middle of the word 'ruckus.' Everyone started hooting and laughing, and the name 'Ruckus' stuck forever, as good names always do.

"But if there was ever a *knight in shining armor* putting it all on the line, it was that day, and it was Joe," added Steven.

"The shirt I was wearing when I met you was the one Ruckus wore that day. It was also the one he died in."

Chapter 16: The Frame

The corner blocks of the violin were shaped and glued onto the mold soon after Steven finished telling the Luthier about Joe Reber. While the glue was drying, the Luthier cut thin strips of curly maple for the violin's ribs from the wood that came from the *Bon Homme Richard*.

The deep flame (waves in violinmaking wood that look and change color like tiger's eye) was beautiful and the stripes changed colors as Steven moved them back and forth in the light. After the ribs were cut, the wood remaining was just large enough to make the back of the violin.

While Steven watched the Luthier cut into the piece of wood, he noticed how different it was from all the others hanging from the ceiling. He gazed up and asked the Luthier, "Where does all *that* wood come from?"

The Luthier looked up from his work and answered, "There are only a few select areas around the world where the trees can grow properly."

The Luthier stood up and led Steven to the back of the shop, "This spruce tree will make bright, silvery sounding bellies; it lived in the Tyrolean Alps." He walked a few feet and pointed to another section of wood and explained, "These trees grew in Bosnia. It is possible to carve backs from them that can cut people's hearts and make them bleed at the back of the largest concert hall."

Steven walked with the Luthier while he pointed to each group of wood, told him where it came from and the character it would give each of his instruments.

"This spruce came from Italy. It will give bellies a pure,

sweet voice, while these others came from Cedar Mountain, only fifty miles north of here. Their voices are sweet and gentle, giving a peaceful character to any instrument. This German maple, on the other hand, will make backs with a forceful, disciplined sound and this tree that grew right next to it has a carefree, capricious nature."

Steven could tell that the Luthier lived in a world of his own. He figured the Luthier was a little crazy, yet he was envious of someone who lived for and loved something so much.

"And my personal favorites," finished the Luthier with obvious, personal bias, "are these." He pointed up at two very large sections of spruce and maple hanging from the ceiling.

"This magnificent spruce comes from Eastern France. Within its fibers is the daring, bold love of the French people. The maple beside it comes from central Canada. Realize that I can choose different molds and then carve any of these woods in a way that will change or compliment their character, yet this maple remains rich and full with a lush, passionate feeling no matter what I do.

"I also have pieces of wood from trees that grew by themselves in other parts of the world, but it is truly rare. Rare enough to be considered a miracle. The wood must come from trees of particular species and they must grow properly to assure the quality of the instrument, but after that, it becomes a matter of taste and the *needs* of my individual customers."

"How often do you make violins out of wood that came from pirate ships, naval vessels, and temples?"

The Luthier took one last, lingering look above his head before answering, "This is the first time."

"The first time?"

The Luthier nodded.

Steven hadn't noticed any other wood that looked like his. "How many more pieces do you have?"

The Luthier walked back over and picked up the wood

for Steven's violin and held it in his hands.

"These are the only pieces that are capable of making a violin, Steven." The Luthier looked down and smiled like he would at his own child in his arms.

"Why me?" he asked as he looked back up at the other wood hanging from the ceiling.

"Because it is what you need," answered the Luthier.

Steven could not believe that this was the same man that had *beat him to a bloody pulp* only two days before.

"My father loved the sea, Steven. His idea of heaven was a large sailing ship floating across the ocean with its mainsail filled with friendly breezes. He enlisted in the Navy during World War II so, if he gave his life for his country, it would be at sea.

"He loved seeing the world from the deck of a ship. Most of all, he loved working the rigging and riding the wind with the spray of saltwater against his face as the prow cut through the water, with the waves lapping over the bulwarks onto his feet. He also loved hunting for lost treasures and rediscovering precious things that were lost.

"You asked me to share my father with you. These pieces of wood will not only remind you of who you are, they will also remind you of him."

The Luthier sat down at his bench and started working again. Steven thought about the special wood while the Luthier peeled away its old, rough, weathered surface. Each stroke of the plane seemed to magically reveal silky-smooth, creamy-white wood just waiting beneath.

The Luthier next cut and scraped the violin's ribs to thickness. They each ended up measuring about one millimeter with the calipers, but not exactly.

"I make each of them the *right* thickness," he explained. "The secret to making a great master instrument is not cutting each piece to an exact dimension, but carving each piece until it is the best it can be. Every piece of wood is different, lived its own life, and therefore it must be treated differently in order for it to *live* in the instrument.

"People born in the same country may have similar

characteristics, yet each retains their own individual personality and each one must be treated differently if they are to reach their full potential. Even though these pieces of wood may look the same to you, each one is very different."

The Luthier smiled, "If a nun had come to the violin shop two days ago for a violin and advice, I would not have taken her down the path and drug her through the rocks and cactus by her hair. Yet I believed it was what you needed."

Steven smiled back at the Luthier as he imagined a nun hanging from the rock ledge and facing the rattlesnake.

The Luthier bent the violin's ribs to match the shape of the mold on an old bending iron. The heated piece of metal was just hot enough to bend the thin pieces of wood without burning them.

When the ribs were finished, the Luthier cut, planed, and scraped twelve small strips of wood, then also bent them to match the inside curve of the ribs. The Luthier called them linings.

The Luthier explained, "These linings will widen the glue joint inside the instrument and also give the corners of the violin extra support and strength. Later, I will carve half of their wood away in order to allow the ribs to flex and move with the vibrations of the instrument. This gives it more strength, and at the same time, a fuller sound than would otherwise be possible."

The process seemed very smooth and systematic to Steven. It amazed him that by lunch time the violin was beginning to take shape.

"At this rate my violin could be done in a week," declared Steven.

The Luthier shook his head. "The things that people think should take so much time are really quite simple and go quickly. It is the things that they don't even know about that take the most time and effort."

Steven knew by the way the Luthier looked at him that he was talking about the process of changing his life as well.

That evening was relaxed and uneventful and Steven went to bed early so he could finish catching up on his sleep.

The next morning, the ribs were re-bent and allowed to relax to perfection. Then they were glued to the corner and endblocks that were attached to the mold. By late that evening, the ends of the linings were mortised into the cornerblocks and glued to the ribs using dozens of small clamps.

The Luthier worked tirelessly, day after day, while telling Steven about the great men and women in history and the ideals they stood for. Their only breaks were when Sheryl brought lunch, or while eating dinner at the Luthier's house with his family.

The Luthier spoke in vivid detail and his words seemed to bring each person and event he spoke about to life. Steven had never even heard of many of the people, and there were many times that he wondered if any professor in any university ever had, either.

As time went by, some of the events and places he spoke about were so ancient, remote, and obscure that Steven couldn't imagine how the Luthier could have possibly know about them. But he listened and learned all that he could, amazed at the knowledge that he had passed by his whole life.

Steven started to understand Booker T. Washington's passion for education and learning, then Martin Luther King's dream for the chance to use it. Somehow Steven himself felt like he was a slave to his circumstances and now he was trying to rise up out of his own ignorance.

Some days, when the Luthier's voice started giving out, he would take a break and play different kinds of music or turn on the radio. Some of Steven's most important lessons about women and relationships started with *Dr. Laura's* radio program. Sometimes, after the show was over, the Luthier would continue with her topics late into the night.

Steven remembered getting bored very quickly in school, and yet he could sit and listen to the Luthier talk for

hours. It was always the Luthier who would finally say
that it was time for bed, not Steven.

One evening, while the Luthier was turning off the lights
in the shop, Steven asked quite bluntly, "Why aren't you
boring?"

The Luthier didn't even hesitate, "Because I love
everything that I talk about."

Steven awakened early the next morning, feeling that
something was different.

As he walked on the road winding along the valley floor,
he admired the beautiful gardens. He listened to the birds
singing in the trees like he had for the last couple days,
but today they seemed more mellow and tranquil. A
squirrel stopped in front of him and stood in the middle
of the road. It held something between its front paws
and started nibbling at it.

Steven found himself walking to the side, so he wouldn't
disturb the animal's meal. When the squirrel didn't move
and looked up at him with its big, dark-brown eyes, Steven
smiled.

As Steven continued up the hill, thinking of how
secluded and peaceful the valley was, he was startled by
a large, four-point buck. It came out of the trees and
walked across the road, not more than fifteen feet in front
of him, its hooves clicking on the blacktop. The deer
only gave Steven a haphazard glance as it continued
across the road and into the trees on the other side.

Even without the squirrel and the deer, Steven realized
that he hadn't felt this way since he was a young boy
walking with his mother. He opened the violin shop door
and immediately asked the Luthier, "Is today Sunday?"

The Luthier smiled back and replied, "It is."

"Do you go to church?" asked Steven.

"Normally, yes," answered the Luthier. "Would you like
to go?"

Steven hesitated. "I don't think I'm quite ready for that
yet."

"That's all right," commented the Luthier. "I won't be

going today, either. Sheryl suggested that I should stay with you while she took the children."

"Are we going to work today, then?" asked Steven

"No, not really," replied the Luthier. "Let's go for a walk, instead."

Before leaving the shop, the Luthier took Dianne's viola out of the large wooden box and carried it outside. When the rays of the sun shone upon it, the Luthier smiled.

"How do you keep such a good attitude when working with people like Dianne?" Steven asked. He still couldn't believe how arrogant and self-righteous the woman had been.

"That's a very good question, but I'll save the answer for later," replied the Luthier.

Steven followed the Luthier up the ladder that led to the roof and watched him place the viola on its stand. As soon as the Luthier stepped back, Steven had a strangely profound feeling about it.

He was thinking about some of the comments the Luthier had made about ancient Egypt and other civilizations that worshipped the sun. Ever since he met the Luthier and began living in the valley, he started having different feelings and dreams. Different than he had ever had before.

After descending the ladder, the Luthier began headed out through the sagebrush.

"Are we taking the path again?" questioned Steven.

"Yes," replied the Luthier.

Steven tested his left shoulder. He was pretty sure he could hang onto the rock ledge if he had to, but it would still be very difficult and painful. Then he wondered how much of the first night's events the Luthier was going to repeat.

The Luthier sensed Steven's apprehension but just kept walking in silence toward the cliff.

As the Luthier approached the edge, he turned and followed another path that ran along it. He commented, "I still question why God allows us to follow others we should be able to trust until we blindly fall off a cliff."

There was irony in the Luthier's words.

Steven was glad when he realized that they were not taking the same path, and now he relaxed while the Luthier continued, "Some people are given fathers who hate them and drag them down as far as they possibly can, mercilessly breaking their spirits and taking away their options in life. Few ever realize it like you have, and when they do, even fewer ever find the courage to climb their way out.

"Others are given the greatest fathers in the world. Fathers who love them and teach them all they can, leaving it up to them to decide for themselves whether to walk a good path or fall off the cliff. But if they fall, it is with their eyes wide open."

Steven shook his head while looking over the edge of the cliff. He didn't know why; he just knew it was true from his own experience.

As they walked along, they looked at the trees and gardens below. It was fall and the leaves were starting to turn the valley into a rainbow of radiant colors. It reminded Steven of the sunset he watched after playing the game of *Bone Guys*.

While he walked and listened to the Luthier, Steven tried to imagine what it would have been like growing up with the greatest father in the world. Then to have a beautiful woman at his side, loving him and helping him each step of the way while he worked at an occupation that he loved and was successful at.

Steven looked down at the Luthier's house. He couldn't imagine what it must be like, living every day of his life in a beautiful valley like this with everything that he could possibly need.

"Has your life always been like this?" asked Steven in amazement.

"No," replied the Luthier.

As soon as the Luthier said the word "no," he turned from the path and headed out through the cactus and sagebrush. After a short walk, the Luthier stopped and looked down at the ground. Steven came up beside him and looked also. There, deeply embedded in the sand and almost totally hidden by the sagebrush, were two twisted, steel I-beams covered with rust.

"This is where I lived when I was thirteen," the Luthier told him.

Steven looked at the Luthier, then back down along the two steel beams buried in the sand. He finally realized that the I-beams were all that was left of an old trailer house.

Bill had visited with the Luthier's father and told Steven about it. He stopped by their house in California and said that it was one of the nicest in town, built on a large, elaborate lot surrounded by trees. Bill hadn't mentioned anything about a trailer house in the middle of the desert.

"My father loved extremes," explained the Luthier. "As I grew up, his occupations and our life-styles went from one extreme to another. In less than a year's time he went from developing explosives to designing jet engines. The next was spent growing grapes on a vineyard then making stepping stones in our own factory. The year after that, he was a nuclear physicist.

"I have told you about a few of his hobbies, but I have not even started to allude to his many occupations.

"My father could choose a new occupation one afternoon and within a month have a small factory producing goods at a profit. He could land almost any job on earth, no matter what the requirements or credentials needed, then be one of the top men in that field within a year.

"Of all his occupations, he was a nuclear physicist longer than any of the others. Possibly because it was mentally challenging and very diversified. From lasers and cryogenics to intercontinental ballistics. But, after a few years, he quit the aerospace industry, sold our large home in California and we ended up here." The Luthier pointed down at the steel beams.

"There was nothing else around when this trailer was literally drug out here. No road. No other houses. No water. No electricity. No phone. Nothing. On top of that, this trailer was being hauled to the dump when it broke in half and drug on the freeway until it stopped the semi that was towing it. My father was the only one that could move it because he had a ten-wheel-drive *deuce-and-a-half* army truck. He wrapped a huge chain around it and drug it out here with the back loaded down and all ten wheels spinning as he went.

"The army truck bogged down right here and this is where I lived until the day I left home."

Steven's eyes were wide. The Luthier's story was starting to paint an unbelievably surreal picture in his mind.

The Luthier continued, "The occupations started changing almost monthly after we moved in. He rented a shop in town and set up a machine shop. Then he went into hydroponics, raising vegetables. Next, we were spinning and casting pottery hung with macrame ropes. He got the designs from an old sea captain and our most successful pot was shaped like a pirate ship that hung from hemp."

The Luthier smiled and added, "We even tied some of the ropes so it looked like your pirate ship's rigging. But, just like all the other occupations, we stopped making the ships just when all the equipment was paid off. At the end of each year, when the land payment came due, my father would consult for large manufacturing companies so he could pay the bill, then have just enough money left over to start into the next set of business ventures and occupations.

"We became lumberjacks and spent two summers logging in Washington. We made roll-a-hoop games for kids. We did development work on electric cars in-between fixing and reconstructing human skeletons for different universities. He bought earth moving equipment and more land, then constructed a subdivision. He even planned on buying the rest of that mountain (the Luthier pointed toward the town of Leeds) and this valley, so he could make them into an amusement park some day.

"I will try to complete his list of occupations, but you would need to talk to my oldest brother, Michael, if you want them all.

"He helped make the amusement ride at the *Hershey Chocolate Factory* in Pennsylvania. He made the automated, mechanical gorilla in the bottom of the *Tokyo Tower* in Japan. He restored classic cars and reupholstered furniture, bought and ran a rock quarry and did masonry work, bakery, silk-screening, finish carpenter, general contractor, we ran a punch-press shop, painted murals at rest homes, made kung fu stars, manufactured the cases for 50-caliber machine gun solenoids, wrought iron furniture, silver and opal mined, jewelry making, sculpting, rubber extension cord holders, metal boxes for holding firewood, and he made plastic cases for walkie-talkies."

The Luthier finished the list in one large breath.

Steven didn't know what to say. He had heard of "jacks of all trades," but that usually meant a few, not literally *all* trades.

The Luthier continued, "Realize that most of these occupations were done together as a family. These were not hobbies, they were occupations. He had *many* more hobbies than he had occupations.

"Most of the professions he pursued only made a few dollars by the time the equipment was paid off, but that was all right with my father. He loved to add another tool to his collection, whether it was a microscope or a dump truck. My father didn't do everything in this world before he died, but everything he didn't have time for was still written on his "to do" list. And he instilled that attitude into each of us children."

The Luthier stood silent for a minute and let it all sink in.

"I don't know why he did it. Maybe it was just who he was. Some of the occupations came about just like the hobbies did; because one of us was interested in it and he took it to heart. Others seemed to make no sense at all, with no logical reason why. He just did it.

"As I look back on his life I have to believe in destiny. For there has never been another father like him, and I could not be a Master Luthier without having him as my father."

Chapter 17: True Love

"Destiny," Steven repeated while looking from the remains of the trailer house, into the Luthier's eyes. "Do you really believe it's possible for Mary and I to have true love at first sight? You said you knew of only five cases in the history of the world."

"I said that I have *heard of* five cases in the history of the world, Steven. I *know* of only one."

Steven's face went pale. "Then why did you agree to help me?" he asked in disbelief.

The Luthier walked to the other side of the frame and turned around. Then he pointed to the ground at his feet.

"Because it happened right here."

"I know that I call him the greatest father in the world, but rest assured, Steven, my father was no saint. He was the hardest worker I've ever met in my life, but he was also a hard man. He was sometimes even ruthless, and showed no mercy. He also claimed that no one could ever beat him or break him."

The Luthier looked over between the old steel rails and continued, "Maybe "no one" could, but this trailer house did.

"After living in it for a few years, he fell into a deep depression and fits of despair. And I, his faithful son, went with him.

"We had tried so many occupations that made only enough money to pay for the equipment that we were eventually left destitute. He could have still gone out and landed a great-paying job at any moment, but he referred to working for other companies as though it were slavery. He often called it 'the forty-year grind.' So he just sat in this trailer house and got more depressed as time went by."

The Luthier walked between the two rails and spoke as though the trailer house was still there, "Don't underestimate what we went through, Steven. The first couple years were spent with no running water, no electricity and no phone; basically no comforts of life. Even though we eventually dug a trench and ran electricity and a phone line here, we were too poor to buy a heater or a cooler and there were still rats chewing away at the walls and ceiling while we tried to sleep at night.

"Skunks dug their way up through the floors and sprayed at us, making life miserable, and the odor gave us the worst headaches imaginable. The temperature ranged between five degrees in the winter and a hundred and eighteen in the summertime. Some days the temperature changed over seventy degrees while other times it remained so hot through the night that it seemed to bake our brains.

"There were many other things that were much worse, and all of them put together finally drug us down into depression. This depression reached an unbelievable low the summer after I graduated from high school.

"No matter what I did, I felt like my life was worthless. I couldn't find anything worth living for, and my father would look back at me and reaffirm my depression with his own. I dyed all my clothes black even though it reached a hundred and ten degrees almost every day that month. My father, who was a man of extremes and raised me the same way, got even more miserable until he and I finally got so depressed that we couldn't think straight.

"We just sat on the couch, feeding on each others' misery while my mother worked away at her housework and chores. Then we started fighting and it escalated until I finally ran away from home.

"I headed away from this trailer house that summer

afternoon with the sole purpose of trashing my life. But I ran out of gas a few miles from Las Vegas and was brought back by the police. When I returned, I was put right back beside my father on the hot, sweaty, miserable couch again. The only real difference was one more broken window in the trailer house because my father had thrown a chair through it while I was driving away.

"In this day and age I am sure that the social services and health department would have brought a quick end to our misery, but not back then. We were free to go as low as humanly possible. And we did.

"Feeling that my life was worthless, and when I was as low as I thought a human soul could possibly go, my oldest brother, Michael, showed up on the front porch. He slid back the broken, twisted, sliding glass door held together with duct tape, and peered in at us.

"Though it was a hundred and five degrees outside, the large, round thermometer on the kitchen wall read a hundred and fifteen when he stepped in.

"'Hi, Mom and Dad,' he said. Then he turned to me, 'I have a surprise for you, Jonathan.'

"He pulled a violin case out from behind him and held it up so I could see it.

"I was glad to see Michael, here at the trailer. I always liked Mike, but I was still too hot and miserable that day to show him that I cared.

"It was the middle of July and it had been a typical day: I had worked on a farm in Leeds in the early morning so I could earn money to fix my car. I came home and worked on the old *Mustang* until the sand and my tools got so hot they could blister my hands. Then I went into the trailer house so I could bake and sweat with my father on the couch for the rest of the day.

"Michael's next statement was very simple and to the point. He said, 'If you will play this violin, you may have it.'

"I wondered why he was offering me a violin. I hadn't played in months and decided to give up the violin all together. So I remained where I was, slumped down on the couch, and looked at him with my eyes glazed over in depression.

"Michael didn't let my lack of enthusiasm stop him. He put the case down on the small kitchen table and pulled out the violin. He tightened the bow as if to relieve me of any extra effort that I may have to put out and held it up, ready to play. Then he offered it to me again.

"'Try it,' he said, with a pleading, almost desperate look on his face, 'just a few notes.'

"No matter how tired I was, or what excuse I might use for someone else, I could not refuse Michael. While all my other brothers had gone through their phases of picking on me and beating me up, Michael had always been kind and thoughtful. He was a lot older than I was and when I was young and had been thoughtless or rude to him he was always kind back to me.

"I slowly stood up. My old, cheap, German copy of a Stradivari was back in my bedroom and I showed as much enthusiasm as if I were about to pick it up."

The Luthier walked over between the two steel I-beams where the living room would have been and closed his eyes while he continued, "I only glanced at it before putting it under my chin, and Michael watched as I placed the bow upon the strings.

"I immediately started to cry and my whole life changed in that one moment. It was as though I had walked through a door and stepped into another world; a beautiful world of joy, with wonderful feelings beyond description. It lifted my soul and I floated above the miserable, pitiful world that I had been living in.

"I kept playing, and passages that had been impossible before, now became effortless. It was as though the violin was pulling my fingers along its strings, faster and faster, lifting my spirits higher and higher as I went. It pulled me further and further into its wonderful world until I was no longer satisfied with reality. In a way, it *showed me reality* for the first time in my life.

"When I stopped playing, Michael told me that the violin was mine, simply because he knew I needed it. The violin was over 300 years old and at that time valued around fifty-thousand dollars. But much more important than that, it was a master violin with a soul capable of lifting the most downtrodden person, from the depths of despair and torment, to heaven."

Steven was amazed; he had never heard anyone talk about musical instruments like that before. He had only thought of them as wood and strings that played songs, not as souls and feelings like the Luthier had described.

Steven stood looking at the old trailer house frame when he realized that the Luthier was standing in a different place than when he had said "right here."

"I thought you said it was over there?" questioned Steven.

"It was," replied the Luthier with a smile. Then he continued, "I played... No, I *lived and breathed* that violin every day, from morning until night. I couldn't put it down. I became part of it and it became part of me. I lived for it and now it lived for me.

"I played every song and book of music that I could find. I couldn't afford new music so I ended up playing my mother's piano music and World War II love songs. Amazingly enough though, after about a month, my violin and I fell right back into another deep fit of depression.

"My violin had carried me to a whole different world. It showed me all that was possible. I felt all the great feelings that music can give."

"So what happened?" Steven asked.

The Luthier replied, "I started playing the love songs. I became obsessed with them until they possessed me. Finally they tormented me when I realized that I was alone.

"I kept playing the old master violin, but now the music became sad and more depressing as each note was played and as each day passed. With the help of its voice and the wanton music I chose to play, I was now able to reach unbelievable new depths of despair and sorrow, *with a passion*.

"My only other outlet in the trailer house was an old

record player back in my bedroom. Before the violin came,
I had used it to play hard, pounding music at full volume
until my head was numb and senseless. Then, at the
very lowest level of my new-found depression, I decided
to give the stereo a try again.

"First, I decided to play an old record that I had found
that summer called "Angels in the Sky" by *The Crewcuts.*"

The Luthier asked Steven, "Have you ever heard of it?"
Steven shook his head.

"Neither had I," the Luthier commented. "Never in my
life."

"It starts with these words;

> Talk to the angels, let them hear your plea,
> tell them that you're lonely,
> get down upon your knees
> and pray the lord will help you...'

"And it ends with;

> ...the Lord will always hear you,
> talking to the angels in the sky.'

"The style of the song was old and outdated but the
words spoke to my soul and gave me hope. As soon as
the music faded away, I taped the arm of the old record
player so it would play "Angels in the Sky" over and over
again.

"I probably listened to it a hundred times before I turned
it off and dropped to my knees. I couldn't remember the
last time that I had really prayed."

Tears rolled down the Luthier's face as he continued, "I
was seventeen years old and I was poor. I lived in a broken
down trailer house in the middle of the desert. I knew I
was no one, and I still felt like my life was worthless, but
I got down and begged God for someone that night. I
promised him everything, and I held absolutely nothing
back. I fell asleep in the early hours of the morning, still
praying on my knees.

"I was awakened by my mother's voice coming down the narrow hall of the trailer, 'It's time to get up and go to church.'

"I was so tired that I couldn't keep my eyes open while I put on my black shirt, black pants, black socks, and black shoes. We were always late for church, so I stumbled over the plywood covering the large hole where the trailer was broken in half and headed to the front door without stopping for any breakfast."

The Luthier walked over to where the front porch of the trailer house would have been and continued, "It was 8:03 am, Sunday, August 12, 1979 and I rubbed my tired, swollen eyes as I slid open the door. When I put my hands down and opened my eyes I was looking straight into the eyes of an angel.

"She was standing right here, in front of this trailer house, looking back at me and smiling. She was the most beautiful thing that I had ever seen in my life, or have ever seen since. She had flaming red hair that looked like gold with the morning sun shining through it, and she wore a sky-blue dress with white, lacy trim. That angel's name was Sheryl and you met her your first night here.

"No one has ever fallen more deeply in love than I did that instant. I knew right then and there that she was an angel, and I knew that God had answered my prayer as she stood looking into my eyes."

The Luthier walked away from where the trailer once stood and back to the path that ran along the edge of the cliff. He looked out across the valley and continued with a smile, "That angel came to church with me that morning, just over that hill." The Luthier pointed beyond the valley where his house was.

"We walked into the meeting late, and every head turned and wondered who the beautiful woman was by my side. Realize, I was seventeen years old and considered an outcast, while she was a magnificent-looking woman.

"She sat down on the bench, and I sat down beside her about a foot away. She turned and looked at me with a serious, questioning look on her face, mixed with disappointment. There was even sadness in her eyes.

"I looked back, not knowing what to think or what to do. And it must have shown, because her expression instantly changed to that of understanding. With playful smile, she gracefully slid her elegant form over a little more than the one foot that separated us until her hip pressed firmly against mine.

"She looked toward the front of the church for a moment as though to say, 'Everything's normal. Nothing special's going on back here.' Then she turned and batted her eyes at me and her face lit up like only an angel's can.

"I looked into her eyes as she gently pulled my nervous, trembling hand over and held it between her calm and loving ones for the entire service.

"She faced forward and listened to the preacher most of the time, but as each member took their turn and stared at us as though to ask, "Who is she, and why is she sitting next to Jonathan?" she would respond by looking at me as though I was the most important person in the world. When a couple of the older boys and a few men looked in her direction, she made it very clear that she was here for me, and me alone.

"That afternoon I packed my violin and belongings into my car and told my mother and father good-bye. Before that night was over, I had driven almost three hundred miles from the trailer house with Sheryl sitting by my side.

"We slept in separate apartment buildings, but spent every waking minute together while she gave my life direction and taught me what this world was really meant to be like."

The Luthier became solemn and choked out the words, "She changed my life and healed my soul." Then the Luthier smiled, "She also taught me many other truly important things, like how to kiss."

Steven couldn't help but smile back at the Luthier.

"She then became my best friend in the time it took to make all the arrangements for a prim and proper wedding.

"My life changed completely with her by my side, and within a year I was carving my first violin. In the tradition of my father, I chose different occupations along the way to gain experience and pay for the violins, but now each occupation was highly successful and there seemed to be no limits to what I could accomplish."

The Luthier put his hand on Steven's shoulder, "Yes, there really are angels. I am married to one. Yes, there really is true love at first sight; I have experienced it. And yes, there really is *happily-ever-after.*"

After a few minutes of silence, the Luthier turned to Steven and added, "Whoever or whatever you believe God is, I owe him *big time.*"

Chapter 18: Religion

Steven and the Luthier continued along the path until it began descending into the trees surrounding the Luthier's house. Steven glanced back and asked, "What happened to the trailer house?"

The Luthier turned and smiled.

"As soon as Sheryl and I were married, my father started recovering from his depression. It wasn't long before he got off that couch and decided to build another subdivision to earn some money. He payed off the land, built my mother a nice home and bought her the Steinway grand piano she had always dreamed of. They moved in a few months before he died.

"It's right over there," the Luthier added, while pointing to a large, *Frank Lloyd Wright*-style home. It was constructed of large rock pillars and glass walls, complete with an indoor swimming pool. The house was within sight of the old trailer house frame.

"Half the town of Leeds came over and joined in with our family celebration. We beat the old, rat infested trailer house with sledge hammers and crow bars, shot it with guns, blew it up with cannons and dynamite, then my mother lit the remains on fire and burned it to the ground. It was a large party and there was dinner and dancing afterward."

The Luthier beamed with pride and satisfaction as he turned and continued down the path,

Steven took one last glance at the I-beams and couldn't help thinking about the old military phrase, "the enemy is dead."

The grass was short and smooth on the east side of the Luthier's house.

"It looks like a putting green," Steven commented, after seeing it through the trees.

"It is," replied the Luthier.

When they reached the yard, the Luthier walked over and lifted up a flag, then placed it in a small hole in the middle of the grass.

"Skyler's flight was moved up at the last minute. He must have gotten the call before he finished playing."

Steven then noticed that there were shutters over the windows and a few small dents in the siding. This Luthier was a serious man, but he also liked to cut-loose and seemed to have no limits. "Looks like fun," Steven commented.

"When your shoulder feels better, we'll have to play," offered the Luthier. Then he added, "This is the library," as he swung the door open.

Steven could tell that it was no ordinary library. In addition to a vast amount of books lining the walls from floor to ceiling, there were printing presses, photographic equipment and a binding area. Steven was enthralled with the bookmaking equipment, but it was the far corner that caught his eye and instantly received his full attention.

Many of the books there were sealed in airtight cases while others weren't books at all. There were clay tablets and rolls of ancient papyri in airtight containers, also metal plates bound together with rings sitting next to other books that looked like stacks of leather. Between the different *books* were artifacts and curious-looking items from many different civilizations and cultures, ancient and modern. It seemed out of place, but a row of unmarked video tapes were lined up on a shelf in the middle.

Steven stopped in the center of the library. He felt like he was standing in the middle of a room filled with treasure.

The Luthier let Steven take as much time as he wanted

inspecting the artifacts. He even gave short explanations of where they came from and from what period of time. Steven picked up and inspected each and every one, and asked many questions.

When Steven had finished, the Luthier announced, "It's time we got serious, Steven."

Steven looked at the Luthier like he was joking. "What have you called the last few days? A picnic?"

The Luthier smiled and continued, "That's what my father would say. Even when we were almost finished with a tough job that had gone on forever, he would announce, 'It's time we got serious'."

Steven looked at all the books that surrounded him. Visions of a grey-haired Steven Miller wearing thick, *pop-bottle* glasses began running through his mind.

The Luthier interrupted his thoughts, "You mentioned going to church with your mother and you said you liked it, then you painted *I hate Jesus* on the back of your helmet in Vietnam. You tell me you didn't mean it, yet if I understand correctly, you haven't stepped into a church in decades."

Steven shook his head.

"Well, we need to start somewhere, Steven. If you had to choose a religion, what would it be, if any?"

Steven looked at a large group of religious books sitting on one of the shelves. "My mother took me to a few different churches. The last one was Methodist, but I didn't notice much difference between the sermons. I liked to hear about Jesus more than anything and most of the preachers seemed all right."

"Anything else?" the Luthier asked. "Good or bad."

Steven pondered the sermons that he had heard as a child; at least the things he could remember.

"I didn't care for a preacher in one of the churches. He talked a lot about Moses and his buddy's army killing people and destroying everything for God just because they were different.

"I don't know why, but that thought haunted me at night while I slept with my M-16 in my hands. I'm sure I'm looking at it all wrong, but every time I thought of religion and that preacher, I thought of killing people for a bloodthirsty God.

"I have no problem killing people to defend my country. I could even live with going overseas and killing people to stop the spread of communism because I knew that the communists wanted to kill freedom. But to go kill someone simply because they were Buddhist or Atheist or whatever, crosses the line for me."

The Luthier nodded his head in understanding. Then he commented, "It was Joshua."

"Who?" asked Steven.

"Moses' buddy," the Luthier answered.

"So, is it fair to say, that if anything, you are a Christian?" asked the Luthier. "Give or take the Old Testament for now?"

"Sure," replied Steven.

The Luthier tone became deep and somber, "Now let's get real serious. What religion is Mary?"

Steven stared at the Luthier with a blank look at first, then he smiled and replied, "Mary's a Christian too. Tom's a Catholic and he told me that they go to each other's church sometimes."

"That's good," responded the Luthier. "That makes this next part a whole lot easier."

The Luthier turned and pulled a very small book off one of the shelves and handed it to Steven. "You'll need this." It was a small, military copy of the New Testament.

Steven looked at the book and raised his eyebrows.

"Think of it as your field manual, Steven. What else did Tom tell you?"

"Only that Mary goes to her church every Sunday and is really strict."

"Define 'really strict,' requested the Luthier.

Steven tried to remember all the things that Tom had said. "Mary has never smoked or done drugs, and she doesn't drink. Not even coffee or tea. When Tom talked about Mary's diet, it reminded me a lot of Hardcore's, only worse."

The Luthier's head went back and he rolled his eyes. "Oh, man!" he exclaimed.

"What?" asked Steven.

After a minute, the look on the Luthier's face began sinking in.

Steven feared what the Luthier was going to say next and he held up both of his hands in protest, "Wait just a minute!" He knew of Catholics that smoked and drank.

He looked up at the books on the shelf and asked, "What if Mary's Catholic, like Tom, and just goes to another church?"

"Then you'll also need these," replied the Luthier and he pulled down an old Catholic Bible, a prayer book and Catechism reader."

"Can I smoke and drink?"

"No," replied the Luthier.

Steven was confused and quickly became desperate. "What if I had said that she was Jewish?"

"Then I would have handed you this," the Luthier replied, after pulling down an old copy of the Tora.

"Could I have smoked and drank?" asked Steven.

"No."

He thought he understood where the Luthier was going, but he still kept trying, "What if she was Buddhist? Baptist? Hindu? Hopi Indian or Hare Krishna?"

With each religion Steven mentioned, the Luthier pulled a book or set of books off the shelf and showed them to Steven with the same reply.

"Your telling me that whatever religion Mary is, that's what I have to be?"

The Luthier nodded.

"And whatever morals and standards Mary has set, I have to live by them?"

The Luthier nodded again.

Steven's eyes went wide, "Why?!"

"Because you both wish to live *happily-ever-after*," replied the Luthier. "Haven't you been listening to anything that *Dr. Laura* has said?"

The Luthier stood up straight and announced, "From

this moment on, you will not smoke, you will not drink alcohol, tea or coffee, and you will not take drugs unless a medical doctor prescribes them to you."

Steven cringed and gritted his teeth. He was afraid of what was coming next.

"This is a direct order," the Luthier firmly declared.

"Oh, man!" Steven deliberately used the same phrase that the Luthier had earlier. "Tell me that I can have one last cigarette, right now. I just need one last cigarette before I start," he pleaded.

The Luthier shook his head.

"No, way!" moaned Steven.

"Yes, way," replied the Luthier.

Steven twisted and writhed at the thought of it. How could he do it?

"No way!" he repeated.

"Yes. Way," was the Luthier's response.

"OH, MAN!" was Steven's final cry as he dropped into a chair and wretched his head from side to side. Against the Luthier's suggestion, he was still silently thinking of much different words while he said it.

"Isn't it good that we already covered the swearing part before, so you weren't hit with everything all at once?"

Chapter 19: Smiley

*T*he wind had definitely been taken out of Steven's sails. The Luthier sat down beside him and let it all slowly and painfully sink in.

"I don't know if I can do it," Steven replied in a low, despondent tone. He put his head in his hands and shook it back and forth. Gloom seemed to possess him.

His tone was somber and pathetic, "I've smoked since I was fourteen."

He stared into space while continuing, "I'm not a drunk, but there are times when I don't think I could make it through the day without a drink, especially not lately."

"Why on earth no tea or coffee?" he questioned, not really expecting an answer. "I can give up the drugs. I never felt like I *had* to have them."

After his last comment, Steven realized just how much he had been using lately. Over the past three months, he had been experimenting with some very hard narcotics and stimulants.

Then he thought about the coffee again and asked, "No cup of coffee in the morning?" with a pleading tone in his voice.

The Luthier shook his head.

"Is true love really worth it?" Steven asked.

The Luthier nodded, "If it is true love."

"Do you really think that I have true love for Mary?" He was now starting to question it.

"I will only know the answer to that question when you succeed or fail," answered the Luthier.

The Luthier could see the doubt and desperation in

Steven's eyes. He stood up and paced back and forth in deep thought. He stopped after a minute and announced, "I am going to give you the option, just this once, Steven. I will release you from your word of honor right here and now, if you ask it."

Steven looked up to see the expression on the Luthier's face. It was pity.

"I am still willing to be your guide, but you must realize what lies ahead of you now."

The Luthier looked down at Steven. Steven had lowered his head again and was staring at the floor.

"Do you remember my words in the violin shop?"

"Pretty much," Steven answered without looking up. "You were pretty dramatic about it."

"The road I have chosen is longer, harder and bloodier than any battle field ever was. Many brave men's bodies lie dead and mangled on it. I will suffer more than I have ever suffered before, more than I ever thought possible."

The Luthier nodded, "The words are close enough. But now I must add others."

Instead of changing to the harsh military tones that he had used in the violin shop, the Luthier's voice now became sad, "I know you were a hardened soldier when you were younger. I know what kind of training a Marine goes through and what he must endure. I also know how calloused and numb men can become during war on the battlefield, and I believe that you have been about as deep as a man can go. But..."

The Luthier waited until Steven was looking him in the eyes before continuing, "I guarantee that even *you* will cry like a baby and beg to die before we are through. Your soul will become so torn and mangled that you can not possibly stand by yourself, no matter how hard you try. And in order for you to continue down this path, you must now give up your freedom."

Steven jerked and sat up straight in his chair. "What do you mean?"

"Until we are finished, you will not be free and you will have no rights. You will literally be my slave and have no life of your own. No honor, no dignity, nothing," replied the Luthier.

"You will also have to tell me absolutely everything about yourself and anything I ask of you, no matter how personal, irrelevant or embarrassing it is."

"Do you know what you're doing?" asked Steven. There was real concern in his voice.

"I *hope* so," replied the Luthier.

"Have you ever done this before?" He was genuinely worried now.

"No one has ever gone this far," replied the Luthier.

The Luthier sat down and it was a long time before either of them spoke.

Finally Steven looked at the Luthier and replied, "My answer is still the same. I don't care how bad it will get. If you believe there is any chance I will make it to the other side, I'm ready to go in. Not just for Mary, I want this for me, now.

"I've always wanted to know what I was made of and who I would have become if I had only been given the chance. It's time I found out, once and for all."

Steven stood up and declared, "I will ask no mercy and I will take no quarter, SIR!"

The Luthier turned away and shook his head back and forth. Instead of responding to Steven's declaration, he softly whispered the stanza, "Though I've belted you and flayed you by the living God that made you, you're a better man than I am, Gunga Din."

"What's that?" Steven asked.

"*Gunga Din*," replied the Luthier. "A poem written by an old military man, *Rudyard Kipling*. It's right over there."

The Luthier pointed to a red, leather-bound book sitting high on a shelf behind the oldest printing press. "We'll read it together sometime. But right now, we need to take care of a few things while your resolve is high."

Steven followed the Luthier out of the library with the New Testament still in his hand.

The Luthier led the way to where Steven's motorcycle

had been parked since the day after he arrived. The Luthier opened the garage door and pulled over a fifty-gallon barrel used for burning weeds. He tossed paper and small pieces of wood into the bottom and said, "Let's get started. Give me your keys."

Steven reached into his pocket, pulled out his keys and handed them to the Luthier.

"Have a seat," the Luthier offered, while pointing to a bench taken out of a van the Luthier once owned.

Steven sat down. He had a feeling about what was coming. The Luthier unlocked the chains, put the keys into his own pocket and started unpacking.

The first bag contained the old, rotten, jungle boots, the shirt with one sleeve and a few miscellaneous items of clothing. The Luthier laid them on a bench and carefully inspected each item before putting them back.

The Luthier held out his hand and said, "Dogtags, please."

Steven pulled off the three dogtags from around his wrist and tossed them over to the Luthier. The Luthier dropped them into the bag and set it aside. The next black leather container started out the same, with each item being withdrawn and inspected on the bench until the Luthier removed a carton of cigarettes and motioned toward the trash can. Steven looked at them and nodded.

The Luthier tossed the cigarettes into the barrel, then continued extracting more items.

The next thing thrown into the barrel was a switchblade. Steven almost shook his head and commented when the Luthier went to toss it in. Then he realized that it was illegal, relaxed back on the seat and nodded his approval.

Some clothes and other items were placed on the bench while others were tossed into the barrel.

Next came the saddle bags. The Luthier selected the items that would remain on the bench first, before pulling out the others. There were about twenty magazines, almost all of them with nude women in them.

The Luthier spoke while he threw them in, "Women are the finest of all God's creations, and they are to be treated with respect at all times and in all places. From now on, you will not buy or look at anything that displays women's bodies disrespectfully.

"Women can choose to be in those magazines, but you will do anything, even kill or be killed if necessary, before you will allow anyone to misuse a woman or her body against her will. This is a solemn vow that every true gentleman takes."

Steven nodded and replied, "Yes Sir," in a humble voice.

"Don't misunderstand, Steven. My father taught me that I should be willing to lay down my life, but he never meant for me to throw it away. If you are forced to fight, fight smart and always fight to win. It is honorable to die trying, but it does much more good for the people you are trying to help if you win. That's what my father would say."

Steven nodded his head again and smiled this time. He liked the Luthier's father even more now.

"You will protect women, *no matter what*, even if you have to compromise other objectives to do so."

The Luthier paused a moment before adding the name, "Hardcore."

"You know about Hardcore and the girl?"

"Don't forget, Steven, I have known Hardcore almost as long as you have."

The four remaining members of the platoon were *mashed* into another until *fresh meat* (new recruits) could be brought in to replace the *KIA's* (killed in action). The mood on the hill was a whole mixture of feelings, like it always was: sorrow for the fallen, celebration to be alive, comradeship for the survivors, and as usual, it ended up in a wild party until utter chaos took over and everybody crashed. Except Tiny, of course.

It was decided that Joe *Ruckus* Reber's field commission of Lieutenant would become official and he was assigned as the platoon's new commanding officer while the other survivors were all advanced a rank.

The replacements eventually arrived; eight *green*

Marines ready for action. They had their problems and needed broken in by the others, but they were all good men. All of them, that was, except Smiley. He had been given the name because he was anything but smiley.

Smiley was mean and ugly. Inside and out. He cared for no one and no one could stand to be around him for more than a few minutes. The other men found it impossible to say anything to Smiley without him biting off their head or knocking them to the ground; though he hadn't challenged Chip yet. He griped and complained constantly and vulgarly, even to the point of disgusting the other men who had lived in the jungle for months and did their own share of complaining and swearing.

When the other men asked why Smiley had enlisted, he told them that he had joined to become a war hero. So he could go back and crawl into bed with every woman he met.

Those kinds of comments were not uncommon in Vietnam, but when Smiley said it, it was in the foulest, most repulsive way possible, and when he said the word "women," the others could swear by the tone in his voice that he was talking about dead rats.

A few weeks after Smiley arrived, the *Four Vipers*, as they were now known in the jungle, sat around a tree eating lunch and talking.

"That's one sick dude," Ruckus commented.

No one even had to ask who he was talking about.

"He seems to take any honor there might have been in fighting this war and flushes it down the toilet," commented Slaughter, just before he spooned some more food out of his C-ration can.

"The man has no honor," Chip took his turn, "He's..."

"Ugly as a #*#@!" interrupted Tiny Tim.

Everyone turned in astonishment.

"His soul," clarified Tiny. "The man's soul is black as coal."

There was silence for a minute. No one had ever heard Tiny swear before.

"Seems pretty judgemental, Tiny. What about walking

in his boots first?" questioned Chip between mouthfuls.

"I will never walk in that man's boots," replied Tiny, "I might get some on me."

All four of them nodded in agreement to that.

Ruckus started looking around and asked, "Where is the *@*#! anyway?"

Chip stood up and looked around. He then questioned the other men scattered through the trees. Smiley was nowhere to be found.

"Private Smith is AWOL (absent without leave), Sir," Chip reported to Ruckus.

"The *vill'* isn't more than half a click away, *November-Whiskey* (northwest). Find him, Miller," ordered Ruckus.

"Yes, Sir," replied Chip less than enthusiastically. It wasn't the first time Smiley had stepped out of bounds trying to find a prostitute. Smiley was already walking on thin ice, and the ice didn't get very thick in Vietnam during the summertime.

Chip headed northwest a few hundred meters until he reached the clearing. It had been quiet the last few days and this was a friendly village, but he was as cautious as ever. He surveyed the clearing around the small grass-roofed hootches, then he carefully scanned the edge of the jungle with his field glasses.

He caught a glimpse of Smiley's helmet just before it disappeared into the foliage.

"Oh, #*@!" commented Chip as he put away the field glasses and headed across the clearing.

He stayed alert, constantly looking from side to side. No matter how friendly a village was, anything could still happen. After making it to the other side safely, he entered the jungle where he had seen Smiley just a few minutes earlier.

Chip had to get down on his knees and push aside the leaves to follow Smiley's trail. After twenty meters, he could hear some commotion ahead and he laid on his stomach and crawled toward it.

"Hold still!"

Chip recognized Smiley's rough voice and crawled to

the edge of the clearing for a look. Smiley was holding down a young Vietnamese girl and tearing off her clothes.

Smiley's rifle was behind him on the ground with the rest of his gear. Chip quickly surveyed the clearing and headed toward them.

He quietly walked over and put his foot on Smiley's M-16. Smiley turned when he heard the rifle crunch into his pack.

"What's happening, Chip?" asked Smiley in a friendly but reserved voice.

"Not this," he answered.

"What's your #*! problem, Chip? She's probably just a Gook that shoots at us at night anyway," replied Smiley, getting more defensive with every word.

"Let her go. That's an order, Private!" Chip demanded.

The girl fought and twisted. There was blood on her face. Chip couldn't tell if it was from her broken nose or from Smiley's hand where she had bit him.

It was impossible to understand what the girl was trying to say through Smiley's fingers but the look on her face told Chip everything he needed to know.

"Let her go!"

"Just turn around and go back to the platoon, Chip. I'll be there in a few minutes and I'll make it up to you," Smiley promised with a smile.

He stood debating whether to raise his rifle and aim it at Smiley, or to just wait and see if he would give in voluntarily.

Smiley looked Chip directly in the eyes as his right hand swung around with a pistol in it. Chip quickly raised his rifle, but he was not fast enough.

Before the pistol could aim directly at Chip, Smiley's head exploded.

Chip shouldered his M-16 just as he heard the report. Smiley's body dropped onto the girl and she pushed him to the ground while Chip looked around, trying to see where the shot had come from. The girl got up without a word and ran off, leaving the torn pieces of her clothing on the ground in front of Smiley's body.

Chip was standing in the middle of the clearing and knew he was in someone's rifle sights.

He wasn't sure if it was friend or foe, but he knew by the accuracy and timing of the last shot that he didn't have a chance. He lowered his M-16 and lifted up his right arm and saluted.

When nothing happened, Chip walked over and slowly picked up Smiley's M-16, his pistol, and one of his dogtags. He paused, one more time at the edge of the clearing, and saluted to whoever was there before disappearing into the jungle.

When the platoon got back to the hill, Chip was called into Ruckus' office. There was a Corporal standing beside the desk when he entered, and after saluting and being set at ease, they all sat down together.

"Corporal Hardy has a little story to tell you, Sergeant Miller," offered Lieutenant Reber.

Corporal Bill Hardy turned toward Chip, "I was at my post surveying when I saw Private Smith abduct the girl. I was debating firing a warning shot and reporting him later when you came along. I believed you to be safe at all times but I felt it my duty to report the incident to you and your commanding officer."

Chip grabbed Corporal Hardy's hand and shook it vigorously. "Thank you, Corporal Hardy." He didn't let go until long after he had finished speaking.

"Hardcore," Corporal Hardy replied with a jagged, toothy grin.

"Chip," Steven offered.

Lieutenant Reber broke in, "I'm going to file this report as killed in action by enemy sniper fire. Does that suit you two gentlemen?"

Hardcore replied, "I can live with that."

Ruckus and Hardcore both turned toward Chip. He slowly nodded in agreement.

After Ruckus finished filling out the report, he looked up and asked, "I've heard a lot about you, Hardcore. Off the record, the warning shot you talked about: where exactly were your cross hairs aimed when Corporal Miller entered that clearing?"

"One-half-inch behind and above private Smith's left ear, Sir."

"That's about where I figured," commented Lieutenant Joe *Ruckus* Reber. "Dismissed."

The Luthier told Steven, "If you were not aware, Hardcore was involved in two other incidents like that. One of the men he killed was a Lieutenant and it ended up in a court-martial.

"With his life on the line, his only defense was this statement;

"'I am an American and a Patriot, which left me with only two options: I either had to shoot the Lieutenant or I had to shoot myself. I could not live and continue calling myself an American, and do nothing.'"

Chapter 20: Chains

The Luthier reached into the bottom of the saddle bag, pulled out a bag of paraphernalia and tossed it into the barrel. Steven was embarrassed. It was a serious amount of drugs.

There were two cans of beer and six bottles of hard liquor.

The Luthier poured the beer down the sink. "We'll throw these others in when the fire is going. It should be quite a show, since half of these are well over one-hundred-proof."

Steven was still taking it fairly well.

"I know your resolve is high, Steven. But do not underestimate the effect all of this has upon you," warned the Luthier.

Steven stared at the bottles sitting on the bench. It was starting to sink in. He needed a drink.

The only other item of importance was a stack of hundred dollar bills a little larger than the one Steven had crumpled up and handed to the Luthier. The Luthier pulled off a large chunk of it and put it into a thick, brown envelope. The remainder of the stack looked small and Steven cringed.

The Luthier put it back in the saddle bag and told him, "The first Sunday you get back, you will give that envelope to Mary's church."

Steven nodded.

"This next question is very important, Steven."

Steven thought he knew what the Luthier was leading up to, "Yes, Sir?"

"Is there anything else?" asked the Luthier.

Steven stared at the Luthier.

"My father would say, 'Don't make me repeat myself or I will kick you across the floor and into that wall over there.'" The Luthier's voice was soft and gentle while he pointed to the back of the garage. "Only my father wouldn't say it that nicely," clarified the Luthier.

Steven stood up and walked into the bunk house. He came back a minute later holding a bottle, a pack of cigarettes, and a small baggie. He threw them into the barrel. Next, he walked to the edge of the lawn and pulled a bottle out from behind a tree and brought it back. He opened it and dumped it in.

"I believe this is everything," Steven told the Luthier. Before he had finished talking, he turned toward the driveway.

The Luthier's family drove up and parked in one of the other stalls of the garage. They got out and wandered over to where Steven and the Luthier were standing.

"What's in the barrel?" asked Tessa, right before she looked in. Her eyes widened when she saw some of the items.

"My past," replied Steven, a little ashamed. Then he stood back while Colter and Sheryl each took a peek inside.

The Luthier turned toward Steven, "I will be spending almost all my time with you while you are here. I ask your permission that I may use your life to teach my children what I can."

Steven felt like he couldn't refuse. "Sure," he answered.

"Thank you." Then the Luthier picked up one of the other bottles and poured it in.

"You will have the honor, Steven."

All of them took a step back while Steven lit a piece of paper and tossed it in. The alcohol in the barrel burst into flames. It was a solemn moment and none of them spoke. Even when Steven threw in another bottle and watched it ignite, they all remained silent. The ceremony took about a half hour and all that was left were ashes, a little glass and the metal from his switchblade.

"Lunch will be ready in twenty minutes," Sheryl announced while she and the children headed into the house.

As soon as the side door closed behind them, the Luthier asked Steven, "How are you feeling now?"

"Like I've been kicked in the gut," he responded.

"It'll get worse," replied the Luthier. Then, in a weird, high-pitched voice, the Luthier asked, "Do you want me to make that pain go away?"

Steven just stared at him.

"Didn't you ever see the movie *Major Payne*?"

Steven shook his head.

"You need to get out more," joked the Luthier. "My kids loved it. With your military background, you and your children will also. Maybe we'll catch part of it before lunch. You look like you need to take your mind off things for a while."

After lunch and watching part of the movie, Steven and the Luthier went back to the library. The Luthier pulled out a notebook and began writing while he asked Steven everything about his life.

Steven had forgotten so many things. He had a hard time answering some questions until the Luthier asked in such a way that it brought the memories back to him. The Luthier also asked about Mary. From the name of the street and number of stairs leading into the restaurant to what kind and color of shoes and socks she wore.

The questions and answers went on and on. The Luthier asked about everyone and everything in Steven's life. His past relationships, his feelings and all of his likes and dislikes. They talked right through dinner and continued late into the night.

Every time Steven thought they were finished, the Luthier would start into other topics and ask him a whole new set of questions: about his work, his tools, what he learned, everything from the simple and obvious, to things that no one else would even know to ask about.

Before Steven realized it, the sun was shining through

the slots in the library window's shutters and he was dozing off.

After the Luthier laid the third full notebook down, they went into the kitchen to eat breakfast with the Luthier's family.

When Steven picked up his fork, he noticed that his hand was shaking and found it difficult to hold the fork still. He looked at the Luthier and asked, "What was the real reason for the last few hours of questions?"

"Killing time and distracting you," was the Luthier's reply.

Steven looked back down at his hands. They were both shaking now. No matter what he did, he could not stop them.

"When you told me that you never felt like you *had* to have the drugs and I saw the amount in your saddle bags, I knew it would be hard. With your other addictions to caffeine, alcohol and tobacco, your life will be a nightmare soon.

"I will continue to distract you all that I can and put you into the best conditions I know, but I can only help for a little while longer.

"I am not a professional at this. No professional would ever do what I am going to. Also realize that I could possibly be arrested, but I still believe my father's way is the best. He called it, 'Kill or cure.'

"It's also the quickest way, so eat up. As soon as breakfast is over, we have some blacksmithing to do."

Steven stared at the Luthier in disbelief and it took him a minute to recover. He had always wanted to learn how to blacksmith, but he worried about what the Luthier had in mind by the tone of his voice and his "kill or cure" statement.

Steven continued trying to eat and found it necessary to hold his fork with both hands. Colter and Tessa looked at Steven without saying a word.

When Steven finally laid his fork down and took a moment to relax, he asked, "What will we be making?"

"Shackles," replied the Luthier.

Everyone at the table turned and stared at the Luthier. Then, a moment later, they went back to their eating.

It surprised Steven, that with no explanation, the Luthier's family left the table and were on their way without any questions about the shackles.

If Steven hadn't imagined it, Tessa had quickly glanced at his shaking hands and nodded her approval before leaving the table. It was as if she knew what was going to happen and agreed about the idea of shackles.

After breakfast, Steven traded the army fatigues for a thick hospital gown and slippers. Then they walked up to the violin shop. Steven felt like he hadn't slept in weeks as they made their way up the hill.

The Luthier explained the fundamentals of blacksmithing while he built the fire in the forge behind the violin shop. Steven looked and listened, though he found his attention span wasn't very good. He ached for a cigarette. He even found himself leaning over the fire and breathing in the hot air and smoke.

After watching the Luthier form the rings and eyelets with the tongs and hammer, Steven asked, "Why not just handcuffs or something?"

There was determination in the Luthier's voice, "Rivets cannot be picked and the edges of handcuffs would cut into your limbs. You will also need the image of these shackles in your mind for the rest of your life. Without that, you would probably fail."

"Is it really going to be that bad?" asked Steven.

"Worse," replied the Luthier while he continued hammering on the red-hot pieces of steel.

The shackles were still warm when the Luthier sized and fitted them around Steven's wrists, ankles and neck. After they were just the right size, the Luthier used a grinder and buffer to smooth and polish their inner surfaces. When he was finished, the outside of each shackle was still roughly-forged while their inner surfaces and edges looked like mirrors.

"So no matter how hard you pull or fight, you cannot cut your wrists or ankles," the Luthier explained.

The Luthier took the rings and attached short pieces of chain to them with large, hand-forged rivets.

As Steven knelt down and the Luthier riveted the wide steel band around his neck, he asked, "Why around my neck?"

"So you cannot beat your head against the floor and break your skull, and so you cannot hang yourself from one of your arm chains if I decide to put you on the wall," calmly replied the Luthier.

With this statement, Steven's whole body stopped shaking as fear took over.

"You aren't kidding, are you?"

The Luthier did not reply while he finished riveting the shackles to Steven's wrists and ankles.

It was late afternoon when they finally walked back down the road toward the house. The chains around Steven's wrists and neck rattled, while the ones around his ankles drug on the pavement. It was an ominous sound in the otherwise silent valley.

Steven imagined himself in the Roman days; that he was being taken to the colosseum to be tortured, then eaten alive by wild beasts.

Based on what the Luthier had told him, he wondered if this road led to a worse fate than the condemned Jewish slaves two thousand years ago.

Chapter 21: Shackles

"What am I going to do?" Mary asked. Then she laid her backpack on the sidewalk and sat down next to Tom. It had been a week since she met Steven in the restaurant.

Tom continued holding his cup out until after he heard the clink of two small coins. Then he said "Bless you, Irene," with a smile, and he turned toward Mary.

"Seems to me yous gonna hafta wait 'n' sees, Mary."

"I've waited my whole life, Tom. If this really is my one and only chance for true love, I'm simply going to have to make a decision, once and for all."

Tom had not mentioned Steven's two visits to Mary. He had never seen anyone like Steven change their life around. He had seen a few try over the years. He had even seen some succeed for a while, but they always reverted back to their same old selves, leaving some poor woman destitute and alone to raise the children.

Tom didn't want Mary to give up her dream of meeting someone special, waiting for Steven to change his life. "I thought yous was askin' for Tom's advice?" He acted a little hurt.

"I'm sorry, Tom. I just don't know if I can hold on to hope now that I've seen the man of my dreams."

Mary leaned over and laid her head against Tom's shoulder while tears wandered their way down her soft, white cheeks. She knew that she wouldn't have had the courage to go on many times if it hadn't been for Tom.

Mary told Tom in a soft, sad tone, "A friend of Cindy's found out last night that his name is Steve Miller and he does ride in a motorcycle gang. She was also told that he was their leader."

"Don' gives up hope, Mary. That's what some spunky little girl told me many years ago when my wife, Louise, passed on. If yous don'ts believe in this Steve Miller fellow, then holds out some hope for someone else. But don' gives up."

Mary cried a little more. Tom reached into his pocket and wiped the tears from Mary's face with his handkerchief, "I'd swear you was still ten yearn old by the way yous carin' on, girl."

After a few more minutes went by, Tom held his cup back out and decided to change his tactics, "Maybe he's jus' foolin' with yous, Mary."

Mary turned and asked, "What do you mean, Tom?"

"Yous dresses up and plays like yous someone else all the time down at the Univers'ty. Maybe he was jus' playin'," offered Tom as a consolation.

"He wasn't acting, Tom. No one acts that well." A cold chill ran down Mary's spine as she remembered the expression on Steven's face while he looked at her in the restaurant.

"Jes the same, Mary. Tom's advice is that you don't gives up on love, chil', ever. An' if yous believes in this 'love at first sights' business, don't gives up on him; at least until yous sees him one more time. Now promis ol' Tom."

"I promise," Mary replied. Then she started getting up.

"That's my girl,"

Tom listened while Mary's footsteps faded away in the distance.

After a quick lunch, the Luthier went to work in the back of the bunkhouse with his construction tools. Steven sat on one of the beds and his body began shaking uncontrollably while he watched.

Within two hours, the Luthier had all of the large, steel anchors embedded in the concrete floor and a gymnastic tumbling mat spread out and glued over the top of them. The Luthier had cut holes through the pads so the chains could pass through from the floor to Steven's shackles.

Steven's body not only shook, it felt worse every minute he watched the Luthier make the preparations. He knew something bad was going to happen and he started feeling paranoid. A chill ran through his body and shook him so violently that he could no longer get warm, even with the blankets pulled around him.

The Luthier stopped working and walked over to the thermostat. He turned it to over ninety degrees and announced, "It is time. No matter what, remember that I am your friend."

Steven lay down on the mat and stared at the ceiling while the Luthier put the bolts through the chains and tightened them into the anchors in the floor.

"I must now take care of some things. Sheryl will watch you while I am gone. If all goes well, I will be back before you awaken."

The Luthier laid a blanket over Steven and headed toward the door.

"How long will I be like this?" Steven's voice was sad and he was losing control of his emotions while looking up and waiting for an answer.

"However long it takes," replied the Luthier, "When I was young, my father told me that it took his friend a week."

Steven thought he saw something move under one of the bunks and he quickly turned.

"Are there rats in here?" Steven asked as terror spread across his face and he pulled at the chains.

"No, there are no rats," replied the Luthier in a calm, reassuring voice.

"Remember this, Steven: No matter what you think you see or feel, Sheryl or myself will be sitting right here the whole time. We will not allow anything to harm you. Everything else will come from inside your mind, no matter how real it feels."

The Luthier gave Steven a smile, then he turned and walked out.

Sheryl came in a minute later and placed a small pillow

under Steven's head. He thanked her, and the moment he relaxed and laid his head down, he felt like the whole room was spinning. Then everything went black.

It was a strange, peaceful rest at first. He knew he had fallen asleep and was dreaming, but he felt like he was still wide awake. He could even open his eyes and look around the bunkhouse without the feeling ever changing.

Good things appeared in the bunkhouse around him, one after the other. Instead of Sheryl, his mother now sat on the chair and smiled at him. He sat up and began painting a picture, just like he had when he was a child. Then his friends from Vietnam walked in, sat down and talked with him.

When he finished the painting, his friends unbolted his ankles from the floor and he stood up. After he walked out of the bunkhouse, he could tell that he was still in the valley but it was different now. He turned to go back in, but the building was gone and everything had changed around him.

Steven got worried and started searching for some familiar landmark. He walked aimlessly until he finally found his mother again. She gave him a big smile and held out her arms.

Steven found that all of his emotions and feelings were ten times more vivid than ever before. Tears of happiness filled his eyes while he ran toward her with his arms outstretched.

Just before they embraced, his mother's head exploded from a large caliber rifle shot. He screamed and watched her body fall to the ground.

He looked around until he saw his father sitting on the edge of the mountain, smiling, with a rifle in his hands. Steven screamed at him with every obscenity he knew. He looked back down at his mother as rats came up and started eating her. Then worms devoured what was left of her flesh until it was gone. Her skeleton lay half buried in the soil by the time Steven knelt beside her and began sobbing.

After his mother was gone, he got up and ran toward

the mountain. As he ran, each of his friends appeared in front of him; happy, peaceful, and glad to see him. When he approached them, they were blown apart or suffered some other hideous death, each more gruesome than the last, until it took hours for them to die. Then, when they were dead, hideous monsters pulled their bodies under the ground with their fiery eyes staring and their fangs gnashing at Steven.

The sky turned black and lightning flashed. The valley, or wherever he was now, turned into a barren wasteland. Everywhere lightning struck, blood oozed out and flowed around him.

Steven was experiencing every nightmare that he had ever had. They were all put together, here in this world, only now they were real and he could feel everything. Now he could finish every gruesome ending; even death, without waking up.

The dream raged on until the monsters from the ground and winged demons in the sky came after him. Some of the flying demons carried the things he had burned in the barrel. They offered them back to him for relief, while the monsters from the ground started throwing spears into his body when he started to run away.

He stumbled over the chains that still hung from his ankles until he tripped and fell. When he opened his eyes, he lay just a few feet from the edge of a cliff. He tried to get back up but the demons were chewing at his shoulders and arms while the monsters pulled at his legs from under the ground.

Steven looked back and saw the Luthier aiming his pistol right between his eyes. He struggled to his feet just as the gun went off.

Steven fell backward, off the cliff. He was conscious and he could still feel everything, even though his head was half gone.

He clawed at the air and was trying to reach out and grab anything to hold onto, but found nothing.

When he hit the rocky floor of the abyss, Steven's eyes finally flew open. It was only then that he realized he was still chained to the bunkhouse floor, shaking in convulsions. The chains rattled and tightened as he went through fits of screaming and whimpering, fighting to get free. His whole body was drenched in sweat, but he was still freezing cold.

Once he realized where he was, he tried to relax and control himself. The fits slowly subsided and he settled down enough to finally look around the bunkhouse. The first thing he saw was the Luthier, sitting on the chair by his side, holding a glass of water.

The Luthier wiped the tears and drool from Steven's face and gave him some reassuring words.

After he had taken a mouthful of the tepid water, Steven asked, "How long have I been asleep?"

"An hour," was the Luthier's reply.

"It seemed like days," replied Steven, "and it was so real. Each and every minute of it. I don't even feel like I have woken up from a dream at all."

Steven shook his head back and forth with his eyes wide and staring. "Is it over?"

The Luthier's face saddened, "It has only begun." Then the Luthier knelt down and started unbolting the chains that held Steven to the floor.

"Then why are you unchaining me?" asked Steven, just now starting to realize what the chains were for and what might be in store for him.

"The more you can move around, the better you will feel, and as long as the option is open we will use it," was the Luthier's reply.

"I understand the shackles now," Steven sadly commented. While looking at the chains hanging from his wrists he added, "Thank you."

The Luthier had to smile at Steven's attitude. "The look on your face reminds me of Ulysses returning home from the Trojan War as his men took the wax out of their ears and unbound him from the mast of his ship."

Steven shook his head. He had no idea what the Luthier was talking about.

"Ulysses, the strongest man alive, had heard his whole

life about the beautiful, enchanting songs of the sirens. These elegant creatures with the most beautiful women's faces lived on a group of islands surrounded by treacherous, jagged rocks. The sirens would sing their enchanting songs when ships would sail by and lure the sailors to their deaths.

"Ulysses knew that no man had ever resisted the siren's songs and that many captains had died on the rocks with their men. So he had his men securely bind him to the mast while they all put wax in their own ears.

"When the song of the sirens came floating out from the islands, it was beautiful beyond his wildest dreams and he ordered his men to untie him and sail toward the music. But, because of the wax in their ears, his men could not hear his cries and they continued sailing past the islands until they were out of danger and Ulysses could no longer hear the siren's voices."

The Luthier paused after dropping the last chain that held Steven.

"By knowing his own weakness, he could enjoy the songs said to be more beautiful than life, without losing his life."

While Steven stood, the Luthier added, "What you are doing goes far beyond what Ulysses did. It is a *truly* great man that will allow himself to be chained and tortured in order to become a better person."

Chapter 22: Free

*D*uring dinner, the Luthier's family carried on various conversations. Each one, no matter where it started, ended up with something to do with dreams, chains, or prisons. The Luthier's children tried not to be too conspicuous, but they glanced at the shackles and chains dangling from Steven's wrists while he ate.

Colter finally commented, "My dad gives speeches at the prisons."

The rest of the family turned and shook their heads.

"Well, he does," Colter added.

The Luthier interrupted the silence, "I have a hard time turning them down."

"Does it pay well?" asked Steven.

"No money," answered the Luthier. "It is a debt that I pay.

"I find that I am no better than many of the men I see in the prisons. It is not because I am a better person that I am sitting here tonight with a wonderful family in a nice home while they remain alone behind bars.

"I do not know why, nor do I understand his reasoning, but God has not stepped in and sent them an angel to save them, like he did for me." The Luthier looked over at Sheryl and she smiled back.

Steven could tell that the Luthier's story was true. He also wondered what would have happened if the Luthier had not run out of gas, or if Sheryl had not shown up on the doorstep of the trailer house when she did.

Steven thought of his own life and what it felt like when he looked into Mary's eyes. He started to wonder just how different the Luthier really was, and what they would each be like if raised in the same circumstances. Steven felt a kinship knitting between them that had not been there before; as though the Luthier could be his brother.

The feeling was interrupted when Steven realized that his chains were rattling against the table. A cold feeling of paranoia seized him and started taking over while he looked around the room. He felt like something was going to crawl out of the walls at any instant.

"Let's get you a warm shower before you go back down," offered the Luthier when he noticed the expression on Steven's face. Then the Luthier excused himself and Steven from the table.

After the shower, the Luthier had Steven put teeth guards on with dental adhesive to prevent him from biting his tongue off. Then he bolted Steven back down to the floor and sat by his side.

When Steven's body started shaking out of control, he asked the Luthier, "Will you read me something about Jesus?"

The Luthier responded by picking up the small, military version of the New Testament and replying, "I was hoping you would ask me that."

Steven listened to his favorite stories of Jesus, but found it hard to pay attention as he gradually lost control of his body. It wasn't long before his mind drifted away and the world of nightmares took over completely. This time he did not wake up when he hit the bottom of the abyss, and the dreams continued with the pain and suffering even more acute and terrifying.

The Luthier was by his side, yet Steven was alone in his misery. Through the night and into the next day, Steven got worse and tore more viciously at his shackles. The Luthier tried everything he could think of, but after a while, nothing had any effect at all. Steven could not hear or register with the outside world any longer and the Luthier simply gave him reassuring words and played soft music on his violin just in case he could hear.

The sun came up and the sun went down again, but it

didn't matter to Steven. He still lay on the floor fighting and screaming, living hundreds of lifetimes of pain and suffering. His friends turned into enemies and the nightmares and torture raged on while he went deeper and deeper into the bowels of the dark, hideous world. It didn't matter whether his eyes were open or closed; he could not wake up and there was no way out.

In normal life the body can shut itself down by going into shock, or if hurt severely enough, the mind can shut off the pain and numb itself so the person can endure it without going insane. But in Steven's world there were no limitations. His wrists and ankles were raw, bruised, and bleeding by the end of the second day in spite of the smooth inner surfaces of the shackles.

During brief moments of consciousness, Steven learned through trial and error, that no matter how hard he tried, he could not fracture his skull against the pad and kill himself. But he also found that if he pulled long enough against the band around his neck he could enjoy one or two seconds of numbness before passing out. Even though his neck was raw and swollen and his head felt like it would explode, it was worth it to him and he did it over and over until his strength gave out.

When he could no longer lift his head, he was left without any possible way of relieving the pain, even for a moment. He then fell asleep and went back deeper than ever, into the world of torment and suffering again.

In the afternoon of the third day, Steven regained consciousness. He woke up, viciously straining at his chains and screaming at the top of his voice. There were pools of tears covering his eyes and streaks running down his face. The robe was twisted in knots and he was drenched in sweat. He was barely recognizable as human.

It took a moment for Steven to realize where he was. His body shook in violent convulsions, but finally he choked and gurgled out the words, "Kill me."

They were the first discernible words Steven had spoken in two days and it woke the Luthier up. The Luthier was still sitting on the chair.

"Kill me," Steven begged again. He shook the chains that hung from his arms and legs and strained against the shackle around his neck.

The Luthier looked down in pity but didn't move.

"I can't take it any more," Steven begged. "Hell cannot be worse than my nightmares."

Steven shook furiously and his eyes stared off into space, "I can still see them right now! And the instant I close my eyes, they will sink their claws into me and start tearing me apart again. I can't survive it another time anyway. Kill me now while I am awake."

Steven begged the Luthier again, "Please, kill me."

The Luthier still remained motionless.

"Kill me!" he screamed in torment, now shaking his chains at the Luthier.

The Luthier knelt down and unfastened the bolts that held Steven's neck and arms. Steven contorted and twisted his body into convulsions as he sat up and desperately tried to figure out a way to kill himself with the chains. When Steven finally looked back up, the Luthier was standing with a gun in his hand.

"Do it!" Steven screamed.

When the Luthier hesitated, Steven screamed louder, "Do it, or give it to me, so I can!"

The Luthier walked over and laid the gun in front of a television and video recorder placed on a small table on the other side of the bunkhouse.

"Don't put it over there, give it to me!" demanded Steven while struggling to his feet.

"Not until you watch this," replied the Luthier. He then turned on the television and pressed play.

Steven was just coherent enough to scream at the Luthier, "Turn that #*#@! off and give me that gun, you *#&~*! You can have my #&*! soul!"

Steven strained at the chains, trying to reach the Luthier and the gun. He struggled and fought until he fell to the floor on his knees. He ignored the pain while he jerked and tore at the shackles around his ankles. He strained with every ounce of energy he had left, even though he knew he would tear off his feet before he could break the chains.

He stretched as far as he possibly could, and while he reached out for the gun with his fingers only inches away, he heard Mary's voice come from the television. He looked up and he saw her smooth, delicate face, her sparkling eyes and her scarlet lips on the screen.

"The man of my dreams has almost faded now," Mary whispered.

Another voice came from the television but Steven could not see who it was, "And what man is that, Miss?"

Mary continued with a far away look, her voice was sweet and solemn, "The one I have created in my mind.

"The sort of man each woman dreams of in the most secret reaches of her heart.

"I can almost see him now before me."

Mary then looked directly at Steven. Tears filled her eyes as she continued,

"What would I say to him, if he were really here?
"Forgive me?
"I've never known this feeling.
"I've lived without it all my life.
"Is it any wonder then, I failed to recognize you when you were brought to me for the first time?
"Is there any way that I can tell you how my life has changed?
"Any way at all to let you know what sweetness you have given me?
"There is so much to say, I cannot find the words...
"...except for these...
"...I love you."

Mary choked back the tears, then continued with a smile, "That's what I would say to him...if he were really here."

The television screen went blank and the Luthier turned it off. Steven looked at the Luthier. There were no words that could express how he felt. There was nothing he could say.

His body still shook in torment and pain and he knew where he would be the moment he closed his eyes, but he slowly laid back down on the floor and smiled. Tears were flowing from his face and he screamed when his body went into convulsions again, but he tried to hold the chains directly over the anchors so the Luthier could put the bolts back in.

Steven's arm shook so violently that the Luthier had to kneel on it to pass the bolt through the chain.

When the Luthier picked up the wrench, Steven struggled out the words through his clenched teeth, "Tighten the chains as tight as they will go."

Tears now flowed from the Luthier's eyes while he pulled the chains taut and bolted them only two links away from Steven's wrists.

When the Luthier was finished, Steven closed his eyes and continued in the same violent shaking fits and convulsions as before. He reentered the same hideous world of excruciating pain and torment again. But now he had hope.

"Order's up, Mary," Charlie announced from behind the counter.

Mary picked up the plates and took them over to the table where Steven had sat almost three weeks before. The restaurant was packed and there were a dozen families in the restaurant.

She carefully lowered the plates in front of the mother, father, and two small children, all dressed up for the evening. She couldn't help but envy them with their happy faces and light conversation.

Mary tried to smile and said very little while she served them. She was starting to question if the man wearing the motorcycle leathers would ever come back. All she had to hold onto was the feeling that she had when she looked into his eyes, and that was all mixed up with the emotions she felt when she thought about the rest of him.

She didn't know anything about him, except his name, that he rode in a motorcycle gang and he looked drunk. She didn't dare go to the bars where men like him hung out and ask about him. Mary had never been into a bar in her life and she feared those kind of men more than anything else in the world.

Mary was still trying to keep up some kind of hope, though. If not for this man, at least hope for some kind of love with someone.

She knew she was getting old enough to worry about how many children she could have, and the families sitting together in the restaurant lulled Mary into the same melancholy mood it had each night for the past three weeks.

After the restaurant closed, Cindy and Mary sat and talked.

"You need to start looking again, Mary. You're starting to depress me." They were sitting in the booth where she met Steven.

"I can't help it Cindy. I feel like this is my one and only chance for true love."

"Well, your 'one and only chance' left on a *Harley Davidson* and he hasn't been back to throw you across his lap or drag you away by your hair in over three weeks, Honey. I told you that you might have to compromise your *Prince Charming* image a little, but don't you think this is ridiculous?"

"I guess that's why I'm so depressed, Cindy. Maybe it's not him. Maybe there isn't really *love at first sight* and *happily-ever-after*. Maybe I finally realize that I'm going to have to compromise parts of my dream if I'm ever going to have a real husband and a real family."

"That's the way I see it," agreed Cindy. "But believe me, you can do a lot better than that guy, Mary."

The next Sunday evening, Steven lay on the bunkhouse floor exhausted. For the first time in a week his body lay perfectly calm. The feeling was much like the time he had a large party with too many people at his apartment.

There was a lot of noise and confusion and it ended in a brawl. Then everyone left, leaving his room silent and calm. Only this silence seemed a thousand times more profound.

The Luthier unbolted the chains and helped Steven to his feet. Steven had to steady himself against the Luthier because he was so weak. He shook his limbs and loosened up, trying to get all the circulation flowing again. Before he could stand up straight, he turned and gave the Luthier a hug.

Feelings of holding a brother, or a father who cared, overwhelmed Steven.

Steven took a hot shower and changed into a clean set of the hospital-style clothes one last time. When he came out, he took a good look at the floor where he had lain for a week. Then he looked over to where the television and video recorder had been.

"Was it just a dream, or did I really see Mary on a television over there?"

"It was real," answered the Luthier.

"How did you do it?"

"I...just...did," replied the Luthier. "It was what you needed."

"At least tell me if it was really Mary," begged Steven.

"I do not deal in copies or forgeries," replied the Luthier.

Steven still had to know more. "Does Mary know about all this?"

"As far as I know, Mary still knows nothing of you or what you are doing, other than your first meeting," replied the Luthier.

"Thank you." Then Steven reached over and gave the Luthier one more hug.

Chapter 23: *For You*

Steven stood in front of the large, full-length mirror in the violin shop.

"Remember this image in your mind, Steven. Remember it until your dying day."

Steven let the image of the chains and shackles burn into his mind then he followed the Luthier behind the violin shop to a large anvil.

The Luthier picked up a hammer and a cold chisel. While Steven placed each of his extremities across the chopping block, the Luthier skillfully split the rivets, allowing each shackle to open. As they fell to the ground, Steven felt freer than he had ever felt in his life.

When the Luthier was done, he picked up the shackles and offered them to Steven, "You will want to keep these."

"What for?" asked Steven, not understanding why.

"Hang them on your wall. Leave them there until your dying day if necessary. When you feel the need for drugs or a cigarette, a drink of alcohol or even a cup of coffee, look at them. It will make your decision a whole lot easier."

Steven took them and replied, "Thank you, Luthier."

That night, Steven slept peaceful and calm.

The next morning, even though he was still weak, Steven felt like a new man. The work on his violin started again as soon as he arrived at the violin shop.

While the Luthier carved the fluting on the scroll, he commented, "I believe she is worth it."

"Mary?" asked Steven.

"Yes," replied the Luthier. "From what I can see, she

very well could be the woman of your dreams."

Steven nodded. He still felt the same way.

"And now that you are free, it is time for you to become the man of her dreams," said the Luthier.

From that moment, and for the next two weeks, the Luthier started through a regimented course of study with Steven. He started with how to treat a woman: from being polite, opening doors, taking her flowers, listening to her desires, and sharing feelings, to learning when he should be firm and stand his ground in a caring, diplomatic way.

The Luthier also taught him manners and culture: how to walk and how to talk in a way that would enable him to fit into social circles under any circumstances. Sheryl and Tessa even taught him how to dance.

One afternoon, after a particularly long and grueling day of lessons and studies, the Luthier laid down his tools, sat back and announced, "It is now time you learned how to sing."

Steven thought of how badly he sounded the first time he tried singing when he was a boy. Other than crude, military cadences, he hadn't sung a note since.

"Don't you think there are just some things I can't do?"

"No," replied the Luthier, "I don't. My father taught me how to sing and now I am going to teach you."

Steven was used to this kind of treatment from the Luthier. He nodded his head and waited for instructions, but it was with a less-than-enthusiastic expression.

"Did you ever see the movie *The Sound of Music*?" asked the Luthier.

"No, I missed that one," Steven replied sarcastically. "It must have come out between the time I beat up my father for the first time and when I enlisted in the Marines."

"He still has a sense of humor!" replied the Luthier with a laugh. "There is hope!" Then the Luthier continued a little sarcastically himself, "Do you know your ABC's?"

"Better than you, I bet," replied Steven, still with a little chip on his shoulder. "Alpha, Bravo, Charlie, Delta, Echo, Foxtrot, Golf, Hotel, India, Juliet, Kilo, Lima, Mike, November, Oscar, Papa, Quebec, Romeo, Sierra, Tango,

Uniform, Victor, Whiskey, X-ray, Yankee, Zulu." Steven rattled the military call names off as quickly as any schoolboy would his normal ABC's.

"Impressive," smiled the Luthier, "but let's keep it simple."

Later that evening, Steven and the Luthier were singing *Amazing Grace* while dangling their feet off the edge of the tallest cliff overlooking the valley. Then, after they finished singing, they silently watched the sunset.

Whatever it took to help Steven learn, the Luthier did it. He used many different approaches and techniques for the many different topics and skills they covered. Steven was trying as hard as he could, and even though he made mistakes, he was slowly learning how to be what he thought was the man of Mary's dreams.

They retired Steven's military fatigues after going into town and buying him a new wardrobe. The Luthier even showed Steven the different ways people reacted and treated him when they walked around town in different types of clothing.

Steven had always known that people acted differently depending upon how others dressed, but it amazed him when he experienced it firsthand under different circumstances. People who would have normally snubbed him, now smiled and greeted him. Everyone acted differently than he expected and it was a nice feeling.

Even at the violin shop, Steven dressed in nice, clean, casual clothing because he could tell that it changed his attitude about many things. Steven could feel himself changing daily and he began reading the New Testament before he went to bed each night.

When the Luthier placed the finished scroll of the violin next to the back and ribs, his whole countenance changed. He moved slowly and seemed unusually quiet as he picked up the large, dark piece of wood that would soon become the violin's belly.

"No one knows how old this piece of wood really is," he said while holding it up and looking it over. "Some records

say that the timbers were stored in the basement of
Solomon's temple since the day it was built. Those records
say these timbers were the only perishable things that
survived the fire because they were kept below ground
level.

"Other records allude that *these* cedars of Lebanon were
hauled into the basement centuries later, after the temple
was rebuilt when there was an uprising of religious
fanatics. Regardless, the original forests of Lebanon were
stripped to bare earth many centuries before the temple
was destroyed in 70 AD."

"Where did you get it?" asked Steven, more curious than
ever about the piece of wood.

The Luthier turned it over and smiled, "Someone needed
a very special violin and the music it alone could give,
even more than they needed this piece of wood."

"You traded a violin for this piece of wood?" asked Steven
in disbelief.

The Luthier nodded.

"How much money will you make off my violin?"

"No money," answered the Luthier.

Steven was speechless while he looked from the piece
of wood in the Luthier's hands to the rest of his violin
sitting on the bench.

"Then why are you making it for me?" asked Steven in
amazement.

"Because it is what you need. It is a debt that I pay,"
replied the Luthier.

Steven thought about the Luthier's story and about the
men in prison he spoke of.

"And when will this debt be paid?" asked Steven.

The Luthier did not answer. He just turned around,
clamped the piece of wood into a large vise mounted on
the side of one of his workbenches and picked up a jack-
plane. He adjusted the glistening, razor-sharp, steel blade
and leaned over the wood for the first pass.

Steven watched the plane slide across its surface and
peel the dark, two-thousand-year-old crust off, revealing
the light, creamy-smooth wood inside.

They spoke very little for the next three days while the Luthier jointed, glued, carved and smoothed the belly. Steven just watched in amazement, realizing that this was the most valuable piece of wood the Luthier had ever used.

After the Luthier finished drilling and sawing two rough holes on either side of the violin's belly, he picked up his knife and began carving the f-holes to their final shape.

What Steven thought would take hours was finished in a few minutes.

"Don't you ever worry about ruining it or making a mistake?" he asked.

"No," replied the Luthier. "I cannot. The minute I worry about ruining it, is the minute I am no longer free." While the Luthier was still speaking, he cut the small notches that finished off the two f-holes. He then held up the completed belly so Steven could see it.

Steven admired it for a minute. Then he looked closer and commented, "They're not exactly the same." He acted a little proud of his observation.

"Neither is your face," replied the Luthier.

Steven looked puzzled.

"Go take a good look in the mirror," offered the Luthier.

Steven walked over to the entry while the Luthier continued, "Even the face of Mary, as beautiful as she looks to you, is not the same, side to side. If it were, she would instantly look plain or artificial to you, though you would not know why. All great artists know that the balance of true beauty comes from the entire picture."

Steven carefully inspected his face in the mirror and began noticing the differences: One eye was open more than the other. The wrinkles across his forehead waved up and down and were uneven. His eyebrows were not the same and his mouth was slanted. He looked even closer and realized that nothing was the same!

"Did you realize that women with nearly-perfect faces will add a beauty mark or change their makeup from side to side, to make themselves more beautiful?"

Steven shook his head. He had noticed beauty marks

and different makeup on the women he looked at in his magazines, but he had never realized that they added them or intentionally put their makeup on unevenly.

The Luthier handed Steven a hand-mirror and asked him to hold it across his face while he looked into the large one. That way, he could only see the right side of his face and its reflection.

"Look at yourself for a few minutes, then take the mirror away."

Steven didn't notice the difference at first, but after a minute, it began to sink in. It just didn't look right! After looking at himself for another minute, he lowered the mirror. He liked how he looked a whole lot better after that.

"Now look at the f-holes again," offered the Luthier.

Steven picked up the belly of the violin and took another look. They suddenly looked better than they had before. He realized that it was because they were different and he knew it!

"The goal of art is not to make it perfect, or simply make it different, either. It is to make it beautiful to whoever looks at it. A woman with a true sense of beauty can make herself look more beautiful with small additions of color, or stylish marks in just the right places, while other women will apply those same changes and make themselves look cheap or strange.

"Every face is different and each one requires its own unique touches of style. The same is true with violins. Now look at how the f-holes lie on the shape of the belly itself."

Steven looked at the belly's shape and the f-holes at the same time. While he admired it, the Luthier pulled out another violin and brought it over.

"Now look at the arching and f-holes of this violin."

The Luthier traded Steven the finished violin for his violin's belly.

There was no mistaking it. The Luthier's violin had arching that was fuller and wider and the f-holes were formed to compliment that shape.

Steven realized that, while each was different, they were both very beautiful in their own way. He smiled and nodded.

"These things, and many others like them, are what separate original master instruments from all copies and forgeries."

The Luthier took his violin and put it back in its case. He gently picked up the back, ribs and scroll of Steven's violin and placed the belly on it before placing them all into Steven's outstretched hands.

"Some may love my instruments, some may not. On rare occasions, some even dislike all the other instruments I have made, but love the one I make especially for them. But no one can ever honestly deny that each instrument I make is original and each is art in its own way.

"I am making this violin for you and for Mary. Others may love it or hate it, but I make it for you. From its wood, its shape, its style, its varnish, its sound and its soul; it is all for you."

"Wow," softly exclaimed Steven.

"Exactly," replied the Luthier.

Chapter 24: The Greatest Father In The World

Within a few days, the violin was glued together, smoothed and finished in the white. After the Luthier announced that it was ready for varnishing, Steven realized that he hadn't seen Dianne's viola since the day the Luthier put it on the roof.

"What ever happened to the viola?" he asked.

"Dianne came for it while you were in the bunkhouse," replied the Luthier.

"Did she like it?"

"Like it?" asked the Luthier.

"Did she get her money's worth?" Steven clarified, after thinking about Dianne's statement about paying more than anyone else. Even though she had wanted Steven thrown in jail, he was still curious.

The Luthier's face took on an almost sinister expression. His eyes narrowed while he answered, "She could barely breathe while she played the instrument. She moaned and cried as though it were mercilessly tormenting her soul. It was hours before she recovered and she will never be the same."

Steven stared at the Luthier. He had wanted to strangle Dianne when he met her, but now he found himself feeling sorry for her.

"How could you do that to her?" he asked.

"She loved it," replied the Luthier with a mischievous grin. "When she stopped playing."

Steven almost fell over.

The Luthier explained, "All of Dianne's other instruments and possessions simply gave her a momentary feeling of accomplishment and power. The viola, on the other hand, allowed her to experience mourning and sorrow, failure and grief, misery and dejection, without being stuck in it. She didn't realize what she was asking for when she originally ordered the viola, but it was what she truly needed, so I didn't argue.

"You asked me before how I could keep such a good attitude when working with people like Dianne. Now you know." Then the Luthier laughed. "She's really quite a pleasant person now."

Steven knew there was more to the Luthier than met the eye, and he looked at his violin and began wondering what was in store for himself.

After seeing the expression on Steven's face, the Luthier looked down at the white violin. His whole countenance changed to that of happiness and serenity. "Don't worry, Steven. Each instrument I make is as unique as the people I make them for."

The wild look in the Luthier's eyes was totally gone. He acted as though the discussion of Dianne and her viola had never taken place.

Steven began wondering how someone could possibly have so many different temperaments and act so many parts. He also wondered if it would be a blessing or a curse to be a Master Luthier, or how anyone could do it without going completely insane. Yet, as he looked at his own experience so far, he felt like the Luthier was exactly the kind of teacher he needed, crazy or not.

The next morning, the Luthier put the small wooden peg into the violin's tapered endpin hole and placed it on its stand.

After admiring it for a moment, he turned toward Steven and announced, "It is now time for you to finish high school and get a higher education."

Steven looked like he was in shock, "What?!"

"The money in your saddle bag will only last a year or two, if you are frugal. How do you plan on supporting a family?"

"I can earn enough in construction to get by, especially if I'm not buying drugs, alcohol and cigarettes. It might be tough at first, but we should do pretty good once Mary finishes college."

The Luthier shook his head, "Mary needs to stay with the children while you earn the money."

Steven looked back at the Luthier in shock. He slumped into a chair next to the Luthier's bench and asked, "Where is this going to end?"

"Everything in its own due time, Steven."

"There's more?" Steven asked. He couldn't believe that there was more!

Steven felt pretty good that he had lived through being chained to the bunkhouse floor. Now he had to go back to school? Then what?

"You are past the worse part, Steven. Let's take the rest one step at a time," the Luthier consoled him.

Steven's expression didn't change. He was overwhelmed.

"We will just take it, step by step, and soon you will be at the end of this path," encouraged the Luthier.

The comment still didn't help Steven's attitude.

After a moment, the Luthier's expression changed to a happy, playful one.

"Before we go on, let's have some fun," declared the Luthier. "Is it still calm outside?"

It took Steven a minute to recover from the thought of going back to high school, but the word "fun" finally sank in. He stood up and opened the door. The air was hot and the leaves on the orchard trees were motionless.

"It doesn't get any calmer than this," replied Steven.

"Good," answered the Luthier. "Then let's go play with the cows."

Steven didn't even bother asking. Instead, he let his imagination run wild while the Luthier took his violin up on the roof.

He knew the Luthier well enough to know that the game would involve *real cows* and that they wouldn't get hurt. But he still wondered, while visions of cows flipping over and flying through the air ran through his mind.

After climbing down the ladder, the Luthier led Steven into the trees. In the center of the orchard was a large clearing with an old-fashioned red and white barn.

The Luthier slid the doors open, revealing a matching red and white farm tractor parked just inside. Steven waited while the diesel engine sprang to life and warmed up. Then the Luthier pulled the tractor out and parked it at the side of the barn.

Steven followed the Luthier inside to where a stack of colored cans and paint brushes lined the wall. The Luthier handed Steven an orange set while he chose pink and yellow ones for himself.

He explained, "This paint dries very quickly and water easily dissolves it, even after it's dried."

Steven looked at his can and commented, "It doesn't sound like very good paint."

"It's perfect for what we are going to use it for," explained the Luthier.

The Luthier held up the yellow can and smiled, "They're all non-toxic and this one drives them wild."

Steven could not even imagine what was going on, so he decided to just follow and listen.

They carried the cans and brushes over to a large corral full of cows. Then the Luthier and Steven worked up a sweat in the Southern Utah sun herding two large bulls into their respective chutes.

While standing between the two chutes, the Luthier caught his breath and explained, "We will each paint a large, colored X on our bull. You can have your choice, pink or orange."

Steven looked down at the can he had carried out and responded, "Orange is fine."

"Good," replied the Luthier. Then he opened his pink paint can and dipped the brush into it. The bull turned his head and looked at the Luthier, but didn't seem to mind when the Luthier painted a large pink X across his shoulders.

Steven did the same to his own bull with the orange paint and brush. He tried to make his X the same size and put it in the exact same place as the Luthier had.

"This yellow paint is not as easy," explained the Luthier. "Even though the chutes are narrow, the bulls will move around when it's painted on them, so I will paint both of them. You might think of this stuff as *cow-catnip*."

The moment the Luthier opened the yellow can, the two bulls started to move. Even the cows in the large corral began wandering over. They looked excited, like they were in anticipation of something. While the Luthier painted the sides of the bulls, the commotion got more intense.

Once the Luthier closed the lid and the yellow paint started to dry, they all settled down a little, but Steven could tell they all still wanted it.

"These three gates can be opened by remote control," explained the Luthier. "We will let the bulls out first, then we will open the main corral gate so the other cows can get at them."

"The cows all love to lick the yellow paint, even the bulls. But the bulls don't like being licked by the other cows, so it will keep them on the run while we play our game."

Steven couldn't hold out any longer. "What game?" he finally asked.

"Cow bombing, of course," replied the Luthier as he headed back toward the barn.

Sitting under two grey tarps in the back were two ultra-light flying parachutes parked side by side.

"No way!" exclaimed Steven with a large grin.

"Way," replied the Luthier.

"What do we use for bombs?" asked Steven.

"Large water balloons. Nontoxic and biodegradable of course," replied the Luthier.

"Of course," Steven commented while pulling one of the machines out of the barn.

"I don't know which the bulls like better; getting cooled

off by the water on a hot day like this, or being rid of the yellow paint. Either way, they always seem a little happier when we're done with them."

They were pulling out the second ultra-light when Steven looked at the Luthier like he doubted his last comment.

"Okay," admitted the Luthier. "Sometimes the other cows licking at the bulls can get them upset, but when I give them their special treat for being good sports, they are always happier," the Luthier added with a smile.

He then explained the powered-parachutes, "These are the safest, simplest flying machines possible. The only controls they have are left and right by moving the bars under your feet, and the throttle, which stays constant if you let go of it. They are designed to fly level at about thirty miles an hour. More throttle makes you go higher, less throttle makes you go down."

The Luthier pulled an aluminum rack off the rear seat of one of the machines and put it back in the barn. It had dozens of smooth, wire-framed pockets, specially made to hold water balloons.

Next the Luthier pulled the rectangular parachute out of a large duffle-bag and fluffed it up. He finished off by straightening out all of the lines that connected it to the ultra-light's frame.

After the Luthier gave both machines a thorough inspection and added gasoline, he started the engine on the first one and let it warm up for about five minutes. While it was running, they both put on helmets and set up the radios so they could talk to each other. Then they strapped themselves in.

When the Luthier increased the throttle, the large propeller blew the parachute open and up behind them and they started moving across the ground. The Luthier pulled the throttle all the way back, and in less than a hundred feet, they were in the air. That's all there was to it, and it amazed Steven while he looked down at the ground falling away below his feet.

They circled and flew out over the valley. It was amazing how green and peaceful it looked sitting in the middle of the hot desert.

The Luthier flew over the surrounding area, showing Steven some of the sights nearby. He saw abandoned rock houses and large mines dotting the hills of old Silver Reef just across the freeway from the town of Leeds. There was even an old *Wells Fargo* stagecoach stop in the middle of the ghost town with large, steel doors. It looked like they could still be used to hold off desperados and wild Indians.

They flew past the mining town toward Pine Valley Mountain before the Luthier swung the ultra-light around. The view was unbelievable. Steven had never seen so many colors at one time. The air was crystal clear and he could see into Arizona and Nevada. It felt as close to the feeling of a bird flying free as he could possibly imagine.

After looking around for a few minutes, the Luthier announced, "We better not keep those bulls waiting too long." Then they started descending back toward the violin shop.

The Luthier easily landed the ultra-light behind the barn in a large, smooth, flat area and pulled it around to where the other machine was parked. Steven was mesmerized and it took him a minute to unfasten the straps and step down to the ground.

"Did you have fun?" asked the Luthier.

Steven grinned in approval.

"Well, let's not keep those bulls waiting." The Luthier pulled out a box of balloons and started filling them with water from a faucet in front of the barn. Steven followed the Luthier's example and started filling his own water balloons on a faucet on the opposite side of the doors.

The Luthier reattached the metal rack on the back seat of the first ultra-light and started loading water-balloons. Steven was amazed at the number of balloons it held. "It must be pretty hard hitting the bulls," he commented after filling his own rack to capacity.

The Luthier's only reply was a mischievous grin.

He then continued with the instructions, "Don't fly too

close directly in front of, or behind the other machine because of air currents caused by the propellers. You can fly above or below each other, but still be careful and don't take any chances.

"If for some reason the engine dies, just restart it in the air. But, even if the engine won't restart, it's not a problem. The ultra-light will just float down to the ground. They will still maneuver very well and the landing is only a little bit harder than it is with power.

"Pick up the balloons carefully with your palm wide open. The first person to completely wash the X off of his bull's back is the winner." The Luthier was smiling the whole time and Steven couldn't help but get a little excited about it all.

The Luthier picked up one of his balloons and demonstrated by tossing it on the ground. It splashed a nice wide pattern in the dirt. He then handed Steven another balloon from his own rack and Steven tossed it onto the ground with the same results.

"You now have two extra balloons to practice with, before the game begins," the Luthier informed him.

"The lower you fly, the easier it is to hit the bulls, but if you fly too low you will scare them and they become very hard to hit."

They both buckled themselves in their machines and warmed up the engines another five minutes while the Luthier radioed over to Steven, "Once a player has washed the X off his bull, the other player becomes fair game until all the balloons are gone."

Now Steven understood the Luthier's mischievous grin. When the cow bombing was over, then the dogfighting would begin.

Steven took off first. He had no problem rising into the air before reaching the trees at the edge of the clearing. It amazed him how easy it was to fly. The Luthier followed, and soon they were circling above the corral together.

"First the bulls," came the Luthier's voice over the radio. He reached up, pushed a button on his ultra-light's frame and the two gates opened.

Steven looked down and watched the two bulls charge out of their chutes. The bulls quickly ran away from the corral while the other cows pushed up against the gate in anticipation.

"Go ahead," offered the Luthier as he pointed to the cows all huddled together.

Steven circled around and flew toward the cows with a water-balloon in his hand. He tossed it, and watched it fly past the cows. He had figured that it would take a little getting used to, so he wasn't discouraged.

He circled around and dropped the next balloon a little sooner. It hit the largest cow in the middle of the group. The waterballoon burst and sent a spray of water across three or four cows standing next to it. The cow shook its head while the others scattered, but it didn't seem to hurt or upset them.

Steven circled back up to the Luthier and they both smiled at each other.

"It's a lot harder when they are running," explained the Luthier. He called out, "On your mark, get set, go!" as he pushed the other button on the frame and let the small herd of cows out of the corral.

They stampeded as fast as they could toward the two bulls who had now slowed down to a trot and were trying to lick the yellow paint off themselves. The instant the other cows started licking at them, the bulls started bucking and ran away, faster than ever.

The Luthier radioed over to Steven, "Do you like rock and roll?"

Steven nodded.

"Then push the button on the box above your right shoulder," came the crackling voice of the Luthier over the radio.

Steven pushed the button.

Credence Clearwater Revival instantly burst out of the speakers in Steven's helmet. Steven smiled and nodded in approval while the Luthier pushed the same music button on his own ultra-light.

The two bulls were now separated and headed in

different directions across the desert so Steven and the Luthier turned and went their separate ways.

The Luthier was the first to approach his bull and drop a balloon. It cleanly missed the bull because another cow reached over and licked him at the last moment. Steven took the next shot, missing his bull by a good thirty feet as he tried to judge the speed of the running bull through the sagebrush. They both circled around and went in for another pass. The Luthier hit the right hip of his bull while Steven's landed just a foot or two away, and the game continued.

Steven soon figured out that there was a lot of luck involved in this game, as well as skill. On one pass he approached his bull directly from the side. The bull was standing still while a single cow stood licking the yellow paint off of him. Just before the balloon hit, the other cow lifted up its head and got splashed right across its face.

Steven was sure that the balloon would have hit its mark otherwise. But, by the time he could circle around, the other cows caught up and chased the bull away at full speed again.

Steven looked over at the Luthier's bull and noticed that half of the pink X was washed off and the Luthier was circling around for another pass. Steven loved a challenge and headed toward his bull with the music turned up and determination on his face. He felt the exhilaration of a bombing raid without the worry of anyone getting hurt. He dropped down low with a balloon in each hand, poised and ready to strike.

He was following the running bull out across the desert and lowered the ultra-light right above him. He threw both of the balloons at the same time. One of them hit the ground while the other hit the bull's lower back, splashing water across the X but not enough to wash it away.

When he pulled up to circle around, water balloons splashed into his face and lap. Steven looked up and saw the Luthier smiling and waving down at him.

Steven was drenched. It startled him more than anything, but after a second, he realized that it actually felt good. So he smiled and waved back up at the Luthier and continued his pursuit of the bull. The Luthier waited until Steven let go of his next balloon before pelting him with another set of waterballoons from above.

Steven continued circling around and taking shots at his bull, but was harder now that he knew what was coming. Each shot he took was immediately responded to by a waterballoon in his face.

The game ended when both the Luthier and Steven ran out of balloons. Steven's X was half washed away and he had received six direct hits from the Luthier.

After they landed, the Luthier walked over to one of the faucets. "Since you aren't good enough to hit me yet, I'm just going to have to do it myself." Then the Luthier stuck his head under the faucet and drenched himself.

It was a hot afternoon, and after the Luthier shook off, they both grabbed a cool drink out of the refrigerator and talked about the cow bombing game. They sat in the shade, describing the expressions on the cows faces and laughed until it hurt.

After relaxing, the Luthier got serious again, "My father never *let* me win any game. I still remember my mother getting mad at him because he mercilessly beat me at chess when I was six years old."

Steven drank his cool fruit juice while he listened.

"After three years and hundreds of games, when I finally beat my father for the first time, I knew that I had done it fair and square. The victory was good, because it was real.

"Children who have parents that let them win, never experience the feeling of truly winning. In not wanting to hurt their children's feelings, parents take away the child's ability to learn patience and the drive to compete and reach the very top.

"The difficult part for the parent is doing it the right way, keeping the right attitude and encouraging them on, no matter how many times they lose. Have fun and show your children that you enjoy winning but never make them feel stupid or slow.

"You and I both know that it wouldn't take many games of cow bombing before you could beat me. Children don't look at things that way, unless you show them with the right attitude. Be careful," added the Luthier.

Steven could tell that the Luthier was always thinking about children and how to raise them properly. "When I have children of my own, can I call and ask you things, or maybe even bring them out here?"

"Absolutely," responded the Luthier. "My father taught me that 'the job is not finished until the job is done,' and I will not consider my job done with you until your children consider *you* the greatest father in the world."

Chapter 25: The Man Of My Dreams

After folding up the parachutes and putting the ultra-lights away, Steven and the Luthier saddled up two horses and rounded up the cattle. They washed all of the remaining paint off of the bulls, then gave them the extra-special treat that the Luthier had talked about. Steven found that the Luthier was right. The bulls did look happier now, and he watched them run back into the corral with the other cows with spryness in their step.

As they headed back to the violin shop, the Luthier asked, "How far have you gotten in your reading?"

"It's been tough, but I'm about halfway through," replied Steven. "I finished the first few books fairly quickly, but then they seemed to go slower and slower and got more difficult to read. I must have only remembered the good parts when I was a boy and all those seem to be in the first four or five books.

"I see," replied the Luthier. "We'll talk more about the Bible later, but you may have to finish your religious training with Mary. Sometimes that works out rather well in the end. Unfortunately *we* only have so much time, and we are going to have to start making some tough choices."

Steven thought again of the long road ahead. He knew he was through the most painful part, but to finish high school and learn a trade that could support a wife and children could take him years!

Steven felt like he didn't have the luxury of years. If Mary were waiting at all, she was waiting blindly, not even knowing for sure if he would come back. How long could that last? But he also knew he couldn't chance seeing her again until he was ready or he might blow his chance forever. He started to get frustrated again, just like he was before the cow bombing game.

"If Mary truly loves me shouldn't she be willing to give something up?" Steven finally asked the Luthier. His expression showed his honest frustration.

"She will," answered the Luthier. "Every woman like Mary dreams from her childhood of marrying the perfect man. The perfect man to Mary is all of the things you heard her talk about in the restaurant, added to the things she told Tom. But there is still more. *Much more.*

"Mary dreams of a man who has lived a pure, spotless life. She dreams of a man that has saved himself for her and her alone, just as she has done.

"Mary has no parents to comfort her and she also dreams of marrying into that man's family and taking his name so she can have his loving parents to comfort her like her own parents did.

"All of this still doesn't include the house with a white picket fence, the two cars in the garage and ..."

"Stop," Steven interrupted, "I already feel lousy enough."

The Luthier silently opened the door to the shop and let Steven recover from the reality of it all while they walked in.

After closing the door, the Luthier continued, "I will finish with these two statements, and never forget them:

"If you start now, and continue until the day you die of old age, you will not be able to count all the things that Mary will give up for you.

"The other one is the advice my father gave me, right before I married Sheryl. He told me, 'When you marry her, it is final, *no matter what.* She may change with time and become old and grotesquely ugly. There may

come a day when she turns into an evil witch and decides
to make your life miserable. She may even chop off your
arms and legs and throw you out into the desert to die.

"But if you marry her, it will not only be your duty to
stay with her, it will also be your duty to crawl back to
her on your bloody stumps and ask her forgiveness for
whatever you did wrong, whether you think you did
anything wrong or not."

"Your father really said that?" asked Steven.

"Yes," replied the Luthier, "and he meant every word."

"Your father was pretty hard-core, wasn't he?" asked
Steven.

"Yes, he was," replied the Luthier with a smile.

The next morning, the Luthier made special
arrangements for Steven to take his high school
equivalency test. The test was scheduled so that the
results would come back about the same time the violin
would be completed. Then they studied from morning
until night every day.

"Hi, Tom. I got a part in the play," Mary announced
with a smile. She was standing on the sidewalk next to
Tom on her way home from the university.

"That's wonderful, Mary."

Mary had talked about trying out for the play each
afternoon during the past week.

"What part did they gives you?" asked Tom.

"I'm the head witch," Mary replied. Then she cackled
and screeched.

"You sound so nice, it's hard to imagine yous as a witch,"
remarked Tom. "Yous gonna hafta work on that screech,
Mary."

"I know," she replied. "It was the funniest thing. I don't
know why they chose that part for me..." Mary tilted her
head back, looked up and tapped her finger against her
chin in deep thought.

"Maybe because it was the only part left? I don't care,
I'll take it. I like a challenge. It was really strange, though.
The director only had me read a few dramatic lines from

the script of *Somewhere in Time*, then let me go, and now I'm a witch!"

"Don't let it go to your head," cautioned Tom with a big grin.

"I won't," replied Mary. She screeched again while Tom shook his head.

"Yous still acts like that same ten-year-old girl I mets a long time ago," Tom remarked. The he asked her, "How's your hope stanin' up, Mary? Yous fall in love agin yet?"

"I'm doing okay," replied Mary. She sat down now that the conversation was turning serious. "I haven't seen him again yet, and I haven't fallen in love with anyone else on death row. But I'm okay."

"Cheer up, child. Some things, they jes takes time," offered Tom. "Speakin' o' time, I'm never gonna finish this sandwich Samuel brought me. Yous wants to help me wi' it?" Then Tom held out a large sandwich he had been eating before Mary came by.

Mary reached up, tore a piece off and took a bite. "Thanks, Tom."

They sat and chewed together for a few minutes while Tom listened and Mary watched all the different people walk by.

After Mary finished, she started talking in a thoughtful, far away tone, "When I read that script, it made me think about everything differently, Tom. It was all about 'the man of my dreams.' While I read the lines, I thought about the *real* man of my dreams and I formed a picture of him in my mind. The thing was, I just couldn't put the man I saw in the restaurant into my picture, and I couldn't imagine him with my children, no matter how hard I tried.

"I think Cindy might be right after all. It's time I started looking for a real, live man."

"I suppose yous right, Mary. Yous dont's want to be sitting next to old Tom for the rest of yous life, holdin' a cup o' your own."

"I'll never leave you alone, Tom. I'll always be near by, and with some luck, I'll even bring a little girl of my own to visit you before long."

Mary smiled, picked up her violin and backpack, then headed toward her apartment with determination in her step.

Chapter 26: The Test

It was after lunch when Steven walked into the violin shop and closed the door behind him. His violin was supported by the large wood stand sitting on the bench in the entry. The Luthier had just taken it down from the roof and brought it in. The last coat of varnish was dry and it was waiting for the final smoothing and french polishing before being "fitted up" with pegs and strings.

It looked beautiful and Steven rotated it on the stand and looked it over. He was really starting to appreciate its value and all the things that went into making an original, master instrument.

He was excited. He had taken it easy for the last two days while waiting for the results of his high school equivalency test to come back. He had never done well on any of the tests he had taken in school but he felt like he had passed *this* test when he finished taking it. The only real question in his mind was his reading skills.

It had been tiresome and grueling for the past few weeks. Steven had forgotten almost everything he had learned in school. Added to all the rest of the things he was learning from the Luthier, he felt like his brain was ready to explode.

The Luthier stood up and walked over when Steven came in the door. The Luthier was holding up a folder full of papers.

"We have something serious to talk about," the Luthier told him while he shook the folder.

Steven's eyes opened wide.

"What?" he asked.

"Like, what's wrong with you, *Boy*?" demanded the Luthier as his voice took on a mean, chilled tone. It reminded Steven of his father.

"What?" Steven asked again, now defensively.

"Honesty," replied the Luthier in an even harsher tone. He pulled out a group of papers and shook them at Steven. They looked like police reports.

"What are you talking about?" he asked, trying to imagine what the papers were.

"You not only failed to mention that your mother was a prostitute and a worthless drunk her whole life!" declared the Luthier as he threw them into the trash. "You also failed to tell me that you were a 'freak' and can't read out loud, so you flunked the high school test." Then the Luthier threw another group of papers in the trash on top of the others.

The Luthier clenched the remainder of the papers in his fist and threw the folder in the garbage. He put his nose right up to Steven's and continued in a mean, challenging voice, "You worthless piece of trash! You also never told me that it was *you* who got your three *buddies* killed in 'Nam! You spineless, yellow coward!"

Steven's blood boiled while the Luthier's face got closer and his voice louder with each statement. Steven could feel the spit from the Luthier's mouth spraying on his face; just like his father's did when he was young.

Without even hesitating, Steven's right fist slugged the Luthier in the stomach. He then followed with his left. The Luthier caught it, but could not stop Steven's right fist when it came quickly again and landed home, sending him backwards onto the bench with a crunch.

Steven delivered one blow after the other, fast and furious, with the Luthier blocking most, but not all of the punches. When Steven drew his arm back and swung harder than ever, the Luthier ducked and Steven's knuckles ended up crashing into the wall.

While Steven held his hand in pain, he finally realized what the crunching sound was that came from behind the Luthier when he fell back from the punches.

Steven looked down and flew into even more of a rage when he realized that the violin was destroyed. He yelled at the Luthier, "My mother had her problems, so what? I can't read, that's my problem! But it isn't my fault my friends are dead, no matter what anyone says!"

The Luthier didn't seem to hear Steven. His expression changed from surprise to deep sorrow as he turned and looked down at the shattered remains of the violin.

"This was not the way this test was supposed to go," the Luthier admitted before slowly picking up each of the pieces. He gently cradled and caressed them as a mother would a dead infant in her arms.

After a minute, it started to dawn on Steven. "This was supposed to be a test?"

The Luthier sat down on one of the chairs and nodded, "Your last one."

"What was supposed to happen after you insulted me like that?" demanded Steven.

"You were supposed to say, 'My mother had her problems, so what? I can't read, so what? I did my duty with honor, no matter what you, or anyone else thinks. I can take your insults whether they are true or false because *I* am a real man'. Or something like that," replied the Luthier.

"Then I was going to give you my deepest apologies for putting you through all this, congratulate you for passing high school with a B average, then we were going to go celebrate. Maybe even play that other game of *Bone Guys* we never got to."

Steven stood silent while he looked down at the broken pieces of the violin. Then he slowly sank into the chair next to the Luthier.

"So I have failed," lamented Steven as he looked at the violin and shook his head.

The Luthier sat silently staring at the violin with a look of hopelessness. Out of habit, the Luthier commented, "No one fails until they fail to stand one more time than they fall. That's what my father would say."

"What would your father say about me punching you in

the stomach and ruining the violin?" asked Steven as the weight of the situation sank in.

"He would say, 'You stupid, punk kid, you aren't worth the sweat off my brow'," replied the Luthier.

Steven grimaced at the answer.

They sat together in silence, just staring at the splinters of wood and varnish.

"He would also say that you are a lot quicker and stronger now that you're sober and have had some sleep," the Luthier added, trying to smile. "I am sorry for the insults. I had a very hard time bringing myself to even say the words, but I had to know that you could control yourself, no matter what."

Then the Luthier's expression got very serious, "Life gets bad sometimes, Steven; things can go wrong and tempers can flare. I doubt that Mary would ever say anything like that to you, but if she did, you probably would have just killed her with those punches."

Steven *only now* realized what this test was really about, and he dropped his head in shame. He shook his head as sorrow and deep regret spread through his entire body. It didn't matter who would have said those words. If it had been those words, in that tone of voice, he would have thrown those punches at anyone, maybe even Mary.

Steven thought about all that he had been through and all that he had done, yet he was still Chip inside. His will to go on broke, right then and there.

"It's who I am," sobbed Steven. "I can't help it," he sighed with his head in his hands, and he began crying.

The Luthier remained silent, barely able to hold back his own tears while looking at the broken pieces of the violin in his hands.

Steven lifted his head and told the Luthier, "I will do anything to keep Mary from harm, even if I have to give her up."

They sat silent again, staring at each other. Neither was able to speak for a long time.

Steven looked at the broken pieces again and told him, "I am responsible for the violin. You don't have to make me another or give me any money back."

The Luthier still sat silently looking down at the pieces.

Steven waited for some kind of response, but the Luthier said nothing.

"You've done so much for me and you've spent all your time away from your family for so long. I have failed, and I'm just going to have to live with it. It's who I am."

Silence and despair hung heavy in the violin shop while they looked at each other.

Finally the Luthier whispered, "When a man compelleth you to go with him a mile, go with him twain."

"What?" asked Steven.

The Luthier replied, "When you walked in my door I could not refuse you. I felt like it was my duty to God, and also to my country somehow."

The Luthier looked Steven right in the eyes.

"Do you think I am going to let you fail now?" he demanded with his voice raising in determination. "If your guts are laying on the floor, man, pick them up! If your legs are off at the hips, crawl on your hands."

The Luthier stood up and placed the pieces of the violin back down on the table.

"If I have to carry the dead, bloody remains of your bullet-riddled carcass the last twenty miles of this journey I will do it, WHETHER YOU WANT TO OR NOT!"

The Luthier physically lifted Steven up out of his chair by his shirt and held him in the air, shaking him.

Steven was not a small man. He had never felt a grip like the Luthier's and his shirt began to tear. The Luthier stared into Steven's eyes, looking and sounding crazier than ever.

Steven shook his head and asked, "What are you talking about?"

"You must repair this violin," answered the Luthier. He let go of Steven's shirt and dropped him to the ground. Then he pointed at the broken pieces on the table.

"What?" asked Steven.

"A unit of power, usually electricity, equal to one joule per second," answered the Luthier.

Steven just stared. Now he knew the Luthier was crazy.

"That's *'watt'* my father would say when I asked him 'what' too many times," replied the Luthier. "He was a nuclear physicist, remember?"

Steven still looked at the Luthier as if he were mad.

"Also remember that I am a Master Luthier," he continued. "And I will teach you how to repair your violin so it can sing in the greatest concert halls and melt the hardest of hearts, no matter what it looks like to you right now. And if you are a *real man* and whether you love Mary or not, you will follow my direct order and you will kill the man that walked in my door six weeks ago. AND YOU WILL SHOW NO MERCY WHATSOEVER!!!"

"I can't kill him!" cried Steven. "He's tougher than you and I both put together." Steven said it with tears streaming down his face. Then he sank back into the chair and put his head back in his hands.

The Luthier reached down and grabbed Steven's shirt again and lifted him back up.

"I know," responded the Luthier.

"More than you'll ever know!" Steven shook his head.

"I know!" said the Luthier again, this time even louder.

"IT'S HOPELESS!" cried Steven.

"DON'T YOU THINK I KNOW IT'S HOPELESS BY NOW?!" asked the Luthier.

Steven just stared back, not knowing how to respond.

Then the Luthier yelled, "I KNOW IT'S HOPELESS!!!"

The Luthier's voice then softened and he looked straight into Steven's eyes, "I know it's hopeless because I am only a Master Luthier. But *I* know a Master Fisherman."

Chapter 27: Jesus

𝒯ary checked her mail, walked up the stairs and opened the door to her apartment. It was small, clean and simple, with no signs of extravagance showing anywhere. She placed her backpack on the small kitchen table then carried her violin into the clean, but simple, bedroom. Everything in Mary's life had been small, clean and simple for the past twenty years and even more so since her last date five years before when she gave up "fishing" and "hunting."

There was only one thing in Mary's life that would even hint that she still believed she was a princess and that someday her *Prince Charming* would come to rescue her from her lonely life of obscurity. Her mirror.

Mary walked into the bathroom and closed the door. On the small, clean and simple bathroom wall hung a large, ornate, golden-framed, genuine, silver-backed mirror that covered the entire wall above the sink.

When Mary's mother was still alive, she told Mary to live her life so she could look at herself with a clean conscience. Then her father would tell her, "Never trust anyone unless they are willing to look you right in the eyes; and that includes yourself, Mary."

After the accident, everything in Mary's life fell apart. Mary and her grandmother were faced with the debts of her father's hardware store and the expense of her family's funeral. Then, one week later, her grandmother suffered a stroke that put her into intensive care where she struggled to live for weeks, but never recovered.

Everything that had any value was sold just to pay the

bills that were overdue. Even the family heirlooms and personal items were auctioned off to pay the combined debts of her father's store and her grandmother's hospital bills, including the wedding rings that her grandfather had made.

Mary couldn't believe that they could take everything and not even give her a chance to buy it back someday. She had only been able to keep her violin because it was loaned to her at the time. Everything leftover was carried to her small apartment in two cardboard boxes.

If that wasn't enough for Mary's nightmare, there were also some personal loans that her father had outstanding. Maybe she wasn't legally liable for the debts, but Mary took them upon herself as a matter of honor and slowly paid them off instead of attending college for a few years.

After Mary was finally clear of debt, she started saving every penny to buy *this* mirror. It was in front of this mirror that Mary would ask herself who she was and where she was going, and it was in front of this mirror that she had dreamed of love at first sight.

After talking with Tom about looking for a real man, Mary decided to look in the mirror and see what she really looked like.

The woman looking back at Mary had short, black hair. She had cut it after her last date, so she wouldn't have to spend so much time taking care of it while she was seriously going to school. It was clean and neat, but she realized that it wasn't flowing and gorgeous like it used to be or like the man of her dreams would probably want, so she decided that she would start growing it out again.

She was thirty-seven years old and had lived a hard life, but she looked at herself in the pure, silver reflection, and it showed her face exactly as it still was: beautiful.

Mary wasn't a vain person. In fact, she was the opposite, but she still never liked to look in normal mirrors that made every face look a little grey.

That was why she had bought *this* mirror. The salesman had reminded Mary of her father and after looking at people and their reflections in normal mirrors and then this silver one, she knew that she could never settle for anything less. Besides, the mirror was beautiful enough for any castle and she could take it with her. It made *good common sense*, and that made Mary think about her mother.

Mary was still beautiful, but she had left her face almost as plain as possible other than her scarlet lipstick. As she looked at herself and thought about dating again, she realized that a little color wouldn't hurt, so she pulled out her small makeup case and started playing.

With just a few touches of the colors that she had never dared use before and a little highlight, she stood back and exclaimed, "Wow!"

The difference was astonishing.

"No wonder, *Prince Charmings* have not been knocking at my door, lately!" she thought to herself while marvelling at the improvement it had made.

After a minute, she walked over, peered into her small closet and realized that she had nothing to fit the occasion. The only clothes she owned were the three well-used, conservative sets of pants and blouses that she wore to school, her two full-length church dresses and her two restaurant uniforms.

She had not bought any nice clothes to go courting in for years. She figured that the man of her dreams would see her for what she really was without being *dolled* up. Mary ended up in front of the mirror wearing her white slip and the decision to buy at least two nice, new dresses.

Next, she put on her mother's small, elegant earrings. They were all she had left of her mother's and she had a hard time getting them through the small holes in her earlobes because it had been so long since she had worn any jewelry.

There she was, looking back at herself in the mirror, and she smiled when she imagined wearing different colors and styles of dresses. She knew she was a dreamer, but it didn't take much imagination to realize that, even after all these years, a very beautiful woman was still looking back at her.

Mary glanced down at her bare feet, then at her tennis shoes sitting next to her on the floor.

"And a new pair of glass slippers, of course," she said with a laugh and a smile.

When Steven and the Luthier walked down the hill, the mood was quiet and serious.

After reaching the valley floor, Steven finally asked the Luthier, "How did you find out that my mother was a prostitute?"

"I talked with Hardcore and others," replied the Luthier, "I was trying to find out everything I could so I could help you. Or in this one case, so I could hurt you. I am sorry, but I felt it was necessary."

"That's all right," answered Steven, "You'd think that I would know you better than that by now."

The Luthier apologized again, "My father had the ability to 'get someone's goat' in seconds. I guess I have inherited that trait.

"Hardcore also told me that there was nothing you or anyone else could have done that day, other than simply not gone on patrol. But he never would tell me what really happened, other than you were the only man left. Do you mind?" asked the Luthier.

"No, I don't mind. It's probably the real reason I came here to see you. And now it's the only reason that I am still listening to you," replied Steven.

"Fair enough," replied the Luthier.

Steven had never told anyone the whole story.

"Our company marched back to the hill late in the afternoon after a long hump for some well deserved R and R. When we got there, intelligence had learned from two different vill's that a small band of Viet Cong were making their way through the jungle a few kilometers southeast. It was the same area that we had just come from.

"Ruckus told us that our country was only asking us to go and not ordering us, since we had just gotten back from a month and a half in the jungle. Every member of our platoon immediately replied, 'If our country asks, the answer is, Yes, Sir!'"

Ruckus walked over to Chip that night while he sat behind a wall of sandbags during his *hole watch duty* and informed him, "Lima company was just ambushed and taken out. We don't have an exact location. Get your gear now."

That's all that was said, and within the hour, Chip headed out with all the other men in the company. They didn't know how long it would take. No one ever knew for sure.

After they regrouped in the jungle and set up a temporary camp, Chip's platoon separated from the others. Ruckus was out front leading the way with ten men in the middle, while Chip pulled up the rear as tail-end Charlie.

Back into the jungle they went. Back over the same rough trail they had just come over less than twelve hours before. There was almost no sign that they, or anyone else, had ever been there as they macheted their way through the thick foliage. When they finally stopped marching, all but two of them sat down and leaned against a tree. They fell asleep without taking anything off and without preparing any kind of bedding.

Before sunrise, they had eaten and were on their way. As they broke camp and started marching, they were already part of the jungle again. The rain came down and their bodies were hot and smelly all over. Their feet were still in the height of jungle rot paradise, small bugs were happily playing in their greasy hair, and any cuts or wounds they had were raw and festering in the humidity. Even Slaughter seemed to fit in more this time than any other with sweat running down his face.

When they broke for lunch, Ruckus decided that they should take an hour and rest, so most of the men took off their helmets and leaned against their own personal tree. *Personal tree* meant the tree closest to them at the time.

After the few minutes it took for everyone to take a nice

warm drink of water from their canteen, Slaughter started in, "Chip, did you bring your snow skis?"

"Can't say that I did," answered Chip with a smile and a chuckle.

"Well I brought mine, and I'm heading down an icy-cool, ski slope right now," Slaughter began.

The men kicked back a little bit more and waited for Slaughter to continue.

"There's fresh smelling pine trees all around. I'm in a beautiful clearing of pure, white snow with a crystal-blue sky above my head. It's peaceful and I stop to take in a deep breath of the clean fresh air. Whoa!" Slaughter acted like he was surprised.

"A pretty, little filly just swished by and her skis threw some of the soft, cool, powdered snow up against my leg. Now she's flowing smoothly back and forth, further down the hill. She looks mighty fine. Her long, blonde hair is trailing behind her and my, oh my, is she fine!"

There were a few good-humored whistles and catcalls from around the trees.

"I push off with my ski poles and follow her down the hill. Even though I am a gentleman, I can't help but notice how her slender hips sway back and forth in rhythm as she heads down the cool, white slope toward her small, Swiss chalet, half buried in the snow. There are small wisps of smoke coming out of the chimney and the smell of barbecued ribs in the air." (Slaughter's favorite meal.)

The men started moaning. Slaughter paused to take a drink, then leaned back and continued, "She turns back and gives me an inviting smile while her soft features and rosy cheeks go flush and dimple. Her crystal-blue eyes match the sky and sparkle like emeralds in the sun."

Slaughter's words were almost poetic and the men knew they were really in for it this time, "She gives me a wink with her long, blonde eyelashes, then laughs. Her ripe, red lips pucker up to blow me a......"

"Quiet!" ordered Ruckus.

By the way he said it, there was no doubt Ruckus was

serious. Every man instantly had his haunches on his heels and held his rifle out in front of him, ready for action.

"East, one hundred meters," Tiny reported while pointing off to the left. He signaled that there were two of them.

Ruckus motioned for the men to follow, then pointed at his eyes with two fingers before swishing them back and forth for them to be extra alert. He fell back to the center of the platoon with the radio man right behind him.

"Call in our coordinates, Private," Ruckus quietly ordered. "Three-hundred meters south of checkpoint foxtrot."

The radio man called in their coordinates and informed the company that the platoon might be engaging the enemy. Ruckus knew better than to pursue straight up the middle of the valley, so they followed the two Viet Cong along the edge of the hill to the north.

The platoon headed up the hill and across its face at full speed trying to cut the two Viet Cong off. The two lead men of the platoon were gradually overtaking the enemy, running along the valley floor.

Right after they stopped and squeezed off their rounds, the air exploded with gunfire from the top of the hill. Viet Cong moved in *en masse* while the two lead men turned and fired up the hill and into the jungle in front of them.

Ruckus ordered everyone to fall back when he saw the number of enemy troops and told them to regroup at some boulders they had just passed. He also told the radio man to call for extra support.

Chip was approaching the boulders when the shooting started and he ran over to them. He shot into the jungle on both sides as he tried to cover the other men running back through the clearing.

Each time he reloaded and came back around the bolder, he could see more Viet Cong in the trees and more members of his platoon lying in the clearing riddled with bullets. The air was thick with smoke and the bullets were buzzing through the air, while pieces of rock flew all around Chip every time he pulled back and reloaded. Even though the enemy outnumbered their platoon four-to-one, the thought of retreating and leaving his friends never even entered his mind.

After emptying his last clip and pulling back behind the boulder for the last time, Chip stopped one second to think. He knew he would be dead in less than a minute now that the enemy was starting to surround him, so he crouched down between the rocks and pulled out his 45 semiautomatic and held it in his hand. He had no desire to be a prisoner of war and was ready to take on the first enemy that appeared around the boulder.

Even though the back of his helmet said, "I hate Jesus," Chip found himself praying.

For some reason, he still hoped there was a heaven, and that there would be someone or something waiting for him on the other side in just a few seconds. He knew, deep down inside, he wished it was Jesus, so that's who he decided to pray to.

While Chip took those few seconds to pray, he realized that a single, large-caliber rifle was shooting methodically, between once and twice a second from the other side of the valley. As he continued praying with his eyes wide open and his pistol in his hand, the dirt and number of pieces of rock flying through the air slowly started to die down. By the time he finished, the only sound he could hear was the methodical rhythm of the rifle.

The shots gradually got further and further apart, then they stopped.

After waiting a minute and hearing only silence, Chip crept back around the largest boulder and cautiously looked around. Everything was dead quiet. Everything was dead.

Chip stood up. There were thirty bodies lying completely still in the clearing. Some of them were piled two or three men deep. As he looked around, he saw that there were many more scattered throughout the trees.

Chip crouched down and picked up one of the M-16's and slid a fresh clip into it. There was an eerie, dead-calm feeling that hung so thick in the air he could feel it with his hands. Even though there should have been some movement or some survivors on the ground or between the trees, everything was completely still and the thick haze almost suffocated him.

After quickly looking around, Chip rolled the enemies' bodies off of his friends and searched for anyone who might still be alive underneath. No one was. Not one of the enemy or one of the members of his platoon. He soon realized that the only two people left alive in the valley were himself and whoever was on the other side.

Chip couldn't help believing that his prayer had just saved him. He had no idea who was on the other side of the valley, but Chip decided to give the credit to Jesus. He didn't know too much about Jesus, he just believed that He was good and if anyone had helped him, it must have been Him.

He had never met anyone as good as he imagined Jesus was, but the three men in the world who came closest to it were lying in the clearing at his feet. He wished he could have saved them and he knew that they would have tried to save him if they were put in the same position he was.

Chip pulled Tiny, Ruckus and Slaughter together and leaned them up against some of the other bodies. He pulled a small camera out of Tiny's pocket. The camera was unharmed, and he positioned it on a large rock at the edge of the clearing and set the timer. He then walked back over and sat down between his friends.

He propped them up the best he could with both of his arms until the shutter clicked.

Steven pulled out his wallet and handed an old photograph to the Luthier.

While the Luthier looked it over, Steven commented, "I know it's pretty gruesome, but I felt like I needed something that I could hold on to. Something to remind me about that day when I prayed, and to remind me that there really were people once who I cared for, and who cared for me.

"Not one of those men ever bailed out on me, ever. No

matter what," Steven proudly announced as he pointed to each of the men in the picture.

Steven and the Luthier walked into the library where Steven finished relating the events of that day.

"Hardcore was that large-bore rifle across the valley. He had survived Lima company's ambush because he had been surveying when the Viet Cong attacked. He went running back, but a stray bullet hit him in the leg and he never got there.

"He patched himself up and set up a blind, but he had no radio and no way to get anywhere, except crawl. He decided to wait it out, hoping that a patrol would come by before the Viet Cong. He spotted us following the two Gooks just as *Charlie* (the enemy) came over the hill from the other direction.

"Even though Hardcore was the answer to my prayer, I felt like Jesus had made it happen. So I decided to try and find some answers and change my life. I did try for a little while, but, by the time I served another tour of duty with the Marines' slogan of "kill, kill, kill," watching the nice guys die, the crazy ones stay alive, and listening to "I can't wait for my first kill" from the green Marines, I was so numb that I forgot about trying to be someone, or looking for the meaning of life.

"There is one thing I did change after that day, though." Steven smiled and pulled out another old photograph while he told the Luthier, "I still felt like I owed my life to someone other than Hardcore."

It was a picture of a soldier standing on the side of a hill looking through binoculars. It was taken from behind and the Luthier could clearly read the words, "I love Jesus" painted on the back of the soldier's helmet.

Chapter 28: The Tape

Mary noticed an instant change the first day she wore her new, bright blue, well fitting dress, her new shoes and a moderate amount of makeup. Men started coming out of the woodwork again, some of them barely over half her age. It only took a few days for Mary to realize that she could be quite picky and still have a date any night she wanted.

She had been asked out many times over the previous five years, but it was different after she started accepting offers again. The men were standing in line for her attention, now that the word was out; "Mary is looking."

But it didn't take long before Mary was overwhelmed with the extra attention and began having second thoughts. At first she was "eating up" the popularity and favors, but more and more, as the time went by, she felt like she was a large side of beef on display at the meat shop.

She thought she had learned a lot from dating in her younger years, but some of the men she went out with now were downright mean and she had to ask many of them to take her home early. It also amazed her how much "extra baggage" came with even the nicest men her age. Everything from three ex-wives with half a dozen children to personality quirks that would offend a gorilla.

Mary walked home one afternoon after a particularly bad day of turning down "fish she didn't want to catch" and decided that she had had enough. She was going to start wearing her plain, everyday clothes again and take a break. Maybe not for five more years, but at least for a little while.

She probably would have started wearing her old clothes earlier but she had been hearing rumors about a new transfer student at the university who was about her age, and how he was *unbelievably* nice and good looking. But so far, she had not seen him and she was getting tired of sifting through the others.

As Mary stepped onto the corner of the sidewalk where Tom was, she heard two motorcycles pull up behind her. They were driving on the wrong side of the street.

They were too close for comfort and Mary could feel the thumping from their exhaust pipes. She didn't dare turn around and look. She just moved away from the edge of the sidewalk and walked a little faster.

"Can I give you a ride?" asked a man in a surly voice, as he pulled his motorcycle up next to her.

"Would you like to ride me?" asked the other man, following close behind.

Mary moved to the far edge of the sidewalk and kept walking.

"Too good for us?" asked the first. He rode with his tires skimming along the edge of the curb.

Mary glanced over at two of the meanest looking men she had ever seen. Both of them were wearing black leather vests with nothing underneath, and each of them had chains hanging from their clothes and motorcycles. The first man had large snakes tattooed up his arms, while the second had tattooed ladies running up his neck and onto the side of his face. But the worst part to Mary was the way they were looking at her.

These kind of men and the amount of trouble in the neighborhood seemed to have increased ever since the night Cindy's friend told her that their leader had disappeared. Mary couldn't imagine what kind of person would choose to be part of a gang, but she also wondered if Steven had been a good influence on them somehow.

Mary turned away with a cringe and walked even faster. Her heart was pounding in her chest.

The two motorcycles quickly pulled ahead and stopped

between her and Tom. Mary froze and tried to decide whether to scream, run, or both as the two men stepped off their motorcycles and blocked her path.

They stood side by side in front of Mary. Evil grins spread across their dirty faces and their large, snarly hands were opened wide. As they both took a step closer, she flinched and dropped her violin case to the sidewalk. Then she took a deep breath...

Just as Mary was about to scream, a man came running down the sidewalk from behind the two thugs and pushed them forcefully apart with both of his hands at the same time. He shoved the first man into the wall, while sending the other one sprawling off the sidewalk, into the street. He didn't even hesitate while passing between them and continuing directly toward Mary.

He stopped and quickly whispered in a deep voice, "Stay behind me and you will be safe." Then the stranger turned around and faced the two men who had now recovered and were past being surprised.

They straightened themselves up and headed toward Mary and her protector. The stranger took one step forward and firmly planted both of his feet on the sidewalk. In a loud voice of authority he announced, "Stop where you are."

The two men hesitated a moment while they looked him over.

"Looky here Carl, we have us a hero," was the first man's snide comment.

"Get out of our way," demanded the other. The colored, tattooed patterns moved on his cheek while he spoke. "My mommy told me never to hit a man with glasses."

The first man quickly pulled out a switchblade, clicked it open, and asked, "Are you really willing to fight for her?" while he waved the knife back and forth in the air.

"I am willing to die for her," replied the stranger. Then he pulled off his glasses and slipped them into a case in his shirt pocket. "The question you should both ask yourselves right now is, *are you?*"

Both men stood motionless while they sized him up

again.

Mary started shaking uncontrollably and couldn't breathe. A complete stranger was the only thing standing between her and the two thugs. She felt like she was going to pass out.

She couldn't believe it when the two men slowly backed away. Then they argued with each other while remounting their motorcycles and starting the engines.

As the two motorcycles sped away, the stranger pulled out his glasses and put them back on. After watching them drive completely out of sight, he turned back to Mary and gently asked, "Are you all right, Miss?"

Mary was still trembling and shaking uncontrollably. She stared up at the man, unable to answer.

He looked about her age, maybe a year or two older. His styled, dark-brown hair and grey, well-fitted, pinstripe vest and matching pants immediately set him apart from the ordinary men she had met, while his muscles were large enough to show under a puffed, dazzling white, long-sleeve shirt. He wore a silk tie, and his silver tie clasp, cuff links and the matching frames of his tinted designer glasses all sparkled in the sun.

If this was the man women were talking about at the university, it was all true. He was unbelievably good looking and Mary looked up at him, speechless.

"I am sorry that you had to go through that, Miss. Would you like to sit down?"

Mary's head was light and her knees were still shaking, so she nodded. He picked up the violin and helped Mary over to where Tom was sitting on his bench.

"Would you mind if this young woman sits down next to you for a few minutes, Sir? She has just been through quite a scare."

Tom scooted over and asked in a very surprised voice, "Is that yous, Mary?"

Mary whispered, "Yes, Tom" while sitting down next to him.

"I heard sumthins goin' on over there, but I never thought it was yous," declared Tom. "Who's this?"

After Mary hesitated, they both turned toward the stranger.

"My name is Lorin Delmar, Sir. You may call me Lorin if you wish. It's a pleasure to meet you." Lorin held out his hand until Tom found it and shook it.

"Names' Thomas E. Lincoln. You may call me Tom, and the pleasure is all mine, Sir," said Tom with better English and manners than Mary had ever heard.

After a pause, Lorin asked, "Is there anything I can get you, Miss?"

"Tom's my friend, I'll be all right now," answered Mary in a trembling voice.

Lorin silently waited until Mary finally stopped shaking and took a deep breath. She looked up and said, "Thank you, so much."

"It was my pleasure, Miss."

Then Mary admitted, "Just before I heard their motorcycles, I decided to stop wearing this dress and start wearing my normal clothes again. In a way, I guess I brought it on myself." Mary was quickly becoming an emotional mess while she spoke.

Lorin replied in a calming voice, "Beauty like yours should not be hidden, Miss, but there are times when it must be protected."

Mary didn't know what to say. No man had ever talked to her like that before! She could also tell that Lorin meant it. He was not using it as a line. By his earlier actions and the tone in his voice, she could tell that he was a gentleman and meant every word.

After Mary relaxed and was breathing easy, Lorin bowed slightly and excused himself, "It has been a pleasure meeting you, Miss, and you, Tom. Good afternoon to you both."

Lorin briskly turned and walked down the sidewalk toward the university while Mary stared after him in amazement. She couldn't help herself, she just stared at him with her mouth hanging wide open.

"Where's your manners, girl?" demanded Tom.

Mary, a little embarrassed, finally stopped staring and

closed her mouth. Then she turned toward Tom and asked, "What?"

"Can't yous tell, Mary? That was a real gentleman!" declared Tom. "Are you blind, child? And yous never properly interduced yo'self," Tom clarified.

Mary thought it sounded a little strange each time Lorin had called her "Miss."

"I know yous jes went through quite a deal here, but, if yous gonna get youself a prince, then yous gonna hafta learn some manners, girl," Tom told her as though he were the highest authority on the subject.

Mary stared at Tom in amazement. Then she turned and looked back down the sidewalk until Lorin was completely out of sight.

When Steven finished telling the Luthier about his platoon, they sat down together at a table in the library. It was still early afternoon but Steven's emotions were torn to shreds and he felt exhausted.

The Luthier let Steven relax and gathered his thoughts before asking, "Have you done any more reading in the New Testament?"

"I finished it last night," replied Steven. "But I have to admit, it didn't do a whole lot for me."

The Luthier looked surprised at first, then he asked, "Tell me what you didn't like."

"Just like I said before, I always liked Jesus, plain and simple. But then it seems to go on and on about people's problems and finishes up with flying scorpions tormenting everyone in the end. It almost starts feeling like the Old Testament; kill, kill, kill, problems, revenge and suffering." After Steven finished speaking, he was concerned about what the Luthier's response might be to his comments.

Instead of reacting, the Luthier encouraged him, "Tell me more. Go further."

"This last week I have really tried. I even started to pray. But the whole time I was on my knees asking who I am and who I really want to be, I dreamed of being like Jesus."

The Luthier's eyes widened.

Steven became passionate, "Not like Peter who denied him three times. Not like Paul who talked until people fell asleep. Not even like John, who told everyone how they would be tormented and suffer in the end if they were bad.

"I know this doesn't sound very humble, but I dream of being someone who would stand for Jesus against all odds. I dream of being someone who does so many good things that very few words would be necessary. Most of all, I dream of being someone who can encourage people to seek love and do good simply for the good feelings they would get, and never threaten them with torment and misery.

"But when I look at the whole book, I seem to lose that dream and wonder if Jesus is real after all."

The Luthier told him, "Stay here," while standing up and walking over to a safe sitting next to the shelves where the artifacts were.

The Luthier opened the door and pulled out a large wooden case. He placed it on the table and sat back down, "I find myself to be a very sceptical person also. Just like you, I feel like I need something I can hold in my hand so I can believe, or other times, so I can remember.

"Just like you needed the photograph, Tiny's boots, Ruckus' shirt and Slaughter's knife. I find those kinds of things are also very important to me. I have told you before that I am willing to accept truth from wherever it may come. As long as it is truth." The Luthier then pointed up to all the different religious books and ancient writings sitting on the shelves.

"I find that when preachers tell me that I must 'simply believe,' I am left wanting.

"There are times when I can look them in the eye and know that what they tell me is true, yet there are other times that I find myself like *doubting Thomas,* no matter how much I want to believe.

"I make the finest musical instruments I can, and I try

to make each one better than the last. I am trying for perfection some day, whatever that is, and it is different for different people.

"I have travelled around the world to visit a single, master instrument so I could hold it in my hands and hear its music for myself, with my own ears. I found that some instruments others claimed were magnificent, I found lacking. Other instruments that they found lacking, I found magnificent. But to decide for myself, I had to hold them in my hands and hear them myself."

Steven nodded.

The Luthier pulled a very small box out of the large one and handed it to Steven. "My father told me that there were no limits in life, even when it came to religion. He was a scientist, yet he believed in God. He told me that if Jesus was real two thousand years ago, he is still real today. So, I started searching."

The Luthier told Steven, "Open the box."

Steven saw two small, brown coins with ancient symbols resting on cushioned, red velvet.

"Widow's mites," said the Luthier. "Hold them in your hand."

The Luthier pulled an old Bible off a shelf and read the story of Jesus talking to the apostles about the widow who gave all she owned to the church. All she had was two mites.

"Those two coins you hold in your hand are mites, or *widow's mites* as they are called now. Those two mites were used as money when Jesus said those words. They could be the actual coins that the widow threw into the treasury, though odds say that they are not. Yet, they could be."

Steven looked at them very carefully while the Luthier read the story one more time. After he was finished, Steven nodded.

The Luthier pulled out another small container and handed it to Steven, "Put the mites back in the box and hold this in your hand."

Steven followed the Luthier's instructions, opened the

second box and picked up the silver coin that lay inside. He held it while the Luthier read the next story about Jesus.

"Peter was told to catch a fish and pay the money he found in it to the tribune for their taxes. That could be the actual coin Peter found inside the fish after pulling it from the water. It is the right age and the right denomination, though chances say that it is not the actual one. Yet it could be. You decide for yourself as you hold it in your hand."

Steven felt it with his fingers and wondered. Regardless, it was amazing to hold something that existed when Jesus was alive.

Next the Luthier pulled out a small leather bag and unfastened the string that held it closed. "Hold out your hands."

Steven replaced the silver coin and set it next to the other box containing the two mites, then he held out his hands. The Luthier slowly poured out thirty pieces of silver and commented, "Shekels of Tyre; the exact age that would have been sitting in the treasury when the priests pulled them out and paid them to Judas Iscariot so he would deliver Jesus into their hands."

Steven looked at them while the Luthier read the story of Jesus' betrayal and trial. When Steven inspected them closer, he saw that they were almost untouched, except that some of them had large scratches and nicks on their surfaces.

"Those could be the very thirty pieces of silver that Judas threw down in the temple courtyard before he hung himself. Odds say that they are not. Yet, you decide for yourself. But rest assured, if they are not the actual ones, they were within a hundred feet of Judas at the time. Either way, they are real and they *were* there."

Next, the Luthier read of the crucifixion as he pulled a spear head from the box. He read of the resurrection after placing two Roman helmets into Steven's hands. Then the Luthier went over to the shelf and pulled down a stack of ancient papers. Each was encased in clear plastic and Steven could tell that the words and pictures were all handwritten and very, very old. The Luthier sorted through them until he came to a group covered with Hebrew characters and pictures.

Steven could tell that each of the pictures was from a set of drawings of a large church or temple. The Luthier smiled when he found the one he was after and handed it to Steven. There was a large picture covering the entire page. It showed twelve oxen standing in a circle with a huge bowl of water resting on their backs.

"The Molten Sea," commented the Luthier, "It was built below ground level in Solomon's Temple. It was used to cleanse and baptize people in Old Testament days. Look against the wall."

Steven looked at the picture. Behind the Molten Sea, leaning against the back wall, were rows of large timbers. There were two groups, long and short and each had a hole bored through it. There were also pieces of rope hanging from the wall beside them. In front of the ropes were two beams that were assembled together to form a cross.

"Cedars of Lebanon," whispered the Luthier. "They were the ones used to crucify religious heretics."

Steven thought about the comment the Luthier had made about the wood used for his violin.

"I would show you the only piece of those timbers that survived the invasion of the Romans, but I used it for the belly of your violin.

Steven stared at the Luthier.

"You see, Steven, I believe that you are special. But I also believe that even if you succeed in your quest, you will need something more, at least for awhile. Something to remind you of what you may become.

"It may surprise you, but I agree with some of your comments. And while I read and learn all I can from the words of others, I always turn to Jesus and his simple teachings when I need *real* answers."

Steven then told the Luthier, "All these things are great, and I get the feeling that some of them really were there.

But to change and to be the man I want to be, I feel like I must *know*. Like you, I must really hold it in my hand. Is Jesus real? And what did he *really* stand for?"

The Luthier smiled back at Steven with a gleam in his eye. "I have one more thing to share with you, Steven. More precious than all of these other things combined.

"Some will say it is real. Some will say it is not. Some will understand, while others will not. Though you cannot hold what it represents in your hand, it has been more than enough for me."

Steven looked at the Luthier in amazement. What else could he have?

The Luthier pulled a video tape out of the large wood box and walked over to the same television and video player that Steven had watched Mary on in the bunkhouse. The video tape was plain and unmarked like the others on the shelf, and like the one the Luthier had played of Mary. Steven even wondered if it was the same tape at first, but then he noticed how the Luthier held it and looked at it. He handled it as though it were sacred.

The Luthier sat down next to Steven as the tape began to play.

Steven immediately recognized the man who was walking down a path toward an ancient city. It was Jesus! A very strange feeling came over Steven while he watched. The feeling that it was somehow real!

When Jesus spoke, it was in a different language and Steven could not understand the words.

There was soft, beautiful music floating through the air and Steven found that he didn't have to understand the words. As Steven looked into the faces of the people Jesus healed, he began crying. He began to understand. The tears flowed down his cheeks but he could not close his eyes.

The tape only showed Jesus a few times. Instead, it focused on the expressions of the people's faces as He touched them, or while His hands raised them up. It showed the blind man's eyes when he saw for the first time in his life. The leper as he looked down at his hands that Jesus had held. The cripple when Jesus lifted him up. The women, the children, the multitudes, and then Lazarus. All of them, one after the another. It showed their faces and the look in their eyes.

The tape lasted five minutes, but it changed Steven's life. He now *knew* why he had always wanted to do good. Now that he had seen the look on people's faces when they were helped by the only One who could, he understood.

Steven fell to his knees, sobbing and thanking the Luthier. "So much time I have wasted. So much that I have missed."

The Luthier looked back at Steven and nodded.

Steven was still on his knees and begged the Luthier, "Please, can I see it once more?"

"As many times as you like, Steven. Quality gets better the closer you look at it."

It was late at night when Steven finally rewound the tape for the last time and turned the television and video player off.

Steven never questioned if the tape was real. He only asked the Luthier, "Where did you get it?"

In the same profound voice that left no room for further questions, the Luthier answered, "I just did."

Chapter 29: Miracles

Mary stood in front of her mirror the morning after she was rescued by Lorin. She was wearing the same dark-blue dress and shiny-black shoes.

"Just imagine," she thought, "I almost gave up too soon!" She knew she was getting way too excited, but Lorin had passed the *knight-in-shining-armor*-test, hands down, and she couldn't believe how Tom had acted around him.

They had talked about some of the men Mary had dated before, but Tom had not approved of any of them. Before she left Tom's side the day before, he had told her, "Now there's a fish worth baitin' for."

Mary headed out the door smiling. Somehow, she felt safe walking down the steps and along the sidewalk. It made her feel good just knowing that there were men like Lorin around. Her step had a little lift to it when she passed Tom on her way to school. Tom could hear her coming and was grinning as big as a *Cheshire cat* when she greeted him with a cheerful, "Good morning."

As soon as Mary reached the campus, she walked into the drama department to see the results of the auditions for *Man of La Mancha*. The cast printout was not on the wall so she continued down the hall a little further. While she was looking around, she heard a voice float out of the auditorium. It caught her attention and she decided to see what was going on. Someone was singing *The Impossible Dream* and the voice was bolder and more courageous than any she had ever heard.

It seemed strange since the auditions were supposed to be over with the day before.

Halfway down the aisle Mary recognized Lorin standing
in the center of the stage. She stood motionless and tears
began forming in her eyes while he finished belting out
the phrase, "...to reach the unreachable star!"

"This guy is unbelievable," Mary thought, and she wasn't
just thinking about his voice.

The panel stood up and cheered, then the director flew
up on stage and vigorously shook Lorin's hand. "You are
Don Quixote!" he declared. "I am so glad you showed up
yesterday, even though you were late and the panel had
gone home. I had to talk them into coming back today,
but I think I speak for all of us when I say, 'you were
worth it'."

The five other members of the panel nodded and clapped
again.

The director asked, "What did hold you up yesterday,
Lorin?"

"I sincerely apologize for being late, Mr. Jones. I assure
you that I would have been on time if it wasn't a matter
of life and death."

The panel gave him a puzzled look, then they laughed
at his comment and went on their way.

Mary realized that *she* was the reason Lorin was late
the day before! She knew Lorin was talking about her,
even though he didn't mention her name.

She didn't want Lorin to see her since she was the one
responsible for making him late, so Mary quietly sat down
and waited until he walked off stage. Once he was gone,
she continued toward Mr. Jones and asked him for the
results of the tryout.

"You made it, Mary!" he exclaimed. "You are Dulcinea
and that man who just left is Don Quixote! You two will
be spending a lot of time together as soon as rehearsals
begin."

Mary's mouth dropped open. She knew that she had
done well as the witch in the last play but she was still
shocked. She had not only landed another acting role,
she was going to play opposite Lorin as the leading lady,
Dulcinea!

Mary's head swam and she dropped into one of the aisle seats.

"Are you okay, Mary?"

After a moment Mary looked up at the director and replied, "I'm fine, Mr. Jones."

A few seconds later, Mary flew back out of the seat and exclaimed, "I'm really fine!"

Steven started learning how to repair violins the morning after watching the video tape. The Luthier pulled out pieces of old, broken violins for Steven to practice on, then explained each of the breaks to him. The Luthier even studied Steven's violin, then broke some of the others the same way so Steven could practice the exact same repairs over and over.

Steven already had a rough idea what might be involved in fixing violins from his time spent watching the Luthier build his instrument. But he had no idea that it would take so many special tools, clamps and fixtures to accomplish it. And now he had to learn how to use each tool and technique to perfection before trying to work on his own instrument.

Steven learned and practiced, day after day, meticulously setting up the clamps, aligning the joints, and getting the pressure just right before he glued anything. The glue had to be made fresh every day and the violin shop could have no air movement, so the fan was turned off before each joint was made.

It was an eerie mixture of feelings as the room went still as death while he glued his violin back together, bringing it one step closer to life. Steven even commented to the Luthier how he felt like *Dr. Frankenstein* at times. They had many, diverse conversations while Steven learned each repair, but most of them were about how to help people and how to make them happy. Truly happy.

Eventually, Steven got to the point that he could make the repairs with very little assistance from the Luthier. It was then that they began talking even more seriously about religion.

"What is the best way to devote your life to God?" Steven finally asked the Luthier.

"That is a very good question," the Luthier answered. Then he added, "That's what my father would say when *he* didn't know the answer."

They both laughed at the comment before the Luthier continued, "I believe the answer is different for everyone. We cannot all shave our heads, lead a life of celibacy, hand weave our own clothes and walk barefoot through the world seeking Nirvana.

"Even Jesus had long hair, drank wine, wore sandals and broke a few rules. He even swung a mighty mean whip when necessary, so they say."

After the Luthier mentioned wine, Steven's eyes widened a little.

"Don't give in now, Steven, not the smallest bit. Jesus had a little more willpower than you."

After thinking about the question some more, the Luthier told him, "I still don't know all the reasons, but after I married Sheryl, I knew that I had to be a luthier."

The Luthier then asked Steven, "Which is the greater miracle? To feed five thousand people bread and fish, or to lift five thousand people's souls and hearts with music?"

Steven was amazed at the question at first. Then he pondered it and replied, "It would depend if the people knew where the bread and fish came from."

"Exactly!" replied the Luthier. "It took me over twenty years to figure that out and it took you about ten seconds. Now, if they know where the bread and fish come from, which miracle is greater?"

It only took Steven a moment to answer, "They are the same!"

The Luthier's face beamed and he looked Steven in the eyes, "You are very close to the end of this path, Steven."

Chapter 30: The Children

*M*ary went back to the director's office later that afternoon to ask him for Lorin's phone number and address. "So we can start rehearsing right away," she explained.

She felt nervous and giddy while the director looked up the information and wrote it on a piece of paper. Her hands trembled when she looked at Lorin's name.

"Thank you, Mr. Jones" she said as calmly as she could. Then she walked out of his office and into the hallway.

She read the address and noticed that Lorin's apartment was only three blocks further away from the university than hers. "That's why he was walking down the sidewalk," she thought to herself while heading toward the music room.

Mary opened the large locker and pulled out her violin with a little extra zeal. Then she quickly headed down the hall and out the door toward home.

"Maybe I'll walk the long way to the restaurant this afternoon," she innocently thought to herself with a smile. "No particular reason, I just feel like I need a little extra exercise and fresh air today." Mary blushed a little when she realized that she was not very good at lying to herself.

Less than half an hour later, Mary was walking down the front steps of her apartment building with her restaurant uniform in her arms.

"Hi, Mary," an elderly woman cheerfully greeted her.

"Oh, hello, Mrs. Jolley," responded Mary. Then she gave Mrs. Jolley a big hug.

The woman's face brightened, "It's so nice to see you

your cheery self again, Mary."

"I know," apologized Mary. "I'm sorry I've been so down lately, but things are looking up now."

Without any further explanation, Mary headed briskly up the sidewalk with her feet almost dancing as she went. Mary was a mature woman on the outside, but this afternoon she felt like the last twenty years of waiting had never happened and she was young again.

Her step slowed down as she approached the block where Lorin lived and she started cautiously looking around. She started feeling self-conscious while continuing up the sidewalk, trying to blend in with the scenery the best she could.

Mary wasn't sure what she expected to see or learn by going there that afternoon. In fact, she hoped Lorin wouldn't see her at all. She just wanted to know where he lived and anything else that she could find out about him.

Mary couldn't explain it to herself, but she also wanted to feel that she was near him. She knew it didn't make any sense, but that was how she felt, and that feeling grew stronger as she continued closer.

In the center of the apartment building matching Lorin's address was a playground. Mary turned and walked up the sidewalk, then started looking at all the children. She thought of how much she wanted children of her own and she suddenly felt thirty-seven years old again, and then some.

There was a wide mixture of ethnic backgrounds and ages. Some of the children were playing together in little groups while others were swinging or playing on the bars by themselves. As she continued up the sidewalk, she noticed that two little boys about six years old, were pushing one other and calling each other names. Nothing serious, but Mary thought that they might start hitting each other soon, so she walked over.

When Mary approached, they both stopped and stared at her with angry looks on their little faces.

"Who are you?" one of them asked.

"What do you want?" asked the other before Mary could even respond.

"My name is Mary," she answered. Then she told them in a kind voice, "Please don't fight."

Both of the little boys responded by facing each other again and giving each other a big shove, then a few more mean words.

Mary was shocked. She was trying to decide what to say next when both of the little boys turned toward the front door of the apartment building and yelled, "Lorin!"

What amazed Mary even more was that every other child on the playground said Lorin's name at the same time and was looking his way before the door had fully closed!

Mary quickly stepped behind a bush nearby and watched as all the children stopped what they were doing and ran toward him. Mary hoped that the bush she chose would conceal her well enough while she peered through and watched them. She wondered what would happen next.

Lorin was carrying a stack of books and he walked through the group of small children over to a bench in the middle of the playground. The children all gathered around him, and as soon as he sat down, they all went quiet.

A little girl held up her hand like she was in school. She said, "It's my turn! It's my turn!" as excitedly as Mary had ever seen anyone.

Lorin smiled and replied, "Yes it is, Alice."

Alice was bubbling over, she ran up and gave Lorin a big hug. Then she reached down and picked up a book lying on the ground by the bench.

"I need help reading," Alice announced as she held up the book for Lorin to see.

"And I would love to help you," replied Lorin.

Alice opened up her school book and began reading. She read very slowly and with much difficulty, stumbling over each word. Some of the other children even laughed until Lorin gave them a sad look. As soon as his eyes met theirs, they all immediately went silent and listened again.

Mary couldn't believe the hold and control that Lorin had over all of the children. She was also still trying to figure out what on earth was going on!

When Alice had finished one complete sentence, she looked up and Lorin smiled at her. "I am now going to tell all of you the secret of reading," Lorin said while looking around at each of the children.

Their eyes opened wide and they leaned forward. Lorin leaned down and whispered very quietly to them.

As hard as Mary tried, she could not hear what Lorin told the excited children surrounding him and she found herself yearning to hear his words. She was just as anxious to hear the secret as all the little children, and she almost stepped out from behind the bush. It was all she could do to keep her feet still.

When Lorin finished telling them the secret, they all stood back and nodded with smiles on their faces.

"Now try it again, Alice," Lorin prompted her in a gentle, confident voice.

Alice looked back down at her book for a minute, then she read the line again. This time it was perfect and flawless!

Mary almost fell over in disbelief.

"Try another line," offered Lorin, who sat smiling with admiration at Alice.

Alice looked back down at her book, and after a moment, she read the next sentence flawlessly. Mary's mouth hung wide open as she stared at Lorin from behind the bush. "No one can teach someone to read that fast," she thought to herself. "No one."

"I can do that!" blurted out one of the little boys that was fighting when Mary arrived at the playground.

"I know you can," replied Lorin, "But right now, it is still Alice's turn."

All the other children turned toward the little boy and nodded their heads.

"Don't forget, it's my turn next," the little boy said in a humble tone. He was almost crying.

Lorin told him, "I haven't forgotten, Richard." Then he

gave the little boy a smile and put his hand gently on his shoulder. The boy brightened back up, then waited patiently with the rest of the children while Alice read more from her book.

"Now, will you help me with my homework, Alice?"

Alice looked a little intimidated at first, but then she meekly nodded with wide innocent eyes.

Lorin pulled out one of his books and opened it. Mary could see that it was the script from *Man of La Mancha*!

After telling the children some of the story, Lorin read a few lines of Don Quixote in character. All of the children's faces lit up and the whole mood changed with his words. Next, Lorin lifted Alice up on the bench so she would be standing up and looking down at him. He turned the script toward Alice and pointed at a line.

Alice hesitated for a minute, then she delivered her line with confidence and in character! Lorin's face beamed and he smiled at Alice while pointing to Alice's next line in the script after delivering his own. When Alice had finished her next line, Lorin softly started singing the song "Dulcinea".

None of the children laughed. None of them turned and walked away. Each and every one of them stood or sat silently, spellbound by his song.

While Lorin continued singing, Mary dreamed that *she* was standing on the bench looking down into his eyes.

"If Lorin were the *Pied Piper of Hamelin*," Mary told herself, "I would gladly follow his music into the sea."

When Lorin finished the song, the entire playground was silent and still.

The Luthier looked Steven's violin over very carefully. Steven had just finished removing the clamps and cleaned the extra glue off the last repair. Each and every crack and seam was tightly held together with the finest hide glue joints possible.

The Luthier nodded in approval while he finished looking it over. "No one could have done better," he commented.

Steven let out a long sigh of relief.

"The touch-up process is next," declared the Luthier. "Would you like to take a break and have some fun before we go on?"

Steven smiled. He needed a break. It had taken him weeks to repair the violin.

"As you probably have guessed, there is almost anything you can imagine between this violin shop and the valley. If you could do anything in the world right now, what would it be?"

"Paint," replied Steven as tears filled his eyes. "I have always wanted to paint...

"Look what I did in school today," six-year-old Steven announced as the screen door closed behind him.

Steven couldn't find his mother anywhere, so he walked over to where his father sat drinking a beer in his large, soft, easy chair in front of the television. There were already two freshly crumpled cans sitting on the floor beside him and a bottle of something harder waiting for later on the TV tray.

"Look what I did today," Steven cheerfully repeated, just in case his father hadn't heard him the first time.

His father glanced at the picture in Steven's small hands. Steven was wiggling the bright, blue ribbon attached to it.

His father turned back to the television with a grunt.

"When I grow up, I want to be an artist." Steven smiled while looking up at his father.

His father turned back toward Steven and his face immediately turned mean.

"Let me see that painting," he demanded. Steven's father remained in his chair while he extended his arm and held out his hand.

Steven didn't know what to think, but he knew it wouldn't be good by the look on his father's face. Yet, he knew that he could not refuse.

Steven's little hands trembled. His father grabbed the painting and turned it around so Steven could plainly see the picture while it was torn in half.

His father put the two pieces together and tore them up again, before crumpling them into a ball. "Artists are poor," he grunted.

He dropped the pieces of Steven's painting to the floor and turned back toward the television without saying another word. Then he started drinking his beer again. Steven looked down at the pieces and silently began to cry.

Without taking his eyes off the television, his father added, "And throw that mess in the garbage."

Steven thought about how poor *they* were, but he knew that he couldn't say anything or he'd get beat. But he still stood motionless. He just couldn't seem to move, while looking down at his torn and crumpled picture on the floor.

His father turned back with his mean, unshaven face and yelled, "I told you to throw that away!'

Maybe it was the one second that Steven hesitated, or maybe it was the single tear on his left cheek. His father flew out of the chair and slapped Steven to the ground with the back of his large, right hand. Blood immediately flowed from Steven's mouth and nose, where his father's knuckles had sunk into his face.

His mother came running in the front door just as Steven's head hit the floor. She screamed, "Stop it!" Then stood defiantly between Steven and his father.

It was an hour later before his mother opened her purple, swollen eyes and tried to wipe the blood away so she could see. The white of her left eye was red and she couldn't open her right eye at all when she looked up. Steven had been kneeling silently above her the entire time.

Even though Steven's eardrum was broken with the second blow from his father and there was blood running out of it, he had not uttered a word. He had picked up and thrown away every piece of the painting before he returned to his mother's side and waited for her to wake up.

Her limbs were badly bruised and she could barely stand, but Steven's mother placed Jim's dinner on the

TV tray at seven o'clock just like he expected her to, and Steven never painted another picture.

The Luthier led Steven around to the back of the violin shop, then up some winding stairs to the second level. Steven had never been to this part of the shop before, and he had wondered what was hiding behind the door.

"Everything," was the obvious answer as the Luthier swung the door open. But what caught Steven's attention first were two large painting easels standing right in the middle of the large, spacious room. Between them was an elaborate, open faced cabinet full of paints, brushes, and artist supplies of every description. In front of each easel was an adjustable height chair. It was as though the Luthier had expected Steven's request.

Steven already anticipated the answer, "I just did," and didn't bother asking. He smiled and walked over to the left easel while the Luthier took the right one.

"Would you like a lesson, or would you prefer to dive right in?" asked the Luthier.

Steven stopped to think. Then he answered, "One general lesson first."

The Luthier smiled, "Choose a topic or subject. Anything that pops into your head and I'll paint it."

Steven responded, "A father."

The Luthier's eyes went wide and he skewed his face a little. "What kind of father?"

"Just an average, everyday father," replied Steven.

The Luthier smiled and replied, "That is a challenge," as he grabbed a very large canvas and placed it on his easel.

The Luthier spoke constantly while he painted, telling Steven the importance of seeing the whole picture in his mind. Then about freeing himself until each brush stroke becomes deliberate and expresses the image as well as the philosophy of each of the colors.

In less than forty-five minutes the Luthier stood back and said, "Voilà!" He smacked his lips together and threw out his hand and fingers, signifying magnificence. Then

he declared, "*Molto bella!*" with a large smile as he turned
back toward Steven for his reaction.

The painting was a large, colorful portrait of Homer
Simpson painted in the style of Vincent Van Gogh.

Steven had to laugh, and he asked, "*Homer Simpson* is
an average, everyday father?"

"Yes," replied the Luthier. "When it comes to being a
father, he is honest and sincere, but doesn't have a clue
what he's doing."

They both laughed together after the comment, but only
because they knew that, sadly, it was true.

After they settled down, Steven walked over and grabbed
a medium sized canvas and placed it on his easel. "What
should I paint?"

The Luthier answered, "Close your eyes."

Steven closed his eyes.

"Paint the first image that comes into your mind when
you think of the word 'people'."

The Luthier watched in amazement as Steven
immediately picked up a brush and began painting.
Steven finished in about the same amount of time it took
the Luthier to paint his Homer Simpson.

It was a street scene in Vietnam showing the poorer
market area of a city. There were clotheslines hanging
above the street and people walking or standing in front
of each of the vendors there. The colors of the people's
clothing standing out in the bright rays of the sun shining
between the dingy buildings were unbelievable. It left
the distinct impression of hope and beauty in a miserable
world.

"When was the last time you painted?" asked the Luthier.

"When I was six," responded Steven.

The Luthier stood back and stared.

"You will have no problem earning a living," declared
the Luthier in a slow, confident voice as he shook his
head in admiration and amazement. The Luthier could
not believe what he was looking at and he continued
staring at the painting in awe.

"Your turn," said Steven with a big smile. "Paint

something to go with Homer."

The Luthier picked up another large canvas. Within an hour, he declared much more humbly than the first time, "Finished."

It was a chair, painted in the style of Van Gogh again. Resting on it was a can of *Duff* beer and a donut with pink icing, covered with colored sparkles. Steven smiled and laughed in approval while he placed another canvas on his own easel and closed his eyes.

"A boat," said the Luthier.

When Steven opened his eyes, the Luthier held up four tubes of paint that he had randomly pulled off the rack. "And paint it with only these," he added.

The colors were white, orange, burnt sienna, and chestnut.

Steven was a little surprised, but he looked at the colors and closed his eyes again. He reopened them after only a second had gone by and began painting.

The Luthier watched while Steven's brushes flashed back and forth from the palette to the canvas. There was not the slightest hesitation in his hand as each color flowed from his brush and filled the canvas with peace and serenity.

Steven stood back and laid down his palette after only half an hour.

The painting was of a Chinese junk. The colors and setting effortlessly pulled the Luthier into a serene, peaceful mood. It was magnificent and unbelievable.

"How many paintings did you paint as a child?" asked the Luthier, in disbelief.

"One," quietly replied Steven. "My father tore it up."

The Luthier sat down on his chair and wept.

"It's Richard's turn now," Lorin exclaimed, and all of the children surrounding the bench seemed to wake up from the trance his song had put them in.

Richard eagerly held up a baseball and announced, "I want to be a pitcher."

Lorin took the baseball and held it in his hand. He

closed his eyes and worked his fingers over its smooth, white leather surface, feeling the worn, red threads that held it together. He turned it over and over in his hand.

"Baseball is a wonderful game!" he exclaimed with a smile as he opened his eyes and looked into each of the children's faces. "The feeling of accomplishment when your bat connects with your very first hit." Lorin pretended to take a swing.

"The thrill of hitting your first home run and winning the game!" Lorin added while pretending to watch a ball sail far away into the air.

"Green grass, fresh air and sunny afternoons with your friends all around you. The wonderful smell of popcorn and cotton candy floating in the stands. Your mother and father sitting on the bleachers cheering you on and yelling your name so everyone else can hear how proud they are of you.

"And best of all, to be the pitcher!" Lorin announced as he stood up. "Not only do you get to hit, you get to throw the ball every time your team is in the field. It's up to you, more than anyone else, who wins the game!" Lorin was now tossing the baseball up in the air, over and over again. All of the children's faces smiled and followed the ball up and down.

Mary didn't even care for baseball and she was ready to grab the ball and start playing with it.

Lorin tossed the ball to Richard and excitedly told him, "Wait here!" Then he ran back into the apartment building.

The children stayed where they were and waited while Mary watched the door and wondered what was next.

Lorin came back out a few minutes later carrying a mattress! He walked over to the wall of the apartment building and leaned the mattress against it.

All of the children seemed amazed and Richard asked, "Is that your bed?"

Lorin nodded while he pulled out a large marking pen. He drew a circle in the middle of it a little smaller than home plate.

"The most important part of being a great pitcher, like so many good things, is practice, practice, and more practice," Lorin informed the children while they followed him over to the mattress.

He stood back and showed Richard how to throw the baseball while the other children watched his every move and how he held the ball. Even the little girls were interested and their eyes never left him the whole time. Neither did Mary's.

When the lesson was over, Lorin turned around and announced, "All of you can take turns throwing the baseball, but remember that Richard is in charge, and he will make sure you all get a chance."

All of the children nodded and smiled, including Richard.

"You may use my mattress until I get back. And if you like, I will find another one that you can use anytime."

With that, Lorin walked over to the bench, picked up his books and headed down the sidewalk toward the university.

Mary watched in amazement while Richard practiced pitching the ball a few more times, then as he gave each of the other children a turn and helped them. Even the boy that he had been fighting with earlier!

Mary stood in front of her mirror late that night after work. It had been a long, tiring evening at the restaurant and she was worn out, but thoughts of Lorin had been running through her mind ever since she watched him with the children.

She took a good, long look at herself. There was no doubt in her mind that Lorin would make a wonderful father for her children.

Before she turned out the light, a thought struck her. A thought that had never crossed her mind in thirty-seven years, "Am *I* good enough for the *real* man of my dreams?"

Chapter 31 : An Angel

A few days later, Mary stopped and talked with Tom. "What should I do now, Tom?" she asked.

"Do?" he asked.

"Where do I go from here?"

"If yous talking abouts Lorin agin', go easy," responded Tom. "Don' go rippin his lips off with yer hook."

Mary was sure that Tom was referring to the *more than adequate* amount of perfume she had put on that morning. She knew how well Tom could smell; he had probably known it was her over half a block away.

Maybe she was trying too hard, too fast. After all, Lorin had not even seen her since the afternoon he saved her from the two motorcycle thugs. She hadn't seen him since the day she stood behind the bushes watching him with the children at the playground. For the last few days Mary had only heard about Lorin everywhere she went.

In the halls at the university, she heard women talking about how good-looking he was. Every time she walked into a restroom she heard Lorin's name mentioned at least once, if not a dozen times. They talked about the things he said or how he helped them in some way. They talked about how polite and well mannered he acted and how brilliant he was in class while they added just a little more makeup in front of the mirrors. Even women who normally hated men, seemed to be drawn to Lorin.

Mary debated Tom's advice. Then she thought about the upcoming play and realized that she would be spending a lot of time with Lorin, starting the following Wednesday, when rehearsals began. That made her feel better. After all, it was only a few days away.

"All right, Tom," Mary replied, "I'll take it easy."

Mary saw Lorin that Friday afternoon. She was responsible for turning off the lights and locking up the music department because she was the last teacher giving private lessons. She noticed a light on in one of the rooms and she was curious who was still practicing. Mary looked through the small window just in time to see Lorin close the lid on a violin case.

"This is unbelievable, and too good to be true," Mary thought while she watched him fasten the latches.

Mary couldn't help herself. She quickly walked back down the hall and turned around. She felt a little childish while standing there, but she timed it so she walked right up to the door just as Lorin opened it.

As he came out, Mary exclaimed, "Pardon me!" while acting a little startled.

"No pardon is necessary, Miss," replied Lorin with a smile forming on his face.

Mary looked up at him. "Wow," she thought to herself. "Now I know how it feels when the tables are turned." She was thinking about how some of the shy men's faces looked when they had asked her out.

Mary gathered herself back together and apologized, "I'm sorry for not introducing myself properly, Lorin. My name is Mary Anderson, and you may call me Mary, if you like." Then she held out her hand.

Lorin gently took Mary's hand in his and lifted it as he bowed slightly; almost as though he were going to kiss it. Mary blushed a little, because she wished he would. But then he gently shook it and responded, "The pleasure is mine, Mary."

"Do you play the violin?"

Mary then realized how stupid the question was after looking down at his violin case. She wanted to kick herself.

"A little," was his reply. "My father bought this violin a long time ago and I am just starting to learn how to play it. It's required that I play an instrument while I'm here at the university to get my degree."

Mary nodded. She was teaching three students for that very same reason. Then she thought, "This really is too good to be true."

"Do you have a teacher here, yet? I've taught violin lessons for quite awhile but I've never you seen before."

For all his good manners and politeness, Lorin couldn't help but smile at Mary's mixed up words.

Mary let out a little gasp and turned bright red as Lorin replied, while trying to keep a straight face, "I just transferred here a few days ago."

"I am such a clod!" Mary thought to herself while trying to regain her composure. She decided not to talk again until the butterflies left her stomach.

"May I walk you to the door?" asked Lorin, breaking the silence.

"Yes, please," she responded.

Mary felt like a little schoolgirl as she grabbed Lorin's free hand and walked by his side. It seemed like the ladylike thing to do as she thought of Tom's remarks about manners and men like Lorin.

They walked silently toward the exit. Mary was holding on tight but Lorin almost seemed a little timid about holding her hand.

Halfway down the hall, Mary froze dead in her tracks. All of the blood drained out of her face and she turned and stared up at Lorin when she realized that *she* was the one who had grabbed *his* hand. She had never stopped to think about it before, but now she realized *it* could be a real possibility.

Lorin turned with a puzzled look. Mary was shaking and her eyes were staring wide open with fright. She was trying to decide whether to let go of Lorin's hand or not.

"Are you married?" she gasped out.

Lorin's face relaxed and he smiled, "No. Are you?"

Mary's face flushed. Then she timidly smiled and replied, "No."

Mary then thought of all the *nice* guys she had dated over the years. She had already made a complete fool of herself, so she decided to push her luck a little further and added the word, "Never."

Lorin responded by slowly walking again and replying, "Neither have I."

Mary almost did a touchdown ritual right there in the hall while she screamed the word, "Yes!" in her mind. But instead, she continued to walk to the door as calmly as she could while still holding firmly onto Lorin's hand with a big smile on her face.

While Steven skillfully and delicately used the fine varnish brushes to touch-up the violin, he told the Luthier, "I have decided to dedicate my life to God."

The Luthier smiled, "I have been waiting for you to say that."

Steven smiled too. Even though he felt like he was giving up so much, he knew the rewards would be worth it if he could only touch people's lives and teach them of Jesus. He finally felt like he was now on the right path in his life.

After a moment of silence and seeing the look on Steven's face, the Luthier asked, "Remember how you asked me 'what else' I wasn't telling you?"

Steven nodded.

"I think it is time now," the Luthier announced.

Mary could hardly contain herself while she stood next to Tom, watching Lorin disappear out of sight. Lorin had not only walked her to the front door of the music building, but he had held her hand and talked with her all the way back to where Tom was.

"Tom, you were right. Lorin is the perfect gentleman." Mary announced before sitting down.

Tom just smiled, "I told yous, never gives up hope, Mary."

"You sure did, Tom." Then Mary gave him a big hug, "You sure did."

* * *

The next day, Mary arrived at work early, hoping to catch a moment with Cindy before the restaurant opened.

When Cindy walked in, Mary pulled her aside and told her all about Lorin. Cindy was excited and jealous at the same time.

"So when do I get to meet him?" she asked.

"I'm not sure," Mary responded, "We talked a lot and he's very friendly, but he hasn't asked me out yet."

"Why didn't you ask him, Dummy?" Cindy scolded her.

"Me, ask him?" Mary questioned.

"When you have a good one bitin', reel him in," replied Cindy. "If he's older than you are and has never been married, he's either gay or too shy to ask."

Mary looked back at Cindy in surprise. "There's no way!"

"Then you're going to have to do the reeling, Honey," was Cindy's advice.

Mary spent the whole evening debating between Tom's advice to take it easy and Cindy's advice to reel him in. She drove herself crazy thinking about it while trying to get to sleep.

Once Mary was asleep, it just got worse and much more complicated. She dreamed all night long about Steve, the greasy motorcycle guy.

When Mary got up the next morning and did her shopping, she found herself looking around every corner, trying to see *him*. She also found herself turning around a dozen times while she walked home with her groceries because she thought she saw *him* out of the corner of her eye. That night at work, every time she walked around the wall by the waitress' booth she expected to see him sitting there, complete with his leathers, chains, and tattoos. But also looking at her with *those* eyes.

When she laid her head on her pillow the next night and tried to sleep, she woke right back up and started kicking and screaming in frustration because she was dreaming of Steve instead of Lorin.

The next morning was Sunday and Mary struggled out of bed, staggered into the bathroom and looked at herself. Her hair was tangled in knots and she had bags under her eyes.

She leaned over for a closer look and exclaimed, "Mirror, mirror over my sink, wake me up and help me think!" It was the same line she had used during spring finals, only this morning it was for a different reason.

She had tossed and turned all night while dreaming about Steve again. She dreamed about doing everything with him, from piercing her body with chains and covering herself with tattoos, to riding away with him on the back of his motorcycle to some dungeon somewhere.

There had been many dreams and nightmares over the years after Mary's parents died in the accident. She was used to nightmares and they really weren't a problem for her. The real problem with this nightmare was, she enjoyed it. No matter how bad her dreams of him were, she was still happy!

She pulled out some mascara and painted a large tattoo on her cheek. It was just like the one in her last dream, only now it made her sick to look at it.

"What is wrong with me?" she almost screamed. She clenched her fists and stomped her feet.

She looked straight into the reflection of her eyes and told herself, "Get a grip. There is no true love at first sight."

Mary stood silent for a minute, looking at herself in the mirror.

She was not satisfied with the statement, so she decided to rephrase it, "There *is* true love, and that love gets better and better the more you look at it." Mary looked at herself again, then thought of Lorin. She liked the sound of it and smiled, since she felt like she was well on her way to *that* kind of love.

After scrubbing off the mascara tattoo and putting on her nicest church dress, she headed out the door with her scriptures in her hand.

Tom and Mary went to different churches, but about once a month Mary would walk over to Tom's apartment and take him with her. During the holidays and on special occasions she would also take him across town to attend mass. Tom and Mary were so different, yet they loved and respected each other more than most family members would.

Mary knocked on Tom's door with her special rap and, about twenty minutes later, Tom appeared in the doorway saying, "Guess ol' Tom could use some Jesus this mornin', Mary."

Tom could tell that Mary was smiling when she grabbed his arm and he smiled also. They didn't talk much while they walked, they just enjoyed the fresh morning air together and said "hello" to everyone they met along the way.

After Mary and Tom were seated on one of the back benches, Mary looked up. Lorin was sitting next to the pastor!

"Tom, you'll never guess who's sitting on the stand!" Mary tried to whisper, but it came out fairly loud and a few people turned their heads and looked back at Mary and Tom.

"De Pope?" asked Tom in a loud voice.

There were a few suppressed giggles after Tom's remark, then they turned back around when they heard the microphone click on.

"It's Lorin," whispered Mary as the prelude music stopped and the pastor stood up.

He introduced Lorin as a new member who had just moved into the neighborhood and invited Lorin to stand up and make a few comments.

Lorin spoke for about three minutes, and it was all about Jesus. When he walked down the stairs and sat on a bench near the front, there wasn't a dry eye in the room.

Tom turned to Mary and told her, "Now thars a man who *loves* Jesus."

Mary had not been on a date with Lorin yet, but she knew she loved him. Not for love at first sight. She knew she loved him for the kind of man he was and what he stood for.

After the service, Mary tried to work her way up to the front where Lorin was, but it seemed like everyone at the church wanted to speak with him. Tom lingered behind since he didn't like being in the middle of so many people. Mary decided that as soon as she could talk with Lorin, she was going to invite him over to eat Sunday dinner with Tom and her.

Finally, after meekly making her way through most of the people, Mary could hear Lorin talking. He was accepting an invitation to eat dinner at an older couple's home that evening.

Mary's heart sank. She didn't think Lorin had seen her yet, so she worked her way back through the crowd to where Tom was standing. She was very disappointed.

Mary gently grabbed Tom's hand and walked out the side door of the church with him. She walked very slowly once they were outside and Tom could tell that something was wrong.

Mary finally told Tom, "He's just too popular, Tom. I couldn't even get up to him in time to ask him over for dinner."

"That's all rights, Mary," answered Tom. "Yous jes keeps up hopin, and have a little patience. Mens like that don' jes jump into things."

While they walked along the side of the building, Tom added, "'Sides, Mary, I'm 'vited over t' Samuel's tonight."

When Mary and Tom reached the back corner of the church, Mary looked up and saw Lorin coming toward them from the other side.

"Good morning, Mary. Hello, Tom," Lorin greeted them with a smile.

Mary thought that there was no way he could have possibly gotten out of that crowd so quickly, and the image of Lorin pushing the pastor aside and throwing old ladies left and right ran through her mind. She couldn't hold back a smile when she thought about it and looked up at him.

"Hello, Lorin," Mary replied.

"I was hoping to talk with you inside, but when I turned around, you were gone."

"I didn't think you had noticed me," admitted Mary.

Lorin's face became serious, "I would notice your beautiful face through the fog on a starless night."

Mary's mouth dropped open and she was speechless. If this wasn't *Prince Charming*, then he didn't exist! She also thought about standing behind the bushes at the playground and wondered if what Lorin said was really true.

Mary still hadn't fully closed her mouth when Lorin asked, "I know this is sudden, but would you allow me to buy you dinner and talk?"

Mary looked like she was under a spell as she meekly answered, "Yes."

"Is tomorrow night too soon?" asked Lorin.

Mary pulled herself together and answered, "I'm scheduled to work tomorrow, but I will reschedule if you would like."

Lorin shook his head, "The last thing I want to do is cause you any extra work or inconvenience. What is your next night off?"

"Tuesday."

"Then, may I pick you up at six-thirty on Tuesday?"

Mary simply nodded. After a second, she told him, "223 University Avenue, number 21."

Lorin seemed to make a mental note of it, then asked, "Now, may I ask another favor?"

Mary nodded again. She felt like one of the little children at the playground staring up at him in a trance.

Lorin then turned toward Tom, "Tom, would you mind if I walked with you and allowed Mary to stay for the next meeting?"

Tom smiled, "It would be my honor, Sir."

Mary didn't know what to say while Lorin excused Tom and himself. But the sight of them walking together made her feel good and she found herself secretly hoping that they would both be important men in her life for a very long time.

After they were gone, Mary went back into the church. When she entered the chapel, she noticed that there was a commotion up front.

One of the ladies turned and asked, "Mary, did you see where Lorin went?"

Mary turned back toward the door and answered, "He headed down the sidewalk a couple of minutes ago. Why?"

The lady exclaimed, "We were all talking with him when he suddenly declared, 'I have to talk with an angel!' Then he headed straight out the back. He said it in such a way that no one dared stop him!"

Even though Lorin hadn't mention her by name, Mary knew that he was talking about her. This time, Mary smiled.

Chapter 32: The Pond

$\mathcal{M}$ary found herself daydreaming all through the rest of the meeting.

Every time something was said about being good, it made her think of Lorin. When they mentioned Moses parting the Red Sea, she thought of Lorin courageously pushing the two men apart. When she heard a comment about "standing for the right," she remembered him on the stage singing "The Impossible Dream." At the mention of Jesus, Mary thought of the children gathered around Lorin at the playground.

To Mary's own surprise, she found herself whispering halfway through the benediction, "He's too good to be true! He's too perfect!"

Mary opened her eyes to see if anyone had heard her. Either they hadn't, or they were being polite, so she closed her eyes again and thought more about Lorin.

Mary knew that perfection was what she had always dreamed of, but now she wondered if it was what she really wanted. She began thinking about what it would be like living with the perfect man and it reminded her of the date with Harold Parker. Lorin was different, yet would she have to worry about everything she said or did, and then feel guilty if she wasn't perfect in every way? She found herself wondering what kind of car he drove, and if he would care how she placed her feet on the carpet.

She thought about the upcoming date on Tuesday and what she might find out about him. "After all, that's what dates are for," she reassured herself.

While Mary walked home, she thought about the other men she had dated and all the things she had found out about them after only one evening together. She wondered if there was anything Lorin could do that would disqualify him, or that could be added to the "negotiable" list that used to hang on her wall.

"If he really is as wonderful as he seems, I wonder what he thinks of me?" she wondered.

She questioned whether a *Prince Charming* would have made a list of his own for his princess. She began looking at her own life as she approached her apartment.

Mary looked at the old, paint-peeled building while turning the rusty door handle. Mary was an orphan. She had never thought of herself that way before, but in reality she was, and she lived in a poor neighborhood. She wondered what Lorin might think of it with his obvious breeding, and it really started bothering her.

Mary thought about the fairytales and the way her father had always called her a princess. It made her feel a little better, but she still thought about her own list more seriously now.

As she walked up the narrow steps, she couldn't think of any problems she might have with anyone's "must" and "must not" columns, but by the time she reached her apartment door with two deadbolts and a chain, she thought about the "negotiable" things.

"Age" was the first item listed under "negotiable." Lorin looked a little older than she was, but he loved children and would probably want some of his own. Mary was thirty-seven and she knew that it was starting to become an issue if he wanted even a medium-sized family. She knew that Lorin could choose a woman of any age if he wanted to.

"Looks" was the next item on her list, and Mary walked into the bathroom and critically looked at her short hair. She wished again that she had left it long and flowing like it used to be, but she was just glad that she had not gone back to her plain clothes and no makeup before meeting Lorin.

She walked into the bedroom and looked around. All she owned of any real value was her moderate-priced violin and a few rows of school textbooks. Her income could be quite reasonable after college, but she still had very little money or *dowry* to add to a marriage. Then, if she stayed at home having children, she realized that she couldn't offer much financial assistance, except by giving music lessons or tutoring. It would be nice if Lorin were well-off, yet she would feel much better if she could contribute more.

Mary then took a good look at how she lived. She began to realize that she had a lot of little habits that could be added to any *Prince Charming's* "negotiable" or "not desirable" list.

It made her wonder what she wanted out of life now. Did she really want to be perfect and marry the perfect man?

Mary sat down to eat her simple lunch at her small table and thought about it. By the time she was finished, she decided to go for a walk and try to find the answer...

Mary leaned over and cautiously poked her head around the corner of Lorin's apartment building. She was still wearing her long church dress and had to hold the hem back behind the wall so no one would see her. She was sure that someone as religious as Lorin wouldn't approve of her wearing pants on Sunday.

Lorin was sitting on the bench in the middle of the playground next to a teenage girl. The girl was dressed inappropriately for any day of the week. The other children were playing at a distance and seemed unconcerned. There was a book lying on the bench between them and Lorin was talking. After watching them for a minute, Mary noticed that they were both knitting.

Lorin spoke quietly and the other children seemed to purposely stay at a distance so they could not overhear what was being said. It seemed strange to Mary. Not that he was knitting and talking with a teenage girl, but that Lorin was not showing all the rest of the children how to knit at the same time. Then the girl turned. She was crying.

Mary watched while the girl opened her heart up to Lorin. She couldn't hear what was being said but she could tell that the conversation was very serious. Lorin listened and knitted while the girl went through all kinds of emotions. When the girl's voice raised and became angry, Lorin responded with a sad look and by quietly shaking his head. The girl immediately settled down, then started crying again.

The girl was still crying after she finished talking. Lorin remained silent for a few minutes, then looked up from his knitting and said a few words. She responded by smiling. It amazed Mary how the girl's face changed while Lorin spoke, and she wondered what he could have said to make such a difference.

They looked back down at the book together and continued knitting until the girl's eyes were completely dry. Then Lorin closed the book and looked straight at Mary.

Mary pulled her head back behind the corner of the building by reflex. She couldn't decide what to do next. But after a moment, she realized that she had no choice. She straightened herself up, put on a smile and walked out from behind the building.

Lorin finished putting away his knitting and stood up as Mary approached, "Good afternoon, Mary. Jasmine, this is Mary Anderson. Mary, I would like you to meet Jasmine Wilkes."

They shook hands, then Jasmine quietly walked away without saying a word. It struck Mary as odd, how reserved she became the moment she was no longer alone with Lorin.

As soon as Jasmine was gone, all the children's eyes turned toward Lorin. He held up his hand as though they should continue playing, and they did. Mary still couldn't believe how much influence he had over them.

"What brings you to our neighborhood this time?" Lorin asked.

Mary turned and looked over at the bush she had stood behind when she had watched him with the children. It had looked so much fuller from the other side. There was no way Lorin could have missed seeing her! She reluctantly turned back and blushed.

Mary thought about it for a moment. She almost tried to come up with some kind of excuse, but when she looked at Lorin's face, she realized that she couldn't. He had just as much control over her as he did with the small children. There was something about him that made it impossible for her to answer any other way than the simple truth.

"You do," she shyly admitted.

Lorin picked up his knitting and the book. "Jasmine wanted to learn how to knit like her grandmother did when she was still alive. She was the only person that Jasmine felt ever listened, so I told her that I would learn how to knit with her."

"And listen," added Mary.

"Exactly," Lorin replied with a smile.

As Mary followed Lorin over to the front door of the apartment building, she asked, "What is the secret of reading?"

Lorin stopped and replied, "Can I answer that question a little later?"

Mary responded with a puzzled look.

"And would you mind waiting here for just a moment?" he added.

"All right," Mary curiously answered.

When Mary turned around and looked at the children, she noticed that most of them were looking right at her and smiling. It gave her the feeling that it was now her turn with Lorin and they didn't mind at all. It gave her an idea.

When Lorin came back out, Mary took his hand and led him back over to the bench in the middle of the playground.

As soon as they sat down, she turned toward him and announced with childlike innocence, yet with the sincerity of a full grown woman, "I want to be a princess."

Lorin looked stunned at first. Then, after his face relaxed, he smiled and replied, "You already are one."

"But I'm an orphan and I live in an old apartment building," Mary explained.

Lorin shook his head, "That doesn't matter."

"But I have short hair." Mary reached up and grabbed her hair with both of her hands. Then she added, "No jewelry except these two earrings, and I wait on tables."

"It doesn't matter," Lorin replied again.

"I'm thirty-seven years old, I bite my nails, and I hang my nylons and underwear in the shower!" Mary's eyes went wide; she couldn't believe she had just said that.

Lorin smiled and looked around the playground before standing up.

Mary apologized, "You see, I'm really not a princess."

Lorin put his thumb and finger into his mouth and whistled so loud that it almost hurt Mary's ears.

All the children came running at once, even a few more came dashing out of the apartment building a moment later.

As soon as they were all standing in a circle, Lorin announced, "This is my friend, Mary Anderson."

The children cheerfully greeted her, "Hi, Mary."

Lorin turned and looked at every child, "Mary needs the answer to a very important question."

All of the children went quiet.

"Take a good look at Mary, from the top of her head to the tip of her toes."

All of the children did as he requested. Then he asked, "Is Mary a princess?"

A smile spread across every child's face. "Yes!" they happily cheered. Then they ran up, one after the other, and gave Mary more hugs than she had ever received in her life.

"You see, Mary. It's obvious," Lorin told her.

The way the children all smiled and by the look in their eyes, it made Mary feel like she was a real princess. She couldn't help looking back at them and smiling.

Lorin thanked them all, then he took Mary by the hand and led her over to the edge of the playground.

Mary turned and asked, "Why didn't you say anything when I was hiding behind the bush the other day?"

"Because a gentleman should always think about other people's feelings first," he replied.

"What a contrast to Harold's attitude," Mary thought to herself.

There was an awkward silence. Mary just couldn't get enough of him, yet she didn't know what to say. Lorin looked down the street as though he were trying to decide whether to walk with Mary or let her go.

"Is there anything else, or did you just need to know that you truly are a princess?"

Mary could tell that Lorin meant it. He was looking at her like she really was. He *was* too good to be true and Mary continued looking up at him, unable to say a word.

"I have an errand to run. Would you like to come along and maybe have a little fun later?" Lorin offered.

Mary's thoughts went from elation to concern as she remembered why she had come in the first place. Her family had always been very strict about the Sabbath. "Errands and fun?" Mary asked. "On Sunday?"

Lorin smiled and started walking, "Everyone has different ideas about what things are proper to do on Sunday, Mary. Please, tell me if I cross the line and I will respect any concerns or wishes that you may have. Simply say the word and I will respect your opinion."

Mary was intrigued. Judging from Lorin's comments in church, she wondered what questionable things Lorin could possibly have in mind.

"Sure," she replied. Then she took Lorin by the hand and headed down the sidewalk by his side.

Mary's step was light and she took a deep breath of fresh air. Everything around her looked wonderful and she almost felt like a little girl again.

As they approached her apartment building, an old wino from across the street called out, "Lorin!"

They both turned and looked in his direction.

Mary had noticed the old man in the alley before but she had never talked with him. Her parents had been killed by a drunk driver and Mary found it very difficult to associate with anyone who drank alcohol.

"Fred!" Lorin called back.

Mary was sure that Lorin felt her hesitate, but he headed across the street still holding onto her hand, almost dragging her along.

Fred was sitting on the ground against a *dumpster*. He was filthier-looking than anyone Mary had ever seen and the whole area was littered with broken bottles and reeked of stale alcohol.

Lorin reached down and shook Fred's filthy hand. "How are you doing, Fred?" he asked with a smile.

"Don't know, Lorin. I sure could use a shot of something hard."

To Mary's amazement, Lorin let go of her hand and sat down on a newspaper next to Fred. Lorin reached into his vest pocket and pulled something out. He was carefully hiding it in his large hands so no one else could see.

Mary gasped and was about to say something when Lorin opened a small, pocket-sized New Testament and began reading, "Blessed are the poor in spirit, Fred: for theirs is the kingdom of heaven." After a moment of silence, he added, "...and blessed are they that mourn: for they shall be comforted." Lorin closed the book and put it back into his pocket with a smile.

Fred smiled too. "Not as hard as I expected, Lorin. But I like those."

"Me too," Lorin replied as he stood back up.

Lorin took Mary by the hand and headed back across the street without saying another word. When they arrived in front of her building, he asked her, "Do you have an old blanket?"

Mary was still thinking about Lorin and the wino and it took a moment for his question to register. She finally looked up at him and nodded her head. All of her blankets were old.

"Wait right here," she told him, then she dashed up the stairs.

She came back a minute later with her only bedspread folded in her arms. It was old and worn, like almost everything else she owned, but it was clean and smelled good. She just hoped he wouldn't ask if it was off her bed.

Mary handed Lorin the blanket and they started down the sidewalk again. They ended up at the university and walked right past the bench where Mary ate her lunch and daydreamed, then they continued down the hill toward a small, marshy pond.

Lorin stopped for a moment and listened very carefully before spreading the blanket out on the grass next to the pond. He laid down on his stomach and told Mary, "Jeremy likes frogs. I heard him talking about this place with one of his friends."

Mary assumed that Jeremy was one of the small boys at the playground. She laid down beside Lorin and looked into the moss and reeds in front of her. After a few seconds, she noticed two bulging eyes looking back up at her. When the frog was satisfied that they meant no harm, he turned and looked the other way.

A blue dragonfly hovered directly in front of them for a moment. Mary admired how it glistened in the sunlight, then watched it fly behind Lorin. Mary noticed that Lorin's eyes were still fixed on the frog.

"There must be something about boys and frogs," Mary told herself. She remembered how much her brother Joey loved to play with them when they visited their grandmother. He even put them in his pockets and snuck them into the house so he could have fun with them later on.

Lorin watched while a small gnat unknowingly approached its predator. The instant the frog's tongue hit its target, Lorin burst out laughing. His laugh was so infectious that Mary laughed along with him. "Just like a little boy," she thought to herself.

The frog didn't seem to like his noisy audience. With

one last glance, he hopped into the pond and swam away. Lorin rolled over and started taking off his shoes.

"What now?" Mary turned and asked.

"Those," Lorin answered, pointing to the tall reeds near the shore. "Megan loves baskets."

"You know how to weave baskets?" Mary asked.

"No," Lorin replied. "But I told Megan that I would learn with her." He finished taking off his socks and headed toward the water.

"I could teach you," Mary called after him. "I love to weave."

"I would like that," Lorin replied.

When Mary began taking off her shoes, Lorin stopped.

"Sunday?" he asked with raised eyebrows.

"This is a good cause," Mary responded while wiggling her toes and stepping into the water by his side. "What you're doing with those children is unbelievable."

While they gathered the long grass and reeds, Mary thought it was strange how Lorin only cuffed his pants once at the bottom and stayed near the shore while she pulled her dress up to her knees and ventured further out. She figured that Lorin didn't want to crease his pant legs and it reminded her again about Harold Parker. "Yet he's so different," she thought to herself. "He cares so much about everyone."

After they had gathered what they needed and put them into a trash bag Lorin had stashed in his vest pocket, they walked out on a small dock nearby. It was over twenty feet long, but barely wide enough for them to stand side by side. While they waited for their feet to dry, they began looking around. It wasn't a very romantic setting, but Mary didn't mind. She was just glad that she was there with Lorin.

After a few minutes, Lorin began telling her, "The secret of reading for someone like Alice is very simple, Mary. It's so simple that I only tell it to people when I believe that they are truly listening. Otherwise they may not appreciate it."

"I'm listening," Mary answered in a meek voice. Then

she looked up at him with wide eyes like Alice had at the playground.

Lorin turned and looked back out over the pond, "The secret is to read each sentence all the way through before you say the first word. Then recite each part of the sentence from memory, no matter how many times you have to read it silently to yourself."

Mary thought about it and wondered if the secret really worked. She had never heard anyone mention reading that way before and she had known quite a few people that had a difficult time reading out loud.

"It works," Lorin commented, "if you don't give in. Something eventually clicks and you can then read just like everyone else. Sometimes even better."

Mary remembered how Alice took her time and paused between each sentence after Lorin had told her the secret. "I've heard that you say some amazing things at school, Lorin. Where did you learn it all?"

"From everywhere I can," he replied. "That's why I came to see Jeremy's frog. I figured that once I met his frog he would talk to me. He's a very special boy."

"You learn from little children?" Mary asked.

"Every chance I get," Lorin replied. "Someday I would like children of my own, but I still have a lot to learn."

Mary admitted, "So do I." Then she asked, "How many children do you want?" Mary knew that the question was a bit forward but she felt like she needed to know.

Lorin was still looking out across the pond. "Every woman is different, Mary. I believe that decisions like that should be left up to the wife, based upon what she feels comfortable with and is capable of."

Mary had never thrown herself at any man before, she had never wanted to, but she threw both of her arms around Lorin and hugged him. While still holding him tight, she said, "With every other man I have ever met I was always afraid of what I might find. With you, I'm only afraid that I might miss something wonderful."

Lorin acted uncomfortable with Mary's advance and she thought about Cindy's words again. She looked up into his face.

There were beads of perspiration on Lorin's forehead.

Mary slowly lifted her hand and put it on Lorin's chest. His heart was beating as fast as hers.

She had never dated anyone this shy before, and she decided that she was just going to have to take control of the situation. She carefully stepped in front of him and took both of his hands in hers to see what he would do.

After waiting just a moment, she pulled herself up close against him, tilted her head back and closed her eyes. Lorin took a deep breath and Mary felt his face next to hers just before he quickly pulled away and put something into her hands.

Mary opened her eyes just in time to see Lorin purposely fall backwards into the pond. She looked down at his pocket-sized new Testament while the water splashed onto her feet.

The water was up to Lorin's chest and she was speechless as he straightened his glasses and made his way back over to the edge of the dock. "I'm sorry, Mary. I'm just not used to this yet," he apologized.

"You're not use to what?" she asked. She had no idea what Lorin was talking about.

"Being in love and not being able to do anything about it," he answered.

"Why not?" Mary asked, with a million thoughts racing through her mind.

Lorin cleared his throat and stated very slowly and distinctly, "Because a gentleman should not kiss a woman on the first date. And ours is not scheduled until the day after tomorrow."

Mary's emotions went from relief to frustration.

"What about your clothes?" was all she could think to say.

"They don't matter," Lorin replied. "Honor is remembered long after a nice set of clothes is gone."

Mary knelt down on the dock in front of him.

"Are you always a gentleman?" she asked while bringing her face up next to his.

"I'm trying to be, but it's difficult," he answered. "Especially with you."

Mary placed her forehead against Lorin's and closed her eyes. She whispered, "Where have you been all my life?"

Lorin brought his hand up and touched her cheek, "Waiting for someone like you to save me," he whispered back.

She wanted to kiss Lorin so badly it hurt. "Me too," she whispered.

Her heart was pounding in her chest again and she was losing control. She wasn't used to being in love and not doing anything about it, either.

Mary gently placed Lorin's New Testament on the far side of the dock, removed her shoes and jumped in.

Chapter 33: Dinner

Mary walked out of her apartment wearing her other Sunday dress and carrying her violin. Lorin had asked her to bring it with her, then waited patiently on the front steps while she changed and took a shower.

"What's the violin for?" Mary asked.

"It's a surprise," Lorin answered. Then he took her by the hand and started walking up the street. "Tom told me that you would be alone for dinner tonight."

Mary then realized how late it was. "That's right!" she sadly exclaimed. "You're supposed to eat at the Chamberlin's in less than an hour."

Her countenance sank. It would almost take that long to walk to his apartment, take a shower and go over to their house. She had wanted to spend more time with Lorin and to see what his idea of fun was. Somehow she knew that jumping into the pond wasn't it.

"Would you like to come with me?" he asked.

Mary thought about it with mixed emotions. "It wouldn't be very polite for a guest to invite someone else at the last minute, would it?" she asked.

"No, it wouldn't," he replied.

Mary was puzzled.

Then Lorin said, "Brother Chamberlin told me to expect enough food for five and that Sister Chamberlin takes great offense if people don't eat everything she cooks. I hate to waste food and I do everything that I can to keep from offending people."

Mary didn't know what to make of Lorin's comments and walked silently by his side.

As they approached Lorin's apartment building, he

pointed to the bush Mary had tried to conceal herself behind, "You also need to work on your covert maneuvers."

"My what?" Mary asked.

"If your going to go sneaking around, you need to practice your hiding skills." Lorin then pointed from the bush, over to the edge of the building.

Mary gave Lorin looks that could kill while placing her hands on her hips. Her expression made Lorin laugh his infectious laugh and she couldn't keep a straight face, no matter how hard she tried.

"This is the best part, Mary; Brother Chamberlin apologized for their air conditioner being broken, it's a warm afternoon and I heard Sister Chamberlin tell a friend that they both love violin music. So you see, it just makes good common sense."

"What does?!" Mary asked in frustration.

Mary found herself sitting on the ground outside Scott and Martha Chamberlin's dining room window holding a large serving plate and a dinner fork. There was a large, empty mug sitting on the ground next to her and her violin case was leaning up against the wall. Lorin had retrieved the utensils from his apartment after showering and changing his clothes.

"The words "good common sense" had been Mary's downfall. It was her mother's favorite phrase and Lorin had used it three more times before he was finished explaining what they were going to do.

"I can't believe I'm doing this," Mary told herself while putting her index finger across her lips and smiling back at a complete stranger walking by on the sidewalk. That's what Lorin had told her to do if anyone looked at her.

It amazed Mary when the stranger smiled and walked away.

They were all seated at the table inside and Mary could finally hear what was being said. Lorin had asked to sit next to the window and the Chamberlins both apologized again for the broken air conditioner.

"No apology is necessary. I'm just thankful you invited me over this evening," Lorin responded.

"Well, since you're so grateful, Lorin, would you please offer the blessing?" Scott Chamberlin asked with apparent good-humor in his voice.

Mary listened intently while Lorin prayed. It was a simple prayer and Mary thought it was almost over until Lorin mentioned the poor and needy. Then he went on and on about helping those less fortunate than themselves; those without shelter over their heads, and with empty cups and plates waiting for someone to help.

Mary almost tossed her plate on the ground and stood up. She knew that Lorin was talking about her.

After the prayer, Mary heard the commotion of plates and utensils. She figured it would be a while before Lorin had a chance to sneak her out anything, so she relaxed with her back against the wall.

"This looks like a banquet set for a king," Lorin commented. "You must have been cooking all afternoon."

"It's my pleasure, Lorin," Martha replied. "I'm just glad that you could join us."

Mary heard the sound of a ladle against a porcelain bowl.

"Wow!" Lorin commented.

"I told you, Lorin. I hope you've been fasting for a long time," Scott cheerfully added.

"Mmm," was Lorin's reply. "This is fantastic."

After a few minutes of silence, Lorin asked, "Could you please pass the pepper?"

"Oh, I'm sorry. I must have left it in the kitchen," replied Martha.

THUMP! A large piece of chicken landed in the middle of Mary's plate and almost knocked it out of her hands.

Mary turned and looked up at the empty window above her head. She was glad that she had been holding the plate with both hands when it landed. She looked down in amazement and wondered how Lorin had managed it with Scott still in the room.

"I heard that you're attending the university, Lorin." Martha's footsteps came back in by the time Scott had finished asking the question.

"Yes," replied Lorin. "I've decided that it's time I finally got a degree."

"What kind of work are you in, Lorin?" Martha asked.

Mary thought, "This is great. Now I can find out everything without having to ask him the questions myself."

"This may sound a little strange, but that's why I went back to school," he replied. "To find out what I really want to do."

After eating in silence, Scott asked, "What kind of work have you been doing, Lorin?"

There was another pause. "I haven't had to do very much to support myself," he replied. Then, as if he were sidestepping the issue, he asked, "What kind of work are you in, Brother Chamberlin?"

By the way Lorin answered, Mary began wondering if Lorin came from a wealthy family and didn't have to work.

"Scott's retired," replied Martha. "He was a clock and office-machine repairman for almost forty years. He also used to made music boxes in his spare time."

"Did you make that one over there?" asked Lorin. "It's beautiful."

THUMP!

"How on earth?" Mary asked herself while looking at a second piece of chicken and a hot butter-roll on her plate.

"I did," replied Scott in a solemn voice.

The dining room went silent except for the sound of eating utensils, so Mary pulled out a napkin and began nibbling on one of her pieces of chicken.

A few minutes later, Mary heard Scott almost sob, "Excuse me." Then his footsteps shuffled out of the dining room.

Just then, a stray dog came wandering by. The collie put his nose right up to Mary's plate and she decided that it was necessary to sacrifice one of her pieces of chicken. She tossed it as far as she could toward the edge of the lawn.

The dog chased after it while Martha explained, "The

music box was a wedding gift for our daughter, Kerry. Kerry's husband, John, brought it back over a month ago so Scott could repair it. You see, Kerry died last year."

"I'm sorry," Lorin offered.

"You couldn't have known. You're the first company we've had since John put it there. Scott looks at it every day, but he just hasn't been able to bring himself to fix it. He's going through a tough time. We all are." Then Martha added, "I think John simply wore the music box out. Let's not spoil dinner, I'm sure Scott will be back in a minute."

Mary heard the sound of dishes and utensils again. She was sure that Martha was dishing more food up for Lorin.

After a few minutes, Lorin asked, "What song did it play?"

"A tune called, 'Simple Gifts.' It was Kerry's favorite song."

After another few minutes of utensils clinking, Martha apologized, "Excuse me, Lorin. I better go see if Scott's okay."

A moment later, Lorin was pouring punch into Mary's cup.

"I didn't mean to hurt his feelings," Lorin told Mary as he returned and dished up a large portion of mashed potatoes and gravy.

Lorin came back a few seconds later with some corn, "Do you know the song Martha's talking about?"

Mary nodded just as Lorin disappeared again. She heard both sets of footsteps coming back into the room.

"I'm sorry, Lorin," Scott apologized. "Where were we?"

"Enjoying a wonderful meal," replied Lorin. "With wonderful people."

"And there's dessert," Martha announced. "Two fresh strawberry pies."

"I better save some room then," replied Lorin. Mary could hear him pat his stomach.

"Just finish this last piece of chicken and these potatoes," Martha offered.

Mary could hear the clink of a serving fork and a ladle

again while Martha spoke. Mary was glad she had come, otherwise Lorin would be suffering trying to eat enough to keep Martha happy.

After Mary finished a piece of the second strawberry pie, she could sense that the atmosphere around the dining room table inside was finally content. The sun was setting and Mary sat back and relaxed with a smile. This was the strangest thing that she had ever done, but it had been fun.

Lorin's voice interrupted the silence, "Brother Chamberlin, tell me about Kerry."

There was an uncomfortable silence inside and Mary could feel it. "What is he doing?" she asked herself, almost in horror.

"Scott has a hard time talking about Kerry," explained Martha in a puzzled tone.

"Please, Scott. Tell me about her," insisted Lorin.

Scott began to choke up as he replied, "Kerry was the best daughter a man ever had. A perfect angel, through and through, and she married a wonderful man that loved her. They had two boys, but she always dreamed of having a little girl, and she died last year having it." Scott then broke down sobbing.

"Did the child live?" Lorin asked.

Mary was aghast, "How could Lorin be so insensitive?"

"Yes," Martha finally answered for him.

"Then you need to fix the music box," Lorin insisted.

"Why?" Scott asked. His voice was becoming defiant now and Mary heard his chair slide back.

"So that little girl will know her mother's song and have hope that she will meet her in heaven someday," explained Lorin.

"I don't know what I believe anymore," Scott replied.

"How about miracles, Brother Chamberlin? Do you still believe in them?"

"I used to. But not any more," Scott answered.

After a long silence, Lorin asked, "Will you fix the music box for a miracle?"

"What are you saying?"

"Will you fix the music box for a miracle?" Lorin repeated himself.

Scott quietly replied, "Oh course."

"Then sit down next to your wife, hold her hand and listen," Lorin told him.

Mary pulled out her violin and began playing Kerry's favorite song outside the window.

Instead of going in and visiting like they had planned on earlier, when Mary finished, she put the violin back in its case, picked up her plate and utensils and silently walked away.

Chapter 34: The Date

*D*uring the long hours Steven spent touching up the varnish on the violin, the Luthier told him about Mary's church.

Once the Luthier had decided to find out which religion Mary belonged to, it had taken him less than an hour on the telephone. It was amazing how quickly the Luthier found the answer with directory assistance and a few phone calls.

When the Luthier finished with all the details, he asked Steven, "Do you have any problems with Mary's religion?"

Steven thought about it for a while, then replied, "No."

The Luthier smiled at Steven's answer and let the subject drop there.

While Steven finished smoothing and polishing the violin's surface, the Luthier told him more about his father; the places he went and how he looked at everything. It amazed Steven how much one person could fit into one lifetime.

"Don't get the wrong impression, Steven. My father wasn't perfect and he didn't know everything, but he had the moral character to teach us how to learn from everyone we met, even if we didn't like the people we had to learn from." Then the Luthier told Steven about all the individuals his father had introduced him to and what he had learned from each of them.

The lessons went on and on, and Steven found his attitude about everyone and everything in life changing.

Steven laid down his varnish brushes and polishing cloths one afternoon, let out a sigh and smiled at the

Luthier. He held the violin up and announced, "I believe it is your turn again."

The Luthier took the violin and replied, "So it is."

The Luthier didn't waste any time. He placed the violin on a red velvet cloth and immediately went to work. He pulled out a tapered reamer and sized the four small holes in the scroll where the pegs would go and the hole in the bottom for the endpin. Next he finished shaving the pegs and the endpin to match the holes perfectly.

He carefully carved and fitted a small soundpost made from the Cedars of Lebanon and placed it inside the violin through the f-holes with two special tools. While the Luthier was working, Steven thought about the small ships that were built in bottles.

The Luthier carved a maple bridge from the *Bon Homme Richard* to hold up the strings on the violin's belly, then put on the chinrest and tailpiece. It was later that same evening when the Luthier pulled out a set of strings and began placing them on the violin.

The window in the entry was starting to darken as the Luthier explained, "These are traditional silver-wound, gut strings. They are used when you want the smoothest, sweetest sound possible. They will not produce the most powerful sound in the concert hall, yet if one word could describe what they will add to your instrument, it would be finesse."

When the violin was tuned and settling in, the Luthier announced, "I must now ask you to go outside, Steven."

Steven did not understood, but without saying a word, he stood up and walked out the door. After it closed behind him, he couldn't help noticing that the sky was just as beautiful as it was the evening of the *Bone Guys* game. It was even more beautiful now that he realized where it came from.

"The same place as the loaves, fishes, and all wonderful things," he thought to himself while looking up and smiling.

Just as the sunset began to fade, the Luthier opened the door and invited him back in. Steven looked over at a violin case sitting on the blue, silk-covered bench.

The Luthier turned to Steven and announced, "It is time. Open it."

Steven unzipped the dark Marine-blue, leather cover and unfastened the gold latches that looked like small boat anchors. He looked at the Luthier and asked, "When did you ever find time to make the case?"

"Like a fighting Marine, a Master Luthier does not get much sleep," he answered with a smile.

Steven slowly lifted the lid and looked inside. It was pure-white silk, lined with 24-karat gold fittings. Next to the violin's scroll, in a small compartment made especially for them, sat two unmarked video tapes. Steven turned toward the Luthier, and the Luthier nodded.

Steven noticed that the bow hanging in the lid had a small silver cross inlaid in its frog. He smiled and nodded his approval.

Then it struck him, and he stared down at the violin in disbelief.

It was more beautiful now and he could not see a single repair or flaw on it. Steven picked the violin up and looked even closer but he could still not tell where the cracks had been. He turned to the Luthier for an answer.

The Luthier smiled and his eyes gleamed when he saw the look on Steven's face.

"If others look close enough, they are still there, but now they are only memories to you. This instrument is now as good as any ever made, possibly even better because of what it has lived through."

Steven received his first violin lesson after dinner. The Luthier started at the very beginning and explained all the elementary techniques, then the bad habits to watch out for.

Even though Steven was only able to draw the bow across the strings and do some simple fingering, he could tell that he was going to enjoy playing the violin.

It was late at night when the lesson was over. As he placed the violin back into the case, he appreciated everything that the Luthier had done for him more than words could express. He found that he loved life now, and like the Luthier's father, he was interested in everything.

After the violin case was closed, the Luthier asked him, "Do you still want to dedicate your life to God?"

"Yes," solemnly replied Steven. "More than ever."

"Who are you, Steven Miller?" The Luthier asked it in a way that left little room for doubt in Steven's mind what he meant.

"I am a Christian," he boldly answered.

The Luthier took a moment, looked deep into Steven's eyes and resolutely asked, "Then where are your wife and children?"

Steven shook his head, "What do you mean?"

The Luthier put his hand on Steven's shoulder, "You are now as ready as any man I have ever known, and you have everything that you need." The Luthier smiled and asked, "'What are you waiting for? Christmas?'

"That's what my father would say," added the Luthier with an even bigger smile. "He would also say, 'Come back and visit so I can beat you at that game of *Bone Guys* fair and square'."

Steven just stared at the Luthier.

"I tried to save the best part for last about Mary's church," announced the Luthier. "It's almost their *requirement* that a man of God have a wife and try to have children."

It took him a minute, but Steven's face finally brightened. Then he began smiling.

The Luthier nodded in reply.

Before Steven could say anything, the Luthier pointed to one of two small compartments in the violin case, "This compartment contains the rosin for the bow."

Then the Luthier pointed to the other. "By your actions, I believe that you have experienced true love at first sight. But like Dr. Laura, I still suggest that you both take a little time and get to know each other before either of you make any commitments or get married. Make sure that Mary is not just in love with your eyes, no matter how much you love her. Don't pretend to be anything you are not, and don't do anything while you are courting her that you are not willing to do for the rest of your life.

"Remember the first day you came into my shop? You said that you would be my friend, whether I was yours or not, and look what it's gotten you into. Just imagine the possibilities when you make the commitment of forever with a wife. In the words of my father, you will be doing it, 'NO MATTER WHAT!'"

Steven smiled at the Luthier's drill sergeant's tone of voice.

The Luthier tapped his finger on the last compartment in the violin case and told him, "I would get back to Mary as quickly as possible, but when you get there, take your time and be patient. I suggest that you wait and let Mary open this one."

Steven went down to the bunkhouse and packed his belongings. Before ten o'clock the next morning he had traded in his motorcycle for a four-door economy car in St. George and was headed back up the freeway. He stopped at the violin shop, then at the Luthier's home just long enough to thank him and his family properly, and to promise that he would be back to visit. Steven wanted to stay longer, but he felt like he needed to get back to Mary as soon as possible.

"You were right, Luthier. I can never pay you enough."

The Luthier shook Steven's hand one last time. "*Though I've belted you and flayed you by the living God that made you, you're a better man than I am, Gunga Din.*"

Steven smiled. He had memorized the poem because of Gunga Din's humble attitude and his eagerness to help others.

After giving them all one more hug, he quickly climbed back into the car and drove away. The Luthier's family could see his arm waving out the window until he rounded the bend and disappeared from sight.

As Steven headed up the freeway, he dreamed that Mary was sitting by his side with two or three children playing happily in the back seat.

* * *

Mary looked at herself in the mirror and smiled. She felt like she finally had the man of her dreams within her grasp and she went to bed feeling content. She thought about her life, and was glad that she had saved herself for someone like Lorin. She finally felt like all the years of waiting had been worth it.

Mary fell asleep smiling but started tossing and turning when she started dreaming about Steve, the motorcycle guy again. The words "true love" ran through her mind and when she looked into his eyes, she felt uncontrollable, passionate desire. No matter how much she tried to stop it, the dream went on and on.

At three in the morning, Mary woke up gasping for air. She was sweating hard and writhing in frustration, but when she opened her eyes and looked around, a cold chill ran down her spine. She knew that if the motorcycle guy were to show up someday and look into her eyes, she would want him.

"No!" she burst into tears. "No! What's wrong with me?"

Mary tried to calm herself and settle down, but she couldn't, so she got out of bed and tried playing a hymn on her violin. She said her prayers again, yet when she fell back asleep, she dreamed of his eyes and ecstacy in his arms.

When her alarm went off in the morning, she was a complete mess. She was lying sideways with one arm on the floor and her sheets were all crumpled up at the bottom of the bed, twisted in knots. She finally stumbled into the bathroom and looked in the mirror.

All she could say was, "Ooo."

She desperately started pleading with herself, "Get a grip, girl. Don't throw it all away now!" Both of her hands were on the sink and she was looking herself straight in the eyes. "How come, when you finally find the real man of your dreams, you go crazy and start losing your mind?!" She was angry at herself, yet her heart was still pounding from her dreams of passion.

Mary clenched her fists and screamed in frustration.

The neighbor's dog barked down the hall, but she didn't care and she took a deep breath and screamed even louder. She pulled at her twisted, matted hair with both of her hands and exclaimed, "Aah!" Then she ran out of the bathroom.

A few minutes later, she went back to face the mirror again. She tried to think about what her mother and father would say at a time like this.

Her mother would say, "Choose a gentleman, Mary. One that will treat you right and be a good father to your children." Then she would add, "But don't kiss him on the first date." Mary rolled her eyes when she thought about her mother's kissing comment.

Then she realized that Lorin had said it also. That was really her only complaint about Lorin. Mary wanted the feeling of unrestrained passion in her marriage. She wanted someone that she could lose control with. Even if Lorin was a gentleman, she still wished he would have lost control, taken her in his arms and kissed her like she had always dreamed about.

"Okay! I'm not perfect!" she admitted. "I've waited a long time, and now I want to get carried away. Does that mean I can't have anything good in my life, or that I can't make someone like Lorin happy?"

Mary still felt frustrated and began thinking about what her father would say. "Hold on to your dreams, Mary. Never give them up."

"Which dream?" she begged. "Mr. Right, or passion and love at first sight?"

When no answer came, Mary leaned over and gently beat her head against the mirror.

Mary was surprised when she didn't see Lorin at the university the next day. It was a large campus and she had only run into him twice before, but for some reason, she expected to see him that day, somewhere.

After locking up the last practice-room, she found herself disappointed. The worse part was, when she walked out the door and started to daydream, it was about Steve, the motorcycle guy again.

Halfway across the grass, she stopped and let out a long sigh. She held up her arms and finally asked outloud, "Where is my true love at first sight, and why on earth should I choose him over Lorin?"

As soon as Mary finished talking, she had the feeling that someone was standing right behind her and she turned around. Like every time before, no one was there. "That's all he is," she told herself. "A dream!"

Mary thought about her dreams of riding away on his motorcycle and then the two men that had accosted her on the sidewalk. It made her shudder. It also made her sick to her stomach when she remembered looking at his hair and tattoos while he looked her over in the restaurant.

When she thought about how he might look on their wedding day, or how he would act on their wedding night, it disgusted her. She took one more glance around the campus in frustration and walked away.

Mary sat down next to Tom on her way home. They spoke about everyday things, but she could tell that something was on Tom's mind. She couldn't get rid of the feeling that he was hiding something.

She stopped in the middle of a sentence and asked, "What's up, Tom?"

Tom smiled, "Did you ever see that motorcycle guy again, Mary?"

"No. I haven't seen him since that night in the restaurant," she replied, "and now I'm not sure if I even want to."

It seemed strange that Tom would bring him up all of a sudden, since they had only been talking about Lorin lately.

"Did you ever wonder what happened to him?" asked Tom.

"Are you kidding? I've wondered about him almost every day."

"Well, take ol' Tom's advice on this one, Mary. Don't do anything rash-like, until you look in his eyes ag'in."

"What are you talking about, Tom?"

"All I'm sayin' is, don't gives up hope, Mary."

Tom just clammed up after that and Mary couldn't get anything else out of him, no matter how hard she tried. She finally went home, shaking her head in frustration.

She thought about Tom's comment while slipping into one of her restaurant uniforms. She stood in front of the mirror and straightened up her dress before putting on her makeup. After looking at herself and thinking about how *that* man had looked at her, she blushed. Then she grabbed her things and walked out in disgust.

The minute Mary walked up the steps and into the restaurant, she could tell that something was different.

There were half-a-dozen people scattered at a few tables. Typical for a Monday and everything was in its place, but she still got a strange feeling while greeting each of the employees along the way. It was as if they all knew something that she didn't.

There were no people in her area yet, but there was a family sitting on the other side of the restaurant and Mary began thinking about Lorin again. The picture of him sitting next to her at that table looked very good to her. She turned toward the booth by the kitchen and remembered looking at Steve. The picture of him sitting next to her did not have the same calming effect as the first one did.

She walked back to the waitress' area and started straightening things up a little while she waited for Raúl's signal.

It was especially quiet, even for a Monday, and after a few minutes Mary thought she would take a look to see where the other waitress was. After that one night, a long time ago, Mary looked around the corner of the wall by the kitchen a lot more often, and she always looked before talking with any of the other waitresses.

Mary jumped when she saw Lorin sitting in the booth where the motorcycle guy had been. He was wearing almost the same clothes as the day he had rescued her, except tonight he wore a dark-blue pinstripe vest and pants. His white long-sleeve shirt was a little thicker and pressed even straighter, and his tinted glasses were sparkling gold, complete with a matching silk tie, gold tie clasp, and dazzling, gold cuff-links.

She paused for a moment to take it all in. "Wow!" she thought, and a smile spread across her lips.

Mary filled a glass of water and walked around the corner without even trying to hide how happy she was to see him.

"Lorin, what a pleasant surprise. What brings you here tonight?"

Lorin smiled back and replied, "You do."

Mary's smile grew even larger. Then, for want of anything else to say, Mary asked, "Would you like to order dinner?" as she pulled out her notepad and pencil.

"The question is, Mary, what would *you* like for dinner?" Lorin asked with a smile that melted Mary where she stood.

Just as she was about to ask what Lorin meant, Cindy, who wasn't scheduled to work that night, walked up and said with a smile and a wink, "Have a seat, Mary, and I'll take your order."

It became obvious that she was being set up, she just didn't know for what yet. Lorin stood and offered her a seat. She felt like she couldn't refuse and sat down in the booth.

Lorin sat beside her and announced, "I am honored that you would join me tonight, Mary."

"The pleasure is all mine, Lorin." Then Mary looked at him with admiration while Cindy took their orders. Mary knew the entire menu by heart and didn't look away from Lorin's face while she told Cindy what she would like.

As Cindy walked away from their table, Lorin announced, "Pay very close attention tonight, Mary. Afterwards, there is a test."

Mary wondered what that meant, but she couldn't help smiling when she saw the expression on Lorin's face. He continued, "Tom told me yesterday that your mother asked you to never kiss on the first date. Just so you know, I really do feel the same way and don't consider yesterday a date."

Mary thought about her advances at the pond. She realized that Lorin knew she wasn't perfect, yet here he was and polite as ever. Then she remembered the date Lorin set up for Tuesday night and thought, "If he did this tonight so he can kiss me tomorrow, I'll start puckering now."

When Lorin saw Mary's face light back up, he turned toward the front of the restaurant and nodded. To Mary's surprise, both Raúl and Frederick hurried over to their table and anxiously waited for Lorin to speak. Mary had never seen either of them act like that in all the years she had worked at the restaurant.

"Yes, Mister Delmar? May we be of assistance?" they both asked together with large smiles.

"Would it be inconvenient to open this area up a little?" Lorin politely asked.

Mary watched in amazement while Raúl and Frederick pulled some of the tables and chairs out of Mary's serving area, leaving their booth next to a large, open space. As soon as they were finished, four musicians from the symphony walked in the front door. Within a couple of minutes, and with a few friendly winks, they set up on the far side of the clearing and began playing soft, romantic music.

Mary compared this treatment to the men that she had dated over the years who thought that buying her dinner meant that they had bought kisses and sometimes more. She looked at Lorin and realized that he would not kiss her tonight for anything because his honor as a gentleman was at stake. Mary was falling fast again, and she knew it.

They quietly ate dinner while the romantic music played in the background. Everything was perfect.

After dinner, Mary and Lorin talked about their roles in the upcoming play. Lorin started telling Mary about his hopes and dreams, then he threw in a joke and they both burst out laughing until they cried. He seemed to have the same feelings about everything she did and it made her feel good just to be with him.

As soon as Cindy carried away their plates, the music changed to a waltz. Mary couldn't help glancing over at the clearing, just before Lorin slid out of the booth and stood up. He gently bowed and asked, "Would you care to dance, Mary?" while holding out his hand.

She gracefully accepted and slid out of the booth. As they made their way over to the center of the clearing, the music faded away. There was a moment of silence while they faced each other and Lorin placed his hand in the small of Mary's back. Mary looked over at the quartet just in time to see all four of them smile and wink before playing "Beauty and the Beast."

Mary looked up at Lorin and thought the song was a little ironic. When they began to dance, she realized, "I am the beast, and this really is a fairy tale come true."

Lorin danced wonderfully. Mary could tell that he had been brought up in a cultured atmosphere. She tried to imagine what kind of house or mansion he had lived in and wondered how much he had paid the restaurant and the musicians.

She had not known many wealthy people and Lorin acted nothing like Harold Parker, but as they floated across the floor, she began to wonder. She also remembered how quickly he had pulled out his new mattress for the children to play with and how he had jumped into the pond and didn't mind ruining an expensive set of clothes.

"He must only be living in the apartments while he goes to school," she thought to herself. "I bet he's rich!" That thought didn't hurt Mary's feelings at all, and she knew that it wouldn't have hurt her mother's either. She drank it all in and dreamed of how life would be with someone like Lorin. She laid her head on his shoulder, closed her eyes and smiled.

When the song was finished, they looked at each other. As Lorin lowered Mary's hand, she found herself losing control. She closed her eyes and leaned forward. Lorin turned gently to the side, let go of Mary's hand and guided her back to the table.

Mary was embarrassed. She knew that if she was going to deserve a man like Lorin, she was going to have to make the commitment to put her passions aside and be a real princess. She told herself, once and for all, "I promise to wait until *he* kisses me."

After talking a little more and finishing a light dessert, Lorin's face became serious. "Now for the test," he announced.

Mary couldn't imagine what it was going to be. By the tone in his voice, it sounded like he was a professor announcing an exam at the university. She wondered if Lorin had some great question that he always asked women, and when they failed to answer it correctly, he moved on. Maybe that was why he had never been married.

"That has to be it!" Mary concluded while remembering her conversations with Cindy. "Boy," she thought, "here it comes!"

"I spoke with Tom, Mary. I know about the man on the motorcycle. I also know that you believe you have experienced love at first sight." Then Lorin added with a raise of his eyebrows, "Make that *true love* at first sight."

Mary stared back in disbelief. She didn't know what to think or where Lorin was going with the conversation now.

"You described him to Tom as a dirty nightmare that made you want to throw up. That his greasy hair was past his waist and he wore black leather, complete with tattoos and earrings."

Mary stared at Lorin, still not sure what to think. She realized though, that they were the exact words she had spoken to Tom.

"Tom said that you also dream of a true gentleman. A devoted husband, a good example to your children, someone that you can live *happily-ever-after* with."

When Lorin said, "happily-ever-after," Mary smiled back. She thought of him the whole time he was saying the words.

"I need to know that you understand, Mary. Understand

that I am not going to kiss you tonight, let alone, ask you to marry me. I simply need to know the answer to the question I am about to ask, before I can go any further in this relationship."

Mary slowly nodded and waited for him to continue.

"If you had to choose one or the other, Mary, which would it be?"

Mary didn't know what to say. If this was her one and only chance for a husband like Lorin, she didn't want to blow it. But she also knew that she had to be honest, so she could think of her parents and look herself in the mirror the rest of her life with a clean conscience.

Mary took a minute and thought seriously about the question. Her father had taught her to never give up dreaming, and she had dreamed of true love at first sight her entire life. She also thought about Tom, just that afternoon, telling her to not give up hope on Steve, the motorcycle guy.

She looked up at Lorin again and her heart melted. She knew, deep down inside, that he was the "genuine article." She knew he was the man that she had always pictured and dreamed of marrying. She looked at him and knew that he would give her all the security and love she would ever need.

She then remembered the warm, rushing feeling that she felt when looking into Steve's eyes. It had consumed her entire soul and thrown her into passion beyond reason, and it grew worse every time she dreamed about him.

Mary looked at Lorin for a long time and thought it over. He was the most loving, caring man that she had ever met. Yet she knew that she would still dream of the motorcycle guy at night instead of him. To Mary, it would make her the worst kind of person in the world to marry him knowing that.

With tears gathering in her eyes, Mary finally answered, "I can't choose between the two, Lorin, and I don't know if I will ever be able to." She burst into tears and began shaking uncontrollably.

The whole restaurant went silent; even the musicians stopped playing while Mary's whole body was racked in torment. Cindy had heard Mary's answer and she stood next to the wall by the kitchen with her mouth hanging wide open.

Mary opened her mascara-stained eyes to take one last look at Lorin. She realized that she couldn't take her answer back now and she knew what she was giving up. Yet she still couldn't live with herself if she was unfaithful, even if it was only in her heart. Mary lowered her head and covered her face with her hands while she sobbed uncontrollably, "I'm so sorry, Lorin."

Tears filled Lorin's eyes and he choked up. He could barely get out the words, "You are correct, Mary. *True love* means that you will never have to choose between the two."

Then Steven Miller pulled off his gold-tinted glasses and put them into the case in his shirt pocket. He gently reached up and lifted Mary's hands away from her face so he could lean forward and look her straight in the eyes.

It really was him; the greasy motorcycle guy. Almost instantly, the same passionate feelings came rushing through Mary that she had felt the first time she had looked in his eyes.

She started gasping for air and frantically threw her arms around Steven, then held him while tears of joy flowed down her cheeks. She held him as tight as she possibly could and wouldn't let go.

The quartet, that had been silently waiting for their next cue, started crying and pulling out their handkerchiefs while Cindy clapped her hands.

When Steven finally turned and nodded, the musicians could barely play the music and it was terribly out of tune. Steven and Mary laughed and clung desperately to each other while they listened to a pathetic rendition of "Love Lifts Us Up Where We Belong."

Steven sat back and took in a deep breath. Then he told Mary, "Though I have pretended nothing, my name is not Lorin Delmar and I am far from being a perfect man."

He rolled up his long, white sleeves and showed Mary the tattoos on his arms. Mary suddenly remembered Tom's comments about how Steven may have just been acting the first night they met.

Mary sat back and asked, "If you are not Lorin Delmar, then who are you?"

"If you can ever forgive me for putting you through all this, I would be honored if you will still go out with me tomorrow night and I will tell you everything."

Mary replied by nodding and trying to smile.

Chapter 35: The Saint

"Mirror, mirror on the wall, who am I dreaming of, after all?" asked Mary while standing in front of her mirror later that evening.

While Steven walked Mary to her apartment, he had alluded to some very serious problems in his life. Now, as she looked reality in the face, she wondered who Lorin, or Steven, really was. His own words had helped convince her, once and for all, that she wanted it all. Nothing less. And now she knew it, even if it meant waiting for the rest of her life.

After all, some of the seemingly nice men she had dated before had come up with some pretty outrageous problems. As bad as Steven had looked and as unbelievably good as Lorin had acted, she now wondered what was in store for her the next night.

She asked the mirror again, "Who is he?" Then, after looking at herself for a very long time, she asked herself, "Who am I, really?"

After almost an hour, she went into the bedroom and tried to sleep.

After rolling over a dozen times, she gave up and turned the light back on. She picked up her script from *Man of La Mancha* and started reading it.

An hour later, she firmly slapped the script back down on her night stand and jumped out of bed. She went back into the bathroom, looked into the mirror and declared, "I am not the kitchen tramp, Aldonza. I am Dulcinea, the princess, and if he's not really Don Quixote, he can take a flying leap!"

Mary slept much better after that.

When she woke up the next morning, she decided exactly what she was going to do; find out absolutely everything she could about Steven before their date that night.

Even though it was early, Mary picked up the phone and dialed Cindy's number.

"Hello?" came Cindy's tired voice from the receiver.

"Cindy, this is Mary. I need to find out everything I can about Lorin."

Cindy perked right up. "How did it go after you two left? Is he still there at your apartment?"

Mary screamed in frustration, "Of course not!" Then she told Cindy, "He walked me to my doorstep, then he went home."

"If you're not going to reel him in, Honey, I'll take him off your hands right now," Cindy responded.

Mary was disgusted with Cindy, but she kept talking with her anyway. "How much did he pay for everything at the restaurant last night?"

"Oh, you want to know if he's 'floating in it' before you commit?" asked Cindy.

Mary didn't reply, she just kept silent while impatiently waiting for Cindy's answer.

"He didn't spend a penny, other than the dinners and tip," Cindy finally answered.

"How?" asked Mary in amazement.

"You never saw anything like it. He just walked up to me yesterday, looked me in the eyes and told me that he thought you were the most perfect, wonderful angel in the whole world and asked if I would do you and him a favor.

"I would have slit my wrists and pulled out my hair if he'd asked me to, after the look he gave me. From what the others said, even the musicians, it was pretty much the same thing. He could be rich or poor. Either way, Honey, he can have anything he wants from me."

Mary hung up the phone in disbelief. She told herself, "I don't care if he is rich or poor. But like Tom said, is he just acting, or does he really love me?" She remembered how easily Lorin had landed the leading role in *Man of La Mancha* at the last minute. Then she thought, "Either way though, he is good. Really good."

Next she went and knocked on Tom's door and woke him up.

"Tell me about Lorin, or Steven, or whoever he is," demanded Mary.

"Sos he tol' yous last night, did he?" replied Tom while he sat on one of the two old chairs in his single room apartment. Bedroom, living room, kitchen: one single room.

"He just told me that he wasn't who he said he was. I'm trying to find out who he really is before I see him again," declared Mary.

"Alls I knows is this, Mary: A man comes to me the day yous told me bout your loves at first sights, an he tells me that whos you saw in his eyes was him, and whos you saws on the outsides wasn't whos he really was. Then he says he'll change whos he is for yous, an' fors you to wait and pray for him."

"And you didn't tell me, Tom?"

"I didn't wan' to gets yous hopes up, Mary. I've never seen peoples like him change befores," apologized Tom. "I din't recognized him myselfs until after Sunday meetin' an he tells me whos he is."

"What else did he say?"

"Only thats he's military. Vietnam vet," answered Tom.

"How old is he?" asked Mary. She was shocked at the age he would have to be.

"Don knows fur sure, abouts fifty I recons," replied Tom.

"Fifty!" moaned Mary.

Mary got up and started to leave when Tom called out to her, "He's not that man yous saw that firs' night, Mary. Look at him wit yer heart, not yer eyes."

Mary just kept walking as the words "Vietnam" and "fifty" kept running through her mind. Her next stop was the director's office.

"What do you know about Lorin?" Mary asked Mr. Jones

while sitting across the desk from him.

"Not a lot, Mary," he replied.

"Where's he from?" she insisted.

"Is this really that important to you?" asked Mr. Jones, who had always liked Mary and wanted her to succeed as a musician or as an actress.

"Everything," answered Mary.

He stood up and told her, "Wait here."

Mary tapped her fingers on the desk while he walked out the door and down the hall.

When he came back with a manila folder in his hand, he told her, "You know this is against school policy."

Mary nodded as Mr. Jones opened the folder and started reading, "Lorin graduated from high school in Utah in...," the director paused before he continued, "four weeks ago!" he exclaimed. "He has no other record of further education!"

"What's his real name?" asked Mary.

Mr. Jones acted surprised at the question, then as he looked down through the pages, he looked even more surprised while reading out loud, "Given name, Stephen Graham Miller, born December 9th, 1952."

Mr. Jones looked up at Mary. "He plays the violin, doesn't he?"

"A little," Mary answered. "Why?"

Mr. Jones' voice got serious, "Do you remember the reading I had you do from *Somewhere in Time*?"

"Yes," Mary replied, wondering what that had to do with anything.

"That was because of an urgent request from a friend of mine that makes violins. He even had me counter-to-counter that tape from the airport because it was so important."

"My tape?" asked Mary.

Mr. Jones nodded.

"Then he called back and asked all about you and your parents."

Mr. Jones asked Mary in a very concerned voice, "What's going on, Mary?"

"I don't know, Mr. Jones, but I'm going to find out! What's that violinmaker's name and phone number?"

Mary skipped her class, cancelled the music lesson she was supposed to teach and headed back to her apartment. As soon as she was in the door, she picked up the telephone and dialed the long distance number.

"Hello," was the simple answer over the phone.

"May I speak with Jonathan Dewey?" she asked.

"I am Jonathan Dewey Luthier, Miss," replied the voice.

The "Miss" stood out just a little too much for Mary's taste. "Do you know a Lorin Delmar or a Stephen Miller?"

"My father's first and middle names were Lorin and Delmar. Other than his, I have never heard the two names together before. I do know a Stephen Miller, though. He just purchased a Master Violin for you, Mary. I believe it to be one of the most special instruments in the world, though I can tell that you have not played it yet."

Mary dropped the phone.

She stared down at the receiver while it lie silently on the floor next to her feet.

When she finally picked it up with trembling hands and held it to her ear, she asked, "Who are you?"

"I am a Master Luthier," came the answer over the phone, "and you are Mary Anderson," the voice continued. "And now I will tell you who Stephen Miller was, and is."

The Luthier told Mary about Steven coming to the shop because he wanted to change his life. He told her of the things that Steven had gone through while he was with the Luthier in vivid detail. He told her of Steven fixing the violin as well as his life for her.

It tore Mary's heart in pieces while she listened to the pain and suffering Steven had gone through. She found herself crying uncontrollably while the Luthier spoke of Steven being chained to the bunkhouse floor.

After a moment of silence, the Luthier finished with these words, "There are two video tapes in Steven's violin case, Mary. One is the *only* thing that kept him alive and gave him hope when he was in chains, and the other is *who* he is now and what his life represents."

Mary hung up the phone and walked slowly back to the university. She asked herself, "Can this all be real, and really happening to me?"

She walked by Tom without saying a word. Tom softly called after her, "I love you, Princess. Good luck."

Mary's whole life seemed like a blur while she walked across campus toward the music department. As the door to the practice room clicked shut behind her, she looked over at the locker where Steven kept his violin. She looked down at the master key in her hand and debated whether she should open it or not. Even though she was authorized to, Mary had never opened a locker without the student being there before.

Mary slowly lifted up the key, turned the lock and lifted the handle. She had to know if all this was real and if Steven was real. She then pulled out the violin case and placed it on the table.

It was one of the large practice rooms with its own video recorder so the students could watch recordings of concerts and critique their performances. Mary wouldn't have to go anywhere else to see the tapes, if they were there.

As she opened the violin case, she was afraid of what she might, or might not, find inside. She knew the answer would affect her for the rest of her life.

It was dazzling white inside. Whiter than any material she had ever seen, and it was accented with the sparkling luster of pure-gold. When the lid was fully open, she noticed everything was there, just like the Luthier had said.

She reached for the first video tape and slid it into the machine.

When the tape started to play, Mary saw her own face appear on the television screen. She remembered the Luthier's words and thought of Steven's raw, bleeding wrists and ankles, writhing and shaking in pain as he lay back down to be voluntarily chained to the floor again, knowing that he was going back into Hell *for her*.

How could she have known? But she knew it now.

When the first tape was over, Mary pulled it out and put the second one in. The Luthier had told her that it was "who he is now" and "what his life represents."

The moment Mary saw Jesus walking down the path she began bawling uncontrollably.

When she saw each of the people's faces as Jesus lifted them up, she thought of the children at the playground and how their faces lit up when he was there. She wondered what her own face must have looked like when he protected her on the sidewalk or when the children told her that she was a princess.

She knew what all the students looked like when they talked about him at the university. She thought of Jasmine, then the feeling she had after playing the song at the Chamberlins' house. She realized that Steven was living his life trying to do the same as Jesus would for everyone he met.

When the second tape finished playing, she turned the machine off and wiped her eyes.

Mary lifted the violin out of its case and looked at it. It was more beautiful than any violin she had ever seen, but when she held it up next to the light and looked closely, she could just make out the small repairs under the varnish. She thought of how Steven had repaired it, as well as his life, for her.

She looked at the small silver cross inlaid in the frog and thought of his words about Jesus. Mary tightened the pure-white Arabian Stallion hair and could easily picture herself growing old with Steven at her side. Then she imagined their grandchildren gathered around to listen to him teach them and tell them stories.

The hair looked like it needed more rosin so Mary reached down and opened one of the two small compartments in the violin case. Nestled in the pure-white silk, were her mother's and father's wedding rings that her grandfather had made.

Mary wiped her tears after a good, long cry, then she tried on her mother's ring. It was just as she remembered it, but now, after all these years, it fit her perfectly. She thought of her mother and left it on while lifting up her father's ring.

She had not seen her father since she was seventeen and it was a long time before she could lay it back down in the case. She wondered how anyone could have found them after all these years.

After opening the other compartment, she swiped the hair across the fresh cake of rosin. It was the finest violin bow that she had ever held and she realized that Steven had bought it *for her*.

With the first note she played, the violin reminded her of Steven and she closed her eyes in ecstacy. The sound was so full and powerful, yet so sweet. She savored the music and it improved with each note she played until it was unbelievable. It made her think of how much he had improved his life since the day she first met him.

Even though she would have cherished the instrument, no matter what it sounded like, the violin really was unbelievable. Mary played her favorite hymn and she felt like she was in heaven. It was everything that she had always dreamed a violin could be and the music from it filled her soul.

She thought about the wedding rings again and couldn't keep from smiling and crying at the same time. That's when she felt like everyone and everything she needed to live *happily-ever-after* was in the room with her. The feeling became so real and intense that she opened her eyes and turned around.

Steven was standing in the practice room with Mary. She had been so carried away with the music that she had not heard him open the door.

Mary quickly looked down at the wedding ring on her finger. Then she looked over at the videotape still in the VCR. She was unable to speak and started shaking while she held the violin up for him to take.

Steven shook his head, "It is yours, Mary. If you truly love it. Just as I am."

Mary looked from the violin in her outstretched hands to his eyes and began crying again.

Steven continued while shaking his head, "Before you decide, Mary, realize that the violin you hold has had many serious repairs." He dropped to his knees, "I am yours, Mary. If you truly love me. But realize that I have had many more repairs than the violin, and many of my scars still show." Then he pulled up the sleeves on his shirt and showed her his arms.

Her gaze went from the large, colorful tattoos to the violin's scroll. The Luthier had told her that it was made out of a pirate ship and she thought of all the things the Luthier had told her about Steven's past. She also realized that there were many things that she would never know.

She looked at the violin's back and thought of John Paul Jones bravely fighting and never giving up, even when his ship was sinking. It made her think of how Steven had fought his battle against all odds, in spite of his upbringing, his addictions and everything else that had happened in his life. She knew that he would stand by her and never give up.

Mary turned the violin over. The Cedar of Lebanon's fine, straight grain reminded her of Steven's life now. He was trying to live his life like Jesus and had sacrificed everything to do it.

The newest requirement for her *Knight in Shining Armor* had been that he be like Don Quixote, who was willing to "march into Hell for a heavenly cause." Not only had Steven been willing to march into Hell, he had done it. And he had done it for her!

Mary choked back her tears and gently laid the violin and bow down. She picked up her father's ring and looked Steven in the eyes. He was still kneeling on the floor, humbly waiting for her answer.

The finest man that she had ever met was kneeling at her feet. It was far better than any fairy tale she had ever dreamed of.

Mary offered Steven her hand and told him, "Now that I know who you are, I love you more than life, and I will try with all my heart to be the woman of your dreams."

After Steven rose to his feet, Mary looked up into his

eyes and continued, "But from now on, I will call you Stephen." Then they fell into each other's arms and kissed.

Not just any kiss. It was their very first kiss and they embraced each other without holding anything back and without any reservations. It was the kiss that Mary had dreamed of her whole life and it was more passionate than anything she could have ever imagined. It reaffirmed all the feelings they both had the first time they met. They knew beyond any doubt, that theirs truly was the *kiss of true love at first sight.*

Stephen thought of the Luthier's words while they looked out over the valley together. He now *knew* that this kind of kiss had happened at least *twice* in the history of the world.

With Mary still in his arms and her lips pressed tightly against his, he couldn't help thinking to himself, "But this has got to be the best of all," and he smiled.

Mary found herself smiling also. When their lips parted, she leaned her head back and looked up into Stephen's eyes again.

Then she corrected herself, "...Saint Stephen."

Epilogue

There is someone, deep down inside each of us, who is far greater and has more potential than we can possibly imagine.

To order autographed copies of "Two Trees" and/or "Choice of Loves":

Please send $12.95 for each book (price includes shipping and handling to the continental U.S.).

Example:
1 book = $12.95 = $12.95 total

2 books = $12.95 X 2 = $25.90

Signature will appear on the title page.

For special inscriptions or dedications up to fifteen words, please add $1.50 per book and write neatly.

Please send check, money order, or credit card number (Mastercard, Visa, American Express) along with the card's expiration date.

No cash or C.O.D.'s will be accepted.
For quickest delivery, please use your credit card.

Expect delivery within 1-1/2 weeks with credit card orders, 3-4 weeks with all others.

Kevin Lee Luthier and Lee Instruments reserve the right to change the price and availability at any time and for any reason.

Or order from our website:

kevinleeluthier.com or leeinstruments.com

Comments about the books are welcome at: leeinst@infowest.com

Send orders and make all checks payable to:

Lee Instruments
P.O. Box 460999
Leeds, Ut. 84746-999

Two Trees: #_____ Choice of Loves #_____ Total # _____

Total amount: $_____

Payment: Mastercard ___ Visa ___ American Express ____

Check ____ Money Order ____

Credit card# _____

Expiration Date: _____

Signature (with credit card):_____

Name:_____

Address:_____

City:_____ State:_____

Zip code:_____
Special requests or
comments:_____

_____

Large, color, trifold brochures for the violin shop are also
available for $3.00 ea (shipping incl).   # of brochures _____
(Just add dollar amount to that of books above).
Please realize that apprentice instruments are currently $5,000.00 -
$10,000.00 while master instruments with case and bow range from
$35,000.00 - $85,000.00 as of Spring 2001.

Authorization to copy 'this' page is granted without copyright
infringement for ordering purposes only.

                              ...and please tell a friend.

Next in the Luthier's Diary Series:
Book 3

Clay Angel
(The Book of Dreams)

It takes more than money to buy happiness.

Sheila Whittaker is constantly dreaming of the ultimate news story and the respect she deserves as an anchorwoman.

Edward Giles, after accumulating billions of dollars and three ex-wives, dreams of something he has never had; a simple life filled with love.

Julia Karr's hope and innocence were forcefully taken from her when she was young and has lived in despair and torment ever since. She dreams of comfort and peace.

Cassandra Empey, devoted and self-sacrificing as anyone has ever been, only dreams of the good in other people.

The Luthier, on the other hand, dreams of everything.

Clay Angel, "The book of dreams."

ABOUT THE AUTHOR

Kevin Lee was born in Renton, Washington, U.S.A. and the first few years of his life were spent playing among the evergreens and along the shores of Puget Sound in Federal Way.

His family made several moves while he was young and after living on a vineyard in Lodi, California for a year, they moved to Thousand Oaks where he started playing the violin at age six. His first lessons were taken from his second-grade school teacher in elementary school.

His childhood cannot be considered "normal" by anyone's stretch of the imagination and with it came many of the unique experiences that have helped him in the arts of violinmaking and writing. (Everything concerning the Luthier's father and the Luthier's childhood mentioned in this book is true.)

Kevin officially became recognized as a 'Master Luthier' and had the title appended to his name before the turn of the last century, when his original violins were appraised higher than any living maker in the history of the world.

While the books are written in novel form and some liberties are taken, the Luthier's true life story is interwoven throughout the series.

As mentioned in the first book "Two Trees," he now lives a life of dreams on a vineyard in Southern Utah with his beautiful wife, Sheryl, and their three children: Skyler, Tessa and Colter.